THE HIKE

THE HIKE
SURVIVORS

A novel by
QUENTIN ROGERS

QT FOTOGRAPHY

For information contact; www.thehikenovel.com

Book and Cover design by Quentin Rogers

ISBN: 978-0-692-84527-1

First paperback edition March 2017

This book is dedicated to my children:
Mariah - *Fourteen years old*
Kaylee - *Eleven years old*
Coltin - *Seven years old*

Several strong women in my life (grandmother, mother, and wife) saved it; and Jesus gave me hope. I pray that you show others the hope and love that has been bestowed upon you. Dream big.

PREFACE

CRASH! A DINNER plate exploded against the dining room wall. It left a large dent in the drywall and paint where it had impacted, and small fragments of the porcelain flew in all directions across the room.

Mackenzie's dad had raised his elbow and slightly ducked in an evasive maneuver when the plate had whizzed by his head from over the bar in the kitchen. He now lowered his elbow and stood up straight as his bewilderment at what happened turned to anger.

"What are you doing?" Mackenzie's dad half-yelled across the room to her mom.

"You're not doing this Patrick!" Mackenzie's mom yelled back at him. Her normally well-kept sandy-blonde hair was frazzled and wavy around her face. Her cheeks were flushed and her eyes were locked in focus on her husband.

From Mackenzie's vantage point sitting at the kitchen table, she couldn't see her mom's hands from behind the countertop, but she was sure that her hands were balled up in fists from the way that her arms were straightened.

"You're not taking her on that stupid trip!" her mom screamed this time and spittle flew from the corners of her mouth. Mackenzie had only seen her mother upset like this once or twice before and she wasn't sure how to react to it. Her little brother James sat in his high chair next to Mackenzie and from the expression on his face she could tell that he hadn't ever seen his mom in that state of anger. Although James normally was Mackenzie's nemesis, the look on his face touched her teenage compassion somehow and she reached out and put her hand on his wrists to give him some comfort in the moment.

"Listen Mary," Mackenzie's dad started to say, but then raised his elbow to his face and slightly ducked again as another dinner plate sailed through the air at him. This time the aim was better and he had to fully duck to avoid being struck by the plate as it crashed against the wall like the other had.

This time though Mackenzie's little brother James began to wail immediately after the plate had struck the wall and left another similar size dent in the dry wall.

"Mary!" Patrick said forcefully. "Now that's enough!"

Mackenzie seen blood begin to trickle down the neck of her little brother and she exclaimed his name as she jumped to her feet to get a better look at where the blood was coming from. At her reaction, Patrick turned his attention to James as well and began lifting his son's short hair in patches to try and determine what the source of the blood was. Mackenzie seen something flash in the hair as her dad was moving James' hair around and reached in and grabbed a small piece of porcelain that had lodged into the boy's hairline just above the back of his neck. He shrieked and continued to sob as Mackenzie extracted the fragment and held it up in front of her nose looking at it.

Her dad grabbed the small piece from Mackenzie's fingers and held it up to Mary with a righteous look on his face. He didn't have to say the words for Mary to get the point that he couldn't believe that she had done that to their son. Before he could say anything, she was across the room and in between Patrick and James inspecting his wound for herself. After Mary quickly surmised that there wasn't any real damage or issue, she began unlocking the tray from the high chair to get James out of it.

"Mary…" Patrick started.

The first syllable no longer left his mouth when Mary dropped the high chair tray turned around and screamed "Just LEAVE!"

Patrick's eyes widened and he stood motionless for a moment.

Mary took a breath, closed her eyes and then opened them. "Patrick," she said with a reserved calm in her voice. "Just leave," she repeated.

Patrick stood for a moment longer, looked to Mackenzie as if he was sizing up her well-being; then he turned and left. Mackenzie seen him start down the stairs and then heard the front door slam behind him. Mary had finished unstrapping James from his seat and began carrying the still sobbing boy towards the hallway bathroom.

"Mom," Mackenzie called out from her place still in the dining room.

"Not now Mackenzie," her mom said back to her somewhat calmly but not looking back as she continued down the hall.

Mackenzie made her a plate of spaghetti from what was on the dinner table being careful to ensure there were no pieces of broken plate in her food. She grabbed her iPod from the counter and took the plate of food with her down the hall to her bedroom. She could feel the adrenaline begin to subside and she began to physically shake.

She sat the plate of food down on the end table next to her bed and collapsed onto her comforter. Mackenzie felt the wave of emotions spill over her and she began to cry herself. She didn't want to go on the trip with her dad. She couldn't understand why he was risking whatever at his work that her mom was worried about, or why he would make her mom so angry over something that Mackenzie didn't even want to do with him. Her dad was mad because he repeatedly chose work over her, and now he wanted her to do things with him that Mackenzie despises. It just wasn't fair.

Her iPod dinged from under the blankets that she knew meant was a text message. Mackenzie dug around under the blankets until she found it and stared at it through the tears in her eyes. It was a message from her dad:

Is James OK?

Anger burned in her and she felt her stomach clench. She thought about not responding to him, but she couldn't bring herself to be that way.

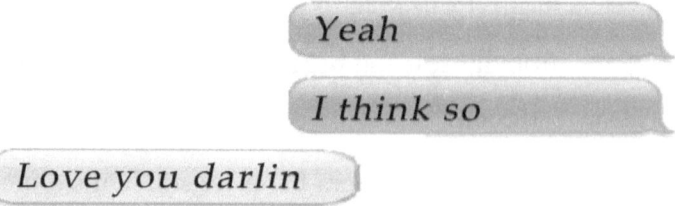

Yeah

I think so

Love you darlin

Mackenzie felt her anger subside a little and her stomach relaxed some. She knew that her dad loved her. But she still wasn't going on that stupid trip with him.

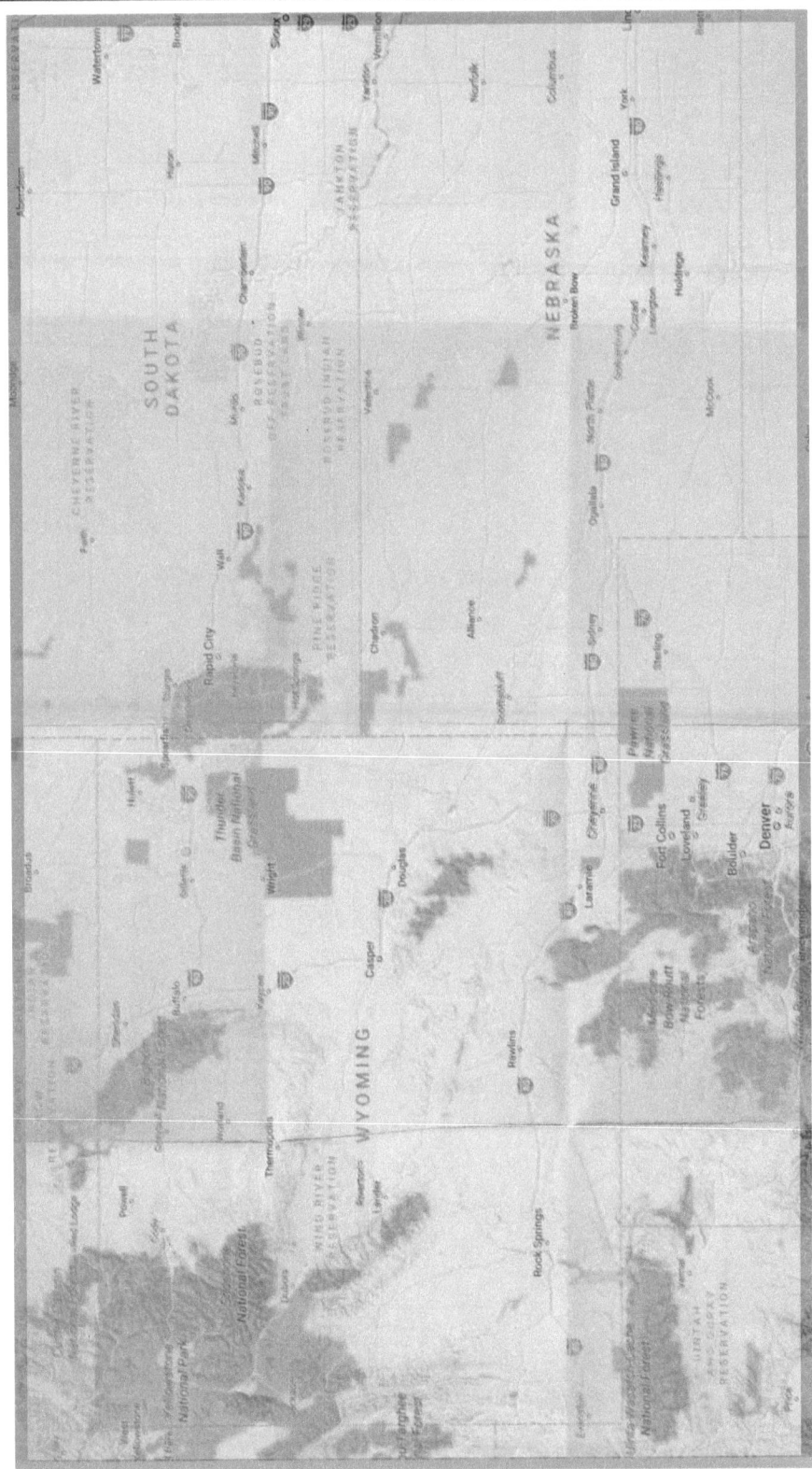

PART 1 –

THE

HIKE

CHAPTER 1

EVERYONE HAS CERTAIN triggers that makes their heart melt just a little. Not a major melt like the smell of a newborn baby or a young puppy licking your face does; but a melt just the same. Patrick Kincaid's does that when he sees the sign that they put next to the interstate and highways for the state of Wyoming that has the bucking bronc on it with the mountains in the background. Patrick had been born, raised, and had since lived in Nebraska his whole life, but somehow that sign always stirred something within him. He knew that it was kind of sappy and he wasn't exactly sure why it had that kind of effect on him, but it always seemed to bring back memories of happy times and the thoughts of restful days.

"Mackenzie..." Patrick said as he adjusted the volume on the radio dial down some as he could just make out the sign in the distance. A quick glance to the passenger seat showed that she still had her ear buds in and was staring out the passenger window trying to will herself somewhere far away from her dad and this car. "Mak…" he said a little louder along with a nudge from his forearm.

The only reaction he got from her was a half-hearted "Yeah" as she pulled one bud from her left ear by yanking on the wire.

"You know when I was a kid that sign used to say 'Welcome to Wonderful Wyoming' instead of 'Forever West'" he told her with a little reverence inflected in his voice.

"That's awesome" she disinterestedly stated in a monotone that only teenagers seem to pull off as she put the misplaced ear bud back in her ear.

So much for telling her about the memories he had of that sign. He was going to tell her about how his mother always used to say "pick your feet up" as they passed by that imaginary line so that they didn't drag dirt from one state into the next. Or the one when his dad and Patrick did a twelve-hour road trip to a family reunion with the radio blaring, and his dad singing along with the radio to an oldies station. That was quite a story if you knew Patrick's dad and how singing along to anything really wasn't in his personality.

Patrick thought about nudging her again and making her listen to his reminiscing of his road trip memories of when he was a kid, but looking down at her disinterested face with that ever-present hate in her eyes he decided to keep his memories to his self for a while. He turned the radio dial back up to a volume that helped to pass the time.

The miles went by and the radio droned on with popular country music that Patrick had no interest in. His mind turned to projects at work; where his marriage went wrong; how it was ridiculous to think that a backpacking trip with his daughter would repair their relationship; and many other dismal train of thoughts that seemed to fill his thinking time of late. All the while the rolling plains of Wyoming rolled by outside the windows, and Mackenzie sat in the passenger seat with that infernal iPod plugged into her ears.

Patrick loved his wife with something deep in his soul. He also knew that Mary loved him. But the last couple of years had been rough. Patrick was sure that it was mostly due to their differences in parenting. Patrick believed that strong boundaries with consequences were essential to raising kids. Mary's beliefs weren't too far from his, but she felt that it was okay for Mackenzie to run around with the dark brooding friends that she has and spend all of her free time staring at the small screen on her iPod. Mackenzie was a good girl with a caring heart, but she could recognize the growing rift in the differences of their parenting styles; and she had been driving a wedge between them every chance she got to earn more freedom that every teenager desires.

"Hey Dad, is that Butt Mountain?" Mackenzie asked an hour or so after they had passed the Wyoming sign. She had to speak a little louder than normal to be heard over the radio. She again had pulled the one ear bud from her ear and was looking out the windshield to a large hill on the horizon on the south side of the interstate that rose abruptly out of the nearby plains. This time though she was sitting forward with only a partially disinterested furrow on her brow.

It took Patrick a minute to register what she was talking about, but then it came back to him. When she was young, probably around eight years old; they had taken a camping trip to the mountains above Sheridan, Wyoming. For whatever reason at the time, she had decided to call the large hill "Butt Mountain". Her little cousin that went with them was only five or six years old at the time and he thought that was the funniest thing he had ever heard. Patrick couldn't recall where the reference came from or how many laughs she had gotten out of that single name, but it went on for miles. After a while he had playfully told her that wasn't the correct name for it and that she should quit saying crude things in front of her little cousin. All the while her mother and dad were snickering in the front seat. That kept the game going on for even more miles while that infectious laughter from her and her nephew made the time fly by.

As Patrick remembered the reference, he couldn't help the grin that tugged at the corner of his mouth. He reached to turn the radio down so that they wouldn't have to strain to talk over Rush Limbaugh's opening monologue, but stopped short when he glanced over to see that the ear bud was firmly fixed back in her ear and the glazed over stare of discontent was back on her face. With that one look, Patrick's grin was gone.

He knew that she didn't want to come along on this trip. She would have rather hung out with the delinquents that she calls friends, or even just sat in her room with her electronics for the weekend in that make believe social media world. If he would have given her a choice, she probably would have said that she would rather "kiss a creeper's foot" instead of spending three days in the mountains with her dad. Whatever that meant. Although he knew that she didn't want to be here, Patrick knew that she needed it. He needed it. He didn't really think that one backpacking trip would take her out of that teenager know-it-all attitude, but he had to at least try to break through that hardened heart somehow and show her what life and love truly was. If he could get that special five minutes of openness while secluded with her in the beauty of the Rocky Mountains to impart a kernel of wisdom and love in her heart, he thought that it could infect her life. As a father, he had to hope and try to create that one special moment. And then try to recognize and take advantage of it when it happened.

His wife Mary had other opinions about the trip. She thought that it would further stress their father daughter relationship while Mary stayed back at the ranch with their three-year-old boy, Piggy the dog, and a forty-hour a week job of her own at the newspaper. Patrick spent plenty of good-will capital with his boss as well. They had several deadlines coming due next week, and Patrick was the only engineer that knew enough about the projects to get them done. Patrick was confident that he could complete the work on time, but his boss wasn't as trusting. He didn't care for Patrick taking a four-day weekend to traipse across the country for personal time with such large deadlines looming. But Patrick felt that this trip was needed. That the trip was worth the cross looks and discouragement from his wife and boss, if it worked. And it had to work.

A couple of hours more on the road and they exited the interstate to a little town called Buffalo. Makenzie had long since drifted off in a late afternoon nap and didn't wake as they pulled off the interstate and into the sleepy little town as the sun began to set. The Big Horn Mountains (part of the Rockies) enveloped the horizon and caused Patrick to pause in awe after turning the ignition off in front of the motel that he had previously booked. He almost couldn't wait to get up there and briefly thought about skipping the motel to drive up to a campground instead. Patrick had been on this hike a couple of times as a kid, and the memories of the beauty and comradery were ingrained in him. The trail went high up to the top of the mountain range where it zig-zagged around a dozen small glacial lakes. The rugged beauty and solemnness of the trail was something that had impacted him deeply as a kid, and he held out hope that it would do the same for his daughter.

Instead of waking Makenzie up before going into the motel to check in, he let her rest in the car with her head up against the passenger window. The air still had a definite chill to it in mid-June, and whatever cobwebs and doldrums had been affecting his brain after ten hours on the road were long gone by the time he got back to the car. Patrick had stiffly slid back behind the wheel and was planning on asking his daughter what she wanted to do for dinner when he realized that she was gone.

First fear and then anger rose to Patrick's chest and shoulders as he looked quickly around the parking lot to see where she might have gone. Mackenzie was always doing something like this to infuriate him. She never seemed to have respect for others now that she was a full-fledged teenager. He left the car parked under the overhang in front of the motel and walked towards the gas station that was immediately adjacent to the motel's parking lot. He thought that was the most likely place that she would have wandered off to.

Halfway across the gas station's parking lot, he saw her standing in line at the checkout counter inside the station. The fear that had gripped him quickly subsided, but it was immediately replaced by more anger.

He continued to walk towards the gas station's entrance, and met her at the door as she was exiting. "Hey Dad," she said smugly as she walked past him.

"What the --heck are you doing!" Patrick half yelled at her as they marched back across the parking lot to their vehicle.

"Getting a coffee," she said lifting her cup with a gesture so that he could see it.

Patrick was beginning to see red, and knew that whatever he said next wouldn't be good for either of them. But he couldn't help himself. "You don't just wander off by yourself in a strange town to go get coffee! And coffee? Since when did you start drinking coffee?" He continued to half yell at her until they reached the car.

"Geez Dad! I just went to get a coffee while you were checking in," Mackenzie partly yelled and otherwise screeched back to her dad as she opened the door and got back into the passenger seat.

Patrick didn't allow himself to open the door right away as he saw through the side window that she had put the ear buds back into her ears. Instead, he spun around and muttered several things through clinched teeth that he wasn't even sure what they meant. He took two deep breaths, then opened the door and got back behind the wheel.

Patrick turned to his daughter, pulled the wire to the closest ear bud and pointed his finger at the startled Mackenzie. "Listen here," he started. "I know that you think that you're fully grown up and you can do whatever you want, but I don't care if you're an eighty-year-old grandma; you're not allowed to wander off by yourself without telling me where you're going."

Mackenzie didn't respond. She knew that she should have said something, but she was old enough to go across the street to get a coffee no matter what he said.

"Do you got me?" Patrick asked.

Mackenzie let the question hang in the air a little too long before saying "Mom said you'd be like this."

Patrick felt himself physically biting down on his lip enough to hurt. "I said 'Do you got me?'" He repeated.

Mackenzie let the question hang just long enough again to show her discontent and then answered with as much smugness as she dared, "Yes. I got you."

Patrick started the car, put his seatbelt on, and turned to ask his daughter what she wanted to do for dinner. Instead, she had her ear phones back in and he said to himself "Tacos it is then."

CHAPTER 2

"**YOU READY?**" **PATRICK** asked as he slung his pack over one shoulder. The backpack was a twenty-year-old external frame pack that was still in good condition. It was packed with gear that was a lot heavier than it probably should be for a three-day excursion, but Patrick didn't ask Makenzie to bring her share of the heavy stuff because he was anticipating the whining and complaining to be at an all-time high without adding any weight to her pack. A deep breath of crisp fresh mountain air made him forget about the extra weight on his back and got his heart pumping in anticipation of the hike. Patrick was not even close to as good as shape as he had been the years before when he last made this hike, but he had been putting in countless hours on the treadmill for the last few months trying to prepare for this trip. It was downright chilly for mid-June, with their breath just barely visible in the early sunlight.

"Hey –" Patrick said as he bumped Mackenzie's shoulder because she of course couldn't hear him with her ear buds in and her iPod cranked up to whatever it was she was listening to. "You ready?" he asked as she pulled one ear bud out long enough to hear him and nod in response. He didn't see that hate in her eyes that morning that was usually there staring back at him; just solemnness. The blank stare and few words was most likely due to lack of sleep and her teenage body not used to waking up before the sunrise.

"I'm going to put the keys…" Patrick started to say but realized that those buds were back in her ears and she wasn't paying attention again. He thought about telling her that there was a rule on this trip of no electronic devices until they make it back to the vehicle, but he decided against it. If he did that, it would just add to her disdain for being up here with him. The batteries in all her electronic devices surely couldn't last the entire trip anyways. It would be nice to have a peaceful and quiet hike without the complaining. Up to Lake Helen at least. Patrick went ahead and put the keys to the vehicle up under the back bumper and made a mental note of telling Makenzie where he put them once the ear buds were surgically removed from her skull.

He threw the other shoulder strap over his shoulder, situated the load a little, and tightened the chest and waist straps to get ready for a long walk up the mountain. Patrick motioned with his hand for Makenzie to follow him and walk the couple of hundred yards along the edge of West Tensleep Lake to the trailhead where their journey was to begin. The sign at the trailhead was just as he had remembered it from his youth. It was a dark brown painted sign supported by two wooden posts. It had a map of the trails in the area, some Forest Service information, registration cards, and a pencil tied to it. Patrick filled out the personal information on the registration card and stuffed it in the box so they would know who was on the trail and where they would be in case there was an emergency. He looked around to make sure Makenzie was situated and ready to start the hike, but she wasn't there. Patrick couldn't believe that she'd taken off again. He felt the anger rising in him. He called out a few times for her at a level not to disturb any fishermen or campers near the lake, but she didn't answer.

With his heart racing from fear and anger, Patrick began to trot back down the trail to where he had last seen her. He was moving a little too fast and not paying enough attention to what he was doing. Patrick didn't pick his right foot up high enough and stumbled on an exposed root on the well-worn trail. With his internal balance being off center from being strapped to the heavy backpack, he couldn't catch himself in time and he fell like a rock. He landed hard on his right knee and hands. The pain was sharp, but not unbearable; and it only took him a second to stand up and get trotting again.

Within a couple of hundred feet he could see the vehicle where he had left it, and standing in the same place as when he had left was Makenzie. Patrick was no longer nervous and worried for her well-being, but rather he was just filled with anger and he could feel his jaw tighten as he walked the last hundred feet back to the car.

"What are you doing?" Patrick scathed as he yanked on the cord of her ear phones to pull them from her ears.

"Hey!" she said.

"Where have you been?" he said as he glared at her. He then lifted his right foot to the back bumper of the car and hiked his pant leg up over his knee.

"What happened to you?" she said as they both inspected the damage. There was some slight scrapes and contusions on his knee cap, but the thing that bothered Patrick the most was that it was already beginning to bruise dark on the inside edge of his knee cap. And of course, once he saw the injury, it seemed to ache twice as much as it had before.

"I fell on the trail running back here to find you." he said crossly as he reached out and pushed a little on the bruise to see how tender it was. A sharp pain shot up his leg and he let out an involuntary snort with it. "I told you to follow me up to the trailhead. What are you doing back here still?" Patrick said with his jaw still tight from anger and the pain in his knee.

"I thought you were still getting ready" she answered somewhat defensively. "I told you that I was ready, but you didn't say anymore."

With his blood boiling, and with what he was sure was a cold stare from his eyes he told her "No more electronics or ear-phones while we're hiking." Patrick pulled his pant leg back down over his knee and told her in the same cool voice "Now, let's go." Patrick turned and started back to trailhead anticipating a whine or some other flak, but he didn't hear any. His knee now was throbbing and ached enough that with each step that he put weight on it, he noticed himself limping on it a little.

After a few steps Patrick didn't turn around to see if she was following, but he could hear her trudging along behind him. She muttered something that Patrick couldn't understand, but he thought that he would just let it go. As they walked past the trailhead sign and got onto the main hiking trail, Patrick remembered thinking that this trip was starting out just like his wife had told him it would go. If the rest of the weekend was this fun, Patrick didn't know if Makenzie would ever even speak to him again. His anger was beginning to subside and give way to his concern over the pain in his knee.

This wasn't the hike that Patrick had pictured in his head when battling Makenzie and his wife about taking the trip. He somehow thought that once they just got up there on the trail with the sun shining and the fresh mountain air in his lungs, he'd visit that place in his mind where he went when he was a kid. That place where there wasn't a single care in the world. Pure bliss. This hike was anything but that place. The sun was beginning to shine, the air was as fresh as ever, and the chipmunks would bark in the background; but pain filled Patrick's every step and bitterness oozed from every breath and snort from Makenzie as she trudged along the trail behind him.

As they reached a small crest of a hill on the trail, another hiker and his son passed the two while they were heading the opposite way down the mountain. Patrick stepped off the trail to let them pass, and he motioned for Mackenzie to do the same. Patrick saw that they had fishing poles strapped to their packs, so between his gritted teeth he asked them if they had any luck. The man responded without slowing and while looking over his shoulder at them as they passed by "They're biting like piranhas up there. We were using 'hoppers, but they're so hungry I bet they'd hit a bare hook if they see one."

Just at the crest of the hill where they passed the other hikers was the perfect sitting rock. "Let's take a quick break." Patrick told Makenzie. They were only a mile or so from the trailhead, but his knee felt like it had just walked to Kansas and back. Patrick took the lead and carefully sat down on the rock with the weight of the pack on his back. He dug the water bottle out of its pouch on his side, took a swig, and offered it to Makenzie. Without looking up, she just made a "fffftt" sound from between her lips as she also carefully sat down on the rock next to him.

"At least it sounds like we'll be able to catch something and won't have to eat oatmeal every night" Patrick said.

Still nothing from her. She just kept her eyes down and her hands on her knees.

He gave up on trying to change the mood and decided to inspect his injury. He pulled up his pant leg over his knee and was in awe with how much worse it looked than it had just a short time ago. The scrapes and contusions looked the same, but the swelling on the inside of the knee cap was now huge and it had begun to seriously bruise. It looked like he had eaten a purple apricot, and instead of going through the normal digestive tract; it somehow got wedged next to his knee cap. Now that he saw the damage, Patrick had serious thoughts about whether they should continue or not. If it got any worse, he'd hate to be stuck on top of the mountain with his daughter and not be able to get back down.

Patrick gritted his teeth and braced himself for the pain as he gently touched the apricot with his finger. It was extremely tender, but not as bad as he thought it would be.

"You alright?" Makenzie quietly asked with steel in her voice yet.

"I've had worse blisters on my lips and never quit whistling" Patrick said as he slowly and carefully pulled his pant leg back down over his knee. "You want to take the lead for a while?"

"I don't know where I'm going" she responded.

"There's nothing to it. There's only one fork in the path between here and Lake Helen; and we're taking a left" he said as he was trying to get up.

"OK" she said. It wasn't much, but at least she was talking instead of snorting.

The rest of the hike was uneventful. Except for when she stopped at the fork in the path to make sure they both were going left, Makenzie was barely visible to Patrick on the trail ahead as she was walking faster than his bum knee would allow. Mackenzie wasn't in great physical condition, but she played enough soccer and softball during those seasons to make up for her slothfulness the rest of the year. Patrick thought that from the bounce in her step and the way she would whip her head around every once in a while to make sure that he was still behind her, that she was at least slightly enjoying herself.

Patrick didn't catch up to her until they reached the lake and Mackenzie was standing at the edge of it just off the trail. Despite the pain in his knee telling him to sit down and rest, Patrick had to take a deep breath and let his eyes soak in the beauty of Lake Helen. The lake was right at timber line, so there were pine trees randomly scattered about the edges of the lake; but all around and above the lake were boulders and the majestic peaks of the Big Horn Mountains. It was late afternoon by the time they arrived at the lake, and the sun was just above the ridge line to the West which created a shimmer so bright that it was difficult to look at on the water's surface. While this was a popular destination as far as back country hiking goes, there wasn't another soul to be seen or heard around the lake.

Makenzie was still gazing at the lake when the pain in Patrick's knee over took his bewilderment of the lake's beauty and he sat down on a large boulder behind her. He massaged the area around the hurt knee while he waited for her to take in the sight.

After several minutes, he noticed that she had those ear buds back in her ear. That's probably why he hadn't heard as much as a whine or complaint from her on the hike up here. He decided to let her disobedience go this time. Instead of chastising her, he picked up a small, smooth, flat rock instead and attempted to skip it across the lake in front of her. As soon as the rock hit the water the first time, Makenzie jumped straight up in the air; back pack and all. Before she landed, her head had swiveled back towards her dad to see where the projectile had come from. Once she had realized that Patrick had thrown the rock, the expression on her face went from wide eyed startled wonder to disdain just as her feet landed back down on the rock she had been standing on.

"What are you doing?" she asked somewhat scolding, startled, and out of breath. She pulled the ear buds from her ears and took the few steps back to the rock Patrick was sitting on. "You scared me half to death" she said as she sat down next to him with her pack still on her back.

"Just seeing how many skips I could get. I've never really been good at skipping rocks. That was probably one of my all-time records with four or five skips," he said as he was staring down between his feet looking for another flat stone. "My dad always told me that the trick was finding the right rock, but nothing ever seemed to matter when I did it. I guess a good rock doesn't make up for poor throwing skills."

Patrick found a stone he liked and continued to impart wisdom of skipping rocks to her "You're supposed to get a flat, light rock; and then throw or flick it with the flat face as parallel to the water's surface as you can get it." He gave that one a flick, but it didn't come off as graceful as he had envisioned.

"You're such an engineer Dad" Mackenzie said half-joking.

The two of them continued to attempt to skip rocks from that boulder for too long. It was almost dusk when they decided to setup the tent and make camp.

CHAPTER 3

BOTH HIKERS HAD good intentions of rising early the next day and breaking camp so they could make it up to Misty Moon Lake early enough in the afternoon to be able to fish some. As a result, they both opted for lukewarm oatmeal from the camp stove the night before, and turned in early. The thought of eating fresh trout out in the mountain air sounded great to them both. However, Patrick could tell that they probably missed their opportunity for much fishing when he opened his eyes for the first time that morning. He could tell that the sun was mostly overhead from the way that it shown through the tent.

While he could tell that he was much older now than the last time he slept on the ground, Patrick didn't think that it was that bad. He was dreading moving his knee this morning because he was sure that it had gotten stiff from laying in a sleeping bag all night, but it wasn't that bad either. It still was painful as he crawled out of the sleeping bag, but it felt a little better than it had when he had turned in last night.

To Patrick's surprise and chagrin, Makenzie wasn't in her sleeping bag or even in the tent. He unzipped the door to the small backpacking tent and got dressed. He hurried more than he normally would have as he realized that Makenzie wasn't in camp or by the lake that he could see.

While Patrick's knee felt better than it had the day before, it let him know that it still didn't want to carry all his weight after he finished dressing and stood up for the first time. Just when his adrenaline started to pump again as Patrick realized Makenzie was not within sight, he saw her walking back to camp from the other end of the lake. She had her pole slung over her shoulder and it looked like she had a couple small trout on her rope stringer that she was awkwardly holding a little too far out in front of her. Seeing that adrenaline was no longer needed, he felt his heart begin to slow down and he sat down on the rock where he had sat the night before for dinner. He massaged the area around his knee until Makenzie sauntered back into camp. While she was trying to look grown up and professional, she was grinning ear to ear.

"Nice catch" Patrick said as she got closer. "Are those rainbows…. or sardines?"

"Ha…" she said flatly while the grin remained plastered to her face. "If you help me clean them, I'll let you have one for breakfast."

"You catch 'em; you clean 'em" he told her as she reached camp and held the stringer out to him at arm's length. Even though he just looked at her and didn't make a move to take the fish from her, she remained still. As soon as the grin that he'd been holding back reached the edge of his mouth, he took the stringer from her and they both chuckled a little.

Patrick's knee was still tender, but it did feel better than it had the day before. He could almost keep up with Makenzie on the hike up the steeper climb to Misty Moon Lake. This part of the hike was high in elevation and was totally above the tree line, so he could keep his eye on his daughter even if she got quite some ways ahead of him. His pack was heavier than it should have been, but he felt like he was getting his stride because almost nothing was bothering him as much as it had the day before. By the time that they hiked past the tiny Lake Marion, Patrick could feel a glisten of sweat on his brow and still felt like he had plenty of gas in the tank yet.

Patrick could tell that the trip was working. Even though Makenzie and Patrick weren't hugging and giggling like little school girls, he could tell that the tension between them was not as heavy as it had been in the last few months. Over breakfast that morning, he even saw a reluctant grin or two break through her scowl. They weren't there yet, but the pure beauty of the wilderness and close quarters of backpacking were having an effect. Patrick would bide his time until just the right moment to have a heart-to-heart discussion with her about her friends and where she may want to go with her life.

Makenzie decided to take a break before the last long hill up to Misty Moon Lake. She was leaning back on a large boulder to take the weight of her pack off as Patrick caught up to her. She pulled one headphone from her ear as he approached and pointed to a boulder field a hundred feet away. "What are those Dad?" she asked.

It took a second for his eyes to adjust and focus on what she was pointing at, but then he saw the furry tan creatures ducking in and out from around the rock piles. "Whistle-pigs," Patrick responded as one of the small dog-sized creatures stood up on its hind legs on top of a boulder to get a better look at them.

"What?" she asked assuming that he was pulling her leg.

"Whistle-pigs," he repeated matter-of-factly. "That's what my dad called them. I think that most people call them rock-chucks or varmints. Back east they call them; or something like them, wood-chucks."

"They're cute" she said as she wrinkled her nose trying to get a better look.

"If you're real quiet you can hear them whistle or chirp," he said in a hushed tone so she could listen. Patrick dug around in the side pocket of his pack that he could reach and pulled out some small binoculars. After looking through them for a second, he handed them to Makenzie. She peered through the binoculars at the whistle-pigs for quite some time.

"They like to live up here above timber line. As we get higher, they'll come out in the hundreds." He spotted another boulder field that had another clan of them and pointed those out to her as well. "They also make a tasty snack for bear."

"Ooooooh. Daaaad!" she said as she shoved his shoulder before they stood back up and headed up the long hill.

When they reached the top of the hill to the lake Patrick stopped and pointed to the north-west corner of the lake where two other pack tents were setup. One of the tents had a bright yellow roof on it as theirs did, and the other was entirely a fluorescent orange. Their colors made them standout like a sore thumb against the entirely grey boulder backdrop. He said "I was hoping we could get that spot over there. It's the nicest one up here, but there's another good one over on this side of the lake by the outlet."

"Where do you think the other campers are?" Makenzie asked as she fell in line behind her dad that had started walking over to the secondary site.

"I'm sure that they're either up at one of the other lakes fishing like we're planning, or they might be trying to summit Cloud Peak" he replied as he pointed back over to the peak behind the other tents. "Cloud Peak is the highest point in the Big Horns, so a lot people come up here just to see if they can make it to the top."

They reached the level spot that Patrick had used as a camp site years ago when he was a kid. They shook their packs off as soon as they stopped. It was late afternoon, but they had made better time than Patrick thought they would have. "You know, if we hustle to get camp setup I bet we can still get a little fishing in up at one of the lakes if you want" Patrick offered.

"Why don't we just go now and setup camp when we get back?" Makenzie asked.

"Darlin'... when it gets dark up here, it gets dark. I don't know how many camps you have set up in the dark with a flash light hanging out of your mouth, but it's no fun. If we hustle, we can get everything done in twenty minutes and not have to worry about it if the fishing's hot up there," Patrick explained in his father-knows-best voice.

"Okay" she said flatly, but with no sign of the scowl that has been oozing resentment for the last few months.

Patrick clutched his chest and feigned a heart attack as he gave her a hard time "What? No smart-aleck comeback or pouting fit? Just general agreement from the teenage daughter about words of wisdom from her father?"

"Stop" she chuckled as she gave him a light push on the shoulder. "Let's just get this done so we can go fishing."

They started setting up the tent as Patrick said "Have I ever told you about Bomber Mountain?"

"Yeah I think so, but I don't really remember the story behind it. Is that up here?" she asked.

"Yeah. It's right up above where we'll be fishing," Patrick answered. They continued to talk as they went through the motions to setup the small two-man pack tent. "I don't exactly remember the story either, but I read a book about it when I was a kid. During World War II, a bomber left somewhere west of here and was heading to Nebraska to stop and refuel before heading over to Germany. But it never made it there. It was quite a mystery for a few years until some cowboys seen something glinting from one of the peaks up here one winter, and they made a trek up the mountain the next spring to check it out."

Patrick thought that it was nice being able to work with Makenzie and not have either of them yelling at each other. Since they had already put up the tent together the night before, they just fell into doing the same tasks that they had done previously while Patrick continued with what he remembered of the story. "I don't remember how many airmen were on board, but I think it was close to a dozen. They think that most of them didn't make it through the crash, but the story has it that one of them was found with his bible in his lap leaning against a boulder not too far from one half of the plane."

"That's terrible," Makenzie answered solemnly. "Do they know why it happened?"

"I don't think that they know for sure, but probably the pilots were off course somewhat in bad weather and ran into the mountain. Half of the plane ended up on the west side of the ridge and the other half ended up on the other," he concluded the story as they finished pitching the tent and he zipped the rain fly up.

"How'd they get the plane down from here?" Makenzie asked as she gazed around at the rough terrain and remembered the long hike up from the car.

They started getting their fishing gear together and put what they thought they would need in a large fanny pack that Patrick planned to carry up the hill. "It was still there when I was a kid," Patrick told her.

"What?!" she exclaimed in excited disbelief.

"Yeah. You could tell that time was rough on it and people had taken pieces of it as souvenirs over time, but the big pieces of fuselage were still there," he told her. Patrick was glad to see that she was genuinely interested in something besides dark music and hanging out at the strip mall.

"Can we go see it Dad?" she asked without hiding the excitement in her voice.

"Sure. I don't think that we'll have time today, but I'm sure we can go up there first thing in the morning if you want," he told her as they started the short hike up to the other small glacier lakes. Although Patrick was somewhat tired and sore from packing the last two days, it felt as if he was as light as a feather without the heavy pack on his back. The pain in his knee was only a dull throb.

Patrick could tell that Makenzie was somewhat disappointed to not be able to go up to the remains of the bomber immediately after he had just gotten her excited about it. So, he told her "There is a little plaque up at Florence Lake that talks about the bomber mission and the people that died. We should be able to see that at least today."

"Why can't we go up there today and look at it Dad?" she asked.

They came to the top of a slight ridge and he stepped to the side of the trail so that they could stand next to each other and look ahead for a second. The view was glorious. They were in the glacier bowls of the Big Horn Mountains and there was not a mark that man had made on the country for as far as you could see. To their right was the valley that they had spent the last two days hiking up, and the afternoon sun shown an orange hue on the wilderness below. Patrick was certain that if he had strong enough binoculars you could have seen all the way back to the trailhead from there. Straight ahead of them was a magnificent ridge line that still had quite a bit of snow pack on top of it, even though small waterfalls cascaded down the face of the ridge from the melting snow. From where they were, the trail continued straight ahead for some ways past Gun Boat and Fortress Lakes, then turned left and made a steep climb.

Patrick could tell that Makenzie was just as enamored with the view as he was when she let her breath out, but forgot to breath back in as she stepped up next to him on the trail. Patrick didn't say a word for a few seconds and let her take in the beauty, but then pointed up the steep hill that the trail took up towards Bomber Mountain. "Florence Lake is right at the top of that hill you can see," he told her. Patrick then moved his finger to point at the summit of the ridge above the hill and said "The bomber is up above the lake across those boulder fields. I don't think that we want to try to navigate those boulders in the dark." He didn't even have to use my father-knows-best voice this time, she just started along the trail again.

"Well let's get some fishing in at least before it gets dark" she said back over her shoulder to him. Even though he couldn't see her face, he could tell there was a little bit of a smile in her voice.

The climb up to Florence Lake was steep, but both had a little bit of bounce in their step since they didn't have their heavy packs on any longer and the thought of a fresh trout dinner was on their minds. The sheer beauty of the mountain and the whimsical whistle-pigs that lined the trail made Patrick think that he had stepped onto another planet made up in fairy tales. They didn't stop at all on the steep climb up to Florence Lake, but Patrick could tell that Makenzie was taking all her surroundings in as well. Her head was on a swivel going back and forth looking at the whistle-pigs ducking and diving behind the boulders, and staring at the huge ridge lines covered in snow to their right and in front of them.

As they topped the steep hill along the trail to Florence Lake, there was a perfect sitting rock just to the right of the trail. They decided to rest on it while they assembled their fishing gear. From that rock they could look back down the trail and steep hill that that they had just climbed, or look down the other side of the hill towards Florence Lake. The lake was another hundred yards down the trail and maybe thirty or forty feet in elevation drop. The trail continued past the lake. They could see another glacier lake up another steep hill called Golden Lake, but the trail was hard to make out from a distance in the midst of the boulders.

Makenzie and her dad decided to both use variations of spinner baits to start out with and began walking down to the lake. Patrick had forgotten just how small Florence Lake was, even for upper glacier lakes. Sheer granite walls surrounded the far half of the lake, so only a portion of the lake was accessible by rock hopping around one side of it. There was no vegetation around the lake either, so trying to sneak up on wily cut-throat trout seemed next to impossible. "The best way I think there is to fish this lake is to get to where you want to be, sit quiet for a little while, and then cast across it. Do you think you can handle that if I go over on this side of the lake?" Patrick asked Makenzie in a tone not much louder than a whisper.

"I think that I could cast across it with a Snoopy pole Dad," Makenzie said rather offended, but with a quiet voice so the fish weren't spooked.

"I meant the being quiet part," Patrick said as he started around the left side of the lake hopping from boulder to boulder while Makenzie started around the other side.

Even though the lake was small, it sure was deep. The water was a deep green against the far side of the lake against the granite walls. Patrick reached the boulder that he wanted to be at where he could cast in a few different angles and most likely make it across the lake near those granite walls and into the deep water.

"A Snoopy pole...." Patrick muttered under his breath. Mackenzie could strike his funny bone or push his buttons sometimes more than anyone else on the planet. He thought that maybe his wife was onto something when she would tell him that Makenzie was just like him.

Patrick cast the spinner bait and allowed it to sail through the air towards the other side of the lake. The line was traveling too fast and he had to pull back on the pole to put some drag on the line so the spinner bait didn't crash into the granite wall. The tactic was successful in that the spinner didn't hit the wall, but instead of gliding into the water silently it made a rather large plop and splash when it landed. He glanced over to see if Makenzie was laughing at him, but she hadn't seemed to notice the splash at the other end of the lake. Patrick hoped that she didn't think that his rusty fishing skills were the correct way to go about it. It had been a long time since he had been fishing. Even though his skills needed to be polished, all those reasons why he had passed on the fishing trips didn't seem as important now as they had at the time. The monthly report to the boss; the broken piece of equipment; the upset product engineer from Germany wondering why the schedule had slipped by two days; along with the hundred other regular occurrences that kept him from fishing and these backpacking trips with Makenzie felt insignificant even though they were almost insurmountable at the time.

They fished for an hour or so and didn't get a hit. They both changed spinners a couple of times, Makenzie ended up using salmon eggs, and Patrick tied on a clear bobber and dry fly, but they still didn't have any luck. Patrick was just about ready to ask Makenzie if she was ready to head back to camp when he felt the earth move under his feet. His arms instinctively shot out from his side to help his balance as he looked down expecting to see the rock that he was standing on sliding into the lake. The rock didn't look like it had moved and his mind couldn't comprehend what was happening. Patrick's body was on full alert. It felt like his heart had jumped up into his throat. It wasn't until a split second later that he saw Makenzie had her arms out like a tight rope walker as well, and he realized that it must be an earthquake.

"DAD!" Makenzie involuntarily yelled.

Patrick had never been in an earthquake before and wasn't sure how to react. He continued to hold his arms out for balance as the rock beneath him continued to quake. He could see small stones and rocks start to move, and some of them slid or jumped into the lake at its edges. They weren't in any danger of anything falling on them, but he wasn't sure how a boulder field on top of the Rocky Mountains would react to an earthquake.

The whole thing only lasted for several seconds, and it was over as sudden as it started. "It was an earthquake," Patrick yelled back across the lake to Makenzie. He started to reel in his line in and go over to her when he got a strong bite. The fish hit it hard and started running. Patrick's rod tip bent almost to the water's surface as he instinctively set the hook. Patrick wasn't sure where it was swimming to in a lake this small, but the fish must have been diving down to the very bottom. Patrick looked over to Makenzie to tell her that he had a fish on and saw that she was fighting one too. He couldn't see her facial features very well from across the lake, but he could see that her fright from the earthquake must have dissipated and she was smiling from ear to ear. Since she seemed okay now that she had a fish on her line, Patrick decided to get his fish on the bank as well before heading over to her.

Both anglers were using extremely light tackle, so even though the fish they were catching were less than a foot long they felt like they we were catching blue marlin in the Gulf of Mexico. They kept fishing since the fish now seemed to be biting on anything that they threw into the lake. Patrick had four and Makenzie had three on stringers when the light began to turn a deep orange from across the top of the ridge to the west. Even though he couldn't see the sunset from where they were below the ridge, he could tell that they probably didn't have time to make it back to camp before it became dark. Patrick reluctantly began breaking down his pole and putting the tackle away from the boulder he was standing on. Patrick made hand signals across the lake to Makenzie to do the same and meet him back at the trail.

As Patrick began to hop back from rock to rock over to the trail, his knee reminded him that it was still too tender to stand in one place for several hours then get jolted from jumping and extending. The pain was bad, but it was more of a shooting pain from being stoved up, and he could tell that it was considerably better than yesterday. When he finally made it over to the trail he saw that Makenzie still hadn't stopped fishing yet. Just as he was going to yell at her, he saw her rod tip bend again as a fish hit and she set the hook. Instead of calling to her, Patrick decided to walk back to the top of the hill and wait on that sitting rock so he could take in some of the sunset from the top of the Big Horns.

As he neared the top of the hill and the rock that they had sat on while coming over to the lake, he could tell something wasn't right. Although he wasn't sure what was wrong, that nervous feeling you get in between your shoulder blades and down the back of your neck was in full effect. As he reached the rock and could begin to see over the top of the hill, it dawned on him that the color was wrong. The color of the sunset and the light hitting the rocks was a deep orange. He had seen plenty of orange sunsets in his life, but this deep hue of orange was different and somehow wrong.

Patrick looked back at Makenzie and saw that she was just landing the fish that she had caught, so he turned his focus back to the sunset. His adrenaline was pumping from the paranoid sensation he was having, so instead of sitting on the rock and taking the weight off his injured knee he continued to stand and just leaned against the rock. As his eyes adjusted and he scanned out across the landscape back to their camp, he saw what was causing the change in color and his concern. A thick dark yellow cloud was moving across the earth. It appeared to be a dense fog or cloud that was hugging the ground. The cloud was probably ten-foot-high at the leading edge that was moving east and grew much taller and thicker back to the west. It was so tall that it was blotting out the sun and causing the weird orange color to envelope everything. Patrick had never seen anything like it and his mind raced trying to reason it out and explain what it was.

From a glance back over his shoulder, Patrick could see that Makenzie was breaking down her pole and tackle. He turned his attention back to the cloud and continued to be awestruck. While there was only a slight breeze where he was standing, the mustard-colored cloud seemed to be moving extremely fast and was blanketing the entire landscape now. The cloud appeared to gracefully slide across the mountainous terrain, and he was amazed at the speed of how fast it moved. In a matter of seconds, it had passed from the area where they setup their tent to the ridge past Florence Lake that had taken them nearly an hour to hike. It seemed that it wasn't able to reach the very peaks of the ridges as it thinned out along the hill Patrick was standing on. From the feeling in the back of his neck and the adrenaline coursing through his veins, he knew that it was wrong; evil somehow.

Patrick was mesmerized at the sight of the cloud and the colors that it was creating as the sunset was trying to shine through it. It seemed as the whole earth was becoming the color of an amber traffic signal. The top and edges of the cloud were less dense and the color of hot dog mustard, while the center and thick portions of the cloud blocked out the sun rays entirely and were the color of expensive stone ground mustard with traces of deep orange. Patrick was so awestruck that he didn't hear Makenzie approach.

"Dad! What is it?" Makenzie exclaimed in bewilderment as she reached the rock that he was leaning against.

"I don't know Darlin'" he responded.

"Is it a forest fire?" she asked.

Although he knew that it wasn't, he said "I suppose that it could be." After a few seconds, he continued "If it is a fire, I think that we're okay since there isn't a tree for miles up here above timberline." They both stood silently and watched the cloud move and grow. Even though it lay as one thick blanket now across all that they could see, one could tell from the various yellow hues that it continued to move quickly across the ground.

The sun was almost totally set or blotted out before Makenzie asked "What are we going to do Dad?"

Patrick didn't know how to respond. He did know that they weren't going anywhere near that cloud. "I'm not sure Mak. It looks like the cloud or smoke can't make it up this high. I've been watching that edge closest to us since I first saw it, and it's stayed about fifty feet down the trail the whole time." He looked around at their surroundings in the growing darkness to see if there was a better place that they should be, and didn't see anything in the massive boulder field. "I guess we hunker down and see what it looks like in the morning," he reluctantly told her.

"What? How are we supposed to stay up here all night without our sleeping bags or stuff?" she asked challenging the reasoning.

"Well, I don't know what else we can do," he said. This time it wasn't his father knows best voice that came out of his mouth, but the one where he tries to explain his reasoning even if he's totally not sure of himself. "If that is a forest fire, that smoke is so thick that we'd have smoke inhalation problems before we could reach the tent. If it's something else, I don't think that we need to be near it either."

"Won't we freeze up here Dad?" Makenzie asked with her voice rising slightly in pitch and her words starting to come out faster and faster. "What are we going to eat? How long do you think we'll need to stay up here?"

The light was becoming so dim Patrick was having difficulty seeing her face even though she was only standing a few feet from him, but he could still tell that her eyes were opened wider than normal and her eyebrows were raised. He thought that she may calm down if she could keep busy. "Darlin, we'll get cold alright, but we won't freeze to death up here tonight." Patrick stretched out his hand with the stringer of fish in it to Makenzie and said "Why don't you run these back down to the lake? If we keep them cold enough, they will keep until tomorrow until we can get back to camp and use the stove."

"What are we going to eat tonight?" she asked with the excitement still in her voice.

"I think that we can get by with a granola bar or two from my fanny pack for one night, don't you?" he told her. Patrick flipped the fanny pack around to the side of his waist and began to rifle through it as she took the stringer from his hand. Patrick found a headlamp in the main compartment and helped her situate it on her head. Without any other words, she began to walk down the trail towards the lake carrying both stringers.

It was almost totally dark and the light from Makenzie's head lamp bounced up and down in front of her as she walked down the path back towards the lake. The setting sun could no longer penetrate the yellow cloud with its light, and it resembled the last embers of a dying campfire on the horizon. Patrick began searching around in the fanny pack again for another light source, but couldn't find anything other than the water tight container of kitchen matches that he always carried in the woods. He decided to leave those in the pack. It was so dark now that he couldn't make out the cloud down below him or even make out the rocks below his feet, so he decided to sit down on the sitting rock and try to figure out what they should do until Makenzie made it back to him with the head lamp.

Patrick's mind was racing and a tight feeling between his shoulder blades made it hard to concentrate. He closed his eyes, tipped his chin up towards the sky, and tried to take in three deep slow breaths before righting his head and opening his eyes. Makenzie was about half way back down the trail to the lake with the beam of the headlamp continuing to bob up and down. Every now and then, the light would dart to the left or the right as she turned her head to look at some unknown noise. Patrick could still feel some adrenaline coursing through his veins, but his mind had slowed to where he felt that he could reason some. His first thought with the somewhat clear mind was to pray.

He knelt on his good knee and leaned against the sitting rock as he faced down the hill towards Makenzie. He bowed his head and prayed in a quiet voice "Lord, I thank you. I don't know what that ominous cloud is from or what it is for, but I thank you for protecting Makenzie and me from it." As he said those words, he began to realize just how lucky they were to not have been caught in that cloud. From Patrick sleeping in this morning, to deciding to go on the late afternoon hike, to catching all the fish right after the earthquake all seemed to matter somehow. "I pray that You continue to protect us tonight and be with us. I also pray that You're with our family back home as You protect and comfort them. Please watch over my Mary and my little guy. In Jesus's name, Amen."

When Patrick opened his eyes and sat back up on the rock, Makenzie had reached the lake and was doing something at the edge of the lake. She must have been looking for something, because instead of the light bobbing up and down as it had when she was walking down to the lake, it was swinging from left to right almost in a frenzy. He closed his eyes again and tried to reason out what they should do and what precautions they should take. Patrick had made up his mind that they weren't going anywhere near that cloud, so that meant they were going to need to spend at least one cold night up there in the boulder field with their camping gear back down the trail.

They had plenty of water in the bottle in his fanny pack and Makenzie's bota bag for one night; and if they needed more, they had some iodine pills in the fanny pack. He ruffled through the fanny pack again and verified by feel that he had three granola bars left in there. If they got real hungry they could always have sushi, but he figured that they would need to be extremely hungry before that would happen. They both only had light weight jackets on and he knew they were going to get downright cold before the sun came up. Patrick could feel the warmth coming off the sitting rock through his legs and hands as he sat on it, but it would sap the heat from him once it cooled off enough. They had matches, but there was no fuel up in that boulder field for a fire.

Makenzie finished putting the stringers in the lake and was making her way back up the trail. She would look up towards her dad occasionally, and the light from her headlamp would point right at Patrick. He turned around on the rock and sat facing the cloud again so that his night vision wouldn't be as effected from Makenzie's head lamp. His mind drifted back to wondering what the cloud could be caused by. If Makenzie was right and it was smoke from a forest fire, they may need to stay up here for a day or two until the smoke dissipated enough. At least stay long enough to make sure there wasn't danger of being caught in the fire on the way back to the trail head. Patrick's gut told him that it wasn't a forest fire though. He could hear his wife's words from their argument about this trip echoing in his head when Makenzie reached the rock again.

"I couldn't find anything to tie the stringers to, so I just put a heavy rock on top of the leads," Makenzie reported as she plopped down on the sitting rock.

"That should be fine," Patrick said somewhat disconnected.

Patrick reached up and turned Makenzie's headlamp off so she would quit blinding him when she looked at him. As he did, he saw that she must have been crying for most of the walk down and back because her cheeks were streaked from tears. "Dad... I was thinking," Makenzie said as the light snapped off.

"What's that Darlin?" he asked still only half-listening.

"It's going to get super cold up here and there isn't any way to build a fire," she started without any real confidence in her voice. "What if we were to find what was left of that plane and stayed in it for the night?" she asked.

Patrick didn't respond right away and she let the quiet set in. He was still pondering what could have caused the cloud and didn't really register her question. After maybe a minute or so, Makenzie asked again "Do you think we could find that plane?"

"That's probably not a good idea Mak. It's been twenty years since I was up there last and it's hard to find in the daylight. We only have one flash light, and one of us will probably break a leg if we go boulder hopping in the pitch black," he said in his father-knows-best voice. It was utterly pitch black. Makenzie was only a couple of feet next to him on the rock, but he couldn't even make out her silhouette with the headlamp off.

"What are we going to do then?" she asked with a little bit of a quiver just on the surface of her voice. Patrick reached over and took the headlamp off Makenzie. He turned the lamp on and shown it in his lap as he unzipped the fanny pack to take stock of what all they had to work with. The fanny pack was organized with stuff in different pockets that included a GPS, a pair of binoculars, a short piece of para-cord, three granola bars, bug spray, iodine tablets, a camping saw, matches, fishing tackle, a water bottle, and a foil emergency blanket. There wasn't a T-bone steak hidden in there anywhere, but Patrick took some comfort in knowing that they had some things to work with.

Patrick didn't answer her right away, because he frankly didn't know what to do. The more he thought about trying to find the bomber, the more it made sense. It would give them both something to do and concentrate on so that they didn't sit there and go stir crazy waiting for the sun to come up. The fuselage would also give a little bit of a windbreak if they had to stay up there for a few days, and by hiking up there they would stay moving and wouldn't get near as cold.

"Maybe you're right Mak," he told her as he reached over and helped her fix the headlamp back on her head. "But if we're going to try to find the bomber, we have to work together and agree to some ground rules so that we don't get hurt." He pushed her chin to the side as he squinted and told her "The first rule is that you can't look at my face when you have that headlamp on." She giggled a little bit and he felt the tension in his neck relax just a little bit at the sound of it.

They walked down the trail to the lake where Makenzie had left the stringers of fish. While they walked, they talked about how it was important that whoever was wearing the headlamp had to keep the other person in mind the entire time. Patrick let Makenzie come up with the signals that they would use to communicate with each other while they were hopping from boulder to boulder. Since it was pitch black and they only had one light, the person in the lead would need to shine the light to the next boulder they were going to, jump over to it; then shine the light back to where they had been standing so the person behind could jump over to where the first person had been. It sounded complicated enough; but add being tired, being scared, a recovering knee, and a teenager into the process and someone was bound to get hurt.

Regardless of the danger, they had decided that they were going to find the bomber and that is what they headed out to do. Makenzie made up signal words for things that they would expect to need to communicate during the process. Patrick didn't know why he agreed to her silliness, but "Glurp" was what the person in front was going to say when they were going to shine the light to the next boulder in front of them. "Nip" meant that the person in back had moved and settled on to the next boulder so the person in front could shine the light somewhere else. Makenzie came up with a few other signal words that they didn't use or forgot by the time they had been moving for a few minutes. As expected, Makenzie would sometimes forget that Patrick couldn't see without the light so they came up with the signal word "Slerk" for Patrick to yell at her when he needed the light and she wasn't paying attention.

They found the memorial plaque near Florence Lake for the bomber site and decided to start straight up the boulder field from there. The bronze plaque's engraving was difficult to read in the darkness using the artificial light, but they were engrossed in the moment and determined to read the memorial. They stood a little longer than they normally would have and helped each other make out the words on the plaque that read:

THE FOLLOWING OFFICERS AND ENLISTED MEN OF THE U.S. ARMY AIR FORCE GAVE THEIR LIVES WHILE ON ACTIVE DUTY IN FLIGHT ON OR ABOUT JUNE 28, 1943. THEIR BOMBER CRASHED ON THE CREST OF THE MOUNTAIN ABOVE THIS PLACE.

The climb up the boulder field was considerably worse than what Patrick had remembered. Not only was the climb steep and somewhat treacherous across boulders and up granite outcroppings, but in the dark they couldn't pick or choose their route. Several times, they had to stop and back track to find another way around a cliff edge that they couldn't safely make it up. The silly signal words that Makenzie had come up with made the difficult trek more bearable for them both. Anyone listening to the exchange on the high mountain would surely have thought that aliens had landed.

"Glurp" … "Nip" … "Glurp" … "Nip" … "Glurp" … "Nip" … "Glurp." "Slerk!" … "I said Slerk!" … "Nip"

It was a monumental achievement, but just as they saw the first light of the sun gleaming on the horizon, they had made it to the top of ridge. They both were utterly exhausted and sat down to catch their breath. Because they had backtracked and changed their route so many times up the climb, Patrick wasn't sure where they were with respect to the memorial plaque down by the lake. He also wasn't sure whether they should walk up the ridge toward the peak or slowly make their way down the peak of the ridge.

"We did it Dad," Makenzie said with a victory in her voice as if they had cured cancer.

"We sure did kid," Patrick replied as he reached out and ruffled her wind-swept hair with his hand. "But the first rule was not to look at my face when you have that head lamp on," he told her as he turned her head by pressing on her chin again. They both chuckled for a second, but then she stopped abruptly and stared into the darkness. "What is it Darling?" he asked.

"I thought I had seen something," she said as she continued to peer into the darkness and pointed in the direction she was looking. As she moved her head slightly, Patrick saw it too. Something glinted just at the end of the headlamp's beam.

"I bet that's it kid," Patrick said as he squeezed her thigh, stood up, and headed in the direction of the glint. They did their best to walk side by side over the boulders along the crest of the ridge toward the glinting object using just the light of the headlamp. While the sun was coming up, it seemed to be taking longer than it should and the light from the headlamp was still necessary.

"That's it Dad!" Makenzie exclaimed before giving him a quick hug as they got close to the wreckage. She picked up the pace considerably and was almost running on her exhausted legs for the last few yards.

After reaching the fuselage, they both stood and looked at it as Makenzie panned the light from the headlamp from one end of the plane's remains to the other. It looked pretty much the way that Patrick had remembered it. It was just crinkled bare aluminum with metal pieces and parts littered among the rocks and boulders surrounding the large remaining piece.

"That's it Dad?" Makenzie asked a little disheartened as she took a good look at what was left of the bomber.

"Yep," he said without much emotion. "It looks like some scavengers have taken some pieces of it over the years, but it's pretty much the way I remember it. What were you expecting?"

"I'm not sure exactly," she said with disappointment in her voice. "And now that we're here, I'm a little creeped out that people died in there."

"I'm so tired that I don't care if there's a grizzly holed up in there," Patrick said as he got on his knees and began to crawl underneath the aluminum shell. He couldn't see a thing, so he was relieved when Makenzie joined him a few moments later with the head lamp.

There really weren't any flat or good spots to lie down underneath the plane, but they each picked out a spot where they thought they could rest and used the fanny pack to lay their heads down on. With the weird cloud, potential danger, and uneven granite rocks Patrick didn't think that he would get much rest, but he immediately fell asleep.

CHAPTER 4

PATRICK AWOKE WITH the sun glaring in his eyes. There was a porthole in the fuselage just above his head that he hadn't noticed when they laid down. As the sun made its way across the sky, it shown directly down onto his head. The sunlight was blinding, but he could tell through squinted eyes that Makenzie was still resting and wasn't stirring. Patrick slowly crept out from under the plane's remains by bear crawling backwards along the rocks and boulders until he was outside far enough to stand up. While his knee was stiff and sore, his back was almost as sore after the climb up the ridge last night and the few hours' nap on the uneven granite.

When he was free of the plane and could survey his surroundings, he was awestruck. The view was utterly mesmerizing. From the top of the ridge, it seemed as if he was standing on top of another world. Only Cloud Peak to the north was higher than where they were. The yellow and orange cloud had engulfed everything. Only the few peaks and ridges that were higher than Florence Lake stood above the cloud. It was as if he was standing on a foreign planet with the sun directly overhead. Patrick stared out at the wisps of the cloud that danced at the edges of the ominous mustard colored fog. He looked in the same south-west direction that they had last night when they had first seen the cloud, but now it was hard to judge how far Lake Helen, the trail-head, or anything was in the opaque yellow fog.

When he could break his trance from the scene, he walked and hopped the couple of hundred yards to the crest of the ridge where he could see to the east. The scene to the east was burned into his brain from when he had looked out from that same spot when he was a kid. On a clear day, he remembered that you could see almost forever from that ridge. You could easily make out the Town of Buffalo at the foot of the mountains, see the buttes that were south of the town of Gillette sixty miles away, and if you squinted you could even make out "Butt-Hill Mountain" near the Wyoming border. But what he saw this time was totally different. For as far as he could make out, it was nothing but the yellow-orange fog that was just as thick as it was to the south-west. It felt to Patrick as if he was staring out onto a yellow-orange ocean of evil from their secluded island. Patrick stood there mesmerized for a long time and was not sure how long he had been there when Makenzie approached. The sun was a little further across the sky, but it seemed like it was still early afternoon.

"You scared me," she said. "I couldn't find you anywhere," she continued with no emotion in her tone. She was just as mesmerized as her dad was at the lack of the landscape below and the rolling cloud.

After a few moments, she said more than asked "It's not a forest fire, is it?"

"Nope," he said without any emotion.

She nudged his shoulder and handed him a granola bar as she opened one as well. They both ate the bars and stared off in a trance at the cloud.

Patrick wasn't sure how long it had been when Makenzie yelled "Dad! Come look." He still had the granola wrapper in his hand, but the sun had moved almost all the way across the sky and was sitting just over the western horizon. He turned and saw that Makenzie was back at the wreckage and was looking in the direction of the sun.

"Dad," she called again and he began to briskly walk over to her. As he approached her, he could see what she was excited about. The cloud looked like it was partially dissipating to the west. At least it might be. He couldn't concentrate on what she was looking at totally until he reached where she was standing because he kept having to look down to watch his footing along the boulders. But it looked like the cloud wasn't as dense on the western horizon as it was in front of them.

"I think that it's breaking up," she said with a little bit of excitement in her voice as he reached her. She had gotten the small pair of binoculars that had been in the fanny pack and was looking in the direction of the setting sun. She pulled them back and offered the binoculars to Patrick.

He took the binoculars from her and pointed them in the same general direction that she had been looking. Patrick had to adjust the focus on them to try and make out what she was looking at, but it did seem that the cloud wasn't as dense on the Western horizon and that it was beginning to become thinner. It was hard to tell, but he didn't think that the cloud reached up as high on the ridge as it had when had looked at it earlier today. "It's hard to tell Darlin', but I think you're right," he told her as he continued to look through the binoculars at the cloud.

They both sat down and leaned their backs up against the wreckage of the bomber as they handed the binoculars back and forth and watched the edge of the cloud until the sun touched the far horizon. That eerie deep orange color filled the sky as the sun shone through the mustard colored cloud.

"What are we going to do Dad?" Makenzie asked.

Patrick had spent all day staring at the cloud and surveying the surroundings, so you would have thought that he had rolled all the possibilities around in his head and came up with the most prudent solution for their predicament. But he hadn't. He didn't even know if he had a single coherent thought from the time that he had crawled out of the bomber wreckage that morning.

"I'm not exactly sure Mak," he told her directly. "We'll take shelter here tonight and hope that the cloud dissipates overnight."

"Why don't we head back down tonight Dad?" she asked with some excitement in her voice. "If we make it down to Lake Florence tonight, we could head back first thing in the morning if the cloud's gone."

"Nah," he told her after little contemplation. "I don't think that the head lamp batteries will make it another night, and I think that we both could use some more rest before hiking out of here."

He could tell that she didn't like his plan from the way that she looked down between her bent legs, but she didn't argue the point at all. Instead she rifled through the fanny pack after a few moments and pulled out the last granola bar and unwrapped it. She tore it in half and handed one-half to her dad.

"You go ahead," Patrick said nodding to the half that she offered him.

"No Dad. We both need to keep our strength up," she said and kept the portion of the granola bar extended out him. Patrick somewhat reluctantly took it while she ate the other half.

Unlike the previous night, Patrick wasn't able to sleep. They had both turned in at the same time after dark, trying to share a portion of the shiny emergency blanket. However, his mind was fully engaged and racing now about their predicament and the nature of the cloud. When he realized that it was fruitless to lay in the make shift shelter any longer, he left Makenzie lay and he paced in the darkness outside the bomber wreckage that was dimly lit by the stars and a sliver of a moon.

Patrick had purposely left his cell phone in the vehicle when they had left for the trailhead because he didn't want any distractions from their bonding experience. There wasn't cell coverage on the mountain anyways. He now wished that he had brought it though just to occupy his time by watching the service bar while he wandered around the top of the mountain. He also didn't wear a watch anymore, so he could have pulled the phone out every few minutes to check the time to see how long they had until sunrise. As it was, he didn't have anything to draw his focus and attention away from the cloud and what their next steps should be.

A few hours before dawn, the stiff breeze that had been nearly constant since they reached the top of the ridge turned into a stiff wind. The pacing that had been keeping him warm in the breeze now wasn't enough in the stronger wind, and he hunkered down on the east side of the wreckage to escape it. Even though the whistling of the wind through the wreckage was loud in the otherwise perfect stillness, Makenzie seemed to sleep through it.

After a while, Patrick's nose caught the hint of an odd smell that he couldn't place. It was an odd odor had been carried along in the wind. Most flatlanders would think that you would smell pine and other woodland earthy smells while on the mountain, but Patrick was always amazed that above timberline there is a distinct lack of smells in the air. So the new distinct odor caught Patrick's attention rather quickly. While his senses couldn't place the odor, he could tell that it was out of place. It reminded him of a burnt-sweet smell. It was almost like that of sugar when it first begins to burn on a crème brulee or when his wife tried to make caramel for caramel apples for the first time and cooked the sugar too long. Almost like that, but not quite. The smell stayed in the air for a while, but it left almost as quickly as it had arrived, being replaced by the absence of smells in the clean crisp high mountain air.

Even though the wind was just as strong as it had been and the temperature hadn't increased at all, Patrick made his way back around to the west side of the wreckage at the signs of first light. The cold couldn't keep him from looking to see if the cloud had broken up anymore or if what they had thought they had seen last night had just been wishful thinking.

Makenzie stirred and then joined him outside as the first signs of light increased from the eastern horizon. They still couldn't make out any details of their surroundings when she exited the wreckage while rubbing her upper arms and making small bouncing movements to stay warm.

"Sleep okay?" he asked her.

She looked up at him with sleep still in her eyes and an almost painful look on her face and said "Not really."

They both waited in silence while staring to the west for the sun to rise enough to illuminate the landscape to see if the cloud had receded or not. It only took a few moments, but it seemed like hours. Patrick slowly paced around in a small circle and Makenzie bounced up and down while they waited. Neither of them took our eyes from the ridgeline to the west where they thought they had seen the cloud receding the night before.

The light came up gradually with the sun, and both Patrick's eyes and brain strained to make out what they were seeing. Makenzie's younger eyes must have been considerably better than her dad's because she was sure of herself when she exclaimed with jubilee "It's gone! It's totally gone!" Her slight bouncing to stay warm turned into jumping up and down for joy. She quickly turned and wrapped her arms around his chest, but her legs continued to jump.

Patrick slowly broke her grasp and removed her arms from around him so that he could concentrate on what he was seeing. His eyes were still trying to bring into focus the far ridge and find the cloud. As the light increased, it was evident that the cloud had receded much lower on the far ridgeline than it had been last evening. Looking down the valley towards the south, it looked like it had receded almost to Lake Helen. Even down there, it had dissipated in thickness and became much less opaque. It now looked more like a haze or smoke instead of a dense cloud. Patrick picked up the binoculars and looked down the valley at Lake Helen and the remains of the cloud. Through the binoculars he could see that the stiff wind that they had been experiencing on the ridge was down at the lower elevations too, and that the wind was carrying off the remains of the cloud.

"It's not gone, but it sure is leaving," he told Makenzie with relief, but not with near as much exuberance as she was exhibiting.

They collected their things, took one last look at the bomber wreckage, and began their trek down the ridge towards Florence Lake. Patrick wasn't sure why, but his knee bothered him a whole lot more coming down the ridge than it had going up. He had to stop several times to rest and pick different routes to reduce the amount of times that he had to bend his knee just to keep the pain in check. He could tell that Makenzie wasn't happy with the delays from the way that she would shift her weight back and forth and furrow her brow when she stopped and waited on him. Because of the delays, it was close to midday by the time they reached Florence Lake and the plaque from where they had started. They both sat and rested for several minutes without speaking to each other. Once rested, they gathered the fishing poles up that they had left near the plaque.

"Do you think the fish we caught are still good?" Makenzie asked.

"Oh yeah, I would think so. The temperature has been cool and I bet that lake water isn't too far from freezing," Patrick responded as his empty stomach growled when he started thinking about the fresh trout. He grabbed the stringers of fish and they both hiked up the hill to the sitting rock along the trail.

Makenzie didn't slow when she reached the top of the hill and the sitting rock, but Patrick grabbed her elbow gently and told her to wait a minute. He dug the binoculars out of the fanny pack and scanned the valley below looking for remnants of the yellow cloud. He couldn't see any clue that the cloud was still there no matter where he looked.

Patrick offered the binoculars to Mackenzie to look through as well, but she huffed and said "Let's just go Dad," as she started off on the trail back to their campsite where the tent was setup. Patrick didn't respond, but just fell in along the trail behind her. His knee continued to bother him even walking down the trail that was considerably less steep than the Bomber Mountain ridge that they had just descended. This time though, Makenzie didn't slow or stop to wait for him. She just continued at a quick pace along the trail such that she was out of sight by the end of the hike and had made it back to camp several minutes before Patrick arrived.

When he reached the tent, Makenzie had the camp stove setup and was rifling through Patrick's backpack looking for cooking supplies. She had already dawned her jacket and changed clothes, and Patrick began to do the same. He had expected there to be a residue or soot covering the tent and everything from the cloud when it left, but there wasn't anything that could be seen or felt.

By the time that the two cleaned, cooked, and ate the fish with some oatmeal it was late in the afternoon. They both were ravished and had made short work of the trout. Neither of them spoke during the meal preparation or consumption of it, and Patrick could feel Makenzie building that wall of anger back up between them. When the meal was finished and they were cleaning up, she began to pack her sleeping bag and other belongings up.

"It's going to be hard to make it back to the trailhead before dark," Patrick commented to her.

She immediately snapped her head around, cut her eyes to him, and responded sharply "I knew it. I knew you were dragging just to keep me up here one more night."

"That's not it at all," he said defensively. "I want to get back just as much as you, but my knee is killing me."

Makenzie continued to pack her belongings while her dad cleaned up the stove and stowed it. After a few minutes, he told her "Why don't you go over to the camp across the lake and see if those folks know what that cloud or fog was from? I'll stay here and break camp so that we're ready to head down when you get back."

He could see the tension ease somewhat in her as she realized that he was willing to at least break camp. She started off around the lake to the other camp and then came back immediately. She then grabbed the water bottles and purifier before heading off again along the trail to the other campsite where they had seen when they first arrived at Misty Moon.

She wasn't gone very long at all and Patrick had just finished breaking the tent down when she returned. Makenzie handed him a filled water bottle that he placed in his pack and asked what the other hikers knew about the cloud.

"Nobody was there," she said.

"Huh. Maybe they saw the cloud coming in and broke camp before it rolled in," he said half wondering.

"No," she said. "The camp was still up with their bags and packs all around. Just nobody was there."

Makenzie helped her dad with stuffing and stowing the tent and they both went through and looked over their packs one last time. Patrick transferred a few of the things over to Makenzie's backpack from his to make the weight being carried a little fairer. He had Makenzie get her flash light and raingear out and put them in side pockets where she could get to them in a hurry if they were needed. There was still plenty of light in the sky, but it was late afternoon and they didn't have much time before the sun would set. Patrick rubbed his sore knee again quickly before they hoisted their packs and quickly adjusted them for the hike back down to the trailhead.

"Now I know that you want to get back down to the vehicle as fast as possible and get off this mountain, but let's make sure that we do it safe. I would hate to spend another night up here nursing one of us with a broken ankle, because we were trying to move faster than we should," Patrick instructed. Makenzie turned to start the hike and after a couple of steps he added "Oh. And don't put that iPod back in your ears so we can communicate if we need to." Makenzie didn't say anything in response or even look back, but Patrick was sure she rolled her eyes at his last request.

Makenzie was in the lead, and just as her dad had worried she set a very fast pace. They weren't quite jogging down the trail, but almost. Much of the trail wasn't extremely steep, but it was downhill. Patrick's knee was still functioning okay after it limbered up some, but it let him know that it didn't like going downhill every step by sending dull pain messages.

Patrick wasn't sure how fast they were going, but he guessed that they were going down the trail three or four times faster than what it had taken them to hike up it the few days before. At the speed they were going, they might make it back to the trailhead just after dusk if one of them didn't twist an ankle and his knee decided to hold together.

When they reached Lake Helen, Makenzie stopped for the first time at a rock near where they had camped the first night. Patrick joined her by leaning up against the rock, rubbing his sore knee, and looked out across the lake trying to take a mental picture of scene.

"You know," Makenzie began while she stared out across the lake as well. "I don't remember seeing any of those rock chuck thingies on the way down."

After thinking about it for a little while Patrick told her that he didn't remember seeing any either. Neither of them offered any guesses of why that might be, but instead they each took a long pull from their water bottles and headed back down the trail.

The further they travelled, the more his knee was bothering him and the harder it became to keep up with Makenzie. By the time dusk fell, Makenzie was a couple of hundred yards in front of her dad clipping along at the same pace that they had started at. They had walked far enough that they were back down below timberline, and Patrick could only catch glimpses of her brightly colored light blue jacket through the trees occasionally. Now that they had entered the trees, the dusk was turning to early darkness and Patrick was debating whether to dig his flash light out of a side pocket on his back pack when he heard Makenzie scream.

CHAPTER 5

IT DOESN'T TAKE long for new parents to recognize the different whines, cries, and coos that their new born baby makes. Patrick's wife Mary could even usually tell if her children's diapers were wet or more soiled just by the pitch of their voice when they would cry. The same type of recognition is still there even when they get older. Patrick knew before Makenzie's scream was half-way over that she just wasn't startled, she wasn't excited about something, and she wasn't playing around. Something was wrong.

All his senses were immediately alert and his heart was pounding even before he started sprinting towards her voice. Patrick didn't recall undoing the buckles or taking the shoulder straps of his backpack off, but it was no longer on his back and he had left the trail to run straight to where Makenzie sounded like she was at. Patrick's body took over all action instead of his mind thinking what to do as he shirked limbs, ducked under branches, and jumped rocks and down trees while sprinting to Makenzie.

Her scream had only lasted a couple of seconds and had stopped well before Patrick reached a small clearing that intersected back with the trail. He slowed ever so slightly as he reached the edge of the clearing and surveyed the surroundings. He broke into the clearing on a rise where he could see across the small meadow of tall sweet grass sprinkled with spring mountain flowers. Patrick's senses were on overload as he tried to pick out any sign of Makenzie and whatever had caused her to scream, but there was no sign of her. The light was getting even dimmer, and he thought that he should have caught up with where she had been. His pounding heart leapt up into his throat and another wave of fear washed over him.

"M-A-A-A-K!" Patrick yelled for all he was worth as he dug in and sprinted across the meadow towards the point where the trail exited the meadow.

As he hopped over a fallen tree in the middle of the tall grass, he caught a glimpse of her light blue jacket on the ground on the trail only several feet past the clearing. As he closed the few hundred-foot distance between him and the jacket, he began to see it better in the waning light and he realized that the jacket was moving. Makenzie was wearing the jacket with her backpack still on and was down on all fours kneeling over something. She turned her head around to look at Patrick while remaining on her hands and knees when she heard him approaching. Patrick could see pure fear on her face and in her eyes. There was also a small amount of blood dripping from her nose in a small stream.

"Dad..." she almost whimpered as he reached her and half dropped, half slid on his knees to her. Patrick wrapped his arms around her and squeezed for just a brief second before turning his attention to what she had been kneeling over. Having Makenzie back in his arms started Patrick's crash back down from his heightened state of awareness and fear. Almost immediately he felt his heart pounding in his ears not from fear, but from physical exertion. His injured knee began to scream with sharp shooting pain that seemed to be non-existent when jumping over logs and rocks just moments ago,.

Looking down, Patrick saw what had instilled fear in his daughter. It was a dead man. A day hiker by the looks of it. He was laying on his back in a somewhat awkward position with one of his legs folded under the other. He had a blank dead stare that looked off into the timber to the right of the trail. He wore jeans, hiking boots, a light rain jacket, and had a tan camouflage fanny pack around his waist.

"What happened?" Patrick asked turning his attention back to his daughter. They both were still kneeling next to and over the top of the dead man as Patrick turned her head up to the sky using his hand gently on her chin. He was trying to see what had caused the blood coming from her nose. He couldn't see any real damage or cuts as the blood was coming from inside her left nostril and running down the curvature of her upper lip in a thin stream. After a second she pulled her head back and away from Patrick's hand, buried her face in his shoulder, and started to sob.

"I fell…" she started between sobs. She started a few more times, but couldn't get out more than those couple of words between her heaving breaths.

"Whoa, whoa" Patrick said trying to soothe her by holding her tighter. "Slow down. It's okay Darlin'. Slow down."

"Is… Is he… Is he… okay?" she stammered between sobs.

"I don't think so," Patrick told her in a low voice. He could tell immediately when he first saw him that he was gone. Patrick hadn't seen many dead people in his life, but once you had seen death you could recognize it easily. "Slow down now. Deep breaths," he continued to coax her while he held her close.

The dead man looked to be in his early thirties. He was slender with no real apparent striking features. Patrick assumed that he didn't spend much time in the outdoors based on his designer jeans and the rain jacket that appeared to be brand new. Just looking at him while comforting his daughter, Patrick couldn't tell what caused his demise.

After a moment or two, Makenzie got her breathing under control and pulled her head back from Patrick's shoulder some and looked up at him. Although she thought she was a teenager going on an adult, she looked to her dad in that moment like his little four-year-old girl that had fallen and scraped her knees while trying to learn to ride her bike without training wheels for the first time. Her nose had mostly stopped bleeding and was now mixed with tears and snot that she began to try to wipe off as she started to tell her dad what happened.

"I was just trucking along, trying to get back to the car" she started again with only a few small sobs breaking up her words. She leaned back on her haunches and then slowly stood as she continued with the story. "It was getting kind of dark, and I tripped and fell." She gently kicked the dead man's outstretched leg with the toe of her right hiking boot to emphasize what she must have tripped on. "I fell and hit my head hard. When I opened my eyes, I saw …him," she said looking down at the corpse. She gingerly touched the side of her face where her nose and check meet and continued "I must have hit my cheek on his chin when I fell, because when I opened my eyes his face was right there." Her last words trailed off a little bit and she didn't move or breathe for just a second. Patrick started to imagine how this incident was going to impact Makenzie.

Patrick leaned his weight back and tried to stand as well to better comfort Makenzie. But his injured knee physically gave out and let out a loud pop when he was about half way up. Intense shooting pain shot from his knee all the way up his back as he fell backwards to his rump and let out an uncontrollable groan of agony. Though Patrick's eyes were tightly closed, he saw intense white light. The pain was almost unbearable as he lifted his body and tried to situate his leg so it wasn't bent back behind him like the dead man lying next to him.

Makenzie was there trying to help her dad, but Patrick couldn't open his eyes or even tell himself to breathe until he was firmly sitting on his rear and his leg was stretched out beside him. As soon as he was situated, the sharp pained numbed somewhat but he felt bile rising in the back of his throat. Patrick leaned over and away from his body just enough, right before he vomited most of the fish and oatmeal that he had eaten earlier in the day in a few short heaves. Afterwards, Patrick leaned all the way back onto the ground, and clasped his hands together over his face. He squinted his eyes and gnashed his teeth trying to make it through the pain.

After a few short moments, Patrick collected himself enough to be able to tell that Makenzie was kneeling beside his head on the opposite side of the dead man and vomit. She had her hand on his chest and was sobbing again.

"Sorry, Mak," Patrick said through gritted teeth.

"What are you sorry for?" Makenzie responded. "I heard your knee pop like a branch breaking. It was my fault that we're even up here. It's my fault that you fell in the first place and hurt your knee." Her voice rose with each sentence and her tone became terser as she finished "and it's my fault that I tripped over this dead guy!" With that she collapsed over the top of her dad with her face on his chest sobbing again.

"Whoa," Patrick said. He put his arm around her the best that he could while lying on the ground and her laying over him in an awkward position. Patrick chose his words and rate of speech carefully because it felt as if he spoke too fast, he most likely would vomit again. "Listen. None of this is your fault. I'm sorry for dragging you up here, for spending the night on top of the mountain on a rock, that you had to even see this dead guy, and for what I'm about to ask you."

She lifted her head from her dad's chest and sniffled her running nose while looking at him in the eye. After a second, her questioning gaze turned from wonder to defiance. "No," she said somewhat defiantly. "No. No. No. No. No." she said in quick repetition and hid her face in her hands.

"Listen Mak…" Patrick started, but she jumped to her feet with her face still hidden in her hands.

"No Dad!" she half-screamed. "I'm not walking back to the car in the dark by myself after just tripping over this dead guy!"

Patrick let her words hang in the air for a moment while he gritted his teeth and tried to make it through the next wave of pain from his knee. "Okay Makenzie. Settle down Darlin'" he said trying to soothe her some. "First thing's first. Why don't you drop your pack, get your flashlight out, and walk back up the trail and see if you can find my backpack." After looking at him almost distrustfully out of the corner of her eyes for a few seconds she started to comply.

"I'm not sure where I left it, but if you just follow the trail and look back through the woods towards this spot I'm sure that it can't be that hard to find," he told her. It was almost fully dark and Makenzie's LED flashlight cut easily through the darkness as she found it and snapped it on. "I'm going to need the Ibuprofen out of the first aid kit in my backpack if I'm going to make it through this pain," Patrick told her as she put stuff back and resituated her back pack.

She stood and looked back down the trail that she had just walked minutes ago and appeared hesitant to take the first step. "It's okay," Patrick said trying to comfort her. "My backpack can't be that far. You were just out of my sight when you tripped, so it is probably just off the trail up in that next stand of trees." After another moment of hesitation, she started back down the trail slowly and cautiously without saying a word.

Patrick collapsed back and closed his eyes. The waves of intense sharp pain were starting to subside, but they were replaced with a steady dull pain that was different. Not any better, but just different.

CHAPTER 6

IT WAS DARK. The stars were starting to come out, but the moon wasn't anywhere to be seen yet. Mackenzie's flashlight was the only thing that let her see the trail in front of her. Mackenzie remembered one night back in Nebraska when her dad had told her about how cool the stars were up in the mountains, but she didn't really understand what he meant until that first night at Lake Helen. That night at the lake the stars filled the sky, and Mackenzie had been amazed how you could somehow see so many more stars than you could back in Nebraska. The stars were just coming out, and as Mackenzie left the little meadow that she had been in the stars didn't shine through the trees at all.

She walked slowly and carefully down the trail and moved the flashlight beam back and forth across the forest floor looking for her dad's backpack. All she could think of was opening her eyes and seeing the dead man's face in hers. That and the feeling of his lifeless body beneath her. Mackenzie realized that she normally would have been freaked out and scared half to death of wolves and bears if she was traipsing along in the forest at night by herself, but that dead man's face was all she could think of. The more she thought of it, the more weirded out she got. Now Mackenzie was only moving a few steps forward at a time because she was shining the flashlight down at her feet to move forward, then stopping and shining the flashlight through the trees looking for the backpack. That way she wouldn't trip over another dead man on the trail.

Mackenzie had gone a lot further than what she thought she could have when her freak out meter hit maximum and she was just about to turn and run back to her dad without finding his backpack. While thinking about the dead man's face again she got the willies down her spine, and her shoulders uncontrollably shook back and forth. When Mackenzie shook, the beam of the flashlight moved quickly across something yellow that reflected quite some ways off the trail. She stood like a statue on the trail because she wasn't sure what the yellow reflection was for sure. Mackenzie was hopeful that it was her dad's backpack, but all the animals and creatures that she could dream up in a matter of seconds that could lurk in the middle of the forest filled her thoughts and pegged her freak out meter way above maximum.

Mackenzie was sure that it was only seconds, but it felt much longer as she forced herself to slowly move the flashlight beam from the ground to the area where she had thought she had seen the reflection. Nothing. Maybe she had imagined that she had seen it in the first place. If it was an animal or creature, maybe it had moved and was stalking her as she stood there frozen in the middle of the trail. She got the willies again and the flashlight shook in her hands. This time she saw the reflection again considerably left of where she had thought she saw it before, but she was immediately able to tell that it was her dad's backpack.

Mackenzie made her way back through the forest to the backpack very carefully and slowly. She swung the flashlight left, right, and behind her as she walked towards the pack. It was eerily too quiet, and she was sure that something wasn't right. On the hike up the mountain a few days ago, Mackenzie had been listening to tunes most of the time, but when she didn't have her ear buds in she noticed that there was always some kind of sounds from squirrels, birds, or other critters living in the forest. There weren't any of those sounds now. Mackenzie's breathing and heart beating were the only things that she could hear when she stopped and concentrated. When she stepped on the pine needles or snapped a twig on the ground it seemed like it was the only noise in the forest.

Mackenzie finally reached her dad's backpack and it surprised her how heavy it was when she hoisted it onto her shoulders. It took almost all her strength to lift it onto her shoulders, and she wasn't sure if she could even make it back to her dad with all that weight. She argued with herself about whether to just walk straight through the woods to him as he had done when he heard her scream, or turn back around and walk to the trail again the way she had just came. Even though it was probably quite a bit further with the heavy backpack, Mackenzie decided to walk back to the trail so that she didn't risk getting lost and started that way. The backpack wasn't adjusted for her, so the part that is supposed to go around your waist hit Mackenzie in the butt with every step. It wasn't just annoying, but it began to rub a raw spot on her butt by the time she made it back to the trail. She found out that if she leaned way forward the backpack wouldn't rub on that spot, so she made her way back down the trail towards her dad hunched forward awkwardly. She shown the flashlight just the few feet in front of her so that she could see.

When she reached her dad and the dead-man, she flung the pack off her back and plopped down on the ground next to her dad immediately.

"You okay?" her dad asked between gritted teeth. While Mackenzie was away, he had scooted back away from the dead man a few feet where the trail sloped some so that he could rest at an incline. With the flashlights beam, Mackenzie could tell that he was still in a lot of pain. His face was completely flushed and beads of sweat lined his forehead even though it was cool in the early evening. She didn't answer right away because she was winded and was trying to catch her breath. "Slerk!" he said as he raised his hand up to cover his eyes from the flashlight's beam that was shining at him. It took a second for Mackenzie to realize what he was saying, but then she remembered the climb up to Bomber Mountain and she chuckled a little. Her dad always had a way of making her smile.

Feeling a little more at ease from her solo adventure, Mackenzie moved the flashlight's beam towards his injured knee and asked him how it was doing between her winded gasps.

"Hurts bad," was all he would say about it. "How come you are breathing so hard? You okay?" he asked.

"Your pack's heavy," she responded now starting to get her breathing under control.

Mackenzie stood and pulled the pack over to him to where he could reach it from his somewhat sitting position. She sat down next to him and shined the flashlight so he could see what he was doing. He first grabbed his head-lamp out of one of the side pockets and put it on his head.

"Slerk," he said smoothly as he pointed to the headlamp and nodded his head with pouty duck lips. This time Mackenzie did more than chuckle. She did a full-out belly busting laugh followed by a full set of giggles as he continued to go through his pack. The giggle fit was just coming to an end as he washed several Ibuprofen down that he found in the first aid kit with a big swig from his water bottle.

He continued through his pack and pulled out a belt knife. He un-sheathed the knife and cut through his jeans just above his injured knee. He grimaced and groaned as he moved his leg back and forth to work the knife around, and when he was done the cut edge remaining on his jeans was extremely crooked and ragged like a little kid had done it.

The light from her dad's headlamp and Mackenzie's flashlight shown on his knee while they both bent forward to inspect it. It was swollen, but it really didn't look any worse than it had a couple of days ago. His knee looked better than it had when he first hurt it because the scrapes and sores were beginning to heal on his skin.

He held the knife out to Mackenzie and she instinctively reached out and grabbed it. "Put it on your belt," he said in that commanding tone that she loathed.

"What do you mean?" Mackenzie asked. She wasn't grasping what he was trying to tell her.

"Put that knife on your belt. It may come in handy," he repeated.

"Dad," Mackenzie said trying to speak slowly because the pain must have been making his comprehension worse than normal. "I don't know how to use a knife and I don't have a belt."

He stretched his arm back out to her with his palm open and she put the sheathed knife back in it. He rummaged through his pack some more and unsheathed the knife. He cut a few feet of rope off a roll, put the knife back in its sheath, and handed the knife and the rope back to her without saying a word.

"What?" Mackenzie asked before taking the items.

"Take them," he said. "Tie the para-cord around your waist like a belt and put the knife on it."

"What's the big deal?" Mackenzie asked as she took the stuff from him and did as he asked.

"It's just good to be prepared," he said in that authoritative tone again.

He continued going through his pack some more and took the fanny pack out as she fumbled with tying the rope around her waist with the heavy knife hanging from it. He took off his head lamp, put fresh batteries in it, and stowed the used ones back in his pack. He was moving stuff from the fanny pack to his backpack and visa-versa when he saw that Mackenzie wasn't getting anywhere with the makeshift belt and motioned for her to come over closer to him. She took a few steps forward and made sure that he saw her eyes roll back as she did so.

"Don't you remember how I taught you to tie a slip knot," as he had her hold one end of the rope while he made a loop and a knot in the other end.

"Daaad," Mackenzie said. "I was like seven years old the last time you showed me that."

"Well, it hasn't changed since then," he said as he put the other end through the loop and snugged the rope around her.

"That belt knife is a good one," he said. "My uncle gave that to me one Christmas when I was about your age, and I've taken it on every excursion since then." It was a nice-looking knife. Nothing fancy, but it looked functional. The blade was about six inches long and it had a black composite handle with a little bit of a finger guard.

When he finished with the rope, he reached up and slung the fanny pack around her waist as well. She stepped back in fear as she realized what he was doing, and he dropped one end of the belt from the fanny pack.

"No!" she said, and she meant it.

"Listen Darlin'," he started, but she cut him off quickly.

"It took everything I had just to walk back and get your back pack," she spat out quickly. She could feel the sting of tears coming to her eyes as she continued and felt the pitch of her voice rising higher and higher. "I am not walking back to the car by myself through the forest in the middle of the night after just tripping over a dead guy!"

"Listen..." he started again, but she cut him off just as quick.

Her fingernails were digging into her palms from the fists she was making. She almost screamed at him "No! I'm not walking down that trail by myself!" By now her chest was heaving with sobs again and she lost her nerve to fight. She sunk to her knees and leaned in close to him.

She knew that his strong arms would envelope her and make her feel safe even before they did. He just put his chin on top of her head and said "Shh-hhh..." until she caught her breath again. Then he started again "Mak, I wouldn't ask you to do it if I could think of any other option Darlin'. I know you're scared, but we can't leave this guy laying in the trail like this and I'm not up for packing him down the trail." The more he talked, the more Mackenzie could feel her heart slow and her breathing get more under control. "The car can't be much more than a mile from here, and you're bound to run into other hikers or campers before you get that far. All you have to do is explain what happened, and tell them where we're at."

She leaned back some and wiped the tears from her face with the back of her hands. They were still flowing somewhat, but they had slowed down a lot. "But what if there is a lunatic or a grizzly bear out there?" she asked.

"I know you're scared, but you don't have to worry about whatever got this guy" he said gesturing towards the dead body. "I've studied him quite a bit while you were looking for my backpack, and the best that I can guess is that he must have had a heart attack, or stroke, or something. There's not a single injury on him that I can see."

Mackenzie tried not to look at the body again, but couldn't help it as her dad talked about him. She had to catch another quick look at it. He was right. From the flashlight beam, there wasn't any blood or noticeable cuts or scrapes that she could see. Mackenzie turned her head quickly and closed her eyes tight as her dad's gaze turned towards his face.

"I threw everything that I could think of that you might need in this fanny pack," he said. "I did keep out the rest of the Ibuprofen for me, but everything else is in here." He motioned for Mackenzie to stand up again so she could put the fanny pack on, but she silently shook her head no.

"You're only going to have the fanny pack on so you can move quickly. Keep the flashlight shining out in front of you a few yards and just make sure that you stay on the trail." He motioned again for her to stand up again and this time she complied. She could feel her lower lip sticking out in a pouty face as he wiped more tears from her eyes. He slipped the fanny pack back around her waist and was adjusting the tightness as he continued "Like I said, I'm sure that we're not much more than a mile from the car. If you just keep focused and move on out, you should be down to the car in twenty minutes without a problem." He gave the fanny pack one last tug then grabbed her hands in his as he looked up at her. "Talk to the first people you find. Tell them that we're just over a mile up the trail towards Lake Helen and what condition we're in. Now kneel down here with me."

She knelt beside him and they both prayed. Patrick said the prayer out loud asking God to look after Mackenzie and a bunch of other stuff while he had his hand on the back of her neck. She thought the words as he said them, but it was kind of empty coming from her heart. She wasn't quite sure that she totally believed in Him yet. When he finished, Mackenzie leaned forward and kissed his forehead before she stood.

"Just keep focused and keep moving," he said as she stood looking down the trail. She must have stood without moving for too long because he followed it up by saying "You can do this. Just put one foot in front of the other."

So that's what she did. First her left, and then her right. Left, then right. Left, and then she had her head down and was moving out. As soon as she was beyond the sight of her dad, she reached her right hand back to the knife sheath and loosened the button clasp that secures the knife in the sheath. Mackenzie didn't pull the knife out from the sheath, but it somehow gave her a little courage just walking with her hand on its handle.

Mackenzie walked along with the flashlight in her left hand shining straight ahead, and her right hand on the handle of the knife hanging on the makeshift belt. She was so focused on the trail and making it back to the car that she didn't think that she would have noticed an elephant stampede next to her.

After not too long at all, the ground leveled out more and the trees became less dense. Mackenzie thought that she began to recognize some of the clearings. The creek off to the right of the trail became visible, and she knew that she was getting close to the trailhead. The moon had come out and was helping to light the way somewhat whenever it peaked through the trees. She was tempted to break into an all-out sprint, but settled for stepping it up some to a full jog. The fanny pack was rising and falling somewhat as she moved faster, but she kept her hand on the knife handle to steady the load.

The trail was longer than she thought it was, and she started to feel a little winded. She could tell that she had broken a sweat in the chilly night air because she could feel a bead or two of it running down the middle of her back.

Mackenzie was just thinking about slowing down some when she saw the sign for the trailhead up ahead and increased her pace instead. She almost couldn't believe it. She made it. She did it!

Mackenzie skidded to a stop as she reached the trailhead sign. She bent over with her hands on her knees, closed her eyes, and celebrated as she caught her breath for a moment. Mackenzie felt herself having perma-grin and tried to wipe it off her face, but she wasn't having much success. She could just imagine meeting a forest ranger and telling him about her injured dad with a dead guy on the trail while she was smiling from ear to ear. She thought that they would lock her up for sure before checking out her story.

Mackenzie thought that she would have met someone from the nearby campground by now or at least heard some commotion coming from there, but the forest was as still as it had been all night. She had caught her breath and took off towards the direction of their car. She thought that she could try to call out on her dad's cell phone or at least honk the horn until someone came to help. The gravel parking lot wasn't that far from the sign and she felt like sprinting again, but she remembered her dad falling when hurrying back on the same path, so she forced herself to walk cautiously.

Mackenzie reached the gravel parking lot and it looked almost the same as it had when they left it. There appeared to be a few new cars there and a few cars had left since they had started their hike, but the parking lot was still about half full. There weren't any signs of movement at the parking lot. Regardless of the thought of her dad tripping on the same trail in broad daylight, Mackenzie couldn't help it when her legs broke into a full run when she saw their SUV there about half way into the lot. She reached the car with a thud as her hands and arms hit the passenger window. She peered into the window and she saw her dad's cell phone on the center console.

Her heart immediately dropped when she reached out to open the door and found that it was locked. She ran around to the other side before she allowed herself to go into melt down mode and found that it was locked too. Mackenzie ran around the car and tried each handle, while trying the rear latch last. Each of the doors were just as locked as the first.

"No. No. No!" Mackenzie exclaimed as she sat down on the ground and leaned against the rear bumper. She felt tears welling up, but she fought them off because she knew that her dad wouldn't have sent her down to the car alone without being able to get into the car. She just had to slow down and think of what he had told her. She couldn't remember anything that he had said about the car, but she remembered that he had said something about putting everything she needed in the fanny pack. She stripped the fanny pack off without standing up and put the flash light in her mouth so she could use both hands to go through the fanny pack. She went through it looking for the keys like a crazy woman. The fanny pack had one big pouch on the back and several small pockets and pouches on each side of it. There were all kinds of stuff in the pack, but she didn't find any keys.

She felt her eyes watering up, but she fought them back just a little longer because she knew that her dad had to have given her the keys. She went back through the fanny pack slowly and she carefully took everything out of each pocket and then put it back after she didn't find the keys. By the time she reached the last pocket again, she had no hope left and the tears fell. Then the sobs came in full force. She went through the last pocket again and didn't find a key.

She pulled her knees up to her shoulders and hung her head between her arms and legs, and cried for several moments. She wasn't sure what to do next. She beat her fists on the cold hard ground and screamed "HELP!" at the top of her lungs. She stood up frustrated and angry, not sure of what she was going to do. There were several medium sized rocks lining the parking lot that she thought would break one of the windows easily. Mackenzie picked up a decent sized rock about the size of her fist and thought about which window would be the best to break. Before she went any further, the thought of her dad looking down at her with his ever-disappointed expression stopped her in her tracks. The rock fell harmlessly to the ground from her hand.

Mackenzie picked up the fanny pack and headed back to the trailhead sign. The moon was out enough that she didn't need the flashlight to see at all. She stowed the flash light in the main pocket of the fanny pack and slung the fanny pack back around her waist. Mackenzie thought that she better checkout the campsite and ask someone for help before she broke out a window in her dad's car, so she took off in that direction at a quick pace.

Mackenzie put the brakes on and skidded to a halt as she passed a small brick building along the trail when she realized that it was a restroom. It had a men's entrance on one side and a woman's on the other. She stood on the path for several seconds just past the building and debated the morality of having to go to the bathroom instead of sending help to her dad lying on the trail next to the dead guy. She hadn't gone number two since they had been in the mountains, and the longer she stood staring at the building thinking about what to do, the more her body was making the decision for her. It wasn't long before she thought that she wasn't going to make it into the building before messing herself.

She slung open the door and was pleasantly surprised that the stench wasn't nearly as bad as she had expected. It smelled like an outhouse in the middle of the mountains, but the smell wasn't overwhelming. There weren't any stalls in the small room, just one toilet in the opposite corner and a piece of stainless steel acting as a mirror on the far wall. There wasn't any electricity in the building, but small glass blocks near the top of each outside wall let in enough moon light that you could still see good enough to do your business. Mackenzie latched the door with the hasp and hurried over to the toilet, undoing the fanny pack along the way. She began trying to untie the knot that her dad had tied in the makeshift rope belt that held the belt knife. Mackenzie began to think that she was going to mess her pants before she got the knot undone and began to involuntarily hop up and down in place, which made it harder to untie the knot. She began yanking at the rope fiercely, but it wouldn't budge. Just as she was committed to go ahead and mess herself, she had an idea. She took the knife from the sheath and cut the rope around her waist right at the knot in one quick movement. She immediately dropped her pants and panties, and then plopped down on the oversized and cold toilet seat.

Just as her bowels released themselves in one big movement, her jaw dropped to her chest and utter fear gripped her again. She was unable to move as her eyes burned the image in her brain of the dead woman and teenage girl crumpled on the floor in the opposite corner. The moonlight shown in just enough at an angle to see the upper body of the woman and the head of girl. She couldn't move or even really think. She sat there for what seemed like forever while her bowels continued to empty and stared at the moonlit scene. The woman had long curly hair and was dressed as if she had been camping for a few days. Mackenzie couldn't make out any major features of the young-er girl, other than she had short hair and appeared to be around Mackenzie's age.

Mackenzie's fear stricken trance broke when a drop of liquid from the cesspool below the toilet splashed up on her bare butt and startled her out of the moment. She immediately and involuntarily screamed, jumped up, and tried to run to the door. Her pants were still down around her knees and she almost tripped before she reached the door, but caught herself instead. Mack-enzie heard herself scream again, but this time if felt as if it was someone else making the noise. She was pulling her pants up with one hand and trying to work the hasp with the other to open the door. She heard herself let out a full other scream before her fumbling fingers finally opened the bathroom door and she fell forward out of the door. She pulled her pants all the way up with one last tug and bolted around the side of the building with all the speed that she had.

Just as she turned the corner, a large man was standing there in the middle of the path and he wrapped his arms around her in a tackling move as Mackenzie plunged into him. They both tumbled to the asphalt trail with Mackenzie screaming at the top of her lungs and his vise like grip holding her close to his body.

CHAPTER 7

PATRICK HEARD HIMSELF groan as he hit the asphalt square on his back. They slid a couple of inches on the asphalt for good measure and he felt his lower back get road rash where his shirt slid up. Makenzie was still screaming, fighting, and flailing well after they hit the ground.

"Whooooaa!" he told her once he caught his breath. He was sure that she recognized his voice, but she didn't let up. He held her as tight as he could as she had one arm loose and was flailing it and her legs for all she was worth trying to escape.

"Mak, Mak, it's me!" he said. It took several seconds for her to slow down, and as she did she turned in his arms to snuggle and began to sob.

They lay that way for several moments as she sobbed and cried. It was extremely uncomfortable and cold laying on the asphalt in the position that they were in, but Patrick tried to block it out and just give her a while to collect herself. When he realized that she was going to have a hard time stopping by herself, he told her "Shhhh." He gave her one big last hug, and began to sit up.

As they separated some, she sat up as well and slugged her dad hard in the shoulder. "You scared me to death," she said between sobs and after sniffling.

"Sorry Darlin'," Patrick said.

"There's a dead woman and girl in the bathroom!" she blurted out.

"You okay?" he asked unfazed by her statement.

"Yeah, I think so," she replied somewhat uncertain. "Did you hear what I said?" she asked with concern.

"Yeah," he said. Patrick wasn't sure how to tell her what he knew, so he decided to just come out and say it. "There are quite a few people dead up here."

"What do you mean?" she asked bewildered.

"I take it you didn't make it down to the campground?" he asked.

"No, I went down to the car. But I couldn't get in because you didn't give me the keys," she hit him on top of both shoulders with her fists and started to cry a little again.

It took Patrick a second to understand what she was talking about, but then he hung his head when he realized that he hadn't told her the keys were in the bumper. "Sorry Darlin'. I had put the keys in the bumper when we left so that if something happened to me, you could still get into the car," he told her without looking up. "I was going to tell you at the time, but you had those dang ear buds stuck in your head. I was going to tell you later and I guess that I forgot with my knee hurt and everything. I'm glad that it worked out like that anyways."

"Why's that?" she asked after a few seconds.

Patrick began to scoot along his butt backwards to lean up against a large rock that was next to the trail. Makenzie sat and watched as she waited for an answer. After he reached the rock, Patrick began to tell her what he knew. "Not too long after you left, the Ibuprofen really started to kick in and I was able to scoot around on the ground enough to find stuff to make this splint\ crutch thing." Patrick looked down at his injured leg and grabbed the limb for emphasis that he had tied to it with the cut jeans and an extra heavy shirt from his pack. "It's really pretty cool," he said talking a little too fast because he was so proud of his idea. "I used a shirt and the jeans to pad it against my leg so it wouldn't rub, and made it a couple of inches longer than my leg when it's tied on so I put all my weight on it instead of my knee."

"You're such an engineer Dad," Makenzie said with a partial smile.

He went back to telling her the more important stuff, so his tempo slowed accordingly. "While I was looking for a branch to use, I found another dead man just off the trail from where you had fallen on the first one. He was only about fifteen feet away. He was off of the trail, but I don't know how we didn't see him before." Patrick unconsciously stopped talking while he was contemplating the scene and how they possibly could have missed the other body when Makenzie was there.

"Daa-aad," Makenzie said prompting him to continue.

"Sorry. Well, after I found the other guy; I knew something was seriously wrong, so I made this splint and got down here as fast as I could because I wasn't sure what was going on. I went down to the camp first because that was where I thought you would be, and it was…" Patrick trailed off not knowing how to describe it to her. "There must have been two dozen or more people down there that looked like they just keeled over doing whatever they were doing at the time." He stopped again as he remembered the disturbing scene, especially the young boy with his fishing pole.

"Dad!" she said again more impatient this time.

This time he didn't apologize, but just continued. "I called out for you time and time again, but I couldn't find you so I headed back and was going to go down to look for you at the car when I heard you scream in the bathroom."

They just sat where they were at without saying anything for several moments. Patrick thought that they were both contemplating the circumstances and glad to be back together. "Was it the cloud Dad?" Makenzie asked finally.

"I guess so," he responded. He didn't know any other way to explain it, even though the cloud wasn't much more of an explanation. They sat for a few more seconds in silence before he interrupted it by saying "Let's get to the car and get back to the lodge by the highway. We can tell them what has been going on up here."

"Can't we just call the police?" Makenzie asked.

"There's no cell service or land lines up here on the mountain. You have to get almost back to that Town of Buffalo before you can get any signal on a cell phone," he told her.

Patrick started to get up and struggled due to his injured leg being splinted straight. Makenzie saw her dad struggling and helped him right himself. She asked her dad sheepishly as she let go of his armpit and elbow "Ummm Dad.... Can we do something before we head down to the car?"

"What's that?" he asked wondering what she could possibly want to do up here before heading back to the car.

"Can you see if there are any bodies in the Men's restroom? I kind of need to clean myself up a little bit," she continued sheepishly.

After Makenzie finished in the restroom they hiked down to the car. Makenzie went on and on about how she couldn't believe that her dad left the keys in the bumper right next to where she had been sitting and going through the fanny pack. She said she knew that the keys were there somewhere, but she couldn't find them.

Makenzie grabbed the keys from Patrick and used them to hurriedly open the door and check for reception on his cell phone to no avail. She was bummed and exhausted, and only half-heartedly helped him try to get in behind the wheel. It took at least five minutes of trying to figure out how to sit down in the car with his injured right knee before he thought that he was going to vomit again from the overwhelming pain. When Patrick was sure that it just wasn't going to work out, he reluctantly asked Makenzie if she felt comfortable driving the several miles on the dirt road down to the lodge by the highway. She of course said that she would do it, and helped him get into the passenger seat instead which was much easier.

Mackenzie didn't look exhausted anymore as she got into the driver's seat and began to adjust the seat and mirrors. Even though she had almost two years to go before she would get her driver's license, Patrick had taken her out for driving lessons several times on old gravel roads out in the boondocks and down by the canal. She usually did well when she kept herself focused, but he didn't think that she had ever drove in the dark, let alone in the mountains.

She backed out of the parking space okay. As she was looking forward to driving out of the parking lot she had a small smile on her lips even after everything that they had went through. The dirt road back to the lodge was maintained, but it had enough traffic on it in the summer months to make drivers wish that they could blade it just one more time every year. The road was plenty wide, but there were quite a few places where it was wash boarded out so you needed to pay attention to what you were doing. Patrick instructed Makenzie to put the SUV in second gear and just take it slow and easy.

He held his cell phone in his hand and stared at the service bars for most of the trip just in the off chance that somehow a cell signal bounced up to a single spot on the road. The No Service sign at the top of the phone never changed though.

Patrick had taken another batch of Ibuprofen before they had driven off, but it hadn't kicked in by the time they left on the drive. Every bump and wash board that Makenzie hit jolted his knee. She must have heard or felt him wince with the pain because she would say "Oooooh. Sorry," whenever she would hit a big one. Besides those interruptions, the drive reminded Patrick of the times that he had taken Makenzie out on the gravel back roads around their town for her driving lessons. The road had quite a few gentle sweeping curves, and in most spots the trees were thick enough that you couldn't see anything from the road so he cautioned Makenzie to watch closely for deer and elk although they didn't see any.

"Look!" Makenzie yelled as she was pointing straight ahead through the windshield. Patrick had been staring down at his phone and hadn't imme-diately seen the pair of headlights that she was pointing at. They were a few hundred yards ahead of them. She looked over to her dad and was literally beaming with a smile and slightly bouncing up in down in her seat.

Patrick didn't have the heart to tell her that something didn't quite look right about the headlights from what he could see. He couldn't initially put his finger on it, but as they got closer he could tell that the angle that they were pointed was wrong somehow. Mackenzie was driving slow and cautious, but it took a while to approach the oncoming vehicle and Patrick also realized that it wasn't moving toward them. As they got closer and closer Patrick could see that Makenzie coming to the same realizations as the smile slowly left her face the closer they came to the vehicle. As they neared it, you could make out that the vehicle was a seventy something tan Ford Bronco with a red stripe down the side of it. It had gone off of the road and struck a small tree.

Patrick had Makenzie drive up close next to it and roll down her window. The vehicle was still running, but there wasn't anyone around that they could see. The Bronco had some oversize tires and a small lift kit on it, so it set quite a bit higher than the SUV Patrick and Mackenzie were in. The windows were rolled up on the Bronco, but Patrick yelled across Makenzie anyways "Anybody in there… Anybody need any help?"

The sound of the older V8 engine purred, but otherwise there wasn't any other response. "We should check it out and shut the engine off," Makenzie said looking at her dad.

Patrick let her statement hang in the air for probably just a little too long before he responded. "You're probably right Darlin'. But I think that whoever was driving up the mountain in this vehicle probably met their demise the same way all those others did back at that campground. I also don't think that the vehicle will start a fire or anything by the looks of it, so it will probably just die when it runs out of gas. Either way, my knee is too bunged up to get out and back in this car right now. So if you want to get out, check it out, and shut their engine off I'm good with it. But I'll be watching you from right here."

She looked at Patrick for several seconds in almost pure bewilderment. He wasn't sure if her wonderment was from him not doing what seemed like the right thing to do, or if it was because he suggested that she do it by herself instead. Makenzie looked straight ahead for several seconds and then she put the transmission in park and left her door open when she got out. Patrick saw her peek her eyes over the edge of the Bronco door to look into the window. Whatever sight was in there; it must have not been a good one. Mackenzie jumped up and down while spinning in a circle with her eyes closed, a grimace on her face, and her fists pumping up and down. When she turned back to the Bronco, she leaned out with one arm trying to keep as much distance between her and the Bronco as possible, and opened the driver's side door. She then reached in and tried to turn the vehicle off in one quick motion, but she ended up pulling her hand back out of the vehicle like she had been bit by a snake. Patrick had a hard time keeping from chuckling as Makenzie jumped up and down while spinning around again. After she completed another circle, she reached in again but was able to shut the engine off this time. She immediately withdrew her hand from the cab of the Bronco. Almost as quickly, she closed the Bronco's door. She slid into the SUV and closed her door.

"Pretty rough?" Patrick asked.

"Mmmm-Hmmm," she said as she put the car back in second gear and started back down the road.

"Wanna' talk about it?" Patrick inquired.

She just shook her head no and didn't say anything. He decided not to press it right now and went back to watching the road and his cell phone's signal bars.

It took another uneventful twenty minutes to reach the lodge. Patrick wasn't surprised that there were no lights on or activity at the lodge when they pulled into the parking lot as his cell phone said it was a little after 2:30 in the morning. All the same, he had a bad feeling about what they would find.

Makenzie pulled the car up in front of hitching posts in front of the main lodge and shut the ignition off. The lodge wasn't much of a lodge, but more of a large cabin. The other buildings that were arranged in the shape of a large letter 'U' were mainly just single level motel rooms that were probably built in the 1950's or 1960's like rudimentary motor lodges.

Makenzie leaned way back in her seat and looked over at her dad with a fretful look on her face. He saw that she was worried that he would make her go into the lodge while he waited in the car as she had done with the Bronco.

"I'll go in and check this out while you hang out in the car," Patrick told her and he could see the worry leave her face almost immediately. "Would you help me out of the car and with putting that splint back on though?"

It took a few minutes to get out of the car and put the splint back on even with Mackenzie's assistance. It struck Patrick how quiet the evening was. The quietness added to the ominous feeling that he had about not finding a happy ending inside the lodge. The Ibuprofen must have been kicking in quite a bit because his knee was feeling considerably better, although he couldn't put any weight on it. Patrick told Makenzie to stay in the car and lock the doors while he went inside and checked things out.

Patrick hobbled up the front steps using the contraption on his knee, and then along a skinny boardwalk that ran along the front of the lodge towards the front door. There was an eve over the boardwalk and a few wood carved patio chairs were positioned on either side of the front door. It looked like it would be an inviting place to sit on a warm summer day. That night the chairs just took up too much space along the board walk for a man with a crutch tied to the side of his leg and it took much longer for him to navigate around the obstacles than he would have liked. When he reached the front door, he cupped his hands around his face and peered through the upper half of the door that contained a large pane of glass into the main lodge itself. He could see one large room with a welcome desk on one end, with a large table and chairs on the other side. The décor looked like low end hand carved furniture with several cool photographs and paintings from the surrounding area hanging on the walls. Although he could see most of the lodge from the window, he didn't see any movement or sign of life.

After turning to check on Makenzie who was still sitting in the car, Patrick opened the main door to the lodge and said in a loud voice "Hello… Anyone around?" His own voice kind of startled him for how loud it sounded in the quietness. He stood at the threshold with the door propped open for a few seconds and then called out again. There was no response so he put his headlamp on, turned it on, and limped into the lodge. The large cabin was made up of the one room with the welcome desk and table, but there was a wall towards the back of the cabin with two closed doors on it. Patrick approached the door that was closest to the welcome desk and called out again before reaching for the handle. There was no answer so he opened the door and found that it was a small office with a desk on one side of the room and a couch along the opposite wall. He was just turning to go open the other door in the lodge when the light of his headlamp illuminated a dirty white tennis shoe towards the end of the desk that looked odd. He decided to check it out and limped in and around the door frame in the dark with his splinted leg. As he got closer to the shoe, he could begin to see over the top of the desk to the body that was laying on the floor that the shoe belonged to. It was a younger man, probably in his early twenties. He had a short scruffy beard and was dressed in a black concert t-shirt and jeans. This body was different than the others that he had seen because his head lay in a considerable amount of blood that appeared to have come from somewhere near his temple area. Although he hadn't noticed it when Patrick first came in the room, the smell of death was beginning to settle in his nostrils and he was immediately wanting to get out of there. Patrick forced himself to stay for a few seconds to look around the office for a telephone or anything else that they could possibly use, but he didn't find anything.

Patrick limped back out to the main room in the lodge and over behind the welcome desk. There were three keys hung on the wall behind the desk that were obviously room keys. He picked number 24 and headed back out to the car.

Makenzie bailed out of the car and ran over to Patrick as he came out the front door and along the boardwalk again. "So…?" she asked with hope in her eyes as she put her head under his arm pit and helped him down to the car.

Patrick dangled the key that he had picked up in front of her by the plastic green fob that had the room number on it and said "Only a dead guy in there, but I did get us a room."

Makenzie evidently didn't think that joke was very funny. They both rested on the SUV's front bumper and stared at the lodge building for several moments. Makenzie broke the silence by saying "I'm not staying here."

"What to do you mean?" Patrick asked half perturbed at her defiant attitude.

"I'm not staying here," she said again matter-of-factly.

"Listen," Patrick started in a defensive and somewhat condescending tone. "We've been up for almost two days without any rest, hiked up to the top of the Big Horns and back with a tore up knee, and have been through an emotional roller coaster with more dead people than I've seen my whole life. We need to get some rest."

"I'm not staying here," she repeated.

"Darlin', I don't think that I could get in and drive down the mountain tonight even if I wanted to with my knee the way it is," he said trying to reason with her.

"I can drive," she said matter-of-factly without looking up.

"Driving down a gravel road to the lodge is one thing. Driving down the mountain on the main highway in the middle of the night is something totally different," Patrick said just imagining what her mother would say if she found out that he let Makenzie drive down the mountain.

"I'm not staying here tonight," Makenzie said again with just as much certainty as she had a few moments before.

Father and daughter both continued to lean on the front bumper while they thought about the situation and what they should do. Patrick ended up rationalizing allowing Makenzie to drive down the mountain because he knew that he couldn't get in the driver's side of the car, and it probably was safer to get out of there in case that cloud or whatever caused all the death came back.

"Okay," Patrick finally said and Makenzie immediately looked up at him. "We'll try to make it down to Buffalo. But there are a few rules," he said resurrecting his father knows best tone of voice. "You will drive down the mountain, but you won't take it out of second gear. And we will pull over and snooze at the first sign that either one of us is too tired to go on."

"Deal," Makenzie said with a half-smile on her face and stuck her hand out for him to shake.

"Deal," Patrick repeated and shook her hand.

They got back in the car and started down the mountain. Patrick gave Makenzie a lot of instruction, but she seemed to be taking it in instead of getting mad or frustrated. He taught her about not riding her brakes and allowing the car to downshift instead; about slowing down for corners before you get to them; how to watch for animals alongside the road, and all sorts of other things. With her keeping the vehicle in second gear, they didn't really get over thirty miles per hour which made the drive take forever, but Patrick felt somewhat safe with her skills at that speed. Although it was three in the morning on the mountain, they didn't see another vehicle coming or going.

After probably twenty minutes on the road, Patrick turned on the radio to see if they could catch some broadcast that could tell them whether anyone knew about what had happened up there on the mountain. All they heard was static, so he methodically began to tune to each different frequency that the digital tuner in car's radio would allow. Suddenly, a large white Suburban without any lights on appeared in the middle of the lane as they were going around a sharp left corner.

"Look out!" Patrick yelled to Makenzie, but it was too late.

Makenzie hit the brakes hard and turned the wheel to the left quickly, but they still hit the driver's side rear quarter panel of the Suburban with the passenger side of their bumper. Luckily, they were probably only going ten or fifteen miles per hour when they impacted, but it still stunned them both. There looked to be quite a bit of damage to the vehicle as the fiberglass part of the front quarter panel of their car came up at least a foot above the hood from what Patrick could see from inside the vehicle.

"You okay?" Patrick asked Makenzie who seemed to have been frozen behind the wheel. Neither of the air bags went off, but both of their seat belts locked. "Mak! You okay?" he asked again.

CHAPTER 8

'**OH-NO! OH-NO! OH-NO!**' was all Mackenzie could
   think after slamming into the back of that big SUV. She knew that her dad
was going to f-l-i-p out.

"Mak! You okay," he asked.

It took her a second for Mackenzie to get a status check from her body,
but she felt fine except where the seat belt had locked and cut into her shoulder and chest. "Yeah. I think so," she finally muttered.

Mackenzie looked over to her dad and he was putting his head lamp on
and trying to take his seat belt off. He snapped his headlamp on and shown
it on her for several seconds. Then he opened his door and tried to get out.
Mackenzie knew that she should go help him out and get his crutch thingy
situated, but she couldn't peel her fingers from the steering wheel. She felt her
foot slip off the brake and the car moved a couple of inches.

Patrick was leaning up against the car trying to attach his crutch before it moved. He immediately leaned in the door and yelled "What are you doing? Put the car in park!"

That started the water works. Mackenzie willed her fingers from the steering wheel and reached up to the steering column to put the transmission in park. Her tears were streaming down her face by the time her dad started walking around the other car. Mackenzie couldn't really make out what he was doing, but he walked around the passenger side of the other car and was looking in the windows for several minutes. He then limped back over to their car and looked at the damage that the wreck had done to the front end. After a few moments, he reached down and began tugging on a piece of the car's body that was loose and bent up at a weird angle up by the passenger side tire. It took him several tugs to finally pull the large piece of the body from the car. Mackenzie's tears continued to stream and she unconsciously wiped them from her face with the back of her hand. When he had the piece free, he turned and threw it over on the shoulder of the road and hobbled back towards the passenger seat.

"They didn't make it," he said as he tried to settle into the car with his injured leg.

He saw his daughter's face and snapped his head lamp off. "You sure you are okay?" he asked again.

"Yeah," Mackenzie muttered again. "I'm sorry Dad," she said and then the sobbing started.

He leaned over and snuggled her face into his armpit. "It's OK Darlin'," he said as he held her. "These circumstances are a little different than how I expected to teach you how to drive."

After a few minutes, he relaxed his grip on her and she pulled back. "Okay, let's get off this mountain," he said.

Mackenzie chuckled a little from relief, wiped the streams of tears from her face, and put the SUV in reverse. She hated backing up. She never could see good enough and everything always seemed backwards. She did okay though, and then they started back down the mountain. They saw several other cars that were stopped in the middle of the road or had went off and hit the guardrails in the next couple of miles, but Mackenzie was going slow enough to steer around those. Since they hadn't seen any other survivors, they decided to not stop and see if anyone needed help, but instead get down to Buffalo to make sure someone knew what had happened up on the mountain.

After a while Patrick started tuning on the radio again and was getting nothing but static. He switched from looking at the signal bars on his cell phone, to looking at the road, to changing the dial on the radio trying to find some station that would tell them what was going on. Mackenzie wanted to ask him to turn the radio volume down more because the constant noise of static was annoying when she was trying to pay attention to driving, but she decided not to say anything.

Suddenly, there was what sounded like a sonic boom outside of the car and almost immediately the whole car shook. The lights went out on the car simultaneously and it became hard to steer. Mackenzie hit the brakes as hard as she could and turned the wheel to the left, but she had to go from memory because she couldn't see anything. Patrick reached out with his left hand and grabbed the steering wheel trying to turn the wheel even further to the left. They were going very slow to begin with, but it felt like it took forever to stop. Mackenzie's seat belt locked again and rubbed her already sore shoulder and chest.

"What did you do?" Patrick almost yelled.

"Nothing. I didn't do anything," she shot back somewhat unsure of herself. "That big boom happened and then the car shut off."

"Set the emergency brake and pop the hood," he said and then started getting out of the car in a huff. He wasn't very successful as he still had to mess around with his knee and lean up against the car to tie his crutch back on.

Mackenzie did as he told her and then got out to help him with his crutch. He tried to turn his headlamp on to let him see to tie his crutch on, but it wouldn't come on.

"Grab that LED flash light I gave you from the fanny pack would you?" he asked as he continued to tie the branch to his leg.

She turned to go to the rear of the car to get the fanny pack and half-way in her turn she remembered that she must have left the fanny pack in the women's restroom at the campsite. Her heart fell when she reached down to her belt loops and realized that her dad's belt knife from his childhood was also laying on the floor of that bathroom with the bodies of that lady and girl. She just stood in that position for a second deciding on how and what to tell her dad about what she had done.

Before she could decide what to do, Patrick reached the front of the car, opened the hood, and said sternly "Mak! What are you doing? I need that flashlight!"

Mackenzie slowly walked back towards the front of the car empty handed, knowing that she was going to have to tell him what happened. Although she tried, she couldn't raise her eyes up from her shoes. Patrick was leaning over the radiator and tugging on some wires that connected to the engine when she mumbled "I don't have it."

She still couldn't bring her eyes up to look at his face, but she could tell that he still had his head under the hood. He held one of his hands out towards her with an open palm and said "I need the light."

Mackenzie didn't respond right away. She mustered up the courage to mumble "I don't have it" again, but this time a little bit louder than before.

He quit tugging on the wires, came out from under the hood, and stood looking at his daughter. Mackenzie could feel his disgusted stare on the top of her head for a second before he spoke. "I told you three times to go get the flash light from the fanny pack. What is your problem?"

All she could utter is "I don't have it."

"What do you mean that you don't have it," he almost yelled this time. Mackenzie still couldn't look up at his face, but she knew that his cheeks would be red and his brow would have that crease in it just above his nose.

She mustered her remaining courage and said "I forgot your fanny pack back at the bathroom with the dead bodies!"

It took a second for that to set in with him and she braced herself for the explosion that was about to come. Instead of exploding, he leaned up against the grill of the car almost defeated. He didn't say a word.

Mackenzie was trembling, but after several moments she forced herself to raise her eyes and see what he was doing. He was hanging his head staring at the ground with his shoulders slumped. Just standing there. After a few moments, he turned and leaned back underneath the hood and began tugging on different wires again on the engine. Mackenzie could tell that he was super disappointed in her.

"Grab my cell phone off the console. I can use the light from it," he muttered without looking at his daughter.

Mackenzie slunk back to the driver's side door to get his phone. She searched all around on the console, but couldn't find the phone in the darkness. The phone must have flown someplace when they stopped the car suddenly. She felt her heart start to pound because she knew that her dad would flip out even more if she couldn't find his phone. She ran around to the passenger side and began searching everywhere. She couldn't see very well in the darkness inside the car, so she just frantically moved her hands around on the dash and floor trying more to feel for the phone than look for it.

"What are you doing Mak?" Patrick asked from under the hood. Mackenzie could feel his disappointment turning to anger and frustration again, and she made her hands move even faster.

Finally, her pinky touched something cool and smooth on the floor that she knew was his phone. It was down at the base of the console where it meets the floorboard. She reached down and grabbed the object that had that cool feel from the gorilla glass on the front. She hopped out of the car, ran around to the front of the vehicle, and held the phone out to him.

"Here it is," she said. He leaned out from under the hood and took the phone from her. "It was down on the floorboard and I couldn't find it."

He pushed the button on the front and nothing happened. He pushed the power button on the top and nothing happened. He shook it a few times and said angrily "What did you do to it?"

"I didn't do anything to it," Mackenzie said.

After pushing the buttons and shaking it a few more times, he suddenly stopped in mid shake. The crease went away on his forehead and his expression changed to look like her dog Piggy does when she yells at him. Their boxer tilts his head ever so slightly and looks at her with his big eyes wondering what she is trying to convey to him. Patrick turned and leaned against the front bumper staring at his phone without saying a word.

"I didn't mean to do anything to it," Mackenzie said.

He drew back and threw his phone. Mackenzie felt her jaw drop in disbelief as her dad's high-priced cell phone sailed over the road and out of sight into the trees. The thud that it made somewhere in the forest sounded like it surely broke when it hit a tree or log.

Patrick didn't say anything, he just leaned against the bumper with his head hung down. Mackenzie didn't move either; she just stood and stared at him.

After a few minutes, he muttered the letters "E-M-P."

"What?" Mackenzie asked sheepishly.

"E-M-P," he repeated. He waited a second and then explained. "EMP stands for Electro-Magnetic Pulse. Did you hear that big boom right before the car died?"

"Yeah," she said again sheepishly and leaned on the front bumper next to him.

"EMP is like an invisible wave that can fry electronics and electrical systems. I think that big boom we heard was a bomb or something that let off a huge EMP event," he spoke with a defeated tone to his voice that resonated with Mackenzie and hurt her heart.

"What's going on Dad?" Mackenzie asked as she realized just how bad her whole world was spinning out of control.

"I don't know kid. But I think we're walking from here," he said as he put his arm around her and squeezed her against him.

PART 2 –
THE
TREK

CHAPTER 9

PATRICK REALIZED THAT exhaustion will make you do things that otherwise wouldn't seem reasonable. After their vehicle died, the father and daughter started walking down the highway back toward the Town of Buffalo. After only a few hundred yards from their useless vehicle, they saw that there was a small residence on a private driveway just off the highway. Mackenzie was adamant that breaking into the house was wrong and that she didn't want to be a part of it. She wanted to continue walking until they found someone. Patrick reasoned with her that these were extraordinary circumstances and that most people would be grateful to help someone out in their predicament, but she wasn't convinced.

After and during the discussion, they walked to the house and found it locked up tight. The house was built with logs and may have been called a cabin by its owner, but it was considerably larger than the Kincaid three-bedroom home in Nebraska. And built twice as stout. Patrick knocked on the door and called out multiple times, but there was no answer. Patrick ended up breaking a side door's window pane out with a nearby rock to gain entry. He left Makenzie outside while he went in and made sure that it was safe and there were no bodies. Patrick thought that the house appeared to be a weekend or summer home as it didn't seem to have that lived-in clutter or feel to it. The electricity wasn't on, so Patrick had to feel around in the dark to figure out where he was going but he didn't find any bodies. There was a large great room, bathroom, kitchen, and dining area downstairs, and four bedrooms upstairs. By the time that Patrick had hobbled back downstairs, Makenzie had become impatient with him and had already entered the house. She was looking through the cupboards in the kitchen.

"There are some guest bedrooms upstairs," Patrick said as he reached the bottom step.

She took a pop-tart from a box she found and walked by her dad up the stairs without saying a word. Patrick could tell that she was not happy with him, but he decided to let it go until they both could get some rest. He took another pop-tart out of the box that she had left on the counter and limped around the lower floor. There was no land-line phone that he could see, and with the electricity out he couldn't try the television that was in the great room. Patrick decided to sit down on the large sofa and eat a pop tart himself before finding a bed upstairs. After a few moments, exhaustion took over and he fell asleep before opening the foil bag of the pop-tart.

Patrick awoke to the sun shining in his eyes. There were huge windows all along the eastern and southern walls of the great room that allowed the mid-morning sunlight to fill the room. He was amazed at the beauty of the rustic decorum, and the layout of how the windows caught the light in the great room. The overall craftsmanship of whoever had built the illustrious cabin was inspiring. Patrick was an amateur wood worker and liked to build things in his shop back in Nebraska, but he was quite sure that his skills would never rise to the level of whoever constructed the cabin.

A quick inspection of his knee found that it was stiff, swollen, and painful. He had fallen asleep so quickly the night before that he hadn't taken his splint off, which probably made the swelling worse. He undid the splint now and took several deep breaths as he allowed his leg to bend and his knee to flex. Patrick wasn't sure how he was going to get off the mountain without a vehicle.

Patrick sat on the couch and tried to fathom all that they had been through in the last few days, but it was overwhelming. He ate the pop-tart that was lying next to him on the couch as if he were ravenous. Mackenzie came down the stairs as he was finishing up, and he hoped that he hadn't been making odd noises while eating it.

"Grab the box of those things would you?" Patrick called out to her.

Mackenzie still half-sleeping walked over to the counter, grabbed the box of pop-tarts, and shuffled over to the couch. She handed him the box as she plopped down on the sofa next to Patrick that shook his leg violently. Patrick let out an involuntary grunt, and dropped the box as he instinctively grabbed his knee.

"Oh – Sorry, Sorry, Sorry," Mackenzie said as she reached down to grab the box.

"You got to be careful Mak," Patrick said through gritted teeth as he carefully leaned back on the couch again. He took the box back from her and tore into a package.

They sat there in silence for a while as Patrick scarfed pop-tart after pop-tart. Mackenzie leaned back on the sofa as well, closed her eyes, and enjoyed the warm morning sunlight in the room.

"It's real isn't it?" Mackenzie said without opening her eyes.

Patrick stopped eating long enough to swallow and respond. "I guess that it is. When I woke up down here, I thought for a moment that it had all been some kind of dream and that we were staying at some resort."

Patrick peered into the pop-tart box and realized that he had eaten all but the last one. He took it out and offered it to Mackenzie. "No thanks," she said. "I'm really not hungry."

"Eat it anyways please. We may have a long walk ahead of us, and you're going to need some energy," Patrick said even though his stomach was telling him to scarf that one as well. The only food that he'd had in the last couple of days ended up on the ground next to the dead man on the trail after he had hurt his knee.

"Mom's okay, ain't she?" Mackenzie asked her dad as she stared down at the pop-tart.

"I'm sure she is Darlin'," Patrick told her with confidence. "I'm sure she's heard about what happened up here on the mountain and is worried sick about us both."

Mackenzie nodded in agreement and broke off a piece of pop-tart before putting it in her mouth.

"I've been thinking about a few things that I think that we should do right away. But with my knee bunged up, I'm going to need your help," Patrick told her.

"What's that?" Mackenzie asked apprehensively. After the Bronco incident last night, Patrick understood why she would be cautious.

"Well, first off my knee could use some ice and ibuprofen," he told her. "Can you see if there is any ice left in the freezer before it all melts? Maybe put some in a plastic baggy or towel or something, and then see if you can raid their medicine cabinet?"

"Sure," Mackenzie answered. "Can I finish my pop-tart first?"

"Yeah," Patrick said growly as he put his arm around her, gave her a squeeze, and kissed the top of her head. "While you're walking around, keep an eye out for a land-line phone or anything else we can try to communicate with."

"There's a phone upstairs, but it doesn't work. I tried it last night and there is no dial tone or anything on it," Mackenzie told him.

"Try it again this morning to make sure would you?" Patrick asked.

"Yeah," Mackenzie said as she continued to slowly eat the pop-tart.

"After you get all of that done, can you look around for some vehicles? I thought that I saw a big garage outside down by the creek last night," Patrick told her.

"I thought you said that pulse thingy would have fried everything?" Mackenzie asked him.

"Well, it probably did. But if there's a chance that I'm wrong and we can drive off the mountain instead of walk, then I'm all for it," Patrick answered.

"K – want the rest?" Mackenzie offered her dad the last large corner of her pop tart. He thought about telling her to finish it, but his empty stomach got the better of him and he took it from her.

Mackenzie had good luck with the ice and the medicine, but not as good luck with the phone or the vehicles. She did find some keys to a motorcycle, jeep, and motor home; but none of them would start. She did find some dry cereal in the cupboard that they both ate handfuls of while sitting on the couch.

By late morning, the ibuprofen and ice had brought the swelling and pain down enough that Patrick thought he might be able to hobble some more on his leg. He put his splint back on after making a few improvements to it and walked around the cabin to test it out. He checked the phone again even though Mackenzie said that she just had, and it was just as dead as she said that it was.

Patrick also looked around for any firearms in the cabin, but he couldn't find any. He thought that was odd, but then surmised that they may have been locked up or hidden some place. Instead he found a bone handled chef's knife in the kitchen that he commandeered. As he was trying to figure out a good way to carry the knife without causing himself harm, Mackenzie came down from the upstairs again.

"Dad, I have an idea," she said.

"What's that Mak? You about ready to head out?" Patrick asked.

"What if we took that motorcycle in the garage and coasted down the mountain on it?" she asked.

Patrick stopped what he was doing and pushed his lips out into a duck-face as he was thinking about what she just said. "You mean just ride with it in neutral or with the clutch in?" Patrick clarified.

"Yeah," Mackenzie said. "And hopefully it's light enough that I could push it up the driveway, or some hills if we have to."

"How big is it?" Patrick asked.

"I don't know," Mackenzie said. "It's one of those Harley bikes. It's kind of big."

After a couple more seconds of thinking about it, Patrick said "I think that's an awesome idea Darlin'! It's definitely worth a try. Did you find keys to it?"

"Yeah, they were in it," she replied. She was grinning ear to ear. It wasn't often, or maybe ever, that she felt that she had an idea worthy of an 'awesome' from her dad.

"Great! Why don't you find a piece of paper and a pen to write whoever owns this place a note? Tell them that we're sorry about breaking in and eating their food, but that we hope they understand. Give them our name and phone number and tell them that we're good for whatever expenses they feel are appropriate."

"Give them the phone number to the phone that you threw into the woods last night?" Mackenzie asked.

"Funny. Okay, maybe put our address in it instead," Patrick said. "I'll meet you in the garage."

Patrick hobbled out to the garage with his splint attached. He was a little disappointed when he saw the bike that Mackenzie was talking about. He didn't know all the different Harley Davidson models by heart, but the dark blue tank had the words "Fat Boy" scripted in red on both sides. He doubted if Mackenzie could keep the thing from falling over let alone push it up the driveway.

Patrick figured out which chain hanging from the huge garage door opened it just as Mackenzie joined him in the large garage.

"The bike's a little big," Patrick told her as she came in.

"Yeah, but it's cool!" she said. Patrick just shook his head.

"Okay, well why don't you wheel the cool bike on out of here and I'll shut the door," Patrick responded.

Mackenzie turned the keys in the bike's ignition, righted it, and pushed the kickstand up with her foot. Patrick was impressed with her up to that point. He didn't think that she'd ever been on a motorcycle before. Then, as she tried to push the bike with it still in gear and he became less impressed. He took a few minutes and showed her where the hand and rear brakes were, how to operate the clutch, and explained the gears so that she could get it in neutral.

Then she was off. It was painful watching his daughter struggle with the weight of the bike on the level garage floor. The more that he watched without being able to help, the more frustrated that he became and the more he became disenchanted with the idea. She was making slow progress, but it was taking forever.

Just as she got the front tire to the open garage door, Patrick said "It was a good idea Darlin', but I think that the bike may be just a little too big to pull this off."

Mackenzie looked up at him as she was bent over the tank pushing for all she was worth. She had started to sweat, and the hair right around her face was visibly wet. "I can do it Dad," she said. Just as the words left her mouth, the bike tipped to her left. It began to fall in what seemed like slow motion. Mackenzie repositioned herself to try and keep it from falling and to make sure she was out of the way if it did, but it fell anyways.

Patrick felt the frustration grow to a point of anger as he looked down at the bike. It went over easy, but the spill still probably cost hundreds of dollars' worth of damage. Mackenzie looked back at him sheepishly and waited for his response.

"Well, do it then," Patrick snapped at her.

Mackenzie became angry as well. She got on the side of the bike and lifted for all she was worth, but it didn't seem to budge. She tried again to no avail. Patrick was pleased that she had the ambition to keep at an idea that she thought would work even it initially failed. He limped over to her on his splint and grabbed the handle bars to help her lift the bike on her third attempt. Patrick could put more weight and strain on his good leg than he thought, and was able to assist. The two of them barely got the bike upright again, and Mackenzie immediately slung her leg over it. Patrick found that if he stood on the left side of the bike with his bad leg closest to it, that he could lean on the handle bars and help her push it.

Once the bike was clear of the garage door, Patrick limped back and shut it. "Did you remember to tell them about us taking the motorcycle in the note that you left?" Patrick asked his daughter.

"No," she said. "But I'm sure that they'll figure it out."

"Yeah. Unfortunately, I think that you're right," Patrick said with a grin.

It took them more than a half-hour to get the bike up to the highway, and both were sweating and winded by the time that they made it. After a brief rest, Patrick took the splint off his leg and gingerly straddled the bike with his injured knee. Mackenzie sat behind him and held the splint off to the side.

It had been many years since Patrick had ridden a motorcycle, and he couldn't remember ever riding one as nice as that one. He was nervous and hesitant about the ride before he pushed off because of his hurt knee, his daughter being on the back, and just being able to coast. After checking to see if Mackenzie was squared away, he gritted his teeth and pushed off.

The grade of the road was steep enough that it didn't take long at all to build up speed. Just to try it, Patrick put the bike in third gear and popped the clutch. The bike sputtered and spit several times, but it wouldn't ever catch fully and run. After a couple of attempts, he put the bike back in neutral and tried to gather speed to get up over a small hill that was coming up.

Surprisingly, they made it up over the hill without having to stop. After that hill was an even steeper grade downhill. This one was full of sharp corners and abandoned vehicles littering the road. Patrick thought that he did well. He braked probably more than he should have and lost some momentum for the next hill, but they were safe.

For the rest of the way down the mountain Patrick screwed up a few times and took some corners faster than he should have, and slowed down more than he should have a few times. But nothing catastrophic happened. The worst that happened was that they had to get off and push the bike up the last little bit up some of the steeper hills. By the time they reached the outskirts of Buffalo, they both were kind of enjoying the ride despite the dire circumstances. The bike was quiet, the weather was warm, and they were both glad that they weren't walking.

As the bike rolled into town in early afternoon, any pleasant thoughts that they had were quickly dashed. It was evident from the few cars abandoned in the highway and the lack of movement along the streets that the cloud had hit the town as well. Patrick realized that his mouth was agape and quickly closed it as the bike coasted into town.

"All those people…" Mackenzie said.

The momentum of the bike was quickly waning on the flat ground in town. Patrick pulled into the Sherriff station's parking lot that was on the highway just before the downtown area, and applied the brakes.

"What are we going to do Dad?" Mackenzie asked with trepidation causing her voice to quiver as they glided to a stop.

"I'm not sure," Patrick said straddling the bike. They both sat there for a minute before Patrick said "Why don't you stay out here and watch for anybody while I go check on the Sherriff?"

Patrick installed the splint for the umpteenth time and headed into the building. The single-story brick building was quite large for a town the size of Buffalo. The building looked like it had recently been built, and the large white letters on the outside of the building that spelled out "Johnson County Justice Center" looked quite modern.

Patrick knew immediately when he went through the set of large glass doors in the entryway that the Sherriff's office wasn't operational. There was an attendant at a large L-shaped desk prominently in the welcome area. He was of slight build and had dirty blonde hair. He was slumped over in the office chair he was sitting in, and his face and shoulders were splayed out on the desk in front of him.

"Hello," Patrick said from across the room to the body. Part of him had hoped that the young man had just decided to take a catnap while at his post, but he knew better when there was no response.

Patrick limped on his splint into the welcome area and over to the attendant's desk. "Hello!" he yelled louder to anyone within earshot.

Patrick worked his way around the desk and stood beside the attendant's lifeless body. There were three different phone handsets on the desk in front of the attendant, several small video screens, and two large PC monitors. There didn't appear to be power to any of them. Patrick picked up each phone's headset and clicked the buttons a few times, but none of them had any response.

While the attendant didn't have a firearm, he saw that the attendant had a cell phone holster on his hip. He reached down and gingerly opened the magnetically held flap of the holster with one hand and grabbed the phone with his thumb and index finger of the other. As he began to pull the phone out, the office chair that supported the attendant's body began to swivel. Patrick pulled the phone out quickly and tried to stop the chair from spinning around with his other hand, but he was too late. The chair spun under the weight of the young man enough that the body's posterior slid off the chair to the ground. His upper torso whipped back violently enough to make a sound like an egg being cracked on a counter top when the back of his head hit the tile. Patrick stood there for a moment and absorbed the sight of the young man lying on the floor and tried to determine if he was dreaming about the macabre nightmare that they had been living the last couple of days.

When he shook the surreal thoughts from his mind, Patrick turned his attention back to the cell phone he was holding. He whispered "Come on..." to himself before he pushed the power button. He was disappointed, but not surprised when nothing happened.

There were two large doors on each side of the attendant's desk. Patrick tried them both, but they were locked. He went back and inspected the attendant's pockets and belt for any keys that could gain him access, but the locks appeared to be electronic and fail-safed to lock in the event of power loss.

As he was hobbling back to the front glass doors, a large relief map of the area hanging on one of the walls caught his eye. It was a decorative map that must have been at least five feet across and had Wyoming, Idaho, South Dakota, most of Nebraska, and portions of the other surrounding states on it. It was more of a traveler's map with the major interstates and highways listed. It wasn't a topographic map with all the lines on it showing elevation, but it was colored and shaded to depict the hills and mountains.

While he normally wouldn't think of stealing anything under normal circumstances, especially from a sheriff's office in broad daylight, he felt an insatiable need for that map. The paper map was behind a thick glass frame that was screwed to the mounting plaque behind it with four large diameter screw heads in each corner.

Patrick ventured back to the attendant, steeled his nerves, and then rifled through the pockets of the pants of the body for something to turn the screws on the map frame. Patrick couldn't help but look at the face of the attendant now that he was in his awkward position on the floor. The attendant had a shaved haircut and a rather large protruding nose. The most disturbing attribute was that the young man's dry tongue was protruding from his mouth. Not like he was sticking it out to be rude, but as if he had been gagging on something.

Patrick found a set of car keys in the dead man's pockets and returned to the screws. He could loosen the screws enough to slide the map out from the frame for the most part. A part of North Dakota on the top corner of the map tore as he pulled it out because it was stuck to the glass. Patrick laid the map out on the floor in front of the plaque that had held it and inspected it further. He retraced their trip from their home in Columbus, Nebraska to the Big Horns. He looked at several other routes to see how close the next town was and planned on what their next steps should be. He then carefully folded the pristine map up carefully making crisp folds in it that allowed it to be almost as small as a cheap road map you could buy from a gas station. With the map stowed in his back pocket, he exited the sheriff's office to see if Mackenzie had any more luck than he had.

Mackenzie was walking back towards the commandeered motorcycle in the parking lot from across the street as her dad exited the sheriff office's large glass doors.

"Where've you been?" Patrick called out to her as he limped towards the motorcycle.

Mackenzie waited until they were closer to each other and then hooked her thumb to point across the street behind her to an older motel.

"I just walked across the street to see if I could see anything," she said. "I kind of wish that I hadn't." When she reached the motorcycle she asked "What are we going to do Dad?"

Patrick put his arm around her shoulder and squeezed it. "I don't really know Darlin'. Let's walk down town and see if we can find something to eat."

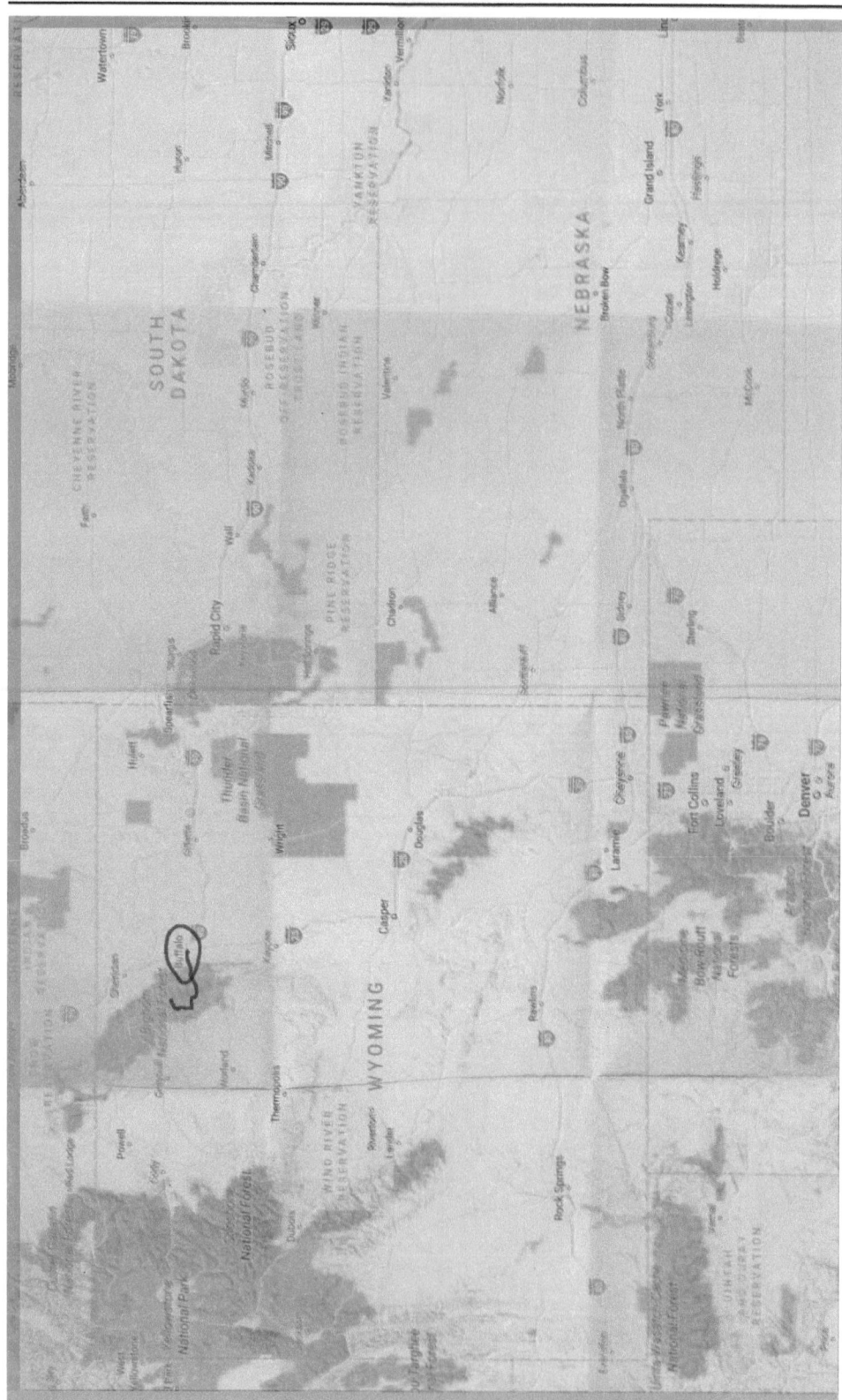

CHAPTER 10

HALF-WAY DOWN THE short and quaint main
street, they had hit the jackpot and found a rather large sports store.
The store looked like it had taken over three or four of what used to have been
individual businesses and buildings along the historic looking main street, and
simply knocked doorways and arches through the walls that had once separated the individual stores. Now each section had something different from
clothes, fishing, camping, hunting, to biking and baseball.

They committed more crimes by breaking and entering and eating several
helpings of granola and protein bars. Patrick and Mackenzie both were becoming more at ease at taking what they needed due to the circumstances.

There were only a few bodies lying around the store, and luckily they were
in the fishing and sporting goods sections that they didn't plan to go into.
Each of them garnered a fresh wardrobe from the available clothes and Patrick

grabbed a large duffel bag to put supplies in. They filled it with foods like trail mix and granola bars, but he also grabbed a small camping stove and freeze dried packages. They also each grabbed a sleeping bag and a multi-tool.

The store also had a rather small display of firearms with some pistols in a glass counter and a few rifles and shotguns in a rack behind the counter. Patrick found keys to each on one off one of the bodies in the back of the store. He selected a .44 caliber short barrel revolver from the case.

"Why are you taking that?" Mackenzie asked.

"Just in case," was all Patrick replied with. He also shopped around the store until he found a holster and ammunition for the pistol.

After their shopping spree at the sports store, they continued to walk down the main street. They came to a large historic hotel that looked like it could have really been something to visit and take the family to under other circumstances. It was a two-story brick building that occupied a whole block across the street from a small open park. The first floor had several doors that opened to the main street from the lobby, a saloon, a restaurant, and what looked like an old-fashioned barber shop.

"Should we check this place out?" Patrick asked.

"To stay the night?" Mackenzie asked.

"Why not?" he asked.

"I don't know. The motel that I looked at earlier wasn't a very nice place anymore," Mackenzie answered. The vivid memories of the looks of the ladies faces in the lobby of the motel had been floating around her consciousness since she had joined her dad back at the sheriff's office. Mackenzie thought that their dull open eyes hadn't been filled with terror, but instead with surprise and wonder.

"Okay. Why don't you let me go in and check it out first, and I'll see what it's like," Patrick said.

"I don't want to stand around out here by myself," Mackenzie said.

"Well just come in with me and stay close," Patrick said.

"I really don't want to Dad," Mackenzie argued.

Patrick dropped the duffel bag he was holding, took a step back and put his arm around his daughter. "Listen, I've thought this through; and I think that this is the best choice. There probably are bodies in here, but the odds are that we can find a room that isn't occupied. If we start breaking into houses, there most likely will be bodies in every one of them."

"I really don't want to Dad," Mackenzie said again this time looking up at him with eyes that conveyed her trepidation.

Patrick took a deep breath, let it out, and then said "Listen, we need to – "

Mackenzie cut him off and said "What if we just pitch a tent over in that park?" She pointed across the street to a grassy area that had a small amphitheater, a restroom building, and the like. She was hopeful that he would go for it so they didn't have to walk past endless dead people again with their eyes staring out in the dark room.

Patrick thought about it for a few seconds and then said "Alright." Mackenzie could tell from his tone that he didn't think that it was the best option, but she was just glad that they didn't have to go into the hotel. "I'll go pick out a spot and start dinner while you go back to the store and find a good tent," Patrick offered.

"Thanks Dad," Mackenzie said as she raised up on her tip-toes to give her dad a peck on the cheek. She turned and went back to the sports store as Patrick limped across the street to the park.

Mackenzie returned to the park with her arms full of more gear while Patrick had the camp stove operational with a large pot of water heating on it. The afternoon was getting late, and the day was beautiful in the park. The sun softly shown with a mid-spring warmth and the slight breeze with the smell of pine filled the air. Patrick was sitting with his legs dangling from the amphitheater's short stage and staring at the map that he had unfolded. He had taken the splint off from his leg and was unconsciously rubbing his knee when Mackenzie walked up.

"How's your knee feel?" Mackenzie asked as she dropped the arms load of loot on the ground when she reached the camp stove.

"Better I think," Patrick answered. "Still hurts like a …. bugger though."

Mackenzie had selected a large three room tent that she had hauled back to the park and began opening the box. Patrick grabbed the splint from the stage and started putting it on.

"I got it Dad," Mackenzie said.

"You sure?" Patrick asked.

"Yeah, I think so," Mackenzie answered. She'd never setup a tent by herself before and she had never seen one like this, but she thought that she could do it. "So, what are you looking at over there?"

"This? Oh, I found a map back at the sheriff's office that I thought might come in handy," Patrick said.

"What will we need a map for?" Mackenzie asked.

"I hope we don't," Patrick answered. "I just wanted to see if there were any other towns close by."

Mackenzie had taken all the tent pieces out of the box and carrying bag, and she was putting the fiberglass poles together. "How many more days do you think we'll have to stay here?" she asked.

"I don't know," Patrick said anxiously watching her struggle with the tent. "None, I hope."

The next morning after breakfast, both Patrick and Mackenzie were restless. They sat on the edge of the stage of the little amphitheater and let their feet dangle. Mackenzie was used to having a television, cell phone, or other gadget to keep her occupied; and her dad wasn't much of a conversationalist.

Patrick suggested that they gather a bunch of wood and other debris, and pile it in the middle of the park so that they could have a signal fire in case they seen an aircraft. Mackenzie made her dad stay on the stage and rest his knee while she assembled all the materials for the signal fire. She went back to the sporting goods store and grabbed fire starters, kerosene, and a camp saw. Then she went around and scavenged all kinds of fuel from a nearby dead elm tree, a blanket from an abandoned nearby car, two wooden chairs from the patio seating at the restaurant across the street, and a few other things. By early afternoon she had made a sizable mass of fuel arranged in a large pyramid in the middle of the park. She stood back and admired her work for some time before joining her dad on the stage again. Patrick was peering at the map again.

"What do you think Dad?" Mackenzie asked.

"It's great Mak," Patrick said without looking up.

After a few moments of quiet, Mackenzie asked "Now what should I do?"

"Ummm…. You could spell out S.O.S in big letters on the ground next to the fire," Patrick said. "Or go see if you can find something to use as signal mirrors," he continued to talk without looking up.

Mackenzie sat with her legs dangling from the stage looking down at her feet. Her dad didn't sound like either of the things he mentioned were of much importance. "You don't think that anybody's coming, do you?" she asked him.

This time he did look up and meet her gaze. He put an arm on her shoulder and said "I don't know Darlin'. I just think that we need to be prepared for whatever."

Mackenzie did do what her dad had suggested. It took her most of the afternoon, but she had found a large full length mirror in the clothes section of the sports store that she had dragged back to the park, and she used all kinds of scavenged materials to spell out S.O.S. in letters big enough to take up the whole block that the park occupied.

They had dinner and then both went to sleep at dark, mainly out of boredom. Mackenzie laid awake in her sleeping bag for hours, unable to keep her eyes closed. "Dad?" she finally asked hours after they had gone to bed.

"Yeah," he replied.

"You still awake?" she asked.

"Kind of," he said.

"I miss Mom," she said.

"Yeah. I do too," he answered. "I'm sure she's missing us too."

After a long pause, Mackenzie said "Dad?"

"What Mak?" he replied.

"What are we going to do?" she asked.

"What do you mean?" he asked.

"Are we going to stay here?" she clarified.

"I don't know. What do you think we should do?" he asked.

After another long pause, Mackenzie answered "I want to go home."

The next day, they both were up with the sun and had an early breakfast from the freeze-dried camping food. The swelling on Patrick's knee had went down considerably and he was trying to walk around the camp gingerly without the splint.

"I was thinking…" Patrick said as they sat in their familiar places on the edge of the stage.

"What's that Dad?" Mackenzie asked. She knew since she was a little girl that whenever her dad started a conversation like that, that something difficult was going to come out next.

"I had seen some mountain bikes in that sports store the other day. Remember the ones hanging in the back by the baseball bats?" Patrick coaxed her.

"Kind of," Makenzie answered. One of the store workers had been back in that area and she had avoided going back there. She even tried to avoid looking back there while her dad walked around in there because she had caught a glimpse of the large man in the forest green vest earlier. He was balding, had a bushy unkempt goatee, and a substantive belly that rested on the floor. The thing that had really bothered her though in the dark back of the store was the way that his mouth was wide open. His cheek and temple were laying on the old hardwood floor, but his mouth was agape with his large tongue and old yellow teeth making the focal point of his face. She had only glimpsed the sight, but had seen enough that she knew that she didn't want to see anymore.

"Well, what if we go grab a couple of them and go explore more of the town. We can make sure that there isn't anyone else in the same predicament as we are; and we can see what we can see," Patrick said with almost a little excitement at the sound of the idea.

"Sure," Mackenzie said. Then she added "Do you mind getting the bikes though Dad?"

"Yeah; I suppose I can. Why's that?" he asked.

"I just don't want to go that far back in the store," she answered.

The two of them walked back down to the sports store and Patrick selected a mountain bike for each of them and wheeled them up to the front of the store. They hopped on the bikes and road them in circles in the main street in front of the store while they made slight adjustments to the seat height, pedals, and a few other things. They didn't waste much time though, and they were off exploring the town.

They pedaled up and down the main street, up the highway towards the sheriff office and then back down the highway towards the interstate ramp. They saw no signs of life or movement wherever they road. There were cars and bodies scattered throughout the streets and the town, just as if they had no notice and dropped where they had been standing when the cloud swept down from the mountain.

The two stopped at a convenience store on the outskirts of town for a short break. Patrick went in and got two warm sodas and two bags of chips. He came back out to sit on the curb with his daughter.

"Thanks," Mackenzie said as he handed her the pop and chips he had selected for her. She was staring up at the large hill that the on ramp to the interstate went up. "How would we go back Dad? If we had to."

Patrick took a deep breath, let it out, and swallowed the mouthful of chips before answering. "There are other ways to go, maybe even shorter ones. But I think that getting back on the interstate and using it for the most part would be the best. If anyone is looking for survivors, that would be the place to start looking."

Mackenzie washed some chips down with a large drink of the warm soda. "How long do you think that it would take us to ride these bikes back home?"

Patrick laughed a little as he said "All the way home? I hope that we wouldn't have to go that far. I think that we could make it to the next big town in a couple of days."

"If we did have to ride all the way back though, how long would it take us?" Mackenzie asked.

"Mmmmm…" Patrick sounded as he put another handful of chips into his mouth and he squinted his eyes. Mackenzie used to imagine that there was a big machine or computer inside her dad's head that was turning gears, bouncing up and down, and blowing steam whenever he would get that look on his face. When she was little she used to tell him that was his thinking face. "Depending on how long and hard we rode, I bet that we could make it all the way back in a couple of weeks."

Mackenzie finished her pop and sat the rest of the bag of chips down on the curb. "Let's do it then," she said.

"You sure Darlin'?" Patrick said.

"Yeah," Mackenzie replied as she stood up.

"Riding for a couple of days straight is going to make the backpacking trip seem like a day at the park," Patrick told her.

"I miss mom," Mackenzie said with determination in her voice.

"And maybe even your little brother too," Patrick said as he finished his soda, collected all the trash, and struggled to stand up with his knee clearly bothering him.

"Maybe a little," Mackenzie said smiling. "But don't tell him I said that."

Her dad reached out and messed her hair.

"Let's go. How far do you think that we can make it tonight?" Mackenzie asked.

"We can't go today Darlin'," Patrick said.

"Why?" Mackenzie said. She felt her breathing speed up somewhat and anxiety filled her chest. "I don't want to stay here again tonight. Let's get going so we can get back home!"

"Whoaa, Whoaa," Patrick said trying to calm her. "We probably only have a few hours of light left. We need to go back to that sports store and stock up on backpacks, tents, jackets, food – all kinds of stuff. We're going to be camping in the middle of nowhere in between towns. We'll get stocked up on things today, and if nobody comes and rescues us tonight, we'll head out early in the morning."

"Why can't we just get ready now and leave today?" Mackenzie asked still not wanting to accept another night of just sitting there.

"It will take all of the daylight that we have left to get ready," Patrick said. Mackenzie could hear that patronizing tone start to enter his voice that grated so badly on her nerves. "And it would be good to stay by your signal fire one more night just in case someone is looking for us."

Realizing that she wasn't going to get her way, she asked "Can we at least ride up to the on ramp there to check it out?"

"You can Mak," her dad said. "I'm going to save my knee for tomorrow."

Mackenzie didn't waste any more time. She hopped on her bike and pedaled out onto the highway. She was kind of upset at her dad and his logic, and pumping the pedals somehow made her feel a little better. The ramp was further away than what she had thought it was, and she was starting to become winded when she turned her bike up the beginning of the ramp. The on ramp was a long and steep incline that rose nearly a hundred feet from the level of the highway below to the flat divided highway above. Mackenzie began to shift gears on her bike as the pedaling became harder and harder with the incline. Each time she shifted it became easier to pedal, but required that she move the pedals even faster.

By the time she was three-quarters of the way to the top, her lungs were burning and she only had one more gear left to go. She told herself that she had to make it. If she wanted to see her mom and little brother again, she had to make it. She was breathing so hard now that she thought that she might pass out. She had to make it.

She began to crest the hill of the onramp and she shifted down a gear. Her lungs were still burning as felt her chest stretching with each gasp. A little further and she shifted down again. The incline was getting less and less. She shifted down again. *I did it!* she thought. *I really did it!*

Mackenzie shifted down two more gears and slowed her pedaling as she topped out on the hill and merged onto the interstate. Her triumph was quickly overcome as she looked out at the expansive country and the interstate that faded into the rolling hills in front of her. The endless length of it made her realize why her dad had tried to temper her enthusiasm.

Mackenzie gradually slowed her speed until she stopped and straddled her bike. She stood that way looking east and longing for the rest of her family. The scenery was beautiful, but terrifying as well as she realized how far away she was from home. She stood there for several moments. After she caught her breath and the burning in her thighs faded, she saw basketball sized black masses on the interstate that stretched across both lanes. It looked as if someone with a huge black marker had marked a diagonal line that was as wide as a house across both lanes of the interstate and into the fields on both sides. Mackenzie got back on her bike and pedaled further down the interstate warily as her mind tried to make out and reason what was causing the wide black line.

It wasn't until she was almost up to the edge of the dark line, that must have been at least forty feet wide, that she realized that the line was made up of the corpses of geese. The large birds must have been flying in a tight pattern when the cloud came through, and they fell where they were. Their bodies dotted the ground so tightly, that their lumpy masses made what had appeared to her earlier as a large black line. Mackenzie stood there straddling her bike at the edge of the line of geese for several minutes. Even though she had finally recognized what was causing the black line across the roads, she had difficulty accepting what it was that she was seeing. She eventually got back on her bike, and turned it back around to ride down the same hill that she had just struggled to come up.

She zoomed down the hill of the on ramp. In a matter of seconds, she was nearing the bottom of the hill that took her at least fifteen minutes to pedal up. The wind was blowing in her face and she felt the adrenaline begin to pump through her veins. As she neared the bottom of the hill, she was going faster than what she felt comfortable with and began to apply the brakes on the handlebars. She slowed somewhat, but she misjudged how fast she was going and began to panic. She pressed harder on the brakes and bike slowed more, but she was still going too fast.

As she reached the bottom of the on ramp and tried to turn onto the highway, she was squeezing both brakes as hard as they would go. Her back tire began to skid as she leaned into the turn. Just as the back tire was skidding out from underneath her, she put her left leg down on the ground in a last-ditch effort to not take a tumble. She hopped three times on her foot trying to not lose her balance, and then finally stood stationary on the one leg. *I just did that too!* she thought.

The two did stop at the sports store on the way back and looted even more gear. They each got a backpack, more clothes, a jacket, camping gear, freeze dried food, and anything else they could think of that they might need. Her dad kept telling her "That looks heavy" and "You sure that you need that?" whenever she picked up something that looked cool.

They also grabbed a few of the rifles that were in the rack behind the glass counter with the pistols. Patrick took a big black machine gun looking rifle that he called an AR, and then he also grabbed a hunting rifle with a large scope on it.

"That looks heavy," Mackenzie told him as he searched the shelves in the dim light for the ammunition to go with the hunting rifle.

"You take this one," her dad said as he handed her a small .22LR that was mainly chrome with a grey synthetic stock. It had a small scope on it as well.

Mackenzie hesitated to take it from him. She wasn't scared of guns at all. Her dad had taken her shooting plenty of times since she was a young girl. She had just never been responsible for a gun all by herself.

"I don't think that I need one Dad," Mackenzie said.

Patrick pumped the rifle in the air as he continued to hold it out to her. "Just take it. We'll secure it to your bike and you won't even know that it's there. Unless you need it."

She reluctantly took the rifle and the ammunition that he found for it. They left another note with their names and addresses on it at the store. They stuck it under the cash register near the front door as they left.

They spent the rest of the afternoon sun sitting out on the curb in front of the sports store organizing and going through the gear that they had taken. Her dad took some of the rope and zip ties that they had found in the store and lashed rifle scabbards and some of the other gear permanently to their bikes. They planned to just keep the rest of the gear in their backpacks on their backs.

It was becoming dusk when they took another short ride around the town to try out how well they could pedal and move with the supplies and equipment. They stopped and adjusted things a couple of times, but for the most part everything worked well the first time.

Patrick stopped at a little gift shop on the main street on their way back to the park. "What are you doing?" Mackenzie asked her dad.

"Why don't you go back and get some water boiling. I'll be right there," he said as he entered the store.

Mackenzie felt a little nervous about riding back to the camp by herself. It was only a couple of blocks away down the main street, but it was getting dark. She thought about staying there outside of the gift shop and waiting for her dad to return, but instead she gathered her courage and rode back to the park by herself.

It took her a few minutes to figure out the camp stove. Her dad rode across the park and joined her just as she was putting the pot of water on the stove. It was almost dark, and she could hardly make out what he was trying to hand her as he walked over to her and sat on the edge of the stage.

"What's this?" she asked.

"Well, it's not a cell phone, music player, or anything else that takes batteries; but it's what I used when I was your age to entertain myself," her dad said snidely.

Mackenzie opened the hard-back book and thumbed through the pages. She peered at the cover, but couldn't make out the title in the fading light. "Very funny. What book is it?" she asked.

"Huck Finn," her dad answered. "It's about a young boy who takes a long journey across the country, and the adventures that he has along the way."

"Yeah, I've heard of it," she said as she checked on the warming water. She seen that he also had a book like object in his hand. Except his looked like it was covered in leather and had a zipper around it. "What did you get?" she asked.

"Oh. I grabbed a Bible. It thought that we could use a little guidance," he said.

The next morning, they both were up just after dawn. They opted for granola bars and trail mix instead of waiting to cook breakfast. They took off down the main street, then down the highway, and then headed towards the interstate.

Mackenzie was pedaling faster than her dad and consistently stayed in front of him. She liked taking the lead. When they had been backpacking up to the lakes, that was her favorite part. When she was following her dad, she had kept her head down and just trudged along with each step seeming like it was work. But when she had taken the lead, she walked with her head held high and it felt like she was blazing the trail in front of her.

"You wanna get a good run at this hill," she turned and called out to her dad as she started up the on ramp. She was still winded and plenty tired as she topped out and merged onto the interstate, but the hill didn't seem like it was near as steep as it was the day before.

She circled around after reaching the top and turned and waited for her dad. He was a little more than half way up, and was struggling to reach the top. She could see him wincing whenever he had to pump down hard with his right knee. "You can do it!" she called down to him.

Patrick kept pedaling and soon reached his daughter at the top of the hill. "Wow," he said between gasps. "I hope that it's - - all downhill - - from here," he made out as he stopped and rubbed his injured knee.

"You gonna make it?" Mackenzie asked her dad.

"I'm tougher than – tougher than you think," Patrick said as he continued to rub his knee.

Once they both caught their breath, they were off. Mackenzie took the lead again and set the pace of the biking marathon. The terrain was rolling hills separated by long runs of straight flat interstate. For the most part, it was slightly downhill from where they had started. While it was exercise and Mackenzie could tell that her thighs were going to be sore tomorrow, none of it was as difficult as that first onramp hill.

There were only a few sparse cars on either side of the divided interstate. Most of them looked like they had just come to an easy stop in the median or ditches along the asphalt roadway, but there were a few doozies that they came across. One small pickup had gone across both lanes and was on its top pointed in the wrong direction in the wrong lane. A Buick sedan had gone over a guard rail on a bridge and landed on its nose on the railroad beneath it, still teetering on its front grill. At first, Mackenzie would peer into the windows as she road by or would even sometimes slow and stop at a car that looked like it was just parked there in the middle of the interstate. After only a few times though, she forced herself to keep pedaling by and tried not to look in at all. The scenes inside the cars were never anything that she cared to see again.

While she didn't know any of them, the people in the vehicles looked just like people that she had seen all her life. One teenage boy that had been driving an older two-door Civic with one prime red quarter panel looked very like one of her best friends back in Nebraska. Although this boy had the same dull look in his eyes that those women did back at the motel, and he had dried blood in a trail down his forehead.

A pudgy lady wearing a grey hoodie looked like she was just sleeping behind the wheel while her van was parked with the front half teetering over a guard rail to a small creek below. Mackenzie could make out two car seats in the middle row of seats and looked away before she saw anything that would have really upset her.

A little before noon, Mackenzie pulled over in a parking area on the top of a large bluff. She took her backpack off and started rummaging through it looking for another granola bar as her dad pulled up behind her.

"How's the knee holding up?" she asked him.

"I think that it's fine," he said slightly winded. "It hurts a little, but I think that the biking might be good for it. Hey – why don't we stop and make something with a little more sustenance? We need to make sure that we keep our energy up if we're going to ride like this all day."

They did take a long break and cooked up freeze dried beef stroganoff. They chatted a little about how the ride was and what they liked about their bikes, but mostly they just ate and read quietly in the books that they had got the day before. After lunch, they stowed everything and hopped back on their bikes.

By early afternoon they were both exhausted. Patrick caught up to his daughter as they neared the Powder River and told her to exit. They took the exit near the river and went down to a small public rest stop. Mackenzie wanted to get back on the road, but Patrick talked her into staying there for the night to rest up and let his knee heal more. They pitched their tent near the river, rested, and read their books until dark.

The next morning, they were up and back on the interstate just after first light. Mackenzie had a drive to cover as many miles as they could, and she pushed her body beyond anything that she normally would have attempted before going on the backpacking trip with her dad. She stopped and rested a few times throughout the day, but Mackenzie set a sustained quick pace. By late afternoon they were reaching the outskirts of a larger town called. They were both excited about making it there and about the possibility of finding other survivors. As they came off the interstate and coasted into town though, their hope was almost immediately dashed.

The scene in that town was grislier than it had been back in Buffalo. There were many more cars and people strewn about in the streets and around the town. They rode their bikes around the town, called out to anyone who was listening, and looked around for things that might help them on their travels. They weren't successful in any of their endeavors. Patrick spent considerable time in a car dealership downtown that had lots of used vehicles in its lot. He had grabbed a handful of keys and gave another handful to Mackenzie to try. They each tried six or seven different vehicles, but gave up after finding that nothing electric or electronic even tried to function.

After exploring the town, they decided to camp outside again instead of breaking into a building. They found a huge park with a lake on the east side of town that they decided would work as well as anywhere. They sat up camp again and read more of their books until dark. Neither of them had much to say and Mackenzie felt like they were never going to get back home.

"What if we're it Dad?" Mackenzie asked her dad. She could feel tears welling up in her eyes as she reclined in the grass on a hillside next to the lake with her Adventures of Huckleberry Finn book opened on her chest.

"What do you mean Darlin'?" her dad asked without looking up. He had his nose in his book and she could tell that he was intrigued by something because he had his finger on a passage while he was reading another one.

"What if we're the only two that lived?" she asked. She could feel her upper lip quiver as she imagined her friends, her mom, and even her little brother as the cloud rolled through their home town. She thought about what each of them could have been doing at the time.

"We're not," her dad said without question.

"How do you know?" Mackenzie asked.

"I've read the back of this book," he said holding his bible up. "I know how the whole story ends. And this isn't it."

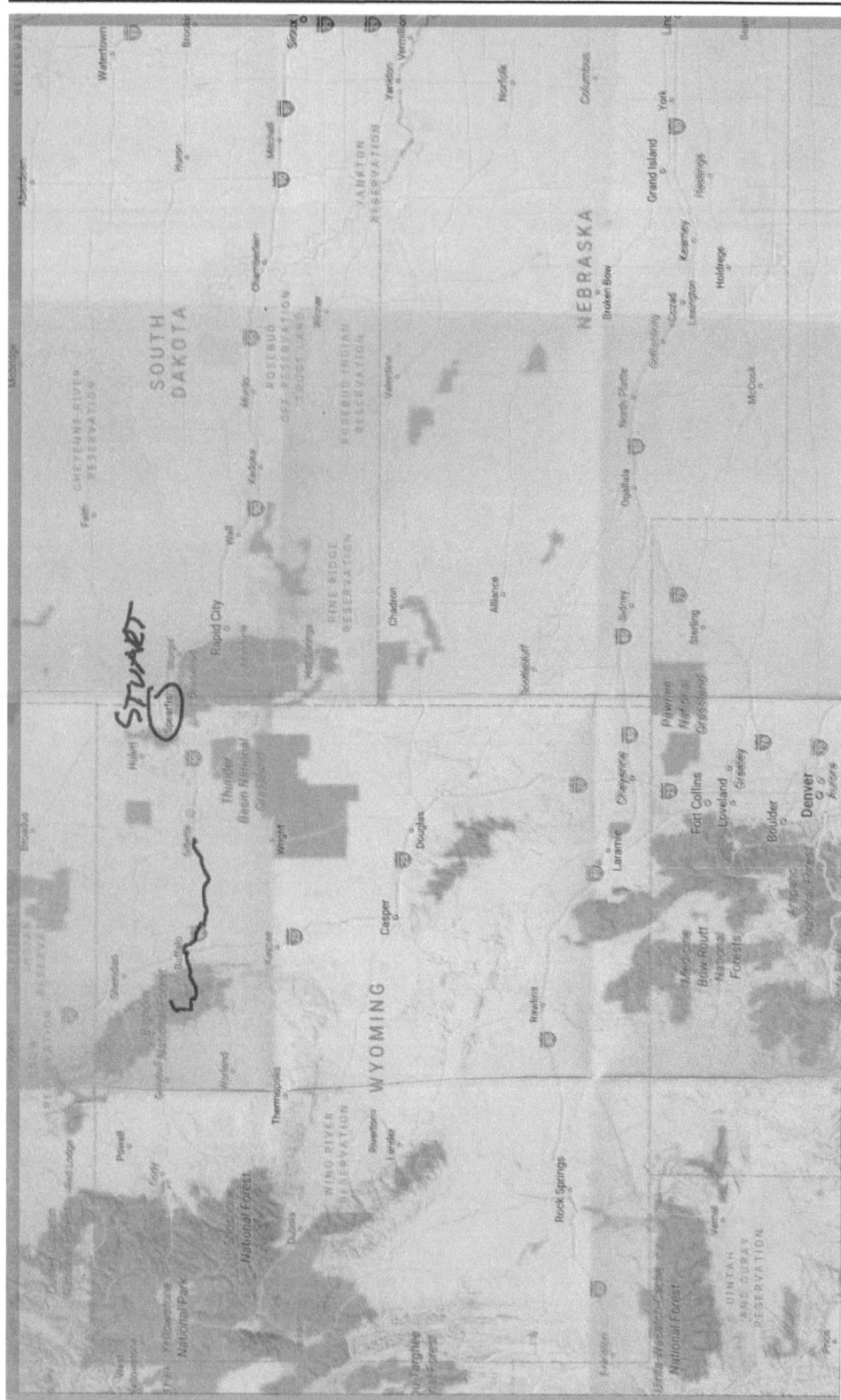

CHAPTER 11

THE EDGE OF Stuart's boot grazed the forehead of Mrs. Wendall's temple as he walked by, and her head rocked back and forth lifelessly as if she were shaking her head no. Stuart glanced down at her sunken eyes and gaping mouth as he turned the corner of aisle nine heading to the canned goods on aisle ten. As he navigated the cart past her large calves and white flats laying lifeless on the tan tiled floor he told her "I'll stop and pick some Crest up for you on the way by Mrs. Wendall. Your breath is getting bad enough to make my eyes water." He made a mental note to drag her body out of the way the next time he came to the store before he got a cart so that he would quit running into it in the dimly lit section of the super center.

Even though it was mid-morning with the sun shining brightly outside, it was quite dark inside the big box store once you got away from the front doors which contained the only windows in the large building. Stuart had been down this aisle several times recently and knew almost exactly how far down he needed to go to reach what he wanted. He was looking for the beef ravioli cans with the easy open lids. He got to about where he thought they should be and took his zippo lighter out of his pocket. He flicked it a couple of times to light it and then held it down to the third row to illuminate the cans enough to make out their contents as he slowly walked down the aisle. The last supply run he made he had grabbed several cans of spaghetti without the easy opener by mistake and it had taken over an hour for him to figure out how to open the can without a can opener.

He finally reached what he was looking for and stooped to grab the remaining fourteen cans of ravioli off the shelf. The cans made rather loud thuds in the stillness of the store as Stuart haphazardly tossed them into the cart and they connected with the six packs of pop and the cart's wire frame. He missed the cart with one of the cans, and it rolled to the opposite side of the aisle where it was even darker. Stuart had to fish his lighter back out of his pocket to find where that last can had rolled off to. While looking for the can, he absentmindedly began whistling the first several notes of *Patience* by Guns n' Roses. He wasn't a big G'nR fan, but that song had been playing relentlessly in his head since he had been stuck in the darkness.

Once the last easy open can was in the cart, Stuart closed the lid of the lighter but didn't stow it away in his pocket yet. The only other thing that he needed on this supply run was near the back of the store where there was absolutely no light.

In the last couple of weeks Stuart had accepted that no one was coming to save him; and with that, no one cared if he took things that he needed. Or took things that he just merely wanted. As a result, he had been around this and plenty other stores in the last couple of weeks raiding whatever suited his fancy. Since he had already looted as much as could, today's trip to the store was simply a supply run. He was out of food, pop, and ammo.

As he continued to slowly push the cart back towards the sporting goods section of the store, Stuart continued to slowly and absently whistle the tune that he had started. As he was walking past one end cap, something caught his eye in the dim lighting and he stopped. "Alright!" he squawked as he realized that the end cap was full of Doritos bags. He grabbed a few of the bags and threw them in the cart, then opened one and began to munch on the chips as he continued back towards sporting goods. Stuart had thought that he had cleaned out all the Doritos when he took the last bag from the chip aisle a week ago, and he was utterly thrilled to find a few more bags were left.

With his mouth half full of chips, he wasn't able to whistle the tune anymore so he began to softly hum and sing some of the lines from the same song as he continued slowly pushing the cart.

He hadn't seen or heard another soul, a critter, or even an insect for weeks; but the dark part of the store was still unsettling in its stillness. The last time he went back this way was to get a bicycle. The stench had been so bad from the remaining bodies and the dairy products that went bad in the non-functioning coolers that he had to change his route to walk in a looping arc around that corner of the store. This time, the stench was still there but had dissipated enough to be bearable, and he walked directly back to where they kept the rifles and ammunition.

Stuart continued to absently sing as he lit his lighter and walked around to the front of the cart to pull it instead of push it in the darkness. After a few steps of pulling the cart, it stopped abruptly and almost caused Stuart to lose his balance. He almost fell, but righted himself instead. Using his lighter, he peered down to the floor at the cart's wheels and found what the problem was. A teenage girl's rotting arm was laying in the middle of the aisle and had become lodged between the wheel and bottom of the cart. Stuart had seen enough bodies by now that he was more perturbed about his supply run taking longer than he had thought rather than thinking about the tragedy that had befallen the girl.

He could dislodge the corpse's arm easily by stepping on the forearm and pushing the cart backwards. As he did, he caught a glimpse of the young girls face and recognized her immediately. Her eyes were slightly sunken in their sockets, her already dark hair was matted with dried blood, and her skull resembled a bruised apple near what had been the impact point of her head and the tile floor. Regardless of her looks, Stuart knew immediately that it was Mary Castlebrock and he felt his spirits lift slightly as he thought about the terror that must have consumed the last few moments of her life. After the years of menacing teasing, unscrupulous comments and actions, and her involvement with his being locked in that unending darkness; he couldn't help but feel some relief that she had been included in the death that had swallowed his town. He wouldn't ever have to see that twinkle in her eye or hear that one-word ooze from Mary's lips again. That word that made him cringe deep down in his soul.

With the Doritos find and now this, this supply run was turning out to be one of the better days Stuart had experienced in the last few weeks. Once Mary's arm was dislodged, he was on his way again. He crooned with his best Axel Rose impression that even he would have admitted wasn't that great. He continued back to sporting goods pulling the cart, but this time he stooped a little closer to the floor with his lighter out to make sure that he didn't run into any other road blocks.

With his supplies loaded up in his overflowing back pack and other bags slung over the handle bars of the red and black dirt bike, he was slowly pedaling and enjoying the sun and breeze of the late afternoon sky. While working to get up the last large hill on route back to the Dungeon, Stuart became slightly out of breath and paused in awkward moments as he continued to sing about patience in a soft voice that only he could hear.

Stuart had been on this route enough in the last few weeks that he went into auto-pilot mode while his mind began thinking about Mary's face again. This time though, her sunken eyes weren't just staring up at him from the cold tile from the department store's floor. The slight smirk that had been at the corners of his mouth since he'd recognized her face in the glow from his lighter faded from his lips. This time those same sunken eyes were staring at him from his memory of the last time he had seen her alive. He remembered how he was down on all fours with one hand holding his abdomen to try and comfort the pain from Brock Donovan's one-two combination to his midsection. Brock and Keith slinked out the partially open door to the Dungeon while Mary stood in the doorway. She was partially illuminated by the moonlight and glared down at him with pure loathing. Only this time, the evil spewing from that hatred stare was through the sunken and half-rotted eyes of the Mary that he had seen laying on the tile floor of the department store twenty minutes ago. While her face was rotted and distorted in this memory now, her voice was just as sharp and cutting as she said "Why don't you stay in here and think about that for a while," as she paused for effect before the word "faggot" darted out of her mouth as a closing condemnation. Mary slipped out of view into the moonlight with wisps of her long stringy black hair following her as she suddenly turned. The open side of the heavy double door swung closed. Then the hard click and bang of the crowbar being jammed through the door handles in the replay of Stuart's memory jogged him back to reality in the nick of time before he missed his turn at the top of the hill. He stopped pedaling and put both his feet down astride the bike to rest a little from the climb, but mostly to recover from the memory.

He closed his eyes and bowed his head as he tried to control his breathing some and change the direction of where his mind was leading him, but he couldn't control either. His chest continued to slightly heave and the memory of the darkness enveloped him…

Stuart was on all fours looking up in utter darkness at the doorway where Mary had just stood when he heard a heavy metal clank on the outside of the door that he knew couldn't be good. He also thought that he heard a faint laugh from Brock or Keith just outside the door, but he knew that must have been his imagination because once those heavy doors were closed to the Dungeon you couldn't have heard a politician with a bullhorn just outside.

The Dungeon was a bomb shelter buried in his backyard that his great-uncle had built back in the 70's when he owned Stuart's family home. Its only entrance was from a discrete storm cellar like staircase from an alley behind Freeway Street, as it was built into the hillside that the rows of houses stood on in Maple Valley Subdivision. When Stuart's family first moved to the house in the summer before his fifth-grade year, his dad had told him the story of the bunker and that his uncle said he had dumped truckloads of iron and steel scrap into the hole before pouring four feet of concrete all around the bunker. His Uncle Dan was an engineer that had been scared to death during the Cuban Missile crisis, and made the bunker for his family and friends to survive the impending all out global thermonuclear war that he was sure would happen. He had spent tons of money and decades of his free time in designing the generator back up system, the sand-and-water air filtration system, the stand-alone sewage and water treatment system, and a hundred other things that made it state of the art for its day.

While the Dungeon may have been all of that and a bag of chips in its day, Stuart remembers visiting his Uncle Dan in the summers when he was younger and always finding him in the bunker with a couple of his senior citizen buddies playing cards, drinking beer, and listening to hippie rock on the ancient sound system down there. They would let him sit on the cot by the door and read twenty-year-old comic books from the stack next to it as they played gin, poker, or crazy eights late into the night. The Dungeon was like a big studio apartment with a bathroom in the corner that was separated by a shower curtain. The décor was a painted concrete floor, enough cots scattered around the room to sleep ten easily, and tin siding covered the walls and ceiling. Besides the card table near the far end of the room by the kitchen, rows of shelving holding boxes and freeze dried food were all the furnishings in the place. Stuart liked thumbing through the old comic books from the stack that was as tall as him, but mostly he enjoyed just listening to his Uncle Dan and friends talk about their yesteryears while they listened to Dr. Hook, Foghat, and Doobie Brothers albums. The smell of the Pall Malls smoke wafting out the open doors up into the night, and the sounds of Budweiser cans being cracked open over the soft laughter of old geezers telling stories about their youth always lightened Stuart's heart and made him feel special that they let him be a part of it.

When Stuart's family moved to Spearfish after his Uncle Dan died, Stuart would come down into the Dungeon with his friends sometimes to play or hideout from his dad when he knew he had a butt kicking coming to him, but it wasn't the same without his Uncle Dan there. As Stuart got older though, he seemed to need more alone time; and the Dungeon provided that. He needed so much alone time that by his senior year in high school, he pretty much lived in the Dungeon. He left for work, school, and sometimes to eat dinner with his parents, but otherwise he was in the Dungeon on his computer that was stacked on his Uncle Dan's old card table. By his senior year, he didn't have any friends and didn't want any. He was living for nothing else but to bide his time to be old enough and save enough money to leave. Leave his family; his house; his town. It didn't really matter where, but somewhere away from here. San Diego or San Francisco would be ideal, but maybe someplace like Daytona would fit Stuart just fine.

Stuart had spent the first several months of his senior year living on the web by putting his application into any college that he thought he might have a chance at when considering his mediocre grades and even lesser finances. Stuart had heard from the in-state school that he had been accepted, and received several other rejection letters, but he still had plenty of options open. Anyplace where he could have a fresh start and had at least a chance at being accepted for being different had to be better than here.

The night that Mary came by the Dungeon, Stuart had just sat down to the card table and was getting ready to turn his desktop computer on to check the status of several application responses that were past due. Stuart had worked at Slappy's Pizza since last summer and had put it down for his mailing address instead of his home so his father didn't intercept the correspondence. He had just finished a six-hour shift and was disappointed when his manager told him that he still hadn't received the two responses that he had been waiting for, so he hurried home to see if he could check their status online. His computer was just booting up when he heard the rapping on the Dungeon's heavy doors. It startled him because nobody ever came out here, not even his dad anymore. Just when he thought that he had been hearing things, the rapping came again. He sauntered over to the door staring at it like it was some strange object that he had never seen before. As he got to the door, the rapping started a third time, but this time it was a little more intense.

Stuart undid the lock and opened the door a crack to peer through. When he saw that it was Mary, he hesitantly opened the door about ten inches or so and said "What are you doing here?"

Mary had worked the same late shift at Slappy's with Stuart, but while he was still in his dirty kitchen uniform, she had changed into tight jeans and a black low cut tank top that was much more revealing than her uniform had been. She held up two envelopes with one hand and pushed the door the rest of the way open with the other.

"I brought you something," she said as she handed him the two envelopes and strolled into the Dungeon. Stuart inspected the letters and she casually walked around the open room peering into and around things as if she was intrigued by its secrets.

When Stuart realized that these were from the two colleges he had been waiting for he was instantly suspicious. He had asked his manager Mike if any mail had been delivered for him just before leaving his shift, as he hadn't seen them on the counter where the mail sits. It would be just like Mary to have some sinister plan to make his life more miserable than it already was.

"Where did you get these?" he asked trying to keep accusation out of his voice, but he was sure he wasn't successful. Neither one of the envelopes had much heft to them, so he thought that they probably didn't contain good news. He opened the one from San Diego state first and saw that the first lines said "We regret to inform you…" so he stopped reading and began working on the one from Daytona College.

Mary acted as if she was too engrossed in the boxes of miscellaneous stuff and other scatterings to hear his question. She kept sauntering around the room with her thumbs tucked in her back pockets and said nonchalantly to him "I haven't been down here since 7th grade. It really hasn't changed a bit has it?"

"Where did you get these?" Stuart repeated. He was still working on opening the second envelope and the tension in his voice was giving away his uneasiness about the situation.

Mary had completed a circle of the room and made her way back to Stuart. "Mike asked me to run them by to you. He said that he found them underneath something right after you left," she said as she watched him wrestle with the second envelope from a few feet in front of him.

Stuart finally got the second one open and began rifling through the three pages. He had to get to the fourth line of the letter before he realized that this was the one. He was accepted to Daytona College! Stuart subconsciously did a fist pump out of pure glee before he remembered that his nemesis Mary Castlebrock was standing in front of him.

"Good news?" she asked as she rose up on her tip toes and tried to peer over the edge of the paper. She was biting the corner of her bottom lip slightly, but grinning with the rest of her face. As she stood up and leaned forward she knew that her low-cut tank top would be revealing more than most teenage boys could resist looking at, but Stuart's gaze didn't leave the acceptance letter as he sped read the last two pages.

"Good news?" she repeated with a little bit of frustration as she settled back on her heals and gave up the enticement.

"Huh?" Stuart asked as he looked up from the letter. "Oh, I've been accepted to Daytona College in Florida!" he tried to say indifferently, but his pride beamed through.

"Wow," she said feigning some amazement. "I'm going to Black Hills State in the fall. Why are you going so far away?" she asked.

If felt weird having a conversation with Mary. Mary usually was talking at him, or about him; but never to him. Stuart was sure that something wasn't right. "Just to get a fresh start I guess," he responded before changing his gaze back to the acceptance letter.

"A fresh start?" Mary asked. Her question just hung in the air for a while. Mary didn't follow up or even move. Eventually, the awkwardness was enough for Stuart that he felt that he had to respond. He folded the acceptance letter up, stuffed it in his back pocket, and walked over to the overfull trash can to throw the envelopes and rejection letter from Sand Diego State away.

"Yeah, you know," Stuart said as he turned back to face her. "A fresh start," he repeated.

Mary had somehow walked towards him while he had been turned and she was now a little too close. She was in his personal space looking up at him with flirty eyes that made Stuart uncomfortable as she said "I think everyone could use a fresh start at some point."

Mary took another short step closer to him and her perfume filled Stuart's nostrils as she continued to make eye contact with Stuart. Stuart involuntarily took a short step backward, but bumped into the trash can and couldn't go any further. He felt his stomach rise in his throat and he wanted nothing more than to find a hiding spot somewhere within the Dungeon to escape this moment.

Mary reached out and looped her two index fingers through Stuarts side belt loops on his work slacks and pulled him into her so that their abdomens were just touching and she had to look up into his eyes. "What do you think Stuart?" Mary asked in a slow soft voice. "Should we give each other a fresh start?"

Stuart's heart was pounding so hard he thought that his ears were going to explode. His mind was racing and he didn't know how to react. After what seemed like too long, he reached down and pulled her hands from his belt loops and tried to step away. Because he was backed up to the trash can, his right heel caught the bottom of the can and both him and the can fell to the concrete floor with a crash. Both of Stuarts legs were left draped up over the can and the refuse spilled onto the floor and his torso.

Mary cupped her hands to her mouth as she began laughing almost hysterically. Stuart laid there for a moment in a mix of papers and month old food remnants from the trash can, and just stared up at Mary as his mind raced to try and figure out what was happening and what to do next.

Mary's longtime boyfriend Brock Donovan and her older brother Keith bounded into the room as Mary began to try and control her laughter. Brock was full blood redneck with an athletic build that seemed to follow Mary at ten paces wherever she went. Mary's brother Keith was a hulk of a young man that was always with Brock when he wasn't on the football field.

"Turning out better than you thought, huh?" Brock asked Mary as he sidled over to her after taking the scene in.

"The best," she said as finally got her laughter under control. "Although I hadn't even told him the best part yet," she said as Brock slid in behind her and rested his chin on her shoulder. Keith just stood behind Brock and his girlfriend looking around the room with a blank look on his face as if he couldn't comprehend what was happening.

With some clumsy awkwardness, Stuart made it to his feet and brushed some of the garbage that had stuck to him off his clothes. "Aren't you even going to ask?" Mary inquired with a deceptive innocence in her voice.

"Ask what?" Stuart said as his focus turned back to Mary and Brock.

"What the best part is," she said as Brock began to chuckle with his head still bent over resting on Mary's shoulder.

After a very pregnant pause, Stuart decided that he wasn't ever going to get them out of here without hearing their punch line. "What's the best part Mary?" he asked with zero anticipation.

"Daytona College," she said and let it hang in the air. She stepped forward from Brock and closer to Stuart as her eyes began to show pure hatred and her facial muscles constricted as she explained what she thought was the best part.

"What?" Stuart asked not understanding what she was implying.

"How could you really think that a nationally renowned college would have any interest in letting you on their campus?" Mary continued with a little too much emotion and fervor in her voice. "A loser like you hanging out on Daytona Beach?" she asked rhetorically. She took another small step forward to where she was awkwardly close to him again, but now hatred and evil was spewing from her gaze and directed solely at Stuart.

Stuart still wasn't understanding what she was getting at. He reached for the acceptance letter in his back pocket and brought it out to inspect it as she continued to rant at him. She snatched it from his grasp and flipped to the last page.

"I wrote this letter you loser!" she yelled as spittle came off her lips. She placed her index finger on a line in the last paragraph and shoved the letter into his face.

Stuart took the letter back and read the last paragraph as Mary began ranting about how Stuart was a waste of a human being and how she had written the letter after she'd intercepted the real letters at work a week ago. Stuart read through the last paragraph two more times because he was having a difficult time realizing that the acceptance letter wasn't real, and that he hadn't realized the letter was a fake when he'd read it through the first time. The paragraph read:

> WE LOOK FORWARD TO MEETING YOU STUART AND SHOWING YOU THE MANY ADVANTAGES THAT DAYTONA COLLEGE HAS TO OFFER. PLEASE REALIZE THAT YOU ARE THE WORLD'S BIGGEST LOSER AND WILL NEVER GET AN OPPORTUNITY TO SET FOOT ON OUR CAMPUS. IF YOU HAVEN'T REALIZED IT YET, THIS LETTER IS A HOAX TO SHOW YOU THAT HOPE IS NOT A GOOD THING FOR A PERSON LIKE YOU. ALL HOPE WILL DO FOR YOU IS DISAPPOINT YOU. YOU WILL BE IN THIS TOWN FOR AS LONG AS YOU LIVE, LIVING UP TO YOUR LEGEND AS THE WORLD'S BIGGEST LOSER.

Mary grabbed Stuart's wrist and made him lower the letter from his face and she stepped in even a little closer. As she spoke, her index finger rose to Stuart's chest and began poking him for emphasis at what she felt were the most important syllables.

"You are a loser Stuart Rappaport, and you don't de-serve a fresh start," and with those words, Mary took a step back and turned towards the Dungeon's door.

Brock Donovan's larger frame filled Stuarts view just as Mary's left it. He stood as close to Stuart as Mary had been, but he spoke with a softer voice so that there was little chance that Mary could hear him from across the room. "I don't know what you did to her to make her that mad; but you are just one big loser," Brock told Stuart just before he doubled Stuart up with a left to his midsection. He then dropped him to the hard floor with an even harder right upper cut to the solar plexus. When he fell to the ground, his right leg extended and knocked out one of the legs to the card table that caused his computer monitor, keyboard, and other paraphernalia to spill to the floor with thuds and cracks that didn't sound as if much could have survived it.

Stuart tried to gasp for air while on all fours, but couldn't make his diaphragm work. He'd had the wind knocked out of him before, so while it was very uncomfortable, he knew what to expect. He looked up to the door and saw only Mary standing there in the doorway. He could feel tears welling up in his eyes, but he could still make out the hatred in her eyes very clearly.

When Mary was sure that Stuart was watching her, she thought of her final words to leave him with and said "Why don't you stay in here and think about that for a while … faggot!"

Mary slipped through the open crack of the doorway and it shut behind her almost immediately. There was a metallic click and then bang from outside the doors that Stuart instinctively knew was something meant to lock him in the Dungeon. With his chest throbbing, his abdomen aching, and his mind reeling; Stuart turned over on the cold floor and sobbed. He sobbed until he fell asleep.

Stuart finished his bike ride back to the Dungeon with little effort, but in a somber mood after reliving the night that Mary had visited him. He didn't know why he deserved that kind of abuse when all he wanted to ever do was get away from this place and those kinds of people in the first place. Stuart knew that he didn't fit in, and he wanted to not be in this town any less than they wanted him out of it.

Stuart left the ammo and some of the other supplies by the bike. He unloaded the bags of food from the bike and took them down the alley way stairs to what remained of the Dungeon doors. He lit his homemade torches on the way in that illuminated the Dungeon.

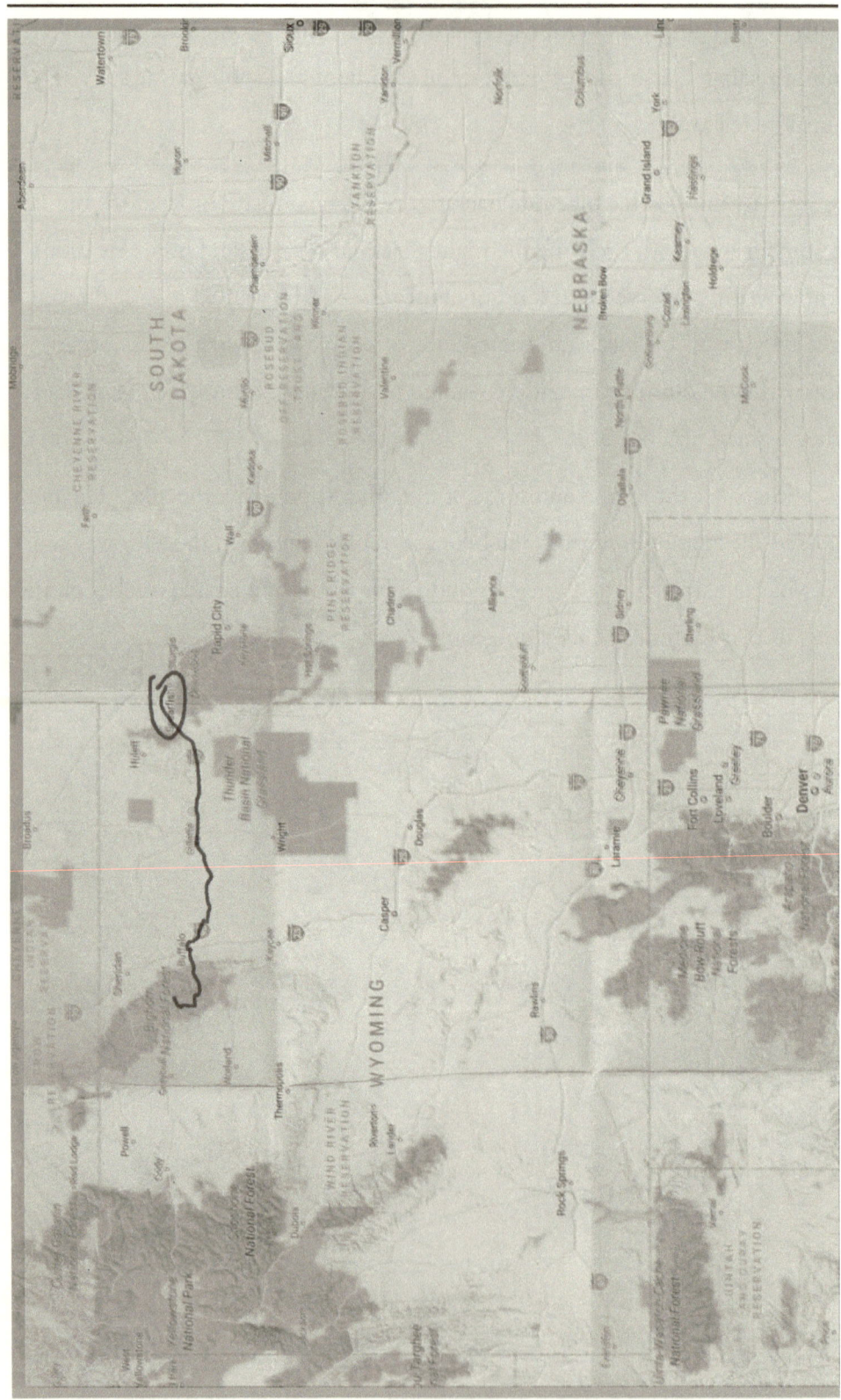

CHAPTER 12

MACKENZIE WAS A few hundred feet in front of her dad coasting down a big hill into the town of Spearfish when she heard it. She leaned over further and strained with her ears to see if she could hear it again, but after another block of coasting, she convinced herself that she was hearing things.

Then she heard it again. She grabbed both hand brakes and skidded to a stop in the middle of the street. She straddled the bike and was fully concentrating again on trying to hear the sound. All she could hear was the wind blowing slightly and the sound of her heart beating.

A few seconds later, Patrick caught up and stopped next to her in the street. He was slightly amused and puzzled at what she was doing. She was standing straddling the bike with her head cocked to one side, and a look of pure concentration on her face.

"What in the world are..." Patrick managed to get out with a little chuckle in his voice before Mackenzie shushed him with a look that meant she was serious.

"Didn't you hear that?" She asked with a monotone whisper.

"Hear what?" Patrick responded in a similar whisper.

They sat there for another ten seconds or so before Mackenzie relaxed a little and stood straight up. "I thought that I heard a..." she started to say and then stopped suddenly. "There! You heard that, right?" She asked her dad now with excitement in her voice as if she had been doubting herself again.

"Sorry. I didn't hear anything," Patrick replied.

"I think that it's coming from up on that hill" Mackenzie said as she stared up a large hill with a few rows of houses built into the side of it. She didn't wait for her dad to ask any more questions or caution her about what she was doing, she just turned her bike in the direction of a side street that looked like it might head to the hill and started pedaling.

Patrick didn't know what she was up to, but didn't think that there was much harm in letting whatever she was up to play out. They had enough supplies and were only turning down into the town from the interstate to find some place to stay for the night. He started after her, but he didn't feel like matching the somewhat frantic pace she had started with, so she began to pull away from him rather quickly as they made their climb up the hillside.

Makenzie was a couple of blocks ahead of Patrick when he seen her turn right on another side street, then he heard what had gotten her all excited. The unmistakable sound of a low power rifle being fired. As soon as he recognized it, his heart jumped into his chest and he could feel it beating in his temples. A wave of feelings and thoughts washed over him immediately. Someone else was alive! He had known that they weren't the only two left on Earth, but some nights he was beginning to doubt himself. Then his thoughts turned to why someone would be shooting, and what could they be shooting at? Then all he could think of was Mackenzie. He could no longer see her, and his dad mode kicked in. He no longer noticed his burning chest and beating heart; he stood up on the pedals, shifted down two gears, and pumped his legs as hard as they could go. His legs pumped harder than even he thought he could go.

He wasn't sure which way she had went now after he had made the turn where he thought she had been, and there was no sign of her. He didn't slow at all though, he just kept cruising. He heard another shot, this time much closer. He could tell that it was coming from a little higher on the hill and a few blocks down yet. He wanted to call out to Mackenzie so bad to see where she was, but as close as that shot was, whoever was shooting would surely hear him.

He didn't slow as he turned his bike up a side street going up the hill and started around the corner when he heard his daughter call out from behind him. "Dad!" she exclaimed in a hoarse voice that made him stop in his tracks.

He skidded to a stop and let his bike slam to the ground as he turned to look for her. She was hunkered down to the ground behind a hedge of some kind looking up the street with binoculars in her hand. Her bike was neatly parked and leaning up against the hedge.

Patrick ran bent over back to her position and slid down next to her behind the hedge. He was breathing so hard that he couldn't speak.

"What are you doing?" Mackenzie asked flabbergasted. "Didn't you hear those gun shots?"

It took a few seconds and several labored breaths before Patrick could start to answer. "Me?" He finally worked out at the end of one breath. "What... do... you... think.... you're doing.... sprinting away" he got the words out with a weird rhythm while he was still trying to catch his breath.

When Mackenzie realized that he was chastising her for taking off, she shook her head and got back into position at the end of the hedge. She looked back through the binoculars just as another shot rang out.

Patrick quit trying to impart his wisdom on her when he heard the shot and instead fully concentrated on his breathing and listening.

"I think that it's just another block up there, but I can't see anything" Mackenzie says without looking at her father. "Who could it be Dad?" She asks.

With his breathing a little more under control, he answers with "I have no idea Darlin'" just as another shot rings out. "I don't think that they are shooting at someone though," Patrick finishes after a couple of seconds.

"What do you mean?" Mackenzie asks, this time lowering the binoculars and turning to look at her dad.

"Just the timing of the shots," he responded still trying to put all his thoughts together and finish catching his breath. "They are far enough apart... and not frantic," he continued. "And with as many of them as they are," he said convincing himself that he was right, "... someone's just target practicing." Patrick had done enough plinking in his younger days that he was sure that was exactly what was going on.

"Who could it be Dad?" Mackenzie asked with the excitement in her voice almost uncontrollable.

Patrick didn't answer her directly, but instead began rifling through her bags tied to her bike leaning next to the hedge. He retrieved the .22 rifle from the center of the pack, loaded a shell into the chamber, put the safety on, and handed it to Mak. "Aim small..." he said waiting for the response.

"Miss small," she retorted almost automatically.

"Stay on this side of the street, and stay back at least 50 feet," he told her matter-of-factly. "Be quiet and keep your eyes peeled," he said with his last instructions as she nodded her head. He bent forward and kissed her hair on the top of her head.

Patrick crawled out into the street to where his bike had toppled and began going through his bags as well. He had always been careful about making sure he could get to his AR rifle easily just in case something happened, but he had been getting lazy with the hunting rifle for the last several days. He finally freed it from the pack, jacked one in the chamber, flipped up the scope covers, and checked the safety. He dug deeper in his pack to find some extra shells.

Mackenzie looked down at her hands as they trembled holding the stainless-steel rifle. She had gotten tougher since she left for the trip with her dad, but she still didn't like the idea of having to aim the rifle at someone. Her dad must have found whatever he was looking for at his bike, because he was scurrying to the other side of the street just as another shot was heard. This time, she heard some glass break almost immediately after the report of the shot. Mackenzie picked up the binoculars again and scanned ahead up the street where she thought the gun shots were coming from.

Mackenzie lowered the binoculars and placed their string around her neck as she watched her dad making his way along carefully on the other side of the street. He was using cars and hedges as cover as he slinked along. She wished that he hadn't told her to stay back fifty feet. She really didn't have any idea how far that was, so now she was worried whether she was too far away or if she should wait a little longer. When Patrick escaped her point of view as he rounded a small blue pickup, she decided she needed to move. She stayed low and tried to creep along as she had seen her dad do, but she felt kind of stupid doing it. She made it to the next driveway that had a large cream colored van parked at the end of it, and peered around the back end of it just in time to see her dad go around a hedge and out of sight again.

The next driveway on her side of the street was empty, so she sneaked quickly past it and continued to the next one where a white pickup was parked in the street at the curb. When she reached it, she seen her dad on the other side of the street frantically holding his palm up and waving for her to stop. He motioned for her to get low just as another shot rang out. This time it was so close that Mackenzie heard herself squeal just a little bit. Her free hand instinctively went to her open mouth and she held her breath. The sound she made wasn't loud, but it sure seemed out of place in this silent wonderland.

She continued to hold her breath and remain absolutely still for what seemed like forever. Her lungs were burning and her legs were aching when she heard another shot. Satisfied and relieved that she hadn't been found out, she let her breath out quietly and carefully slid underneath the pickup truck parked at the curb. She army crawled up to the front wheel well and positioned herself to be able to look around with the binoculars. From where she was, she couldn't see her dad, but when she last seen him he had been directly across the street from her. She also couldn't see the shooter, but from the gun's report and other sounds of movement she could tell that he was in the yard just past the front of the truck she was under. She slowly crept up to the very front edge of the bumper so that she could see around the tire, and then she saw him.

The shooter was a high school kid with a tall and lanky build, and he had dirty shoulder length dark hair that was unkempt. He was half singing, half humming a tune as he slowly waltzed around while reloading his rifle. Once reloaded, he leaned the rifle on a large plastic garbage can and took aim at something further down the street. He loaded a shell in the breach and eventually shot. Makenzie heard glass break again right after the shot. The shooter left his rifle lie on the lid of the garbage can as he lifted both arms in the air as a sign of victory and did a short dance that reminded Makenzie of the Rocky movie when he made it to the top of the steps in Philadelphia.

When the kid's back was turned half-way in his victory dance, another shot from a much larger caliber rifle rang out from across the street. It was followed closely with Patrick's booming voice telling the kid to "Hold it right there. Don't move."

Mackenzie got her rifle ready as well and took the safety off. She couldn't quite make herself train it on the shooter just yet, but she felt that she could get ready quick if she needed to.

The shooter started to turn around slowly and Patrick yelled "Whooa. I thought that I said don't move." The kid complied and remained standing in his Rocky stance with his back to the street, Patrick, and his rifle.

"What are you shooting at kid?" Patrick yelled across the street. The kid didn't respond right away, so Patrick yelled again. "Listen, there's not that many of us left. I'd hate to have to shoot you over something stupid. Now what were you shooting at?"

"Windows," the kid said back, though not very loud.

"What?" Patrick asked.

"Windows. I was shooting out windows of the houses down the street," the shooter yelled back louder this time.

"What's your name?" Patrick yelled.

"Stuart. Stuart Rappaport" the kid yelled back.

"How many are with you?" Patrick asked hopefully.

"Just me. It's just me," Stuart yelled back with a definite sullenness in his tone.

After what felt like a long pause, Patrick told Stuart what he was planning to do. "Okay Stuart," Patrick started. "I'm going to slowly walk across the street and pick your rifle up from that dumpster." With that, Patrick started slowly walking across the street with his rifle pointed in the general direction of Stuart. "Once I have both yours and my firearms, I'll put them both down and we can talk," he stated as he continued walking.

Stuart didn't immediately reply. Patrick stopped walking after what seemed like too long of silence from Stuart. "Are you okay with that Stuart?" he yelled. Now that he was half-way across the street, he didn't have to yell near as loud to make sure that he was heard by both Stuart and his daughter.

Stuart didn't respond. "Stuart, I need to know that you're okay with that plan or we need to come up with another one to get out of this awkward situation." Patrick waited a few beats, but Stuart still didn't respond. "Do you have a better idea Stuart? It just needs to be one where neither you or I get shot. Especially me."

"Okay," Stuart finally responded.

"Okay, here I come then," Patrick said and started slowly walking across the street. He reached the dumpster with the rifle and picked it up. He opened the bolt and leaned both it and his own against a large pine tree a few feet behind him, but closer to him that to Stuart.

"Okay Stuart, we're both unarmed. You can turn around and we can properly introduce ourselves," Patrick told Stuart.

Stuart finally dropped his arms and slowly turned towards Patrick. Patrick's first thought was just how disgustingly dirty the kid was. He would have guessed that the kid was of dark complexion when looking at him from across the street, but up close he could tell that he was Caucasian; he was just filthy. His hair looked like it was some kind of helmet from the amount of gunk in it. His skin had at least several layers of grime covering it, and his clothes surely hadn't been changed since the cloud.

Patrick stuck his arm out with an open hand to Stuart. Stuart hesitantly reached out and shook the outstretched hand. "My name is Patrick Kincaid. I am very glad to meet you Stuart," Patrick said. "I was beginning to think that there was no one else left. Have you found anyone else?"

"No," Stuart answered in a meek voice. "Just me."

"How did you survive it?" Patrick asked.

"I'm not sure," Stuart said as if he hadn't really thought about it yet. "The Dungeon I guess."

"The Dungeon?" Patrick asked for clarification.

"Yeah, come on; I'll show you," Stuart said and began to turn back towards the bi-level home they were standing in front of.

"Uhhhh, not just yet. Let's hang out and talk some more for a minute," Patrick said sounding somewhat unsure of himself.

Stuart looked back at Patrick over his shoulder and said "What are you hiding man?"

"What do you mean?" Patrick asked.

"I mean what are you hiding?" Stuart asked this time with a confidence that Patrick knew he couldn't bluff his way out of.

After another long pause, Patrick spoke in a loud voice "Come on out Mak."

"What? You mean there are two of you?" Stuart said with an excited and higher pitched voice. Patrick could feel the unease coming from Stuart. He looked like he was going to flee, or do something stupid.

Makenzie flipped the safety back on her rifle and army crawled out from under the front bumper of the truck she had been lying under just twenty feet away. Patrick waved for her to approach them and then introduced them to each other, "Stuart, this is my daughter Mackenzie Kincaid. Makenzie this is Stuart Rappaport." They both shook hands and Patrick could tell that Stuart's unease was settled.

"Nice to meet you Stuart," Makenzie said as they finished shaking hands. She took half of a step back before leaning in and involuntarily wrapped her arms around him in a hug. Patrick could see from his vantage point that she was grinning from ear to ear.

Stuart acted like he didn't know what to do with the hug, but he put one arm around her and looked at Patrick with an expression that screamed for help.

"Okay Mak, turn him loose. He was just fixing on showing us a place that he calls the Dungeon," Patrick said as he tapped her on the shoulder.

Makenzie did let him go, but held him at arm's length for just a moment longer as she looked up into his eyes and said "It IS really nice to meet you Stuart."

Stuart awkwardly turned and gestured for them to follow him into the back yard. Patrick picked up his rifle and they followed him a few paces behind. After taking a step or two, Mackenzie gave a little hop and kicked her heels together before putting one arm around her dad's waist unable to temper her excitement that someone else was alive. They walked across the sloping yard and then down a set of steps to a gate at the alley. Once through the gate, they turned and were looking down into the stairs of the Dungeon.

Stuart took his lighter from his pocket and easily lit one of the homemade torches that he had left at the top of the stairs. He handed the lit torch to Patrick and grabbed another one from the pile for himself and lit it from Patrick's. Stuart could see Patrick staring at and contemplating the design of homemade torches made from PVC pipe, a couple of fittings, and cloth wrapped around the tip.

"Did you make these?" Patrick asked Stuart.

"Yeah; the pipe has white gas and petroleum jelly in it with a strip of the cloth for a wick. They work really good," Stuart finished sheepishly.

"That's a really great design. Did you come up with it?" Patrick asked still closely inspecting the pipe.

"Yeah, I don't like the dark," Stuart said with a little more confidence. "Welcome to the Dungeon" Stuart told them doing an Axel Rose impression from another Guns n' Roses song and stretching his arm out like Vanna White. He walked down the stairs and stepped around and over the heavy entry doors that were laying awkwardly on the last few steps into the Dungeon. He looked back and seen that the other two were hesitant to follow him, and were standing partially down the steps. He decided that telling them not to worry and to follow him blindly into the dark scary place probably wouldn't work since they had just met. He decided to just go in and straighten things up while they mustered up the courage.

Patrick handed the torch to Mackenzie and unshouldered the sling of his rifle. He left the safety on it and didn't point it at anything, he just kept it at the ready. Patrick slowly began the rest of the decent of the stairs and motioned Mackenzie to follow him. They could see light from Stuart's torch coming out from the entry way, and they could hear him moving around and busying himself.

"Ughhhh. What is that smell?" Mackenzie whispered to her dad when they reached the doors lying on the stairs. There was a distinct stench wafting up the stairway that made them both pause.

"I'm not sure," Patrick replied quietly. "From the looks of this guy, it may just be teenage boy stench."

Patrick awkwardly stepped on and around the doors, and then held a hand out to Mackenzie to help her balance. As she stepped out across the doors and down the stairs the torch light caught shiny parts of the door where you could tell that something had mangled the hinges and had been seriously scratching at the center latch between the doors. She stooped a little and held the torch closer to the doors while she inspected them closer for just a second.

As Patrick and Mackenzie stepped into the entryway of the Dungeon, they became more at ease; but the stench became stronger and almost unbearable. Stuart had placed his torch in a makeshift holder on one wall and was in the opposite corner of the one large room bent over picking up things from the floor.

It was apparent that Patrick's guess about the stench was correct as their eyes scanned the room. You could tell that the room had been sparsely furnished before the cloud, but now had garbage and refuse from canned meals, cans of pop, milk jugs, potato chips, and numerous other wrappers from consumables heaped in piles around the room.

They stood in the doorway for a few seconds before Stuart realized that they were inside. He quit what he was doing and walked across the room towards them.

"What is this place?" Mackenzie asked clearly dumbfounded.

"It's a bomb shelter isn't it?" Patrick asked Stuart.

"Yeah; my family calls it the Dungeon," Stuart told them as he reached out and grabbed the other torch from Mackenzie.

"Come in," Stuart said and gestured for them to sit in the folding chairs arranged next to the cot. He went over to the large post in the center of the room and hung the torch in the holder there.

Patrick and Mackenzie sidled across the room clearly uncomfortable, and each sat in one of the chairs. Mackenzie tried breathing through her mouth to try and tolerate the stench. Stuart joined them and flopped down on the army style cot that had a few blankets on it that looked like they were just as dirty as his clothes.

"So, you survived the cloud by staying in this place?" Patrick asked.

"The cloud? What cloud?" Stuart asked perplexed.

"Maybe you should tell us your story first and we can try to fill in the blanks," Patrick suggested.

Stuart stood up and grabbed three cans of pop and handed two of them to Patrick and Mackenzie before sitting back down and starting his story. He lounged on the cot and took the next several minutes to tell them about the night Mary had come to the Dungeon, but he left out some of the more personal parts of the story.

"So, they locked you in here?" Makenzie asked still trying to only breathe through her mouth, so that made her sound like she had a cold.

"Yeah. I didn't know what they had done at the time, but they had hung a crowbar through the handles on the outside of the doors. I laid on the floor for a couple of hours before getting up and trying the door. When I realized that they'd locked me in here, it was pretty late so I decided that I would just sleep on the cot wait until the morning when I could text my dad to come help." Stuart paused for several seconds reflecting about his decision and steeling his nerves so that he wouldn't cry in front of the two-new people.

"When I woke up the next morning, I texted my dad; but he wouldn't answer. I sent texts and tried to call my mom, my aunt, people from school, anyone I could think of really; but none of them would respond. I thought that my phone was screwed up somehow," he reached into his pocket and pulled out an older flip phone to show them. "So, when I got tired of banging and beating on the doors, I tried to fix the computer over there to see if I could e-mail someone to come get me. The monitor was trashed from it falling and I started to panic because I wasn't sure what I was going to do. Not only did I miss school, but I was going to miss my shift at work too; and I couldn't deal with getting canned right before college."

Stuart shifted on the cot and became noticeably uncomfortable. They sat that way for several seconds with Stuart trying to get the courage to continue with the story. When the tears started flowing down his cheeks, Patrick reached out and grabbed Stuart's knee. Patrick looked him in the eye and said "It's okay son. We have some of these same stories that we'll share when you're done."

Stuart took a few moments to compose himself, then he continued. "Just when I thought it was bad, it got worse… Everything went dark."

Stuart hung his head for a few minutes, and just when Mackenzie thought that he wouldn't be able to continue, he suddenly stood up from the cot and wiped his eyes. The tears had streaked clean stripes through the grime on his face, but his rubbing them just smeared them all up again. It appeared that anger had replaced his sadness and he began to walk around the room with giant strides from one pile of garbage to another pile of refuse, stopping long enough to pick up or rearrange some of the contents. He began talking as he was walking to finish his story for them.

"I don't know if you realize how dark it can be in a bomb shelter with the doors locked and no electricity, but the word 'utter' comes to mind," Stuart said as he stood up from a pile in the corner and walked over to a shelving unit to put something round up on it. "After struggling to find the generator and fussing with it in the dark for what seemed like a day, I realized that there wasn't any chance of getting lights on in here. The light on my phone didn't even work. So, then I began to work on the doors. I don't really know how long it took me, but I guess that it took four days to pop the hinges enough on the right-hand door for it to fall partially down and let some light in. Once

I got some light in here, during the day at least, I was able to look through the shelves and find some food and get better tools to work on the other door with."

Stuart continued inspecting the piles and moving from one to the next, stopping every once in a while at a shelving unit to put something on it. His mood seemed to improve somewhat as he continued his story. "The crowbar in the door handles didn't let the right-hand door open even after it was off the hinges, so I had to pop the hinges off the other one as well. That took the better part of two days. As soon as the second door fell to the stairs, I sprinted outside so excited that I had finally escaped the Dungeon. I ran to our house to tell my folks that I was alright." He stopped for just a moment and stared at something on the shelf in front of him, lost as if he was somehow reliving the moment again. "For those days sitting here in the dark, I couldn't believe that my parents hadn't come out here to look for me. I made myself so angry about it. For all those days that I had gone over in my mind time and time again about how I would righteously tell them where I had been trapped; how I had escaped; and ask them why they didn't care enough to come find me. But when I finally escaped, I wasn't angry at all. I just wanted to see them, hug them, and tell them that I was all right." Stuart was moving again, but this time he wasn't taking big fast steps as he had before, he was more mulling around and shuffling his feet. "But then I found them and understood why they hadn't been looking for me. Both of them were lying in their bed. Their corpses already rotting."

Stuart paused again with his story, but this time the flood works had let loose. He tried to continue straitening up, but he couldn't help but wipe the tears from his eyes and cheeks every few seconds. Mackenzie couldn't stand it any longer. She sat her pop can down on the ground next to the chair she had been sitting on and went over and put her arms around Stuart. Stuart seemed appalled at first of the human contact and didn't know how to react, but Mackenzie just stood there. After a few moments, Stuart put his arms around her and let all of it out.

Patrick sat awkwardly and watched the two embrace and share their feelings of hopelessness from the last couple of weeks. With the way that Stuart reacted when Mackenzie hugged him, he thought that Stuart may run from the Dungeon never to return if Patrick stood up to hug him.

After what seemed like twenty minutes or more, Mackenzie and Stuart returned to their prior seats. The mood was still solemn, but this sharing of information felt like it needed to continue.

"I have a lot more questions for you Stuart, but what if we tell you our story of how we got here first?" Patrick asked what felt like a rhetorical question. Stuart nodded as he looked sideways over to Mackenzie and asked if she wanted to start out.

Mackenzie did a good job of telling the story and highlighting a few of the details that she thought was important, with Patrick only chiming in a few times with things that she had forgotten or omitted. This was the first time that either of them told their story to someone else, and it was very interesting to Patrick to hear the story from Mackenzie's perspective. He remembered some things differently, and hadn't thought that some of the things that Mackenzie brought up were important at all; but for the most part he just listened to Mackenzie's portrayal of the events. He was most amazed at how much of the silly language they'd made up while boulder hopping that night had made an impact on her. She couldn't help but smile and beam with pride while she told that part of the story, even though it didn't seem like a major event to Patrick compared to all the other stuff they had been through.

Stuart asked a few questions about the cloud, and both Patrick and Mackenzie found it difficult to explain what they had saw. They both vividly remembered that opaque cloud rolling across the landscape, and the colors that had danced in it; and they found that they could use the words to describe it, but they couldn't convey the ominous feeling that they had just watching it from the mountain top. They could tell that Stuart wasn't completely satisfied with the depiction of the cloud, but Mackenzie continued anyways and went through almost comical detail of finding the body along the trail and then the body in the outhouse.

Stuart became visibly excited when they got to the part of the story with the EMP event. "I thought that it must have been EMP as well. Do you think that it was from a nuke?"

"I'm not sure," Patrick replied. "We haven't seen any fallout or evidence of radiation damage, but I guess that doesn't mean much."

"My uncle; you know, the one who built this place" Stuart said rather rapidly as he waved his arms around to make sure they knew he was talking about the Dungeon. "He used to tell me to be careful of the water if there was a nuclear attack. He said that the water would hold the radiation in it much stronger and longer than anything else. That's why I haven't drank any water or bathed since it happened. The Dungeon has a five-hundred-gallon recyclable daily water storage tank, besides the drinking water tank; but I haven't touched a drop of it. You can even use wood or whatever to burn and heat the water for a shower!"

Even though Stuart beamed with pride at his ability to withstand taking a shower for the last couple of weeks, Mackenzie was sitting on the edge of her seat. "What? You mean that we can take a hot shower in here?" Makenzie exclaimed?

"Sure," Stuart replied, "but you take the risk of getting radiation poisoning if you use water."

Mackenzie stood up with excitement "I've been taking frigid showers and baths in streams, creeks, and what's left of motel water tanks for over two weeks! If you have a warm shower, I'm in!" Mackenzie offered to trade her binoculars, her .22 rifle, and several other personal things that she had on her; but Stuart said that wasn't necessary.

Stuart gathered stuff to burn and started the fire under the boiler while Mackenzie walked back to get her bike and bags. It took a little while for Stuart to figure out how to run the shower system, but he finally got it going and Mackenzie wasted no time jumping in. Stuart returned to the cot where Patrick was sitting to finish hearing about the story.

"So, what happened to you guys after the EMP?" Stuart asked almost impatiently.

"Well, we made our way down the mountain on foot for a while and crashed at a cabin. Mackenzie had the idea that we coast down the mountain on a motorcycle that we found, and it worked pretty good. It was almost kind of fun riding the motorcycle down, but when we made it down to the town it was a different story. Nothing but death," Patrick paused with that last statement. He hadn't recounted the events to anyone since they happened, and without Mackenzie here with him, he wasn't having to guard his thoughts.

"I know man," Stuart said.

"Yeah, I bet you do kid," Patrick solemnly replied. He pushed the ugly memories to the back of his mind and continued with the story to Stuart. "In the town there we got some bikes and other equipment and headed east. We've mainly been staying to the interstate and stopping in towns along the way for supplies and to rest sometimes."

"Where are you going?" Stuart asked.

"Nebraska," Patrick said with finality. "A little town called Columbus, Nebraska. That's where our family is."

"What if it's like this when you get there?" Stuart asked.

It took Patrick a moment to respond as he was imagining what it would be like to find his wife and boy lying in their beds as lifeless as Stuart had found his parents. "It won't be," Patrick said matter-of-factly.

"Sorry man, not that I've ever been good at it; but I ran out of wishful thinking a while ago," Stuart said with little feeling.

Instead of debating the merits of their quest and how Patrick 'knew' that this family was okay, he thought for a moment and changed the subject as he heard Mackenzie banging around in the small bathroom. "So, do you know where we can get you a different bike?"

"What are you talking about?" Stuart asked.

"The bike that you had up at the top of the stairs is pretty cool, but it only has one gear and won't go near as fast. There are some times that we make up time by cutting the right-of-way fence on the interstate and going cross-country, but for the most part we try to make time on the paved interstate" Patrick explained.

"I still don't get it," Stuart responded.

"You'll be wore out riding that thing and you won't be able to keep up. It's a dirt bike," Patrick said beginning to wonder if he had misjudged Stuart's intelligence.

"Oh," Stuart said between chuckles.

Mackenzie came out of the bathroom running a comb through her wet hair. She didn't appear to be wearing anything except a long t-shirt. She asked what was so funny as she walked back over and sat in the chair where she had been sitting before.

"Nothing really," Stuart responded. "It's just that your dad thinks that I'm going to go with you guys on your bike ride east."

"Why wouldn't you?" Mackenzie asked continuing to comb her hair.

"Why would I leave the Dungeon?" Stuart asked.

"What is there for you here?" Mackenzie asked.

"Shelter. Food. Water," Stuart replied. And after a second he added, "Even warm showers."

Mackenzie giggled at that and told him that she wasn't sure how to shut off the water so it was still on. Patrick asked if he could use it to since it was still running. Stuart had no problem with it, so he climbed the stairs back out of the Dungeon to get his bike and the bags from it.

Mackenzie and Stuart talked and chuckled for some time while Patrick was in the shower. When Patrick came out clean and in fresh clothes he found Stuart and Mackenzie sitting next to each other on the cot with their backs to the wall looking through comic books and talking in low voices.

"You know Stuart," Patrick suggested, "you really should jump in the shower while it's hot."

"Yeah, you really should," Mackenzie said plugging her nose as she said it. "I think that I'd rather the radiation in the water get all of us instead of your smell slowly killing me and my dad."

"Okay, okay," he said as he got up from the cot and headed to the bathroom.

"If you don't mind, Mak and I will set our tents up on your lawn up above while you're in there," Patrick said.

"Yeah, no problem. Just don't put them on my mom's peonies, those are her pride and joy" Stuart replied without really thinking about what he was saying.

While Patrick and Mackenzie were helping each other setup their tents underneath a couple of pine trees in the corner of the back yard of Stuart's house, Patrick thought that he would press Mackenzie a little about Stuart.

"So, you two seem to be really hitting it off," Patrick said with his voice reflecting more of a question than a statement.

"Yeah, he's pretty cool," Mackenzie responded rather nonchalantly.

"Whew; that's a relief," Patrick said in an acting voice as he pushed the last stake for Mackenzie's tent into the dirt.

"What do you mean?" Mackenzie asked with a smile in her voice.

"Well, the way you two were acting I thought that you were thinking he was cute too and not just cool," Patrick cajoled her.

"Yeah, I don't think so Dad. You are so clueless…" she said in a playful way.

"Hey, listen Darlin'; I don't mind if you think some kid is cute. It's just that he's a little bit old for" he started but Mackenzie stopped him short.

"He's gay Dad!" Mackenzie said with a tone that a parent sometimes talks to a preschooler when they just aren't getting a concept.

"What!?" Patrick replied as he pushed the ridge pole for his tent through the loops to his daughter as they had numerous times over the past couple of weeks.

"Yeah, Dad" Mackenzie continued not believing that her dad was that far out of touch. "He is totally gay. How could you not tell?"

"I guess I don't know. So, that's why he is a loner you think?" Patrick asked as they bent the last tent pole into position and began stretching it tight for the stakes.

"I imagine. Kids in these small towns are probably even worse that the ones in Columbus when it comes to giving kids a hard time that are different," Mackenzie said as they finished installing the stakes.

As they threw their bags into the tents and started back towards the Dungeon, Mackenzie told her dad "Now don't go acting all weird around him now that you know he's gay."

"What do you mean?" Patrick asked his daughter as he put one arm around her.

"Just don't be weird," Mackenzie said again chuckling.

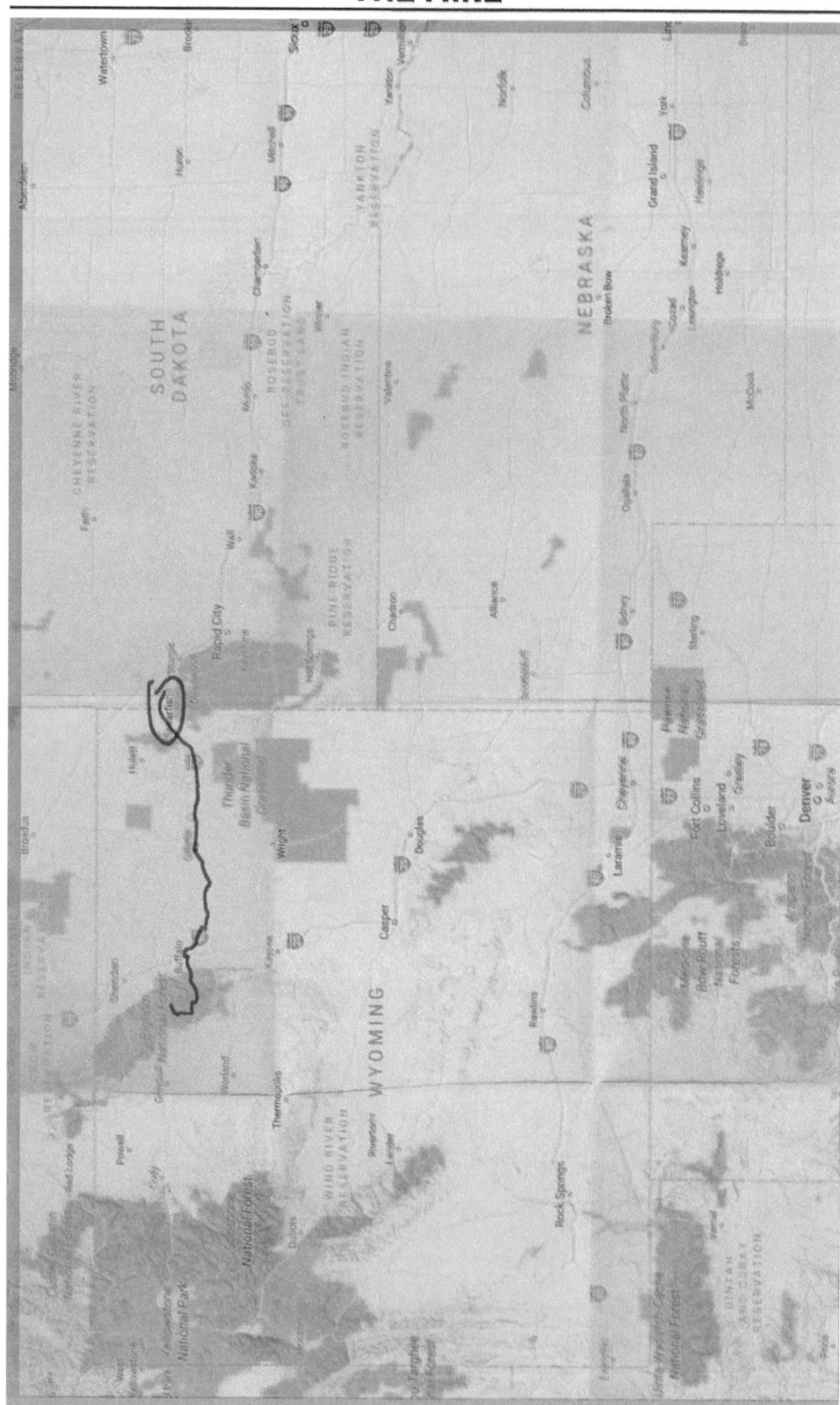

CHAPTER 13

THE THREE SURVIVOR'S spent the next few hours visiting and talking about Spearfish, the rest of the Kincaid family, music, old comic books, and several other topics that had nothing to do with the cloud, EMP, or dead bodies. They each had a can of raviolis and genuinely enjoyed each other's company. Patrick couldn't help but act somewhat weird around Stuart, but Mackenzie gave enough sideways glances to her dad that Stuart didn't seem to be uncomfortable. Even though Stuart tried to talk them into staying in the Dungeon for the night on some of the unused cots that were piled high with supplies and storage, Patrick insisted that they stay in the tents up in the backyard.

Stuart rolled out of bed sometime in mid-morning and felt better than he had in months. He used the restroom and somewhat combed his now clean hair before bounding up the stairs to visit with his new-found friends. Mackenzie was laying on her back reading a book with her head poking out of her unzipped tent, and Patrick was sitting in a folding chair reading a paperback where his tent had been the night before. Patrick was wearing a half cowboy / half safari hat that Stuart thought made him look weird.

"Well, you do sure clean up nice," Mackenzie said as she rolled over onto her elbows as she heard him approach.

"Shut up," he told her while grinning.

Patrick put his book down in his lap and pointed over to one of the pine trees by Mackenzie's tent. "What do you think about that one?" he asked Stuart.

A black mountain bike with electric blue splotches here and there along the frame was leaning up against the tree. It was decked out with hard plastic bags near the hubs on each of the rear wheels. It had big knobby tires, several water bottles at different locations, and two sets of leather saddle bags draped across the main part of the frame. Stuart thought that it looked like something out of one of those Mad Max movies.

"It looks pretty tough," Stuart said walking over to it. "Are you trading up for it?" he asked.

"Nah," Patrick said as he got up and walked over to join Stuart next to the bike. "That one's yours!"

Stuart's great mood fell immediately like a ton of bricks. "Hey – I told you that I wasn't going with you Mr. Kincaid. I'm staying right here."

"I know that's what you said," Patrick said without letting any defense into his voice. "I also understand why you would want to stay here at the Dungeon. But I'm telling you that others survived. Mak and I know in our heart of hearts that the rest of our family is okay; but even if you can't believe that, then you must be able to reason that the cloud couldn't have made it around the world. So if we don't find anyone in Nebraska, we'll keep heading east. Somewhere in Missouri, Kentucky, Georgia, Florida, or somewhere out there is a large group of survivors."

Mackenzie had joined them at the tree and wrapped her arm around Stuart's waist. "It's no use Stuart," Mackenzie started. "He has so much practice getting me up and pedaling each morning that you don't stand a chance." Stuart couldn't help but smile a little bit at that.

"You can make your mind up later," Patrick said. "Why don't you take it for a test spin and check it out?"

Stuart showed some hesitancy before finally grabbing the bike and saying "Where did you get it?"

"There's a bike shop down on the main street with all kinds of cool things in there," Patrick said with a little bit of excitement in his voice.

"He's been gone since early this morning putting that thing together for you," Mackenzie added.

Stuart hopped on the bike and made a few big arcing circles in the alley around some of the waste laying on the ground. Then he started out slow down the alley, but by the time he made the next side street he was standing up and pumping it as fast as he could go.

"I think he likes it," Mackenzie told her dad. Patrick smiled. He had gotten the reaction that he had hoped for.

Patrick sauntered back to where his bike was parked and said "Let's follow him for a little ways. I'd like to get both of our bikes down to that shop and add some of the attachments and bling that they have there."

"Bling?" Mackenzie said somewhat snidely. "I think that you may be a little too old to use that word correctly Dad."

Patrick chuckled a little as they got on their bikes and turned down the alley in the direction Stuart had ridden. "You two sure seem like you are pretty close for just meeting yesterday," Patrick said as they rode side by side.

"What do you mean?" Mackenzie asked.

"Nothing really. It just surprises me that you just met that boy and you act like he's your best friend already. I was just wondering why," Patrick said as they rounded the corner to the street Stuart had turned down. There was a decline to the hill, so both riders padded their brakes some so they could still go slow enough to talk to each other.

"I don't know really," Mackenzie responded after thinking about it for a few seconds. "I guess that he reminds me of some of my friends back home. He's different."

Patrick pondered her response for a little bit and decided not to tell her what he was really thinking and instead allowed himself to coast a little in front of her so he could lead the way to the bike shop. He surmised from the little time that he spent with Stuart that he was indeed different. Different enough that he had been shunned from other kids his age. Mackenzie's other friends back home weren't like that at all in Patrick's opinion. They weren't necessarily different by nature, but instead they tried hard to be different. They did and wore shocking things to be different, regardless of moral fortitude or impacts of others. They wanted other people to notice how different they were. Patrick didn't feel that having that conversation now with his daughter would be productive when those 'friends' may never be seen again.

Stuart found them at the bike shop after a while. He told Patrick that he really did like the bike, and he asked if Patrick could adjust a few things on it while they were there. Stuart and Mackenzie sat outside on the curb enjoying the afternoon shade visiting and laughing at each other while Patrick spent several hours in the little back room shop adding things and changing things to each of their bikes. The shop had enough hand tools and things without motors that the engineer in Patrick had fun for the first time in a long while putting accessories on the bikes and making other adjustments. When he'd finished his tinkering, he walked outside to find the two kids still sitting on the curb visiting.

"So….," Patrick interrupted. "Did she talk you into it?"

"Talk me into what?" Stuart asked.

"Going with us," Patrick explained.

"Yeah," Stuart said with some resignation. Mackenzie shoved him a little with her elbow and giggled. "There's no reason why I can't come back if I want to." Patrick extended his hand to Stuart and Stuart stood up to shake it, but didn't take it right away.

"That's great news son. I think that is the right idea," Patrick said with some confusion as he let his hand drop to his side without Stuart shaking it. Stuart looked down at the ground and appeared to be mustering up the courage to say something.

"Mr. Kincaid…" Stuart started, but trailed off without raising his eyes from the ground.

"Go on Stuart," Patrick said. "Just go on and say what needs said." Patrick was bracing himself for Stuart to tell him about his homosexuality, and Patrick was scrambling on the inside about how to respond. He couldn't tell the boy that he condoned his lifestyle, but he wanted to make sure the kid still wanted to leave here with them.

"There's one thing that I need to do before we leave," Stuart said still staring down at his feet.

"What's that?" Patrick asked. He felt a wave of relief wash over him and he caught himself breathing out a sigh that was probably noticeable to Mackenzie and Stuart.

Stuart's eyes came up to Patrick's as he said "I need to bury my parents."

Patrick paused for a second, then extended his hand back out to Stuart again. "We'll do it tomorrow and head out the next day," Patrick said directly. After just a brief pause, Stuart reached out and shook Patrick's hand.

They all enjoyed raviolis, pop, and each other's company again that evening, and then retired to the same sleeping arrangements that they had the night before. They awoke to drizzly conditions that seemed to damper the already somber mood. After raiding neighboring garages for additional shovels, the three of them started digging a large single grave in Stuart's back yard near his mother's peonies that were in full bloom. When they'd reached a couple of feet deep by mid-morning Patrick went into the house to prepare the bodies while the two kids continued to dig.

He found them both in their upstairs bedroom in bed. There was the undertone of death in the small room, but the smell wasn't unbearable. He went over to a window by the bed and opened it all the way. The window had stuck a little, and the noise caused Stuart to look up from his shovel in the backyard that made both him and Patrick uncomfortable. Patrick left the window and turned back toward the bed to determine how he was going to handle this dreadful task.

Before this catastrophe, he had never seen a dead body other than ones already prepared in caskets. He'd seen enough in the last two weeks though, that he thought that he had become numbed to the sight when he offered to do this for Stuart. But seeing this rotting couple laying here in their bed with their son outside digging their grave was more than his personal defenses could take. He took a moment, sat down on the floor in the corner by the closet and wept. He said a prayer that originally was just asking for strength, but turned into a string of requests to aid him, his daughter, and their new companion.

He wasn't sure how long it had been, but when he stood back up he could see out the window that the grave Stuart and his daughter were digging was getting deep enough. Where Stuart was standing, it looked like he was at least waist deep in the hole.

Patrick looked through the two closets in the bedroom, but didn't find what he was looking for. He found a linen closet in the hallway and took a few of the sheets out that he found in there, but he needed more. He went into an adjacent bedroom and immediately knew that it must have been Stuart's room. It was messy, just like a teenager's room; and the palette of colors of the posters on the walls, the bedding, and the clothes strewn around the room were dark and moody. Patrick grabbed most of the bedding in a big wad and headed back to Stuart's parents.

The task ended being up even worse than he had imagined. Both bodies had begun to rot significantly, and at some point, a mix of dark bodily fluids had run out of them staining the sheets and mattress. Patrick wrapped Stuart's mom up first. He used a blanket from the bed they were on, then used one of the clean sheets to roll her up like a burrito before placing her on the ground next to the bed.

Stuart's dad was more difficult due to his size. He looked to have been a man about the same as Patrick's build or a little smaller, and Patrick had a much more difficult time shifting the body around than he had with Stuart's mom. He eventually had Stuart's dad wrapped up as well, but not near as neat as his wife's blankets were.

Patrick was really looking forward to using the Dungeon's shower after this ordeal. He just felt dirty and unclean from the sweat of his exertion and the unavoidable touching of the bodies that he had to do, but mostly to get that subtle smell of death out of his nostrils.

Patrick looked out the window again and knew that he was out of time. The kids were standing in the hole and leaning on their shovels. The hole was deep enough that he could just see the top of Mackenzie's head and from Stuart's shoulder on up. They both were resting with their hands on the top of the shovel handles and appeared to be talking about something serious.

Patrick didn't want Stuart to have to help carry his parents out of the house on his shoulders, so he began walking around the house looking for ideas. As he walked around, his mind was racing for what he could possibly say as they laid them in the ground. He knew that he couldn't say anything to really ease the young boy's mind, but he felt that something should be said about them.

As Patrick walked around the home, he felt a little like an unwanted intruder. The layout of the home was like many other bi-levels that Patrick had visited in the Midwest, and he felt that he knew what each room was used for before he walked into it. The Rappaport's home was older and dated, but very nice and cared for. Patrick didn't find what he needed upstairs, so he headed down stairs. There he found a small work out room, a home office, and a spare bedroom. The spare bedroom had two floor standing lamps on each side of the bed with metal posts supporting them that were probably five feet in length. They weren't exactly what Patrick was looking for, but he dragged both the lamps out to the garage and fashioned a crude travois from the metal lamp posts, some scrap wood he found in the garage and the electrical wire from inside the lamps.

Patrick used the makeshift travois to drag each of the bodies down the stairs and out to the garage. It didn't work quite as slick as he had imagined, and he was huffing and puffing something serious by the time he finally had Stuart's father in the garage.

After taking a few minutes to catch his breath and allowing his heart to slow some, he went back to the back yard where he found both kids sitting on the edge of the hole and softly singing. It was a song that Patrick didn't recognize, but had a slow catchy melody. Patrick stopped several feet from the hole so not as to interrupt them, closed his eyes, leaned his head back, and just listened. The tone of the song was somewhat like a rock ballad that had a catchy new age pop to it. Neither one of the kids had a voice that would land them a record deal, but the sound was nice just the same. Patrick was learning to appreciate beauty wherever he could find it in this land of horror.

As the two singers finished, they both chuckled somewhat at the things that they felt they messed up during their rendition.

"Why don't you go get cleaned up Stuart and put some fresh clothes on? Mackenzie and I will make arrangements up here and then meet you down in the Dungeon," Patrick said as he had rehearsed.

"Yeah, okay," Stuart replied and headed for the house to get clean clothes. Patrick and Mackenzie waited for him to head down to the Dungeon before going and getting the bodies. They used the travois to hall them one by one over to the grave, then lowered them down into it as gently as possible.

They both grabbed clean clothes from their packs and headed to the Dungeon to clean up as well. Patrick also had grabbed his bible from his pack and began thumbing through it on the walk down the stairs.

"I don't think that his parents were Christians, Dad," Mackenzie said looking at the open bible in her dad's hands.

"Maybe not," Patrick replied. "But I am."

Once they were all clean and in new clothes, they headed back up to the yard for the awkward graveside services and burial. Patrick was extremely nervous about what to say and do, but Stuart seemed somber and steady. The drizzly morning had turned into a sprinkly afternoon as the three survivors stood around the edge of the grave. They all stood there quiet for some time before Patrick broke the silence.

"Do you want to say anything Stuart?" Patrick asked.

"Mom, Dad," Stuart began. "I don't know what happened, but I'm sorry that it did. I also know that you didn't love me the same as you had when we first moved here. And I'm okay with that…" A few tears began to stream down Stuart's face as he continued the eulogy. Mackenzie sidled over from where she had been and stood next to him with her arm lovingly around his back. "I know that you tried; and I know that I disappointed you. But I'm going with these people now."

After a few seconds, Patrick asked Stuart if he minded if he said a few words and Stuart just nodded his acceptance.

"As we lay Mr. and Mrs. Rappaport down to their final resting place, let me read from the book of John," Patrick started as he flipped to a piece of paper that he had inserted as a bookmark. He was looking down at the bible and didn't notice the sideways look that his daughter was shooting him.

"'And as Moses lifted up the serpent in the wilderness, even so must the Son of man be lifted up: that whosoever believeth in him should not perish, but have eternal life. For God so loved the world that he gave his only begotten Son, that whosoever believeth in him should not perish, but have everlasting life.'" Patrick spoke the words not with a monotone voice, but with enough vigor and life that the other two were listening intently. As he continued, Mackenzie remembered back when she was a little girl and her dad used to read her bible stories before bed every night. "'For God sent not his Son into the world to condemn the world; but that the world through him might be saved.'"

They all stood quietly for some time more and then Patrick suggested that the two of them sing that song that they had been singing earlier. They looked at him skeptically at first, but when they realized that he was serious about it they looked at each other and then began singing. Patrick closed his eyes and enjoyed the melody of the song. He said a prayer in his thoughts for Stuart's parents and their son, then just listened to the song.

Mackenzie joined Stuart in his tears by the end of the song. Neither of them were sobbing, but both were showing their sadness. Patrick picked up a shovel and gently threw the first few full shovels of dirt over the wrapped-up corpses. After a little while, the other two joined in and they had the grave filled back in just as the sprinkles turned to rain and the light began to fade. Patrick took a few large stones from the flower garden and placed them on top of the grave, about at the heads of each of the bodies.

THE HIKE

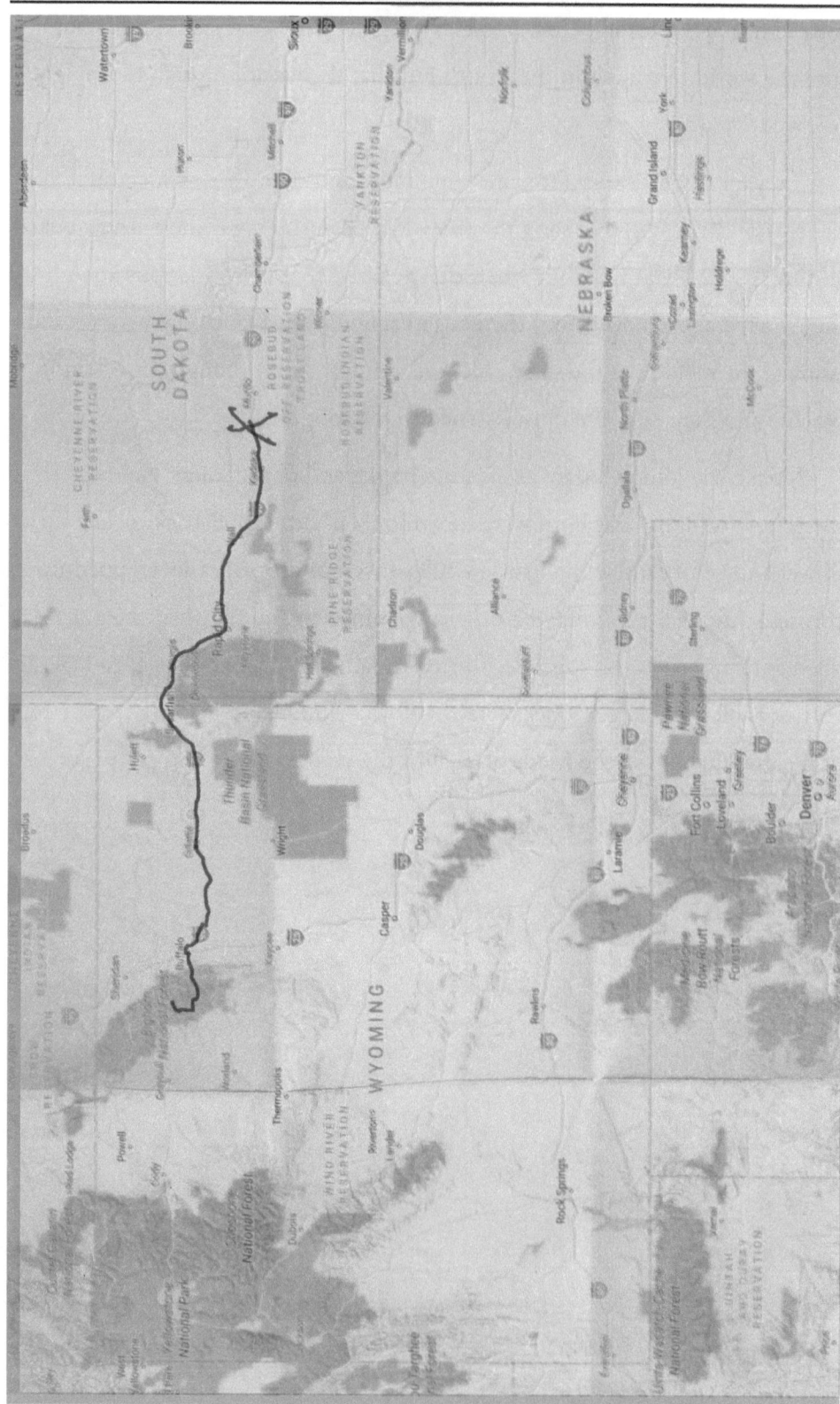

CHAPTER 14

BY THE MORNING of the third day on the road, Patrick was beginning to wish that they hadn't talked Stuart into coming along with them. If Stuart wasn't lollygagging behind to look at something that had no bearing on what they were doing, then he was whining about the food or how fast they were going. Patrick was also sure that even though Stuart lived so close to the Black Hills and the Rocky Mountains, he had never been camping before. Setting up a tent, starting a fire, and many other mundane tasks seemed foreign to this kid.

Stuart wasn't sure that he'd made the right choice to come along either. Mackenzie was always nice enough, but most of the time she was pedaling away up in front and barely visible. All the while Patrick constantly nagged him to keep moving, quit looking around, or about anything else that seemed to be irritating him at the moment. Stuart worked up enough courage to decide that he was going to let the other two know that he was going to turn around and head back to the Dungeon. He thought that they should be close to Murdo, South Dakota by lunch time, and that he would break the news to them when they took their break.

Then Stuart saw Mackenzie off her bike up ahead near an exit ramp drinking from her water bottle and using her binoculars. It looked as if she was waiting for the other two to catch up, so Stuart thought this might be the chance that he'd been waiting for to break the news to them. As he and Patrick approached, Stuart recognized what had caught Mackenzie's attention.

"It's actually pretty cool," Stuart said somewhat winded as he pulled up next to where Mackenzie was standing.

"Is it just a tourist attraction?" Mackenzie asked. She was looking through her binoculars at what looked like an old west town just a few hundred yards from the interstate. There was a white church with a tall steeple, what looked like an old main street with buildings that had false fronts, and several wagons and windmills planted around the scene. A large billboard out near the gas station that sat in front of the attraction said *Experience the West* in front of the picture of a large buffalo.

"Yeah", Stuart replied. "But it's still pretty cool. They have a train that goes around the park, and you can go in and check out the old buildings."

Patrick had stopped next to them and slid off his seat. He was not really paying attention to the conversation that the two kids were having, but instead had unfolded the paper map that he had found at the sheriff's office and appeared to be studying it intently.

"Do you want to go check it out?" Stuart asked Patrick.

Patrick didn't respond or seem to hear Stuart, so Mackenzie lightly kicked her dad's front bicycle tire and said "Dad; can we go look at the buildings?"

"Huh?" Patrick asked before registering what it was Mackenzie was asking for. "No. We can get another couple of hours in before lunch. If we keep it up today, I think that we might be able to make it to the Missouri River before it gets dark."

"C'mon Dad. I just want to take a closer look, it won't take long," Mackenzie pleaded without sounding too whiney. "Besides, the lines can't be too long."

"Yeah, and I think that we all could restock on water and get a snack at the gas station there," Stuart said before he hopped back on his seat and headed to the off ramp before Patrick could argue.

Mackenzie giggled at the look her dad gave her, then stowed her binoculars and water bottle, and headed after Stuart. Patrick stared down the road in front of him and longed for his wife and son. This trek was taking a lot longer than he had anticipated at the onset, and he was getting more troubled by each passing day that they hadn't seen another living thing. He took a deep breath, folded the map up, and started pedaling after the kids.

There were a few cars out front of the gas station, so Patrick wasn't surprised that there were a couple bodies in the store. After calling out to the kids and not getting an answer, Patrick figured that they must be out at the attraction and walked down the aisles seeing if there was anything of value. He picked up some aspirin from one aisle, a couple of candy bars and a handful of protein bars from another aisle, and then two large liter bottles of water from the warm cooler in the back. Patrick headed out a back door that led to the attraction with his arms full of supplies.

Patrick thought the old town was neat. They had a livery stable, a blacksmith shop, an old-time church, a saloon, and just about anything else in the old west that you could imagine. Patrick thought that it was kind of ironic that Mackenzie wanted to come look at this place, because he was sure that if he would have suggested that they stop here on their road trip on their way out to the Bighorns that she would have threw a fit and made them both have a miserable time of it just out of spite.

After walking around some and peering in some of the buildings, he heard voices coming from the saloon. He walked in through the saloon's bat-wing doors and found the two sitting at a large round poker table that they had dragged over closer to a window to catch some light. The room was painted a deep bright red that was so bold it almost hurt your eyes to look at for very long. There were period paintings hanging from the walls, a piano in the corner, and a large bar off to the side with a mirror running the length of it. Patrick felt like he stepped into an old spaghetti western movie, and he liked it. Patrick started walking over to inspect the bar when the tone in his daughter's voice stopped him.

"That's stupid!" Mackenzie half yelled at Stuart before taking a big swig of a pop from a bottle she must have found in the gas station store.

Patrick sidled over and sat his arm load of supplies down on the table that the other two were sitting at. "What's going on?" Patrick asked as he pulled up a chair and joined them.

Neither one answered for a moment. Stuart stared down at his hands underneath the table and Mackenzie stared out the window with pursed lips. Patrick couldn't help but think how much she looked like her mother when she was like that. Before taking another big swig from her pop, Mackenzie finally forced out "Stuart wants to go back to the Dungeon!"

"Why's that?" Patrick asked Stuart. Even though Patrick knew that he couldn't let Stuart go back by himself, he felt a little joy and at ease at the thought of it.

Stuart continued to look down at his hands when he said "I don't know. It's just not working out." He lifted his eyes for a minute to the half-eaten single-serving bag of potato chips on the table in front of him and then back down at his hands.

"What's not working?" Patrick asked.

Stuart leaned back in his chair and folded his hands across his stomach without looking up from them. "I just want to go back to the Dungeon," he said.

They all sat in silence for a few seconds. Patrick was contemplating how to influence this kid. Stuart was trying not to let anything penetrate his passive aggressive shield that he was so good at putting up. Mackenzie was taking drinks from her pop, staring out the window, and trying to not let that heat that she felt welling up inside her make the tears spill from her eyes.

Although it rarely worked on his wife or his own kids, Patrick tried an old standby response to see if he could buy some more time to think about how to sway this teenage boy's opinion. "If you don't tell me what's broke, I can't fix it," he said.

After a few more seconds, Stuart surprisingly responded. "It's just not working out," he said fidgeting a little bit in his chair.

"You gotta give me more than that kid," Patrick replied. "What could make you want to go back to living in solitary, in a lifeless world full of death and despair, instead of going with us to find civilization?"

Stuart didn't respond quickly enough, and Mackenzie blurted out "You Dad." She turned and looked at Patrick with those familiar feelings of hurt and discontent emanating from her eyes. "He says that he's tired and having a hard time keeping up; but mostly he's tired of you nagging him," she finished as the first large crocodile tear that she had been holding back spilled down her cheek.

Patrick absorbed this information for a few seconds and knew that he couldn't let this kid go back. He didn't think that Stuart had told the whole truth to Mackenzie either. He had been riding the kid hard since they left together, but he hadn't given him a hard-enough time to want to go and live and die by himself.

"Stuart," Patrick said catching himself slipping into dad-mode, but letting it happen anyways. "I know you're tired. We are all tired and sore. I'm just trying to get us to make better time so that Mackenzie and I can get back to our family."

Stuart didn't reply. He just sat back in his chair with his invisible shield up and continued to stare down at his hands. Stuart had been in plenty of these types of situations in the past, and he was certain that Patrick didn't know where the chinks in his armor were. He knew that this would be a short battle.

"It's not just that Dad," Mackenzie inserted. She was still trying to control her anger and fear, but tears were running down both cheeks now in a steady stream and her voice was rising with the tempo of her words getting faster. "He's tired of you nagging him constantly about every little thing," she said as she continued to stare out the dirty window. She felt that if she looked directly at her dad, she would lose all control and become unhinged.

Patrick hung his head for a second collecting his thoughts. "You're right Stuart," Patrick said looking up at Stuart from under his brow. "I have been giving you a harder time than you deserve, and I'm sorry."

This statement and the honesty behind it surprised the others. They both looked at Patrick for a few seconds and waited for him to continue. It quickly became awkward and they both averted their eyes again.

After a few more seconds, Stuart felt awkward enough that he had to respond. He felt a little bit of a hole growing in his impenetrable shield and he was becoming nervous. "It's just not working out," Stuart said. He wriggled in his chair for a second and then added "I just want to go back to the Dungeon."

"Listen Stuart," Patrick started. "This is tough. I know that you lost your folks and everyone else that you know in this mess. Nobody should have to go through that, especially a young guy like yourself. Mackenzie and I are trying to get back to our family. We hold out hope that they made it, and I'm trying my best to get us back there as quickly as possible because I can hardly imagine what they are going through. We need to be there to help them. So when I've been nagging and complaining at you to go faster and keep moving it's because I need to get back to them as soon as I can. But I can try to make it easier on you and cut you some slack."

The hole in Stuart's shield was now large enough to crawl through and he felt himself becoming more uncomfortable. "I want you guys to get back to your family too," he said as he looked over to Mackenzie whose face was now full on red with tears still flowing down her face. "That's why you guys should keep going and I am going to turn around and head back to the Dungeon."

"Tell me the real reason why you want to go back Stuart," Patrick said.

With the hole in his shield, Stuart had to give him something. After a moment, he said in a quick blurt "It feels just like high school." After another moment of silence, he said "And I'm sure if we find more people, it will be just like high school there."

"What do you mean kid?" Patrick asked bewildered.

Stuart didn't respond. Stuart didn't know how to respond.

"Is it because you're different?" Mackenzie asked as she turned to look at him. Somehow the raw emotion on her face and the care that she exuded towards him consumed the rest of his shield.

Stuart started nodding at first before feeling his upper lip quiver. He turned his gaze from Mackenzie and shot a piercing look to Patrick before half yelling "I'm gay!" His voice came across a lot louder than he had anticipated, but he held Patrick's gaze with his as he continued. "I see the same disapproval in your eyes and the way you treat me, just like I did in every kid and teacher in high school. Just like – Just like every person in town." Tears started to slowly flow down Stuart's face now as well. His upper lip uncontrollably curled as he spoke. "Just like my parents," he finished in a short burst.

Stuart could feel his chest getting tight and knew that he couldn't sit here with his shield down for much longer. Just as he was about to stand up and leave, he felt Mackenzie's hand on his forearm. She was looking up at him through her tear-filled eyes with real compassion.

Patrick was reeling and trying to strategize about how to continue this conversation so that it was the best for everyone, but he was coming up short. He couldn't go against his convictions and pacify this boy with words that he knew weren't true, but if he told him what he knew there was little chance that he would continue their journey with them. He decided that the only way was the truth.

"Stuart," Patrick started and then took a deep breath. "I am truly sorry that I made you feel belittled or unwelcome. That was not my intent at all, and for that I apologize." Stuart was locked on his gaze now with Mackenzie still resting her hand on Stuart's forearm. Stuart sniffled as his tears had evidently caused his snot to begin to run as well. "But I do believe that being gay is wrong," Patrick forced out. He saw Stuart's body tense and Mackenzie turned to look at him with an almost gaping jaw.

"I know it is wrong, but I don't think that it is your fault," Patrick continued.

"What do you mean Dad?" Mackenzie asked almost unbelieving that her dad would be saying what he was to this boy who wanted to leave anyways.

"My faith says that it is wrong. It doesn't mean that I hate you; wish you bad will; or think less of you. Maybe it's a bad example, but I also know that abortion is wrong. The bible tells us that life starts at conception, not at nine weeks. I don't hate the middle-aged career woman who had one after a one-night stand because it was an inconvenience to her life. And I don't think any less of the teenage girl who had one because she was raped and impregnated by some monster in a back alley. But it is still wrong," Patrick said. He could feel tears welling up in his eyes too, but he had more years of experience keeping them held back.

He could see both Stuart and his daughter relax ever so slightly as they contemplated his thoughts and believed his honesty. With that, Patrick continued with his thoughts "I have a problem with alcohol." He could see Mackenzie furrow her brow as though she doubted him and he chuckled a little bit. "That makes me happy to know that you doubt me on that one Darlin'. My whole family has had problems with alcohol or addiction in some way. Both sides of my family. My father, both grand-dads, a couple uncles, several aunts, and lots of cousins were either alcoholics or at some point had been addicted to drugs of some kind; and it killed them. And I started out the same way."

Patrick felt the tears in his eyes continue to swell, so he stopped for a moment and opened one of the large bottles of water that he had brought in and took a swig before continuing. "When I was a little younger than you, my dad died. I hadn't known him for a few years since my mom and him had gotten divorced, but he was still very important to me yet. He had been the only male figure in my life that I really respected. When he died, I lost it. I got in trouble with the law, started drinking, thought about killing myself…

Really dark days. I went out and partied. I got black out drunk almost every day for a couple of years. I did a lot of things in those days that I'm not proud of. A lot of things that I hope that you never find out about Mak."

With that, Patrick felt the first tear roll down his cheek. He wasn't sure where this was going to end up, but he felt good about it being the truth. This isn't what he had been hoping to have a heart to heart with Mackenzie about when he envisioned going on the backpacking trip with her, but he realized that this truth is what would have made a difference with her. He took another swig of water from the bottle before continuing. Both Mackenzie and Stuart were immersed in his story.

"Stuart, my faith also says that getting drunk is wrong. And many of the things that I did in that condition were very wrong," Patrick continued. He felt a pair of tears now streak his face and he no longer tried to hold them back.

Patrick looked Mackenzie dead in the eyes and said "Your mother brought me some happiness during all of that. She was a light in the darkness of my life at that time that let me stop and think. In that time, I was saved." Patrick changed his attention from Mackenzie to Stuart and continued "Jesus showed me that I was still loved. Even though I had done terrible things; and was still doing bad things; I was loved."

Patrick took another swig from the water bottle. All three of them were fully crying now. Patrick couldn't help but think that if you would have told him before he left on their road trip that in a couple of weeks he would be setting around a saloon table with two teenagers and airing his dirty laundry while crying like babies with them; he wouldn't have believed it.

"I still struggle with alcohol and addiction today," Patrick was concluding. "It's been a long time since I've been drunk, but I still think about it every time I'm in a situation where the opportunity is there or it would be socially acceptable for me to do so. But it's easier now. Every time I beat it back it gets a little easier the next time."

Patrick wasn't sure how to wrap up his speech and see if it swayed the boy's mind about leaving, but he still had Stuart's full attention as he finished. "I have done some terrible things Stuart. I still screw up in many different ways, but I know that I'm loved. When you realize that... When you realize that Jesus loves you no matter what; your whole world will change. It won't get any easier, but it will change. I know that being gay is wrong, but you need to know that you are loved too."

They all sat there awkwardly for a minute not sure how each of them should react. Mackenzie was first as she stood up and hugged her dad. Patrick stood up with her, and she kind of nestled in on his side with her head near his armpit like she used to when she was a little girl.

Patrick could see in Stuart's eyes that he believed his story. Patrick waved with his forearm for Stuart to join them. Stuart immediately stood up, but then hesitated. Patrick waved again to him and he walked over to him. Patrick put his free arm around the boy and they all stood there hugging and crying in the red saloon for some time.

THE HIKE

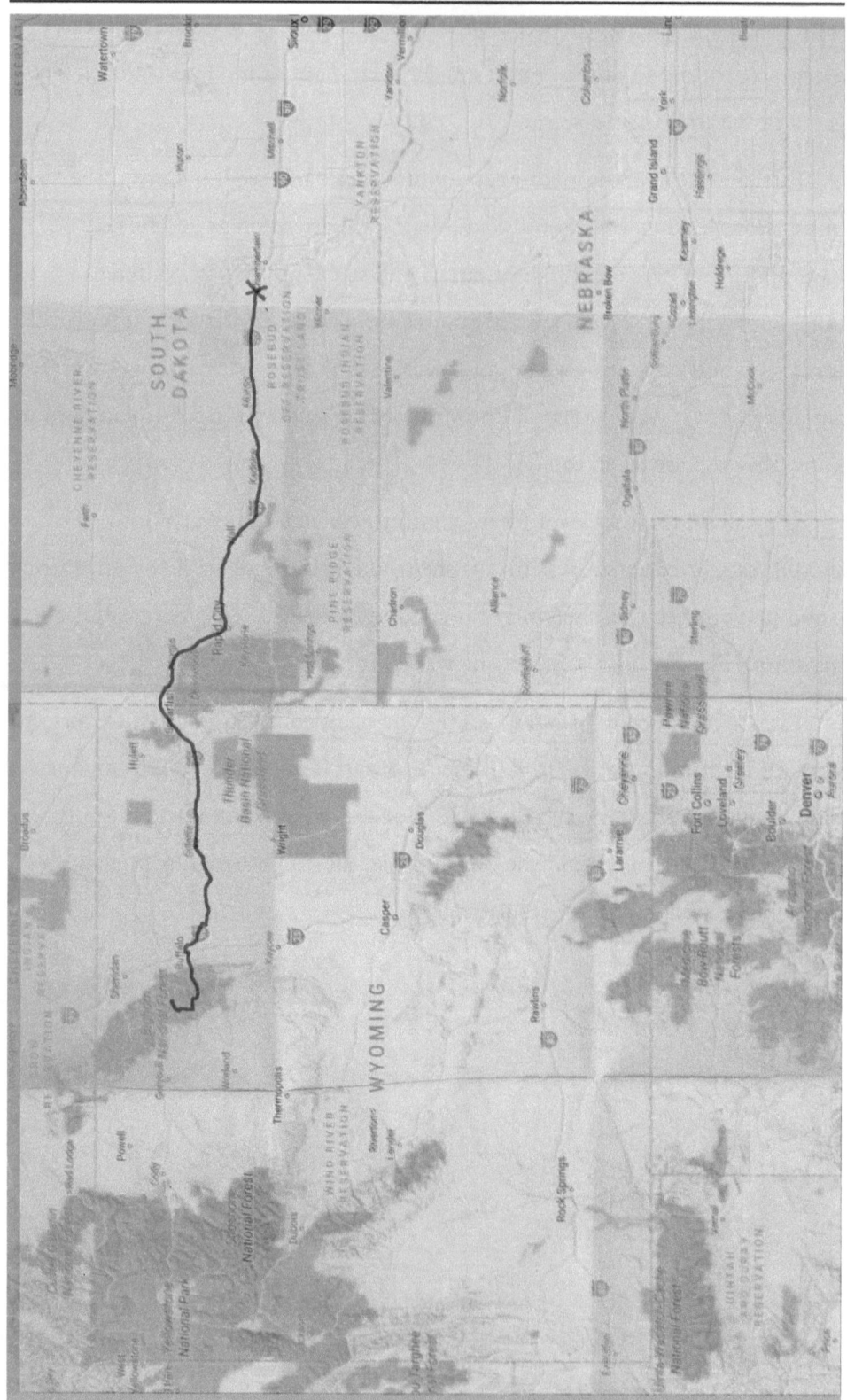

CHAPTER 15

THEY HAD COVERED a lot of ground in the last couple days since they stopped in the western town for supplies. They had stayed over in the town that night while Stuart decided on whether he would continue their trek with them or go back to the safety of the Dungeon. Stuart decided to go on with them, and they all seemed to think that it was going better. Stuart was learning the little things about roughing it that was letting him keep up better, and Patrick was biting his tongue more when he thought Stuart was slowing them down. Mackenzie kept the pace going by riding way out in front, mostly not even seen now that the flatness of South Dakota was being broken up by large rolling hills. The other two would usually only catch up with her for water breaks, and once when she was having a hard time cutting through the barb wire fence at the side of the road to take a short cut.

They had stopped the night before just short of their goal for the day of reaching the Missouri River and setup camp some little ways from the interstate on the crest of a hill amongst some trees. They finished setting up the tents in the middle of a beautiful orange and pink sunset. They were all exhausted from the long day of biking and were asleep before the sun was all the way down.

Patrick was amazed that morning when he awoke shortly after sunrise and came out of his tent. Stuart's tent was no longer where it was the night before; it was nowhere to be seen. Patrick's first thought that the kid had decided to back to the Dungeon after all and he was about to wake Mackenzie up when he seen the boy's bike still parked with the other two down by the interstate where they had left them last evening. After looking around, he saw Stuart sitting by some trees just east of camp on the very crest of the hill. Patrick used his camp stove to make some coffee and took two of their camp mugs over to where Stuart was watching the sun come up.

"I thought that you had left. It isn't like you to get up before me in the morning," Patrick said as he walked up to where Stuart was sitting with his back to a small cottonwood and handed him one of the mugs.

"Couldn't really sleep last night," Stuart said as Patrick leaned up against the same tree.

"Anything you want to talk about?" Patrick offered.

Instead of answering his question, Stuart pointed east and south a little and said "You can see the river from here."

They stayed that way for a little while until the sun was well above the horizon, then headed back and broke camp after waking Mackenzie up. She wasn't as chipper this morning and lagged behind the other two at times on the road.

There were a lot more vehicles on and off the road than there had been going through Wyoming, and they slowed their progress some. The wrecked vehicles just appeared as if all the drivers had fallen asleep at the same time.

Some pickups were on their tops after going through the guard rail, some SUV's were in the right of way as if they had tried to go hill climbing, and occasionally a semi-truck with a full-size trailer would be overturned across the whole interstate. They all learned to try and not consider the vehicles or at the wreckage near them as almost all the scenes were gruesome ones. Old ladies hanging out of sedan windows, little children in the back seats of SUV's, and all other carnage that one doesn't want to imagine. With the increase of vehicles, the number of collisions had also increased that made it more and more difficult to not look at the wreckage. So even though they had witnessed a glorious sunrise and the crisp air of the early morning was enough to get one excited about what the day had to offer, all three of them remained somber and quiet as they continued their quest eastward.

Patrick was in the lead when he topped over a large hill and first seen the river. His heart sank immediately and he put his brakes and came to a more sudden stop than he anticipated. Stuart and Mackenzie were only a few seconds behind him and stopped next to him just past the top of the hill.

"What's wrong?" Mackenzie asked. She could tell by the way that her dad had stopped that something was wrong, but she didn't recognize it.

"They're gone," Stuart answered as he looked down the road the same as Patrick.

"What's gone?" Mackenzie asked this time becoming perturbed that neither of them were clear on what the problem was.

"The bridge," Patrick said as he pointed down to the river. Mackenzie realized what the problem was as she saw that the interstate seemed to just dive beneath the massive river for what seemed like a mile before it arose on the opposite side on a steep hill.

"It's not just that one," Stuart replied after a few seconds. "There was a railroad bridge over there to the right and another bridge for cars between the towns over there," he said pointing to the left of the interstate.

"I don't think that they're gone," Patrick said after looking it over more. "I think that the water level is just so high that they're underwater."

Stuart put his hand up to his forehead to shield his eyes from the early morning sun and peered down at the scene that was becoming harder for him to understand. He could see somewhat from where he was standing that the town across the river was mostly underwater. "Yeah, I think that you're right," Stuart said.

"How could that happen Dad? We haven't had a lot of rain or anything," Mackenzie asked.

"I'm not sure," Patrick replied. "I would guess that they have a dam or hydro plant or something that controls the water level somewhere downstream. It probably is on the fritz with all of the other electronics, or nobody is there to regulate the water level."

"Or both," Stuart added.

After a few seconds, Mackenzie asked the question out load that they were all wondering. "How do we get across now?"

"I'm not sure about that either Mak," Patrick said.

They coasted down the hill to the water's edge for a better look. It didn't take long because the hill was quite steep and there were only a few cars on the pavement. Looking across the river from the water's edge made it look even more daunting. It was more than a mile across, maybe even a couple. Mackenzie got off her bike, took her shoes off, and walked to the water's edge as the other two stared across the seemingly still water.

Mackenzie waded out into the river until she was about knee deep. The water was cool, but not cold. The water was also very murky and dirty looking. She turned back to the other two and said "I bet that we can make it swimming across without our gear."

The thought of having to gear back up didn't sit well with Patrick. Their bikes and gear were allowing them to make much better time than they otherwise would be.

"Do you know this area very well?" Patrick asked Stuart.

"Not really," Stuart replied. "I've been through here a few dozen times probably, but I've only stopped here a couple of times. There is a small town on this side of the river, with a bigger town on the other side."

They continued to look out across the water and internally debate about how they were going to get across it. Stuart pointed out to their right and said "Look! You can just barely make out the top of the railroad bridge."

Just as Stuart said the word "railroad", Mackenzie let out a high-pitched scream and ran high stepping it back to the shore. Patrick jumped off his bike and ran to meet her at the edge of the water. "What's wrong? What's wrong?" he was yelling at her.

When Mackenzie reached him after those few steps she breathed out "Something touched my leg!" She was staring back at the water.

"Did you see it?" Stuart asked now off his bike as well.

"No." Mackenzie said not letting her grip relax from her dad. "It was cold and fleshy."

Stuart took his shoes off as well and rolled his pants legs up. He walked over to an older four door car that was partially submerged in the river just off the shoulder of the road, and pulled off a large chunk of trim from the side of the car that had started to come off already. He waded out into the water about to the same spot where Mackenzie had been and poked around in the murky water with the trim that was a few feet long.

After a moment or two, Stuart jumped back a few feet like he had been bitten and Mackenzie clutched her dad even more tightly. Instead of running, Stuart used the trim in his hand to stir the water beside him until he could see what had bumped against his leg. After finding it and recognizing what it was, he used the trim to push it near the edge of the river. It took a little while to push the mass those eight to ten feet and he gave up once it bottomed out on the pavement, but Patrick and Mackenzie could see that it was a large lifeless catfish from where they stood. Mackenzie relaxed her grip on her dad and walked over to peer at the fish.

"Dinner anyone?" Stuart asked. The fish was very large, but didn't look appetizing. Some of the skin on its side and belly was sliding off exposing its rotting flesh. Mackenzie took the trim from Stuart and began poking and examining the fish in the ankle-deep water as Stuart came out of the water and walked over to where Patrick was standing.

Stuart said to Patrick "I say that we ride into town and see if we can find a boat to get us across."

"Sounds like as good of a plan as any," Patrick replied.

They had to back track some on the interstate to get to terrain where they could easily cut across on their bikes to enter the little town on the west side of the flooded river. It was a very small town that pretty much only had a large truck stop on the north side of the interstate, and trailers and other small houses on the south side of the interstate. There may have been larger homes or other businesses closer to the river, but they were underwater now and inaccessible.

By noon they had pretty much canvassed the truck stop and most of the town looking for a boat to take them across the river. The only thing that they even debated using was a small speed boat that was hooked to an out of state pickup at the truck stop. As they rode back to the truck stop to decide what their next steps were and restock supplies, they argued about whether the one boat they found would work or not.

"How can there not be a single boat in all of this town by a major river?" Mackenzie asked to no one in particular.

"I bet that they have a local marina or dock somewhere where people probably keep their boats, but it's probably under water now," Patrick speculated as they pulled up to the front of the truck stop and got off their bikes.

They walked over to the one boat that they found. Stuart climbed aboard the trailered boat and began going through the contents of the cubbies and cabinets. He found a couple of oars, some water skis and paraphernalia, and a large knee board. While they could all fit on the boat with their bikes and supplies, they had no easy way to get it down to the water's edge.

Patrick wandered into the truck stop and loaded up with supplies and things to eat for lunch while the other two stayed outside in the parking lot looking at the boat. The truck stop was a large one with a restaurant attached to it, and by the number of bodies in the store and booths it had been a popular place as well. The two kids started in just as Patrick was headed out and he stopped them. He handed them some things that he found for lunch and told them that they didn't need to see what all was going on inside there.

They all climbed into the boat and ate their lunches without saying much. Mackenzie was sitting in the bow facing the back of boat with her arms splayed out across the front of the boat and her head tipped back enjoying the sun. Stuart was sitting in the captain's seat staring at the odds and ends that he had strewn all around the boat as he munched his potato chips and Patrick was staring off in the distance as he absently ate a king-sized bar of chocolate.

Without looking up, Mackenzie said "The trestle."

The other two didn't look up, but just nodded. "I'll go as soon as lunch is over," Patrick said.

"Nah," Stuart said. "I'll go. I'm a really strong swimmer."

Patrick thought about arguing with the kid, but decided that it may be best for the group and just agreed by nodding his head and said "Okay."

It was mid-afternoon before the group was back down to the water's edge with their extra supplies. Stuart had made a type of water travois by lashing the long oars and a life jacket to the knee board that he planned to tow behind him with the ski rope. Patrick had gone through and emptied his day pack from anything that would get ruined if wet, but left things like a tarp, multi-tool, water proof matches, some glow sticks, and other odds and ends in it. He helped Stuart lash it to the knee board along with the boy's extra jeans and an extra pair of shoes using a length of paracord that had been in the pack.

All three of them walked the half a mile or so to where the edge of the bank was closest to the railroad trestle bridge. Stuart dragged the knee board along behind him in the water to see how well it would work. It kept getting caught on the bank every twenty or thirty yards, but they all thought that it would do better out in the open water.

Stuart took his pants and shoes off while listening to all the instructions by Patrick. Some of the things Patrick was telling him were pertinent to the task at hand, such as he was to light one of the flares in the pack when he reached the other side. Otherwise, Patrick and Mackenzie were swimming across at first light to find him. He also described the most appropriate boat that would work for them, but to get anything and get back to the other side. The other things that Patrick told him were pretty much just fatherly advice about things to watch out for or not to do that Stuart thought he already had a handle on.

They went over the plan one more time. Stuart was to swim out to the railroad bridge where part of the trestle was sticking a foot or two out of the water. There he could walk along the trestle to the other side towing the knee board. Once on the other, side he would light the flare to let them know that he had made it and find a place to sleep for the night. The next morning, he would scour the larger town on the other side of the river for a more appropriate boat for them, their gear, and ideally their bikes. He could then row back across the river and pick the other two up.

"Should we go over it one more time?" Patrick asked Stuart.

Stuart started rolling his eyes, but was cut short when Mackenzie teasingly shoved her dad and then hugged Stuart. "Be safe," she said before letting him go. "Let him go Dad," she said as she turned back to the bank and Stuart waded out into the river.

The water got deep fast and Stuart was swimming before he made it thirty yards into the water. The weight of the knee board seemed to slow him quite a bit when the slack ran out of the ski line. He felt himself start to get winded and tired with the trestle still quite some ways off, so he flipped over to his back and just kicked his feet. He could see that Mackenzie and Patrick were still on the edge of the bank watching him intently. Mackenzie waved once and he waved back before flipping back over on his stomach and started swimming again. He was exhausted by the time he reached the trestle a few minutes later, so he clung to it and rested for several moments before trying to get up on the steel. He banged his toes hard on something on the bridge under the water that made him wince. He tried to lift his foot out of the water to look at it while he held onto the bridge with one hand, but he couldn't get his foot all the way out of the murky water to give it a look.

The trestle top was made with eight-inch iron or steel I-beams. The start of the trestle where he was at was only a couple of feet out of the water, but it was still difficult for him to pull himself up onto it. Once on top of the steel, he inspected his foot and found that the fourth toe on his right foot was mangled good and that it was bleeding. He managed to stand on the trestle and found that where the water hadn't cooled it off, the top I-beam was extremely warm. He didn't think that it would injure him, but it would be uncomfortable walking the mile along the top of the steel in bare feet. He sat back down on the steel and reeled the knee board over to him and up on the bridge. He unlashed an oar and his shoes before retying everything else back down and lowering it back down to the water. The rope slipped right at the end and he ended up dunking it enough that he was sure Patrick's day pack was drenched. He put his left shoe on, then gingerly forced his right foot with the injured toe into its shoe. He tied the ski rope around his waist and readied himself to try and stand back up on the I-beam. Looking back at the shore, he seen that Mackenzie and Patrick were no longer where he had left them. He couldn't see them from his vantage point, but he was sure that they probably had headed back to the bikes to get their equipment to make camp for the night.

He used the oar to help him stand up and immediately felt the pain from his injured toe. He closed his eyes for a moment and moved the oar back and forth in his hands to try and find its balance point. He opened his eyes and held the oar out horizontally before him to help him balance. He began the longest balance beam walk of his life just as the sun was starting to dip beyond the horizon.

Stuart first began humming, then whistling, then absently singing a familiar tune as he walked along the beam. His Axel Rose impression really hadn't improved much since he had last been alone.

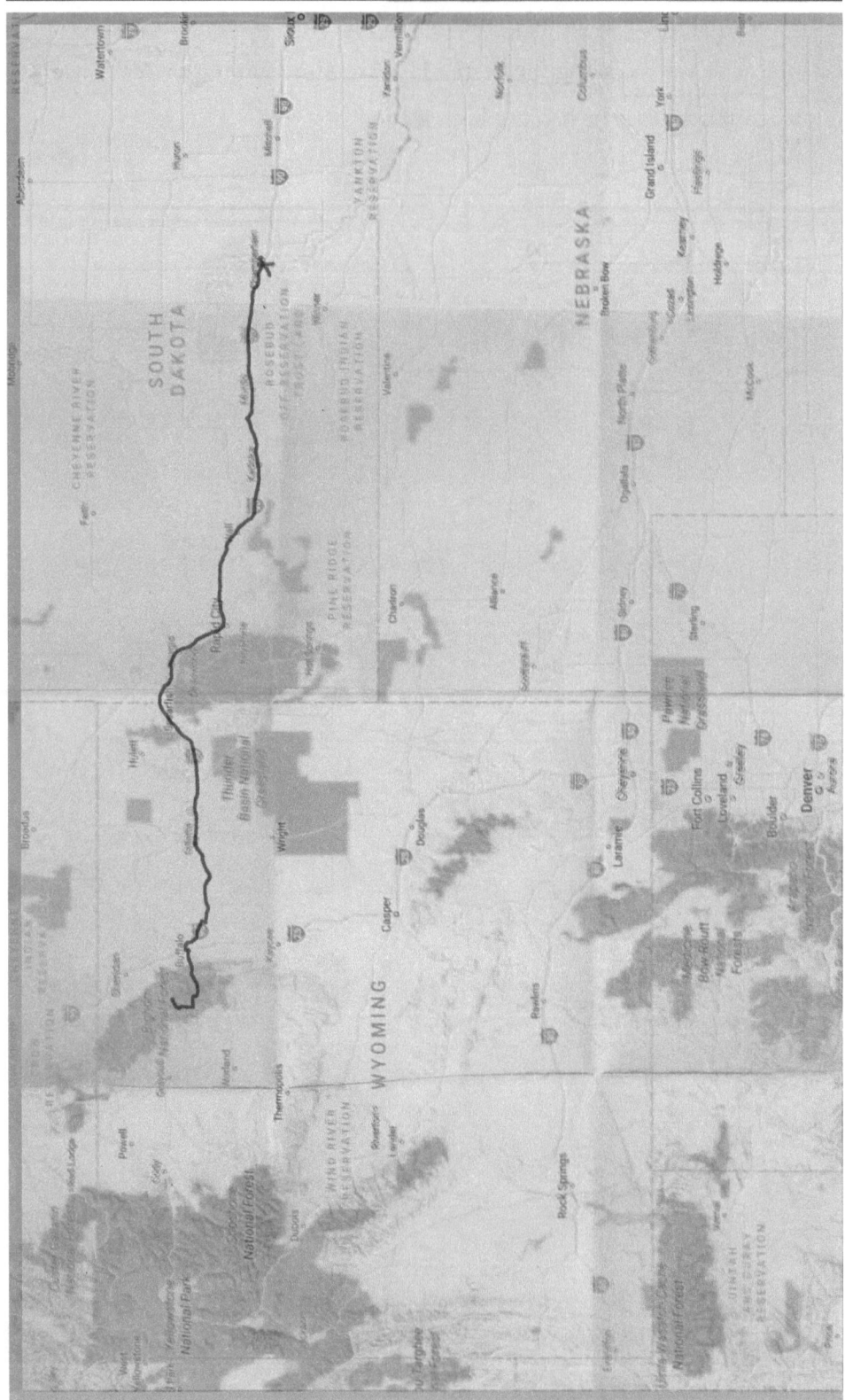

CHAPTER 16

IT HAD BEEN quite a while after dusk since they had lost sight of Stuart when he was a little less than half way across the bridge. A stiff breeze had come up and Patrick was beginning to worry about the boy climbing out of the river with wet clothes on and freezing to death before he had sense to take shelter or find dry clothes.

They had already pitched their tents on a little hill in a stand of trees just up and away from the river where they had left Stuart. Patrick was cooking them some warm oatmeal on his camp stove when he couldn't take it any longer and called Mackenzie over from her lookout spot to finish preparing the meal. He had brought his assault rifle and pistol up to camp from where they left their bikes near the interstate, but he hadn't thought to bring his hunting rifle. He walked back to the bikes in a brisk gait continuously looking over to where Stuart would be when he was supposed to light the flare. After Patrick unstowed the rifle, he headed back to camp in almost a jog. He continued to look over to where the flare should have been, but he never saw it.

Mackenzie had dished up the warm oatmeal and handed him a bowl as he returned to camp. He joined her at her perch next to a tree looking across the river as she ate her dinner. He sat his bowl down on a rock nearby and lay in a prone position with the rifle.

"Dad, what are you doing!" Mackenzie exclaimed as she looked over and seen her dad setting up the rifle's bipod and flipping up the scope covers.

Patrick opened the bolt, ensured the safety was still on, and then peered through the scope. "I'm just trying to see if I can see Stuart down there. I had given him my binoculars in that day pack," Patrick replied as if laying prone in the dirt and aiming his rifle at their friend across the river was a normal occurrence.

The moon was half-full tonight without any clouds, so there was enough light to walk around carefully and do normal functions, but there wasn't enough light for Patrick to see the other side of the river through his scope. He could pick out bits and pieces of the trestle sticking out of the water in areas where the moonlight glistened off the steel, but he was sure that Stuart should have been past those spots by now. Nevertheless, Patrick laid prone staring at the farthest spot that he could make out through the scope for at least twenty minutes before he gave up and decided to give his back some rest.

Mackenzie had gone and grabbed her sleeping bag from her tent and continued to lean against the tree and watch the other side of the river. Patrick joined her and began to eat his cold oatmeal. He was thankful that she offered to share a corner of her sleeping bag as he was still wearing his light biking clothes, and the steady breeze was somewhat chilly.

"You think he made it and forgot to set the flare off?" Mackenzie asked.

"I don't see how. We went over it four times before he left," Patrick replied between spoonfuls of cold mush.

"Do you think he…" Mackenzie started, but stopped abruptly when she thought she heard something. Patrick heard it too as they both looked at each other with wide eyes for a split second before Patrick jumped up and launched over to where his rifle was resting on the ground. He spilled his oatmeal on Mackenzie's sleeping bag when he jumped up, but neither of them bothered with it at the moment. They both were intently looking across the river to see if they could see what had caused a splash.

Though the breeze was blowing and causing some rustling of the leaves and branches in the trees that they were in, the world was still eerily quiet in this new lifeless environment. They both were sure that they had distinctly heard a healthy splash coming from the other side of the river. It was a faint sound, but still easily identifiable.

Patrick used his scope to peer all over the river and bridge, but still couldn't see anything through the scope due to the lack of light. Mackenzie just sat straight up with her arms around her knees staring across the river intently.

"You think that he's okay Dad?" Mackenzie asked.

"Shhhh… I'm sure he's fine," he replied in a whisper. "Let's listen and see if we can hear anything else."

They sat that way watching and listening long enough for Patrick's back to be screaming at him to move. He finally gave in and stood up pushing his hips forward to stretch his back.

"I think that I'm going to head across Darlin' to make sure he's okay," Patrick finally said to his daughter even though he had been thinking it for the last hour or so.

"No you are not!" Mackenzie offered defiantly. "You told him that you would wait until first light if you didn't see the flare tonight. He's counting on that and you're going to stick to the plan, just as he's going to find a way to light that flare." Patrick realized that his daughter was right and resigned himself to sit back down with her and share her sleeping bag.

After a little while more of silence and watching the blackness of the other side of the river, Mackenzie reflected solemnly out loud to her dad "Thanks for taking me on that backpacking trip Dad."

"You bet kiddo. Turned out great, didn't it?" Patrick said facetiously as he rubbed the top of her head.

Mackenzie giggled a little and said "No; I'm serious. I know that I didn't want to go, and the whole end of the world thing is bad and all." She giggled again and continued "But do you remember that first morning before all of this happened that I went off fishing while you slept in?"

"Yeah. You scared me to death when I couldn't find you," Patrick responded. They both continued to lean against the tree and stare out into the blackness.

"That was a beautiful morning," Mackenzie said with her tone turning from solemnness to reverence. "I'd walked along the creek as the sun first came up, fishing the holes and bends in the creek just like you taught me. I find myself going back to that morning in my mind." Mackenzie paused for a couple of seconds and then added "Even if I hadn't caught those monster size fish, it still would have been a good morning."

"Monster size fish?" Patrick exclaimed. "As I recall, we had to supplement breakfast with oatmeal and granola bars," he finished and Mackenzie feigned that she was appalled.

Then they saw it. A red glow came immediately to life directly on the other side of the river from where they were.

Patrick jumped to his feet and his back shot out a signal of pain and stiffness to remind him of his age. He ignored it and scrambled behind the scope of the rifle and zeroed in on the red flare. As he picked up on him, he saw Stuart waving the flare over his head in a big arc staring back across the river towards them.

Patrick got to his knees, unholstered his pistol, and shot it off at a high arc in a safe direction towards another point on the river. He decocked the pistol, put the safety back on, and slid it back in his holster before getting behind the scope again.

"Is he okay?" Mackenzie asked.

"I think so," Patrick said continuing to peer through the scope.

He could see that Stuart had laid the flair on the ground while he was putting his clothes on and shouldering the day pack. By the way that he was moving and carrying on, he could tell that Stuart was cold. Stuart picked the flare up and began walking over to the interstate on the other side of the river.

"He's limping pretty good," Patrick told Mackenzie.

"Can you tell what he's hurt?" Mackenzie asked with concern. She stood and walked over to where her dad was.

"No, not really. It's his right leg that he's favoring," Patrick responded as he continued to peer through the scope.

"Can I take a look Dad?" Mackenzie asked.

Patrick sighed and reluctantly stood up to let Mackenzie stare through the scope. Without looking through the scope, the flare just looked like a small red ember floating through the sky.

"I think that it's his foot Dad," Mackenzie said.

"Could be. Can I get back in there?" Patrick asked.

Mackenzie stood and walked back over to the tree and sat down as Patrick nestled back down behind the rifle. After watching the kid walk for a while, he thought that his daughter was probably right about Stuart's foot being injured.

Patrick watched Stuart intently for the several minutes as he walked towards the interstate, carrying the burning road flare. Not too far from the interstate, Stuart stopped and dropped the road flare. He kicked in the dirt around the flare and waved again towards Patrick and Mackenzie. Patrick fired off another round from his pistol before climbing back behind his rifle. When Stuart heard the pistol's report, he then started walking again towards the interstate.

"Why did he stop?" Mackenzie asked.

"He's still going. He just dropped the flare because it was probably getting hot," Patrick said. "I think that will probably be all of the show for tonight. If he does what I told him to, he'll go find some place to grab some shut eye and warm up."

Mackenzie let out a yawn and Patrick suggested that she go to bed. "Go ahead and use my sleeping bag since I spilled the oatmeal on yours," Patrick offered. After they argued back and forth a few times about who got the clean sleeping bag, Mackenzie conceded and headed off to her tent for the rest of the night.

Patrick leaned against the tree and watched across the river for quite some time. At first his mind raced about what trouble the kid was getting into on the other side of the river by himself. He was worried that Stuart wouldn't have found dry clothes or a warm enough spot to lie down in for the night. By the time that the moon had made an arc most of the way across the sky,

Patrick's body took control over his mind and told him that it was time to rest. He fell asleep while leaned back against the same tree under Mackenzie's sleeping bag.

At some point while it was still dark out, Patrick awoke to sounds of movement in the water down below. Patrick had gotten so used to the quiet of this new world that any other foreign sound put him on high alert almost immediately. After listening intently to the sound with his eyes closed for a couple of seconds, his mind concluded that it was indeed an unusual sound and he was instantly awake and fully alert. He peered down to the river where the sound was coming from and he thought that he seen a flash of green light coming from the river. He dismissed what he saw initially as it seemed ridiculous and he'd just woken up, but then he saw it flash again almost in the same spot that he had seen it before. The light was coming from where the sound was emanating from.

He tossed the sleeping bag aside and climbed back behind the scope. The coolness of the night had zapped the warmth out of the ground, and Patrick was chilled almost immediately as he laid down on the ground behind the rifle. He adjusted his position behind the scope for his right eye to get a full picture, then he panned the scope around in the direction of the sound until he found it. Once he saw the faint green glow a little closer than half-way across the river, Patrick knew immediately what he was looking at. Stuart was rowing a boat across the river along one side of the trestle bridge. Whenever he switched sides with the long oar that he had, the green glow light that was hanging on a string around his neck would flash with a bright green glow.

Patrick's heart raced as he watched the boy paddle for several minutes. From what he could see through the scope in the moonlight enhanced by the glow stick, the boat that Stuart picked out looked perfect for what they needed. From here it looked like it was a somewhat small drift boat setup for fishing and had three rows of seats. Stuart was sitting in the bow of the boat and was using one of the oars that he had taken across with him to propel him across the river. He seemed to be doing a good job at rowing and it looked like he was making okay time in the dark.

Once Patrick realized that Stuart was okay, anger started to boil up in him. He couldn't understand why the boy hadn't followed the plan and stayed across the river for the night. Coming across the water in the middle of the night could lead to any number of accidents. The more that Patrick thought about it, the more upset that he became. Patrick got up from the rifle and walked back to his tent. Mackenzie had taken his sleeping bag back to her tent and it sounded like she was still sleeping soundly. Patrick slipped on warmer clothes and grabbed a jacket before walking down to the bank of the river.

He watched quietly as Stuart rowed the boat closer to the bank. When Stuart got close enough to shore that they could easily see each other, Patrick waved his arm in a big arc above his head. Stuart replied with a similar motion with his free hand.

After several more minutes, the bottom of the boat ran aground on the bank of the river. Patrick stepped into the river with one foot to grab the boat and help drag it up onto the bank. Before Stuart could get out of the boat, Patrick's emotion boiled over and he blurted "Just what in the world do you think you are doing?"

Stuart continued to climb out of the boat without responding. He grabbed a piece of the bow and gave it one more tug onto the bank. When he was done, he stood facing Patrick and said flatly "It's nice to see you too."

Patrick pushed the image back in his mind of trying to bend an eighteen-year-old over his knee. "Listen… We have to have a mutual respect if we're going to make it. When we make a plan-" Patrick started to lecture, but was stopped short with Stuart's response.

"There's something over there," Stuart said flatly again standing still and looking right at Patrick.

Patrick reeled at those words for a minute and his anger left as quick as it had come on. "What do you mean? What did you see?" Patrick asked with a sense of skepticism coming through in his tone.

"I'm not sure. I didn't get a good look at it," he said averting his eyes from Patrick for a minute. "But whatever it was, it wasn't friendly."

Patrick could now see in the light of the glow necklace that Stuart was shivering. He was also favoring his right foot. "Here; let's get you up to camp and get you warmed up," Patrick said now taking pity on the young man that he was ready to teach a lesson about respect a few minutes ago.

Patrick helped Stuart hobble back up the hill to camp, and sat him in front of his tent with Mackenzie's sleeping bag wrapped around him as he began to gather wood for a fire in the moonlight. The commotion woke Mackenzie up and she came out to greet Stuart as well. On one of the trips back to where he was stacking the kindling and wood, Patrick saw that Mackenzie had gotten her first aid kit out and was attending to Stuart's injured toes. Patrick went over and peered down at Stuart's foot in the semi-dark to inspect the damage, but Mackenzie had already bandaged the area and he couldn't see much.

"It doesn't look that bad, but it sure hurts like hell," Stuart said.

After gathering a small pile of kindling and a stack of bigger wood, Patrick made a small fire pit in the dirt a few feet in front of where the kids were sitting and talking. Then he went about starting the fire with some matches. Stuart and Mackenzie were chatting in low tones that Patrick could only catch bits and pieces of the conversation. He made himself have enough patience to wait until everything was settled before trying to piece together the story that Stuart was already telling to Mackenzie. Some of the damp kindling was being difficult to start, and as Patrick was on his fifth match Stuart got his attention and handed him his zippo lighter that he always carried on him. The extra heat from the lighter got the kindling going right away, and within a few minutes Patrick had a good size fire going that warmed all of them. Patrick put a small pot of water next to the fire to make Stuart some oatmeal before sitting down on the other side of the fire and waiting for Stuart to tell him about what happened on the other side of the river.

"Okay, let's hear about your adventure," Patrick asked now fully at attention.

"Well, I was running out of a house near the top of the hill and..." Stuart started before Patrick cut him off.

"No. No. No," Patrick said. "Tell it from the beginning. From where you left us. We have plenty of time."

"Oh. Well, when I reached the bridge, I kicked part of it below the water and split my toe," Stuart started. He made a grimacing face as he thought about the pain of that moment, and then he continued. "You wouldn't think something like that would hurt so bad, but I could hardly walk by the time I got to the other side. You'd be amazed at how long that bridge is when you're actually on top shuffling along it." Stuart paused and took a swig of water. The other two sat quietly and listened intently to the story.

Stuart continued on with the story "I finally made it over to the other side and lit the flare that you guys saw. I had put my shoes on because that metal from the bridge was smoking hot at first. So, I was freezing from the wet shirt and shoes by the time that I started walking into town. I thought at first that I would walk up to that hotel on top of the hill; but my foot hurt so bad and I was so cold that I didn't feel like I could make it, so I started down a side street into town and saw that boat parked in someone's drive way. It looked perfect, and the trailer was lined up and ready to head to the river. I went into that house to find a place to crash for the night, but the scene wasn't good." Stuart paused again and took another swig of water. He was trying to collect his thoughts and figure out how to explain what he saw.

"It's okay. Just tell us like you remember it," Patrick said.

"Well, it just didn't feel right from the time I went in," Stuart started again. "Something was just off. The place was a mess. I walked upstairs and found the kitchen where there was food, pots and pans, and everything just everywhere."

"What do you mean?" Mackenzie asked. "Like pots and pans in the sink and on the counter?"

"No. No," Stuart corrected. "I mean like everywhere. On the floor, on the counters, on the kitchen table. Not just pots and pans, but spoiled food, canned food; I mean everything. I know that you told me not to use the glow sticks unless I absolutely had to, but I had to see what was going on in that place." Stuart took another swig of water.

"Were there any bodies?" Mackenzie asked.

"Not that I saw. I didn't stick around though. I was weirded out enough that I just split," Stuart said. "I walked down the street a few houses and went into a nice-looking home. As soon as I walked in the front door, I seen the same thing as in the first house. I walked in and went into the living room, and it looked like someone had ransacked the place looking for something."

Mackenzie and Patrick were enthralled with the story and sat perfectly still except when Patrick had to stand up to throw more wood on the fire or adjust the pot of water warming next to it.

"I really wish that I would have taken my rifle with me," Stuart said. "I was super freaked out by then and wasn't sure what to do. I dug through the day pack that you'd given me and I found that belt knife in there. I at least felt a little better when I had it ready."

Patrick asked Stuart to hold on for a minute while he prepared the oatmeal from the boiling water and gave it to him in another bowl.

Stuart had a couple of bites and then continued on with the story, "Even though my foot was killing me, I decided to walk up to the big hotel on top of the hill since something wasn't right with the houses. I was cold enough that I had to find some place to get out of the wind and crash for the night, but the hike up the hill was terrible. I don't know how long it took me, but I was froze to death and didn't think that I could take another step on my foot by the time that I got there."

Stuart took a few seconds to finish the oatmeal and Patrick took the opportunity to tend to the fire. Mackenzie sat wrapped in the sleeping bag trying to take all in the adventure that her friend had just been on.

Stuart sat the empty bowl of oatmeal down and continued with the story. "I had a heck of a time even getting into the hotel. It's not huge, but it's big for a town this size. It had three different buildings to it, but they all had their exterior doors locked except for the main entrance. There were several bodies in the lobby and the hallways. I couldn't see really well from just the glow light and was just wanting to find a place to crash, so I didn't check them out too close. I went down the hallway and tried to get into a room, but I didn't have much with me to break in and didn't get too far. I tried a couple others and then gave up trying to break into the doors. There was a huge laundry room about halfway down the hall that had a ton of sheets in the machines, so I just emptied the dryers out, piled the sheets in a corner and flopped down into the pile to sleep."

Mackenzie asked "There weren't any bodies in the laundry room?"

Stuart replied "Yeah; there was a maid near the door, but I was so tired and cold that I didn't think much of it."

"So why did you come back tonight then?" Patrick asked.

"There's something over there," Stuart said. His response hung in the air for a minute.

"What do you mean?" Patrick asked.

"There's something alive over there," Stuart said clearly afraid and not sure how to explain what he saw. He shifted in the sleeping bag showing that he was visibly uncomfortable. "I was dead asleep in that pile of sheets when I heard a huge bang that woke me up with a start. At first I thought that it was a gun shot, but a couple of seconds later it banged again and I could tell that it wasn't a gunshot. It happened a few more times before I could talk myself into going and checking it out. By the time that I got to the hallway it had stopped completely. I stood there for a minute and was about to go back to the pile of sheets when it scared the crap out of me."

Stuart took another drink of his water, but his hand was shaking somewhat as he was recalling the memory to his traveling companions. Mackenzie slid one hand out from her sleeping bag and held his wrist of his free hand in a friendly gesture.

Stuart looked at Mackenzie for a second before taking a deep breath and continuing. "There's a huge window in the hallway that goes almost from the floor to the ceiling about fifteen feet away from the doorway to the laundry room that I was standing in. Just when I thought I was going back to bed, a creature slammed itself into the window and made the huge boom that I'd been hearing."

"What did you do?" Mackenzie asked bewildered and aghast.

"At first I jumped out of my skin. Then I just froze and stood there watching it," Stuart finished.

There was a slight pause while Stuart reflected on the image that was burned into his memory and the other two were trying to imagine themselves in the hotel. Patrick asked "What do you mean it was a creature? Like a big dog or a bear?"

"No. It was almost... human," Stuart said.

"How so?" Patrick asked.

"It was really hard to see through the window into the darkness, but after it hit the window and I jumped; it looked right at me. I had the glow light with me that was dimming, but it must have been enough for it to see me because it looked right into my eyes." Stuart paused as he was picturing the creature and trying to explain what he had seen. "The eyes were human. There's no doubt about it; but the way that it moved just wasn't right. It was hunched over, and it had long hair on its head that made it hard to see anything in the darkness."

"Are you sure about what you saw son?" Patrick asked. "You were exhausted, cold, and just woke up to a loud banging."

"Yeah," Stuart said without hesitation. "There's no doubt about it. After we locked eyes, the thing backed up and ran at the window again; but this time it was even more determined and hit it even faster and harder than before. I had been frozen where I was, but when I saw it hurl itself at the glass and heard that boom; I moved. I ran back into the laundry room, grabbed the day pack, and threw the glow stick in the pile of sheets. The creature was crazy and the pounding was twice as quick as it was before: BOOM... BOOM... ...BOOM."

Patrick suddenly had a chill at the thought of this boy and what he had saw, and stood up to put some more wood on the fire. Stuart took another drink of water as he waited for Patrick to sit back down. Mackenzie and Patrick couldn't think of anything to say to comfort Stuart, but just waited for him to continue.

"Sore foot or not, I ran. As soon as I could tell that the creature had backed away from the window for another run at it, I ran down the hall way and back towards the front door. Even though I was running, my foot was still messed up and slowing me down. It felt like I was running in slow motion; slogging through maple syrup as I heard the booms continuing." Stuart made his arms move like he was running in slow motion as he told this part of his story. "And then…" he smacked his two hands together out in front of him with his arms extended. "As I came into the lobby, I tripped over something and face planted right on the hard tile floor. I hit hard enough that it rang my bell for a second," he said as he reached up and gingerly touched a red spot on the side of his forehead that Patrick and Mackenzie hadn't previously noticed. "The next BOOM brought me to my senses, and I realized that I had tripped over a dead-guy's boot and his face was like right there." Stuart raised his palm up to just a couple of inches in front of his face. Mackenzie shivered and drew her hand back into her sleeping bag.

Stuart's tempo got faster as he continued with the story. "So, I got up and sprinted out the front door. That creature kept it up for a while, because I could still hear thuds as I ran down the hill back towards town. I didn't stop anywhere and just made a beeline for the boat that I'd seen earlier. I had to crack another glow stick and catch my breath some when I made it to the boat, but I didn't take long. I drug and pushed it on the trailer down to the river, which ended up being a lot easier than I thought. It took me a little while to figure out how to get it off the trailer in the dark, but I managed. Once I got into the water and off shore, I realized how wiped out I was. It seemed like it took forever to paddle across the river."

After a couple of seconds, it was clear that Stuart was done with the story. Patrick stood up, walked over to Stuart, and leaned down to put his hand on Stuart's shoulder. "I'm sorry that you had to go through that. I should have insisted on going instead of you." Stuart started to protest, but Patrick shushed him and continued. "Mak and I have a ton of questions for you, but right now why don't you go crawl in my tent in that warm bag and get some sleep. You're wore out and frazzled."

"I don't think that I could go to sleep if I tried," Stuart replied. "I'm so wired that I don't think I'll sleep for a week."

"Well," Patrick started. "Why don't you try anyways? At least rest your body so you don't catch a cold."

Mackenzie reached out from her sleeping bag again and patted his arm. "My Dad's right, why don't you go lay down at least for a while," she said.

Stuart somewhat reluctantly got up and hobbled into Patrick's tent. Patrick helped him lay down and get situated before returning to the fire and sitting down next to his daughter where Stuart had been. He hadn't any sooner sat down and crossed his legs before they heard light snoring coming from the tent. They looked at each other and chuckled a little bit.

"What do you think it was Dad?" Mackenzie asked.

"I don't know," Patrick replied.

"You believe him don't you?" she asked.

"Yeah. I believe that he believes what he saw," Patrick said staring into the fire.

The two sat in silence for a while as the sun started to come up and a magnificent dawn came into view.

PART 3 -
THE
VOYAGE

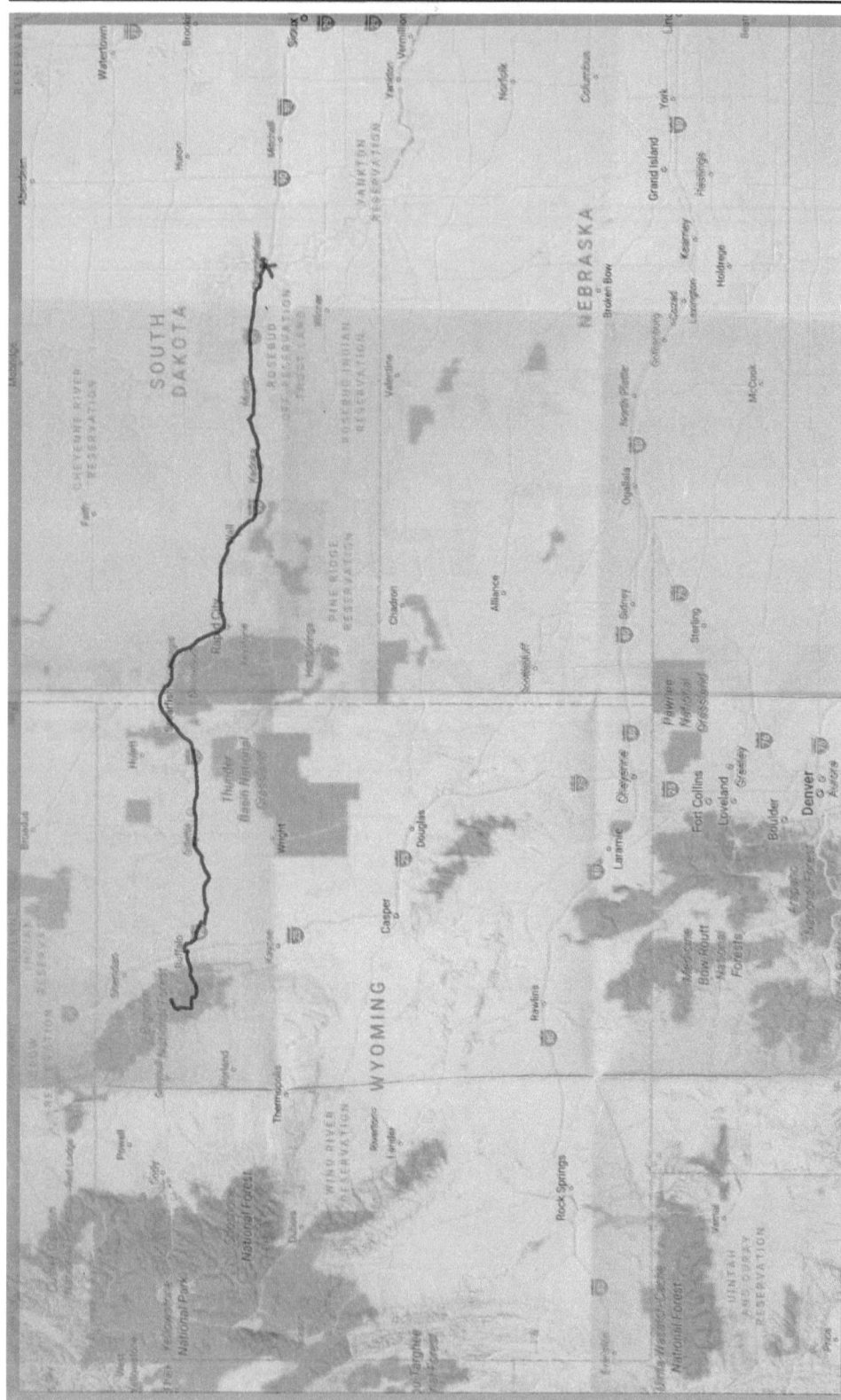

CHAPTER 17

THE BOAT THAT Stuart picked out was perfect for the three of them and their gear. Patrick and Mackenzie spent the morning stowing their gear and lashing their bikes down to the boat while Stuart slept. They both just milled around and waited until Stuart finally awoke in the midafternoon. They finished breaking camp and all gathered in the boat for the next leg of their trek.

Stuart sat in the middle seat with Makenzie's sleeping bag around him. He still was not feeling well at all and looked exhausted. Mackenzie was in the front seat of the boat rowing from the bow and Patrick was in the rear of the boat paddling some but mostly steering. They weren't in any hurry as there was a light current in the river that pulled them along slowly.

Stuart used one of the set of binoculars to peer up at the town and the hotel until it was totally out of site. Patrick and Mackenzie both had a ton more questions about Stuart's adventure, but his somber mood since waking didn't seem to be conducive to a lot of questions. They pretty much floated down the river in quiet reflection.

When it was near dusk, Patrick began guiding the boat over to a small campground along the shore. When they were almost to the campground, Stuart realized what they were planning and stammered "Not here!"

"What do you mean," asked Patrick.

"Not here!" Stuart blurted. "You can't be serious! We can't stay on this side of the river!"

Patrick still wasn't sure what Stuart was talking about until Mackenzie said "It's the creature Dad. He wants to camp on the south side of the river."

Patrick thought about arguing because the campground was setup for what they needed and there were probably some supplies close by, but he thought better of it. He could see the fear in Stuart's eyes and didn't think that it was worth it. Instead he steered the boat back into the river and closer to the other bank. There weren't any good places to pitch a tent in the area, so they drifted on down the river without saying a word until it was almost dark.

They rounded a small bend in the river and found a good camping spot. The bend had caused silt and sand to build up on a bump-out on the corner that made a beach up to the bluffs along the bank. They guided the boat into the sand along the beach and made a quick impromptu camp as the final light of the sun waned. Patrick broke out the camp stove and was beginning to setup to make some freeze-dried beef and noodles when Stuart announced that he still didn't feel well and was going to bed.

"Are you sure that you don't want anything to eat?" Mackenzie asked him.

"Nah. I'm not sure that I could keep it down," Stuart replied. "I think that I'm just going to crash for a while and see if I feel better in the morning."

Patrick and Mackenzie took their warm dinner over to a set of rocks on the bluff overlooking the river to eat. The moon was out and they could make out the river and some of the wildlands around it from there. Patrick reminded himself to come back at sunrise as he imagined it would be a beautiful sight.

"We need to get some more supplies," Patrick said in between bites of noodles.

"Since we're in the boat and don't have to pack as light, can we get some non-freeze dried stuff?" Mackenzie asked.

"Sure. That's a great idea," Patrick said. "I'm sure that we won't find a gourmet dinner in cans, but it sure would be a change of pace." After a few more bites, he added "I'm down to the last can of fuel for the stove, so we need to find a town big enough to have a store with camping supplies."

"Do you think that he can hear us from here?" Mackenzie asked in a lower tone as she was finishing up her bowl of noodles.

Patrick looked back over his shoulder towards Stuart's tent to gage the distance and shook his head no. "Not if we keep our voices down," he said in a low tone as well.

"I'm worried about him Dad," Mackenzie said. "He's not the same guy."

"Give him some time," Patrick responded. "Whatever he saw, or thought he saw over there has him pretty buggered up."

"Do you believe his story?" Mackenzie asked.

"I believe that he thinks that he saw something," Patrick said. "It's just a pretty tall order to believe it verbatim."

"I believe it," Mackenzie said flatly.

Patrick thought for a moment and then said "Then we should take shifts staying guard tonight. I'll take the first one. Why don't you go to bed?"

Mackenzie thought about it a few moments more and then said "Goodnight" before kissing her dad on the cheek and walking back to her tent.

Patrick went back to the tent and grabbed his AR and his sleeping bag, and brought them back over to the rock where they had eaten dinner and settled in for the night. He wasn't really expecting any issues, so he let his mind run rampant thinking about his family, what they should do next, their route home, and Stuart's story. The longer that he sat there, the less he was sure of what they should do. He just knew that they had to get home. Dawn was breaking before Patrick heard a tent unzip and Mackenzie came out to spell him.

"Why didn't you wake me up? I thought we were taking shifts," Mackenzie said still sleepy, but half perturbed.

"Yeah. I probably should have; I'm wiped out. I was just out here thinking," Patrick said as he was getting up from the ground and realizing how stiff he was from sitting there all night.

"Go get some rest," Mackenzie said as she hugged her dad with one arm as he was walking by her.

Mackenzie climbed up on the rock and watched the sunrise over the river. It was so beautiful that she was mesmerized by the sight until the strong colors left the sky and the sun was well above the horizon. She went and grabbed the book that she was reading and came back to the rock. She could already hear her dad snoring as she flipped open to the page that she had dog-eared. She never was much of an avid reader, but she really enjoyed this book that her dad found for her. He had said that it was a classic, which didn't immediately appeal to her but after she had started reading it she realized how good it was and why it was a classic. Even though she normally drifted right into the story and could block out the immediate happenings around her, this morning she couldn't. After several pages, her mind kept wandering to the rest of her family back home; and then sometimes to the creature that Stuart had described. She wanted to ask him so many more questions about that creature that had terrified him.

After sitting on the rock a little while longer, she decided that she needed to have some physical activity. She knew that her dad would probably kill her for even thinking of such a thing, but she thought that she might go check around for supplies and maybe even find a place to clean up a little. She walked back to camp and found the binoculars that Stuart had been using the previous day. She scanned the horizon and didn't see much of anything as far as civilization, other than a few farm houses some ways off on the other side of the river.

She steeled her nerves, grabbed her dad's AR rifle and backpack, and headed down to the river. She loaded up in the small boat and pushed herself off into the wide river. After getting settled in on the middle seat and beginning to row, she thought that she might have bitten off more than she could chew. The river was moving very slowly, but it still moved her off the direction that she was shooting for. She eventually figured out how far upstream that she needed to aim for to make the landing place on the opposite bank that she was hoping for.

It took her longer than she had anticipated, but she eventually landed the boat on the other side of the river where there was a slightly overgrown dirt road that came down close to the water's edge. She jumped out of the boat and pulled it up onto the bank as far as she could get it before unlashing her bike and pulling it out. With the backpack and rifle slung across her back, she walked the bicycle up the dirt path to the road that she had seen with the binoculars from the campsite. She gave one last look back to the campsite to make sure that Stuart or her dad weren't up and around yet before she took off pedaling down the dirt road.

It was mid-morning and beginning to warm up. Mackenzie felt herself start to sweat as she stood up on the pedals and pumped her legs in a quick rhythm as her bike flew down the bumpy dirt road. She had never really enjoyed bike riding all that much before this trip, but after sitting around in camp and in the boat all day yesterday the physical exertion felt great.

It wasn't long before the slight incline that she had been climbing since the river turned into level ground. She could tell that all the ground around here was typically farmed. Even though it was fallow now, she imagined that it normally held rows and rows of corn in the summer. Before long, the dirt road she was on turned into a graveled road at an intersection. She continued straight through the intersection the same way as she had been traveling, but now she sat back down on the seat as the road was a little smoother and easier to ride on.

After a mile or so of passing open fields just waiting for someone to plant them, she saw the farm houses she was expecting up ahead. As she got closer, she realized that the houses were two houses on either side of the road, with several small buildings and barns scattered about them. Neither of the houses were extravagant or very large, but the one on the left side of the road up ahead looked like it might be a little bigger. She continued to check them out as she approached and decided to try out the house on the left first as the driveway was the first one she came to on the gravel road.

As she turned into the driveway and slowly pedaled down the graveled way, she passed an older tin garage or shop that most likely housed tractors and such. Up ahead there was a huge cottonwood tree that dominated the front of the older white-washed two story farm house. The tree had an old tire swing hanging from the main branch that stretched out and seemed to cover the length of the open front yard. Mackenzie road her bike onto the unkempt grass and over to the large tree. She dismounted and leaned her bike against the tree while inspecting the front of the farm house. The house needed a paint job, but overall looked like it was well-maintained. The white paint on the front porch and around the windows of the second floor was flaking and peeling in several places.

Mackenzie took the AR off from around her back and flipped the safety off. She was proud of herself coming this far without the others, but now she was getting nervous. The weight of the rifle was a little too much for her and she struggled holding it out in front of her as she walked slowly towards the front door. She walked slowly and was intently listening for any odd sounds. She could feel her heart beating faster than it should have been as she took slow steps up the front steps and onto the covered porch that ran the length of the house. When she reached the screen door, she stood there for several seconds just listening and tried to gather the courage to move forward.

She used the barrel of the rifle to knock on the door. After listening intently and not hearing anything other than her own heartbeat, she knocked louder and hollered out "Hello!"

After a few silent seconds, she reached out and opened the screen door that made an awful screech when it was pulled open. She hollered one more time before turning the knob on the front door and stepping inside. The windows let in plenty of light in the mid-morning sun and the scene was pretty much just as Mackenzie had pictured it. A living room with a TV and a few out-dated chairs and sofa was just off the main entrance, and a set of stairs in the middle of the house prominently separated the living room from a country kitchen with plain cabinets that was in the opposite corner of the first floor. The little place was somewhat cluttered, but was relatively clean and well cared for.

Mackenzie made her way to the kitchen and started going through the cabinets to see what food stuffs she could find. Since they had the boat now, she didn't have to limit her search to freeze dried items. She got excited when she found a box of macaroni and cheese along with some evaporated milk. She also found some cans of various soups and even a couple of cans of ravioli's that she was sure would bring a smile to Stuarts eyes.

At the edge of the kitchen was a narrow door that Mackenzie opened. It led to a set of stairs with very narrow runners that went down into darkness. She started to close the door, and then remembered her Aunt Heidi's root cellar. Her aunt lived on a small country farm in Nebraska, where Mackenzie had gone and stayed for a couple of weeks every summer. Her aunt canned every fall, and always had food stored down in the root cellar. Mackenzie dug through the backpack and found a single glow light. She snapped it, shook it up, and put the string around her neck so she could carry the rifle easier. She took a deep breath to steady her nerves, then crept down the narrow stairway towards a hope of good food. Each stair seemed to creak louder than the last one as she slowly made her way down to the bottom. She could only see a few feet in front of her, but knew that she was all the way down when she stepped on bare earth.

This farm house had a true root cellar where the ground and walls were mainly just dirt. The room she was in, wasn't much bigger than her bedroom back home, but the walls covered from dirt floor to rafter ceiling with cans upon cans of food. Mackenzie allowed herself to give a little fist pump before closely inspecting the mason jars for their contents. Each one had been painstakingly labeled with what was in it and the date that it was canned.

She went through and found tomatoes, corn, pickles, jams, green beans, and anything else you could imagine canning on those shelves. Mackenzie cracked open a jar of dill pickles and ate through at least half of it as she was holding the glow light up to the shelves trying to decide what she wanted. She could tell that after only filling up the back pack half full that she wasn't going to be able to grab as much as she had hoped because it was already almost too heavy for her to carry. She grabbed a few more jars of what she thought Stuart and her dad might like best and closed the back-pack up tight. It took several minutes for her to figure out how to lift the heavy pack and get it onto her back. She grabbed a jar of blackberry jam and the rifle, and headed up the stairs. The stairs groaned even more on her trip back up to the kitchen, but they held out just the same. Once in the kitchen, she sat the backpack down harder than she meant to and winced at the sound of the jars clanging together. She didn't have the heart to look in it to see which jars hadn't survived. Instead she headed to the kitchen drawers and opened a few of them until she found where the spoons were stored and grabbed one. She broke open the jar of blackberry jam and dug straight into it. She couldn't help her eyes from rolling back into her head as the strong bitter and sweet flavors from the jam rolled around on her tongue. It was unbelievable. She would have eaten a jar of it on biscuits or toast normally, but as it was she was content to eat it straight from the jar. She had a couple more heaping spoonfuls of the nectar before being able to move about.

She slung the rifle over her shoulder and headed up the stairs still spooning blackberry jam into her mouth as she walked. At the top of the stairs there was a hallway with several doors in it. The only open door was at the end of the hallway, and it clearly led to the largest bedroom. Mackenzie gingerly walked down the hallway and peered into the room. As she suspected, there appeared to be two bodies lying in the bed. She quietly closed the bedroom door and walked back down the hallway. She opened the next door and found what she was looking for. It was a small bathroom with a cast iron tub and a small window near the top of the ceiling just above the tub that let enough light in to see. She tried the sink faucet, but as was normal in this new world, it just let out a little water before hissing and guffing, and then finally falling silent.

Mackenzie had an idea and sat her jar of jam down on the bathroom counter top with the end of the spoon sticking out from it. Then she left the bathroom and began skipping down the stairs. She didn't stop in the living room and shuffled right out onto the porch. Her excitement grew as she saw the hydrant in the middle of the front yard that she had thought she remembered seeing there when she leaned her bike against the tree. She leapt off the porch and started jogging over to the middle of the yard when the screen door made a loud 'swap' sound behind her as it most likely had done ten thousand times before. The sound startled her and brought her back to reality just before she reached the hydrant.

The hydrant was an old hand pump that had been painted black, and didn't look like it had been used in quite some time. Her hopes were dashed when she reached it and tried to pull up on the handle, but it wouldn't budge. She let out a deep breath and half-heartedly kicked the pump at its base. When the pump rocked slightly, she seen the handle move somewhat. She took the rifle from her back and laid it on the ground next to the pump. She tried lifting the handle again, except this time she put everything she had into it. The handle slowly began to raise and she heard a slight sucking sound coming out of the hydrant. Once the handle was at the top, she jumped up and put all her weight on top of the handle. She began to work the handle up and down, again and again. It slowly loosened up and became easier to operate. Mackenzie was hearing more and more sounds coming out of the pump that gave her hope as she began to breathe hard and felt herself sweating again. Just when the pump was getting somewhat easy to move up and down, water gushed out of the spout. She pumped it a few more times just to make sure, and clear water spewed out of the hydrant's mouth.

She ran to the large barn that was around the side of the house without picking the rifle back up. When she got there, she found the remains of several animals laying in the pens and around the outside of the barn. She tried to ignore the animals as she looked around for something to hold water in. She quickly spotted a large metal pail and a plastic bucket that she scooped up and jogged back to the hydrant with. It didn't take long and she had filled both containers up and walked them into the house to fill the tub in the upstairs bathroom. After about five trips, Mackenzie was exhausted and the tub was full.

Even though she was excited to use some of the soaps, shampoos, and scrubs that she had found in the bathroom, she almost changed her mind altogether when she stepped into the frigid water. She stood there for several seconds before she heard her teeth start to chatter.

"This is stupid," she said to herself and quickly sat down in the cold water. After sitting there for a few moments, she decided it wasn't as bad as she had thought it might be and decided to stick it out. She leaned back against the tub and reached for the blackberry jam.

Mackenzie spent the rest of the morning soaking, scrubbing, and eating the jam in the tub. Just when she was thinking that she had to get out before she was totally shriveled, she heard the screen door downstairs slam. Mackenzie's stomach immediately jumped up into her throat and all her muscles tightened. It had made the same 'swap' sound as it had with every trip she had made in and out with the buckets of water.

She looked around the room for the rifle and sheer terror filled her when she realized that she had left it on the ground next to the hydrant in the front yard. She didn't know what to do. She just laid quietly in the tub and listened for any sound that would tell her what was going on, but she heard nothing. After a few minutes, she sat up and pulled the curtain around the tub so that she could hide behind it if anyone came up the stairs and into the bathroom.

She continued to sit there and listen long enough that she began to doubt that she had heard the screen door slam in the first place. She decided that she couldn't lay in the tub indefinitely, and had to get out at some point. She began to move and slowly stood up in the tub. She stood there for several seconds taking shallow breaths and listening for any sounds. She stepped out of the tub moving ever so slowly, but the floor board beneath her foot squeaked regardless. Immediately afterwards, she heard what sounded like glass breaking from somewhere on the floor below.

She tiptoed quickly over to the bathroom door and turned the lock on the doorknob. She gathered up her clothes from the floor in one pile and stood there quietly listening. In a few moments, she heard something softly coming up the stairs. Then she heard it quietly shuffling down the hallway, getting closer to the bathroom. She just stood there in the center of the bathroom with her clothes in her hands trying not to breathe loudly or make any kind of sound.

Whatever it was reached the bathroom door and stopped. She heard it touch the door, then heard what sounded like it was trying to smell something from around the edges. Then it put its head to the floor and was smelling underneath the door. It was becoming more excited and agitated as it continued to take in big snorts of air, trying to smell whatever it liked on Mackenzie's side of the door.

Mackenzie stood motionless and utterly quiet. She closed her eyes and wished for her dad. She was pushing her will out to him, begging for him to come save her from whatever creature was on the other side of that door.

Suddenly, the smelling and snorting stopped. She didn't dare make a sound. She continued to stand as quietly as she could in the middle of the bathroom with her now soaked clothes pressed up against her. Her breathing was so controlled and quiet that she couldn't even hear it, but she was petrified that the creature on the other side of the door could hear her heart beating. It was pounding inside her ears and she was sure that it was loud enough for someone else to hear.

WHAM! Whatever was outside the bathroom door had just decided that it wanted what smelled so good on the inside of the bathroom and had hit the door hard enough that it rocked on its hinges. Mackenzie let out a startled yelp after the noise, and she involuntarily lifted her hand to her open mouth to silence anything else that might try to come out.

After another couple seconds of quiet, the creature slammed into the door again. This time it was harder than the last, and Mackenzie seen the door jamb begin to splinter where the hinges were.

Mackenzie didn't know what she should do, but she knew that she had to do something. She put her underwear and t-shirt on just as the thing hit the door again.

She looked up to the small window above the tub, and even though it looked impossibly small and high for her to reach and get through; she knew she had to try. She put her feet on the sides of the wet tub and straddled it enough to reach her finger tips up to the window ledge just as the creature slammed into the door again. This time after it hit, it let out a low groan from the other side of the door that sounded like a man in pain.

She got fingers and palms from both hands over onto the window ledge and pulled herself up high enough to see the window. The window was designed to slide sideways and there was no latch on it luckily. She let herself back down and reached up with one hand to try and open the window.

WHAM! Mackenzie looked over her shoulder and seen that this time, the door had physically moved such that one of the top corners of the door hadn't closed all the way back into the doorway.

One of her nails caught on the edge of the window, and it slid open a few inches. She took a couple of deep breaths and pulled herself up with all her might. She pulled herself high enough for her to put one hand through the window and grab the outside of the house just as the creature hit the door again and let out another loud moan.

She pulled and worked her arm through the window until it was up to her armpit. She pushed again, and with one big heave the window slid open even more. She was pushing against the wall with her feet and edged her head through the opening. The afternoon sun was bright compared to the dimly lit bathroom and it was difficult to see anything, but she was sure that there was no ledge from up here.

She managed to get her other hand and then arm out of the window. She wriggled back and forth through the tiny opening until her waist was balancing in the open window. She wasn't sure what to do from this position as she couldn't turn over and there was nothing to grab a hold of on the clapboard siding. Just then, the creature hit the door again and came crashing into the room. Its momentum carried it across the room and into the tub.

Mackenzie heard the commotion and felt something dig at her left leg that was dangling in the open window. Her fear of the creature took over her fear of falling and she tried to push herself free from the window opening. Both of her feet caught in the upstairs window as she tumbled down. She hit her left shoulder into the house on the way down before landing on her right side in the grass just next to the house.

It took a second for the pain to hit and the cobwebs to leave her after she landed. She opened her eyes and seen the shape of a man's head and shoulders looking out of the upstairs window. It took another second for her to realize that the creature was no longer looking out the window, and then her adrenaline kicked in. She sprung to her feet only slightly aware of the pain in her shoulder and sprinted around the side of the house. Not seeing anything as she rounded the corner, she continued to sprint towards the middle of the yard where the rifle lay on the ground next to the water hydrant.

When she was half-way to the pump, the creature bounded out of the front door and the screen door made a loud swap again. It stopped to look around for a split second before seeing Mackenzie darting across the grass. Its eyes locked with hers and it took off in a path that would intercept with hers just about where the rifle lay. The creature was much faster than Mackenzie and she pumped her legs as hard as they would go. The creature looked like young man, but it didn't run or move like a human. It bounded with rolled over shoulders much like a large animal.

Mackenzie reached the hydrant a split second before the creature, and she slid in the wet grass just like she was sliding into second base. She snagged the rifle as she slid, somewhat shouldered the stock, and pulled the trigger in three quick successive pulls. The man-creature was so close that it didn't matter if she aimed or not, and all three shots hit him at different locations in the torso. The creature let out a loud moan, slowed, and then stood straight up. Mackenzie pulled the rifle all the way up to her shoulder and aimed at the creature's head as her slide came to a stop.

"Stoooop!" she screamed at the thing in front of her.

The creature's bewilderment at the holes in its torso quickly left when it heard Mackenzie scream, and its eyes locked back on hers and it took a step forward. Mackenzie dispatched it quickly with a round to the forehead that knocked it backwards before it crumpled.

Mackenzie was instinctively on her feet with the rifle trained on the creature. As she looked at it she realized that it was a man. Or at least it had been. It was undoubtedly a human, although it didn't appear to be solely human. Its flesh was almost white with a green undertone, and there were black open wounds on its face and all along its exposed parts of its arms. The wounds looked almost as if the flesh was rotting right on the body.

Mackenzie shot two more times into its shoulder and upper chest, then turned her head and violently vomited blackberry jam all over the lawn. She wiped her mouth with the back of her hand and turned back towards the creature. She was sure that the image of that thing lying in the grass would forever be burned into her memory, but she somehow struggled to look away from the creature. The creature's body was lying in a heap with its back arched and its legs bent behind it. Wherever the man-thing's skin was exposed, its dark veins shown through its semi-transparent white flesh.

She slung the rifle over her shoulder and ran back into the house. She grabbed her back pack and hefted it onto her back. The creature must have been down in the root cellar getting food the same as she had been, because there really was no sign that it had been in the house other than the door to the cellar being left open.

She walked as fast as she could back out of the house and back to her bike. She tried not to look at the creature as she walked by, but she couldn't resist herself from staring at it one more time. She swung her leg over her bike and headed back down the driveway, and then down the gravel road back towards the boat. This time she stayed standing as she wanted to put as much distance between her and that thing as possible; and she had not bothered to go get her shorts, so the seat was uncomfortable in her underwear.

As she left the gravel road and started down the dirt path back towards the river, she saw a large shape coming towards her from the direction of where she had landed the boat. She skidded the bike to a stop and unslung the rifle from around her back. By the time she shouldered the gun and looked down the open sights, she recognized the shape as unquestionably her dad on his bicycle heading towards her. She put the rifle back on across her back and headed towards him.

They were still a hundred feet or more from each other when she heard him start yelling at her. "Just what in the world do you think you're doing?" he yelled. As they got closer to each other and he realized that she was half-naked and her shoulder was bleeding profusely, his tone turned from anger to worry. "What happened? Are you okay?" he asked.

She stopped just in front of him and said "I'm okay Dad. We have to get out of here." She stood back up on the pedals and headed towards the boat.

"What's going on?" Patrick asked, more worried than before. "What happened?" he asked as he turned his bike around and followed after her.

Mackenzie reached the boat first and slung her backpack and the rifle onboard. Patrick was right behind her and put both bikes on the boat as she climbed on board. He pushed them off and climbed into the middle seat with the oars.

When they were almost half-way across the river, Patrick stopped rowing and lifted Mackenzie's chin with his hand so that he could look into her eyes. "What happened? Where did you go?" he asked her gently. She started crying, then began to sob. She knelt forward and put both arms around him and they held each other in that embrace as they slowly drifted down the river.

When the sobbing stopped, Mackenzie leaned back and sat in the front seat facing her dad. "I'll tell you about it when we get back to camp, so I don't have to tell it a second time to Stuart," Mackenzie said.

"You sure you're all right?" Patrick asked her.

"I think so," she said as she started inspecting her shoulder. This was the first that she realized that there was a deep gash on the front of her left shoulder a good inch or two long.

Patrick began to paddle back to camp and Mackenzie dipped her hand into the river and scooped water out to put into the wound on her shoulder.

Once back to camp, Patrick helped Mackenzie out of the boat and grabbed her backpack. Stuart had come down to the edge of the river with a sleeping bag wrapped around him. When Mackenzie got to him, she hugged him tightly and he wrapped the sleeping bag around her as they walked back to the tents. Stuart coughed a few times on the way back and he clearly wasn't feeling well.

"Let me get that first aid kit before you start your story," Patrick said as he headed into his tent. After a few moments he came back out with what he wanted and sat down in front of his daughter.

"Okay, now let's hear it," he said as he began to clean up and bandage the wound on her shoulder. She told the story front to back and by the time she was done, the sun was beginning to set. Stuart walked over, opened the back pack, and rifled through it. He found a large jar of pickles, opened it, stuck one in his mouth, and offered the jar to the other two who declined.

Patrick leaned in and hugged his daughter. They both cried for a few minutes and Patrick told her "I'm glad you're okay Darlin'."

"So they're zombies huh?" Stuart asked. "I wouldn't have guessed that from the one that I saw."

"I don't think that they're zombies," Mackenzie said sounding somewhat offended by the comment.

"Sure sounds like it," Stuart said.

"The creature that I saw had definitely been human, but I don't think that he was dead. I definitely wouldn't have even thought to have called him a zombie before you said that," Mackenzie said sure with surety.

"You said that it looked sick. That he moaned. That his flesh was rotting from his bones. Sure sounds like a zombie to me," Stuart said.

"It wasn't a zombie, alright? I know that I said those things, and the way that you say it; it does sound like a zombie, but it just wasn't okay?" Mackenzie said. Her voice was rising and she was becoming agitated at Stuart's insistence.

"Hey," Patrick said to Stuart. "Back off."

Stuart took the hint and didn't say anything more, but fished another pickle from the jar instead. Mackenzie couldn't let it go though. "No. No, it wasn't a zombie. He moved more like an ape. Powerful and fast, not like a corpse ready to fall over," she said almost to herself.

"It's okay Darlin'. If you say that it wasn't a zombie, it wasn't a zombie," Patrick said to her. Then to Stuart he said "You can just claim those pickles for your own." Stuart coughed as he fished a third pickle out of the jar.

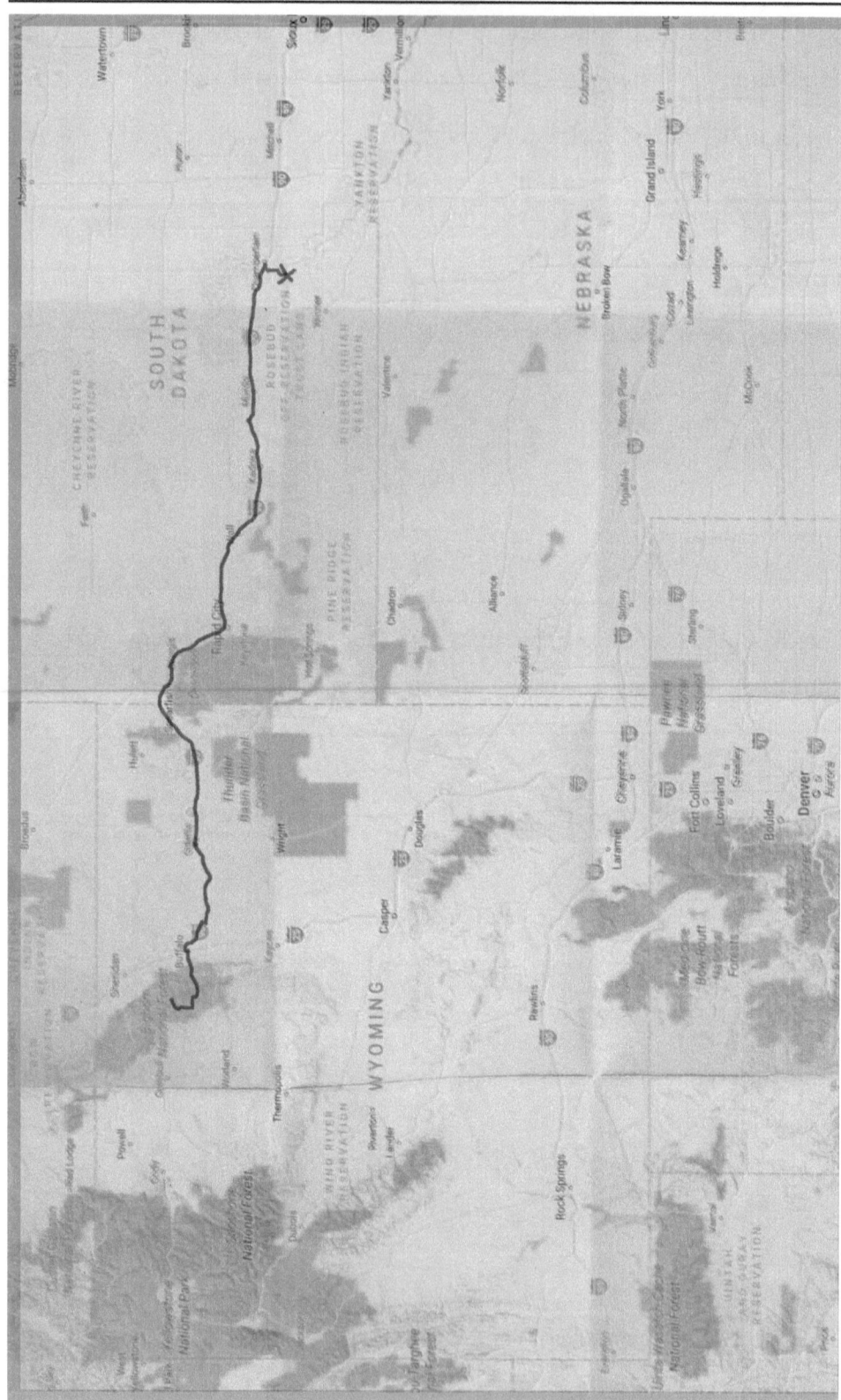

CHAPTER 18

HIS DAUGHTER'S BLOOD curdling scream woke him from his sleep. Patrick grabbed his belt knife from the side of his pillow and jumped to his feet slicing through the side of the tent in one fluid motion. Mackenzie's tent was just two steps from where he was standing and after seeing nothing out of the ordinary from the moonlight, he leapt forward and unzipped her tent. He could see her clearly sitting upright in her sleeping bag with her hands over her face. His mind flashed back to those nights when she was younger and used to wander into their bedroom with the remnants of a bad dream still lingering.

He stepped in and sat down next to her. He put his arm around her and said "Shhhh…" Stuart stuck his head in the open tent doorway, and Patrick waved him off. "You want me to lay down with you for a while?" he asked. She just shook her head yes and laid back down.

Patrick got up and retrieved his sleeping bag through the man-sized gash in the side of his tent wall. Stuart came up to him before he reentered Mackenzie's tent. "She okay?" Stuart asked in a low voice, but with a real level of concern.

"I think so. She just had a bad dream," Patrick said. "You staying awake okay?" Stuart nodded and headed back over to the rocks where he could see out across the bend in the river. He coughed a few times on his way over and picked up his jar of pickles on the way.

Patrick climbed into Mackenzie's tent and laid his sleeping bag out next to hers before zipping the tent. He climbed into his bag and Mackenzie rolled over and snuggled tight to him. His mind was racing with the story that she had told him earlier, and his heart was breaking that she had to go through such a thing without him. He knew that he wasn't going to fall asleep again that night, and decided to just enjoy his daughter wanting to snuggle with her dad.

Stuart sat with his back to the large rock and his sleeping bag wrapped around him like a shawl. He munched on the last bite of the last pickle from the jar that Mackenzie had brought back with her. The pickles were awesome, and their sour juice soothed his sore throat. He felt a little selfish that he had eaten the whole jar, but they were good. He held the jar up to the moonlight and seen that there were pieces of dill, garlic, and other things floating and tossing around in the bottom of the jar. He braced himself, and then took a swig of the pickling juice. He flinched at first due to the strong taste, but then realized that he liked it just as good as he had the pickles. Maybe even better.

He felt bad. His body ached, his throat was sore, and he could feel something settling in his chest. He knew his cold wet walk across the bridge hadn't been good for him, but he was paying the price for it now. Stuart thought back to how Patrick had cared for him and waited on him all day, trying to make his day better. He knew that Patrick felt guilty for not crossing the bridge instead of Stuart, but Stuart could tell that it was more than that. He could tell that Patrick genuinely cared for him. Stuart didn't understand how someone could be so against him being gay, yet still care about how he felt.

Stuart also thought about the creature that Mackenzie had met. Mackenzie was a whole lot tougher than what Stuart had originally given her credit for. To have the guts to run for the rifle when that thing was headed straight towards her was something that Stuart didn't know if he would have had the courage for.

Stuart continued to think about Mackenzie's adventure. He thought about how Patrick had taken care of him all day, the burial that they gave his parents, and whatever else that he could think of to try and keep that image of that creature slamming into the window at the hotel out of his mind. No matter how hard he tried, every now and then when his mind would go idle he still saw that hairy thing leaping through the air towards the window and crashing into it.

After first light, Stuart wandered back to the camp and opened the backpack that Mackenzie had brought back with her. The thing must have weighed sixty pounds or more and was stuffed with mason jars and cans of food. As he was digging around in the pack, he heard the zipper on Mackenzie's tent open and he turned to find both Patrick and Mackenzie stiffly climbing out of the tent.

"Morning," Stuart said to both before digging back into the backpack.

"Hey," Patrick responded. "How you feeling?" he asked.

"Still kind of rough," Stuart said honestly.

"Oh, hey," Mackenzie said with some excitement in her voice as she came over beside Stuart. "I found something special for you," she said as she peered into the bag and shuffled jars around. She pulled out a metal can from the bottom of the bag and handed it to him.

Tears filled Stuart's eyes when he realized that it was a can of his favorite raviolis. He wasn't sure what the tears were about, but he leaned over and gave Mackenzie a big monster hug.

Patrick handed Stuart a spoon from his mess kit and said "You feel up to traveling? We were thinking that we should get down the river a ways and see if we can find a bigger town with some camping supplies." He pointed towards the side of his tent for emphasis. Part of the tent wall was flapping in the wind from the large gash up the middle of it.

Stuart smiled some and said "Yeah, I can hack it."

"What else you got in there kid?" Patrick asked Mackenzie.

After some digging in the backpack she pulled out a smaller jar; she smiled, and tossed it to her dad. "That stuff is good, but I don't think that I'll be able to stomach any for a while," she said as he read the label – 'Blackberry Jam'. They all chuckled and headed over to the rocks to watch the sunrise and eat some breakfast.

After breakfast, they packed up camp and stowed all their gear back on the boat. They left Patrick's wounded tent standing where they had set it up, and they all turned to look at it as they drifted down the river in the crowded boat. They sat in their familiar places with Mackenzie in the bow, Stuart in the middle seat, and Patrick bringing up the rear.

They drifted and rowed mostly in silence until the sun was nearly overhead. Patrick then broke out in a low and out of tune chorus of American Pie by Don McLean. Stuart joined in with him, just as low but much more in tune. Mackenzie joined in the tune for the few words that she knew, and they sang what they could remember of the song a few times through before it got old and they stopped.

"How can such a depressing song make you feel better?" Mackenzie asked.

"I don't know," Patrick answered. "That one just always did."

They drifted and rowed for the rest of the day without seeing towns of any kind along the river. Every few miles or so they would come across a campground or some dirt roads that would come down to the river's edge for access to a beach or a nice coolie for fishing, but other than that it was just the river. The river was beautiful. Green grass grew tall on both sides of the river, with sweeping hills breaking up the scenery on the horizon. If it hadn't been under such dire circumstances, Patrick probably would have spent a paycheck on taking a trip like this down the river with his daughter.

They camped on the south side of the river again as soon as the light started to fade. Patrick slept in Mackenzie's tent again with her even though it was somewhat crowded. They had a cold camp with no fire or stove; they just rested and were up again at dawn and back on the river. Patrick and Mackenzie took the watches, as Stuart was still not feeling well.

Patrick was beginning to worry about Stuart. The cough that he had was now settling in his lungs, and Patrick could tell that Stuart was beginning to lose strength. He was worried that his cold had turned into pneumonia or something worse that could end up really injuring the boy.

"Land Ho!" Mackenzie yelled and startled the other two passengers. She had been looking through the binoculars off and on all morning trying to spot somewhere that they could refresh their supplies, and now she was holding them up to her face while pointing at a spot on the horizon that neither of the two others could see.

"I don't think that is what that term is used for," Patrick said.

"I know Dad. I was being funny," Mackenzie said as she leaned back and handed the binoculars to her dad in the rear of the boat. "It looks like a larger town over there."

It took Patrick a couple of moments to find what Mackenzie was talking about as he panned the binoculars around in the direction that she had been pointing. After getting a good look at the town, he handed the binoculars to Stuart who just waved them off and showed no interest in looking through them.

"That town is quite a ways off," Patrick said.

"How far would you guess?" Mackenzie asked.

"I don't know," Patrick said pondering the distance. "It looks like it is at least a good three or four miles away I would say."

"We should be able to get there and back by lunch then wouldn't you think? There's a campground with a dock just up there a little ways," Mackenzie said pointing down the river. She turned in the boat to look at her dad to gage his expression and caught the glazed look of Stuart's feverish eyes instead. Her heart sank when she realized just how bad he was feeling. "Besides, we can look around for some medicine for Stuart," Mackenzie added. Without waiting for a response from her dad, she began paddling to the dock that she had spotted. Patrick didn't argue and started paddling with her after he set the binoculars down.

Patrick and Mackenzie pitched Stuart's tent on a small beach near the dock while he sat on a nearby picnic table with his sleeping bag wrapped around him. After he was laying down in the tent and they made sure that he was comfortable, they loaded up their bikes with their rifles and empty backpacks and took off up the paved road toward the town that Mackenzie had spotted. As they pulled away, they heard Stuart making a hollow and vibratory coughing sound that made them both cringe.

"Do you think that he'll be okay Dad?" Mackenzie asked when she was sure they were out of earshot.

"I don't know," Patrick replied. "Let's make this trip quick so we can get back to him, but we have to be careful and quiet. If we run onto anymore of your creatures, I would rather that they not even know that we're here."

THE HIKE

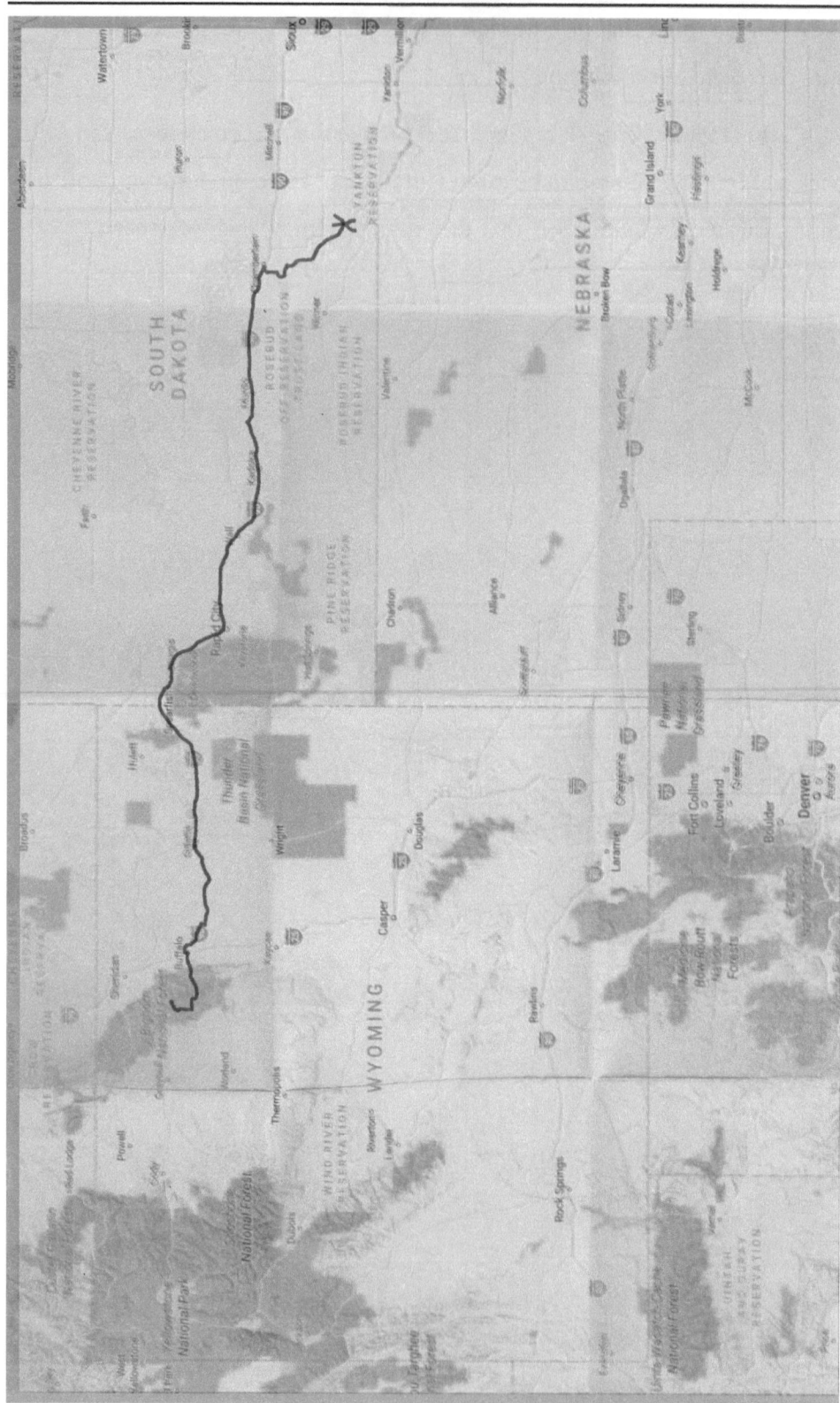

CHAPTER 19

AFTER THEY ARRIVED in the town of Idleville, they realized that it wasn't nearly as big as it had looked from the river. The population sign they saw as they pedaled past said 2,300 people, but the town didn't seem like it was near that large. There were two stoplights in town on the main street that looked like it had originally been built many years before. On one of the corners with the first stoplight was a rather large drug store. They had stopped well short of the intersection and looked over the whole area through their riflescopes and binoculars before approaching the drugstore. One of the large windows by the front door had been broken, and the inside of the store looked ransacked. Intact and broken items were strewn all about the aisles, and more than one of the large shelving units was tilted off its base.

"I don't like this Dad," Mackenzie said in a low voice.

Patrick looked over to his daughter and ruffled her hair with his hand as he had done when she was a small child. He then turned and made his way across the intersection alone while Mackenzie hid in a doorway near the bikes that were kitty corner from the drug store. Patrick had his AR locked and loaded as he briskly walked across the pavement. Mackenzie had her .22 at the ready and swiveled her head back and forth looking for any movement or anything else out of the ordinary. She caught herself holding her breath when her dad was a little more than half way across the street, and made herself exhale quietly.

Once Patrick reached the other side of the street, she could see him standing in front of the broken window for quite some time looking around in the store the best he could. He opened the door and went inside. Mackenzie thought that she heard something a few doors down to her right and immediately looked in that direction. She didn't see anything moving, but continued to stare in that direction. Her heart was pounding up in her throat now as she began to quickly shift her field of view back and forth from where her dad had just entered the drug store and where she thought she had heard a sound. She wasn't sure that she had heard anything. She felt the rifle shaking back and forth in her hands, and looked down to find her hands and arms shaking from nerves. By the time that her dad came back into view in the doorway, she had convinced herself that she had imagined the sound. He was waving for her to advance to the doorway. She looked one more time down the street to where she thought she might have heard the sound, then padded quickly across the street to the drug store.

The inside of the store was even worse than it appeared from looking through the broken window. There was cereal or something like it over the entire floor, glass and broken items were littered everywhere, and only a few of the wider aisles were clear enough to easily walk down. The light from upper windows on the two sides facing the streets let ample light in, that allowed

Mackenzie to see almost everywhere in the store. Besides the massive mess throughout the store, it looked like a hundred other corner drug stores in small towns that Mackenzie had been in or seen on television.

"I'll see if I can find some ibuprofen and antibiotics somewhere. You load up with food," Patrick whispered to her. She nodded her understanding and started to go down the aisle along the outside wall. "Oh!" Patrick said in a loud whisper and turned back towards her. "Look for anything that you think I could burn in the camp stove. I need some coffee." He gave her a slight grin before turning and heading towards the back corner of the store. He had to duck and hunch over to get below the tilted stand of shelves that bordered the aisle he was stepping into.

Mackenzie made her way along the outside wall of the store trying to see where they kept the food. The aisle was mainly makeup, fingernail polish, and other girly stuff that she was sure that she wasn't going to need anytime soon. Instead of following the outside wall all the way to the back of the store, she turned down a middle walk-way and slowly walked along the end caps peering down the aisles looking for anything that resembled food. The aisles were mostly like long caves with the shelving units tipped over and balancing like a row of half-sprung dominoes.

One end cap that she came to had large bags of chips on it, which looked promising. She just ducked into the aisle\cave when she heard her dad yell out for her, "MAK!"

She could tell by the sound of his voice that it was something serious. She bent over and mostly ran down the aisle that she had started down towards the back of the store where her dad's voice had come from. As she rounded the corner at the end, she seen her dad behind the pharmacy counter with his AR up and ready. They locked eyes for a split second before he fired off three quick shots down an aisle that Mackenzie couldn't see down.

The gunshots were deafening in the small store and it took a second for Mackenzie to realize that her dad was yelling for her to join him behind the counter. She hadn't ever seen that kind of fear in her dad's eyes before, so she dropped her empty backpack and sprinted for the open door thirty feet away that led to the pharmacy room where her dad was standing behind the service counter.

Halfway to the open door she passed an end cap full of toothbrushes on it just as her dad fired two more quick shots that exploded packages of toothbrushes all around her. Without slowing, she turned her head to look at what he had shot at so close to her, and she saw one of the creatures that somehow looked like the one she had encountered at the farm. This one had been a teenage girl, probably just a little older than Mackenzie. One of the shots Patrick had fired at her struck the creature just below the left eye socket, and she was collapsing as Mackenzie ran by. If she wouldn't have had the hole in her cheek, she could have lunged and reached Mackenzie for sure.

Mackenzie reached the doorway as her dad ripped off three more shots down the same aisle that he had fired the first time. She tried to close the door behind her, but she realized that the doorjamb had been broken and it wasn't going to close easily. Instead, she readied her rifle and took position next to her dad standing behind the counter. She could see a couple of bodies lying in the shadows down the aisle that her dad had taken to get back to the pharmacy. Even though she had just sprinted across the store, she felt herself holding her breath again and made herself exhale.

"Is that all of them?" Mackenzie asked. She didn't realize that she was that shaken until she heard the quiver in her own voice.

Patrick reached over with one arm, pulled her head towards him, and kissed her on top of the head. "Somehow I don't think that it is Darlin," he said before readying his rifle again.

Patrick suddenly swung the rifle over to the left and shot twice at a creature who had come out of the same food aisle that Mackenzie had ran down. This one was a young man with a beard and a duck brown work jacket on. The first shell hit him in the upper shoulder and knocked him backwards down the aisle so that only his work boots and the bottom of his dirty jeans were visible where he now lay on the drug store's floor. When Patrick had swung the rifle around, he had accidently struck Mackenzie with the stock rather hard.

"Here," he said repositioning himself on the other side of Mackenzie and closer to the open door. "You concentrate on getting anything that comes down that first aisle," he said as he lifted his elbow up and gestured down the only aisle that you could clearly see down all the way. "I'll try to get any others," he finished stoically.

Mackenzie stared down the aisle, looking for any movement. The two of them stood almost back-to-back now as they waited for any more creatures. She could feel her heart beating in her throat again. She saw the rifle sights begin to sway back and forth as she started shaking.

Patrick fired a shot, and the surprise made Mackenzie jump and she accidently jerked the trigger and fired her rifle as well.

"Did you get it?" Patrick yelled over to her without looking.

"I didn't mean to shoot," she yelled back. That quiver was still in her voice.

Patrick shot again; and then again. "Do you have this?" Patrick yelled to her.

Mackenzie closed her eyes and took a deep breath. "Do you have this?" Patrick yelled again with more emphasis.

She opened her eyes and yelled "Yes!" back to him just as she saw a young woman-creature on her hands and feet down the aisle that she was supposed to be watching. The creature-thing seemed to be smelling the leg of one of the bodies that her dad had shot earlier. The woman-creature moved in fast jerky type movements.

Mackenzie trained the sights on the thing's face and held it there for a moment while she tried to steel her nerves enough to squeeze the trigger. The creature suddenly locked eyes with her and Mackenzie recognized that same blank stare that she had seen from the creature at the farm. She squeezed the trigger without any more hesitation, and the small bullet hit its mark. The woman-creature thing cried out with a shriek and spun around to the ground. The small caliber bullet must not have been enough to finish off the creature, as it shrieked and crawled on its belly around the corner out of view.

Patrick fired two more quick bursts and then asked "You still okay?"

"Yeah; I got it," Mackenzie said with more confidence than she had had before.

They both stood there at the ready with their eyes locked in the area away from each other waiting to acquire their next target. The woman-creature was still making noises from somewhere near the front of the store that made it clear she was in pain.

"That noise will probably really bring them in," Patrick said as he debated leaving the pharmacy area and Mackenzie to go finish it off.

Mackenzie then heard a sound that she hadn't heard for weeks. She thought that she must be hallucinating. It was very faint, but it was becoming more and more distinctive. When Patrick didn't respond to the sound, she asked him "Do you here that?"

"That creature howling?" he asked her.

"No," she said. "That motorcycle."

Patrick glanced over his shoulder to see if his daughter was okay or if she was going crazy with all the macabre stuff happening. She didn't look back to him, but instead kept her eyes trained down the aisle. Then he heard it too.

He turned his attention back towards the other aisles and strained his ears to hear the noise over the wailing of the creature at the front of the store. It did sound like a motorcycle, although it was some ways off and was hard to tell exactly what it was. Whatever it was, it was getting closer.

A creature stepped out of the aisle where the work boots were sticking out. Patrick swung his rifle around and fired, but his shot was way off and struck the old man-thing in the leg near the kneecap. The creature spun and fell to the floor. Patrick fired one more shot at the base of skull of the creature as it laid on its side grabbing its knee. That round found its mark and it immediately created a gory mess all over the floor in front of the creature as it made impact.

Then they heard gunshots coming from outside as the motorcycle was wound tight and sounded like it was right outside. The shots were from a larger caliber semi-automatic rifle or pistol because they were being fired in quick succession.

There was a stampede of creatures. Two came running around the endcaps towards the pharmacy door, and Patrick shot multiple times and dropped them to the floor. Their momentum carried them partway across the floor. Two more came around the corner. And then another. Patrick began pulling the trigger as fast as he could.

Three turned the corner into the aisle that Mackenzie was watching. Two teenage boy creatures, and a hulking bald man-creature that ran with a limp. Mackenzie aimed at the fastest boy in front. She shot twice at his head, which caused him to fall on his face. She then turned the rifle to the second boy and began shooting. She had several rounds into him before he finally spun around and collapsed to the floor.

Patrick's rifle continued to fire almost non-stop, and the shots coming from just outside the store were almost continuous as well. The large bald man continued to trudge down the aisle towards the pharmacy and made it about half way by the time the second boy had succumbed to Mackenzie's small caliber rifle shells. The man was garbed in an oily dark blue set of coveralls that had a name badge stitched high on the chest. He had a bad limp with his right leg that required him to almost drag it along behind him as he walked. Mackenzie aimed for the man's large bald head and squeezed off a shot. The bullet hit the upper left cheek of man-creature that immediately caused a trail of blood to flow down its face. Other than causing a small hesitation, the man-creature continued his walk towards the pharmacy undeterred.

Mackenzie held the rifle sights as steady as she could, and trained them on the large man's left eye. She remembered all those things her dad used to say when he took her out to the shooting range: 'Aim small, miss small'; 'Squeeze the trigger, don't pull it'; 'Concentrate on your breathing'. She let her breath out, and slowly squeezed the trigger as the large creature had gotten close enough to read that his name badge had "George" embroidered in red cursive on it. But instead of the normal report or the rifle, it just clicked.

"Oh no," Mackenzie said softly, but it couldn't be heard by anyone but herself over the noise of the other shots being fired and the ringing of her ears. She pulled the slide back on the rifle to see if it had jammed, and she realized that it was out of shells.

She looked up to see George about seven feet away from her limping towards her with those empty eyes staring directly into her. She thought that she saw a small smile at the corner of George's mouth just as blood and gore exploded out of the side of the large creature's head and he crumpled with a thud to the floor at the base of the counter. Mackenzie felt bits of bone, blood spatter, and other mess contact the side of her face in a warm painful ooze.

As Mackenzie involuntarily leaned over behind the counter to vomit, she saw a figure of a man holding a pistol half way down the aisle. That figure must have been the one that finished off George.

"Hey!" the figure in the aisle called out as Mackenzie continued to vomit and wipe at the muck and gore on her face and hair. "Let's get out of here!"

Patrick swung the gun around and trained it on the new comer at the sound of his voice.

"We don't have time for this," the man said. He then turned and ran back down the aisle towards the front of the store.

Patrick grabbed his backpack and Mackenzie by the arm. He half-pulled Mackenzie out of the doorway to the pharmacy and down one of the aisles as she was still vomiting and wiping the mess from her face. Another shot was fired from right outside of the front door to the drug store.

There were creature bodies everywhere that they had to step over and around just to get down the cave-aisles. As Patrick and Mackenzie reached the broken window and burst through the store's door, they saw the young man that had just saved them climbing onto a four-wheel ATV just outside the door. The ATV was camouflage painted and had four large red jerry cans strapped to the rear cargo rack.

The man turned to the father and daughter as they ran from the store. He looked like a strapping young ranch kid to Patrick. He had short buzz-cut hair, and built like he probably played linebacker for the senior-high football team. He had an AR slung diagonally across his back, and was starting the ATV as the two reached him.

Patrick took Mackenzie's forearm and guided her onto the back of the ATV while he yelled at the kid, "Take this road straight down to the river. We have a boat and someone else there waiting for us."

"Dad," Mackenzie said worriedly when she realized that he was leaving her in the care of this stranger.

The boy didn't hesitate, and wound the engine up on the ATV and headed off down the road in the direction of the river. Mackenzie couldn't help but wrap her arms around him, otherwise she would have lost her balance and fell off the back of the vehicle. She felt the boy's muscles tighten and flex as he navigated the ATV around the stranded vehicles and over the terrain. She was dazed. She didn't want to leave her dad alone, but he evidently had planned it.

Mackenzie wasn't sure how fast they were going, but it felt like they were flying. The ATV's engine was whining and its two riders were leaning forward into the wind staring down the paved road that was streaming beneath their feet. It was only after a few minutes when the slope of the ground changed from being mostly flat to going slightly downhill towards the river.

When they reached a hill that Mackenzie recognized was just before the river, she yelled to stop in the man's ear; but he didn't seem to hear or respond. As they crested over the top of the hill and they could see the river a few hundred yards away, she yelled again and hit his shoulder hard twice with her closed fist.

The man grabbed both breaks hard and sent the ATV into a sideways skid. Mackenzie found herself gritting her teeth and gripping his torso tightly so she didn't spill off the side of the four-wheeler. They came to an abrupt halt several feet from where the man had first applied the brakes.

"What's the matter?" he partially yelled to her.

"Stuart," she said flatly peering to locate him down by his tent. She then saw the glint from his rifle laying on the other side of the beach from where his tent was, with him behind it prone on the ground. She pointed to where Stuart was laying, and then waved her arms back and forth over her head.

The man couldn't tell what she was pointing at until Stuart stood up and began waving the hand without the rifle in it over his head as well.

"Hop off," the man said.

It took Mackenzie a moment to understand what the man said, and then another to decide if that was the best thing to do.

"Hop off," he said again, but this time more impatiently.

Mackenzie quickly slung her leg around the seat and slid off the seat. The man gunned the engine and took off back the same way that they had just came without so much as looking back. She could hear the whine of the engine as it sped away and she stood there wondering what happened and where he was going.

She trotted down the hill towards Stuart. When Stuart realized that Mackenzie was okay and now by herself, he left the rifle and sat backwards on a picnic table bench with his blanket wrapped around him again. When she was several yards off, Stuart seen the blood and other gore plastered to the side of Mackenzie's face and hair. He jumped up from the bench throwing his blanket off, and ran the rest of the way to meet her.

"Are you okay? What happened? Did that quad guy do that to you?" Stuart fired off several questions while inspecting her head and looking through her hair trying to find the injury.

"No. None of that," Mackenzie said perturbed and slapped Stuart's hands away from her head. "I'm fine. That's not my blood, it is creature blood."

Stuart paused and took a step back as he only imagined what Mackenzie must have been through to get that kind of mess on her. Mackenzie continued to walk down the slight slope to the boat dock and ramp area.

"What about Patrick?" Stuart asked.

"He's okay," Mackenzie responded as she continued to walk. "I think he is anyways," she said unsure of herself. "Quad-boy snatched me up and ran me back here to the river while my dad was hoofing it back with the bikes."

"What happened, and who is that quad-boy guy?" Stuart asked.

"I'll tell you all about it, but you'd better break down your tent and get your stuff put away first. I've got a feeling we'll be high-tailing it out of here soon," Mackenzie said as she reached the edge of the water. She got on all fours and submerged her head in the water and began to rub at the mess on her face and in her hair.

Stuart did as he was told and had his tent broke down and most things in the boat when he heard the four-wheeler again. Mackenzie was still on her hands and knees at the edge of the river trying to get the last of the blood from the strands of hair at the edge of her scalp.

"Quad-boy's coming back," Stuart told her as he made the last trip to the boat.

Mackenzie finished what she was doing, wiped her hands dry on her shorts and picked up her rifle. She wasn't sure what she was going to do with it, but she wasn't sure who this quad-boy really was or what his intentions were.

It took considerable time for the four-wheeler to appear over the crest of the hill. The two waiting at the river could tell that engine wasn't revved nearly as high as it was before, and they anticipated that the four-wheeler wasn't traveling near as fast as it had before. When the rider did crest over the hill, he was matched with Patrick riding his bicycle side by side. Mackenzie's bike was strapped to the front carriage rack of the four-wheeler and looked large and awkward bouncing there as the duo traveled towards them.

Mackenzie began to walk, but then trotted towards her dad as they approached. She embraced him in a hug while he was still on his bike when they reached each other. After a moment of reciprocating the hug, he swung his leg off the bike and they walked Patrick's bike down to the dock. The four-wheeler driver had driven down to the dock as well, and was off the contraption and was introducing himself and shaking Stuart's hand as the other two walked up.

"My name is Patrick," Patrick said extending his hand as he walked up to the younger man. "We sure owe you for your help back there," he said with full sincerity.

"Sawyer," the man replied and shook Patrick's hand. The young man was wearing a dirty green button down shirt with the sleeves rolled up and the tail flapping about. His jeans had a few holes in them here and there, but they didn't look like they were there when he bought them. He had short sandy blonde hair and Mackenzie thought that he looked more strapping and fit standing out in the sunlight next to her dad than he had back at the drug store. He had a strong jaw line and slightly pronounced cheekbones that made hard shadows on his face in the afternoon sun.

Sawyer turned and looked Mackenzie in the eye and said "I'm sorry that one got so close to you. Are you alright?"

Mackenzie suddenly felt warm inside and couldn't really make the words come out that she was thinking. Sawyer had large brown eyes that seemed to look right into her. After she realized that her lack of response was becoming awkward, she forced out "I'm fine."

Patrick nervously chuckled, messed her hair with a quick rubbing on top of her head, and said "This is my daughter Mackenzie." Then he added "And it looks like you already met Stuart."

"Yeah," Sawyer replied. "So what in the world were you guys doing going into the middle of a town in broad daylight? You must be really hard up for something huh?"

Patrick and the others looked at each other bewildered. "We needed some medicine for Stuart, but what do you mean?"

"What do you mean 'what do I mean?'" Sawyer asked sounding somewhat dumbfounded. "Those scaveys back there would have had you for lunch if I hadn't seen them swarming and headed your way."

"Scaveys?" Stuart asked.

Sawyer looked at Stuart for a moment while squinting. "Where are you guys from," Sawyer finally asked.

"What do you mean?" Stuart asked.

"Where are you from?" Sawyer asked again.

"Why? Where are you from?" Stuart replied defensively.

"Where are you from and where are you headed?" Sawyer asked as he took a half-step backwards so that he was facing all three of them more generally. Patrick could tell that he was holding his right arm funny and seemed to be readying himself for the pistol holster on his hip.

"My daughter and I were on a backpacking trip in the Rockies when the cloud came through. We're headed back home to Nebraska," Patrick told him flatly and quickly.

Sawyer was visibly aghast. "You survived?" he asked in awe.

"So far," Patrick said.

"We haven't seen any survivors. They told us that there wasn't any. That there couldn't be any. Are there any more?" Sawyer continued with the questions.

"Just Stuart here," Patrick replied.

Sawyer stepped backward again and plopped down on one of the benches that made up the picnic table. He was staring up at each of them in amazement. "How did you guys make it?" he asked to no one in particular.

"We'll get to that. But tell us what you know. Did Nebraska make it?" Patrick asked.

Sawyer conceded and said "Part of it. Some of it. The Stafford Line runs from Sioux Falls, and down through Lincoln to Topeka."

"The Stafford Line?" Stuart asked.

Before Sawyer could respond, Mackenzie asked "Did Columbus, Nebraska make it?"

Sawyer wrinkled his nose while he thought for a minute. "I guess I'm not sure where that is at."

"It's north-west of Lincoln a hundred miles or so," Patrick injected.

"I'm sorry. I don't know for sure. The Stafford Line zig-zags down through Nebraska and Kansas, so some little towns are in the zone and others are outside of it," Sawyer concluded. Then he remembered "If it helps at all, I crossed the Line just north of town called Norfolk that was just outside the zone."

"That's just north of Columbus!" Mackenzie exclaimed.

Sawyer smiled some at Mackenzie's excitement, but felt like qualifying the conversation so he added "Like I said, the line zigs and zags through there, so I don't know for sure."

After a brief pause, Patrick asked "Where are you headed? Can we travel together?"

"I'm going the other direction. To the Park." Sawyer replied.

"What park?" Stuart asked.

"Yellowstone. The epi-center," said Sawyer.

"It started in Yellowstone?" Stuart asked.

"Do you mind camping with us for a night? It sounds like we both have a lot of information to share," Patrick inquired.

"Sure, but not here," Sawyer answered.

"We have a boat," Patrick said gesturing toward the dock. "If you don't mind leaving your ATV here, I think there's enough room in it for you. We could find a spot on the other side of the river. We haven't seen any of those creatures on the other side of the river yet."

Sawyer pondered the offer for a moment and then agreed. He got back on the ATV and pulled it into a stand of cottonwoods some little ways off from the dock. He sauntered back with a regular sized grey backpack slung over one shoulder along with his AR. The others were fastening the two other bikes to the boat and making room for Sawyer.

"Oh – I almost forgot," Patrick said somewhat alarmed. He reached down and grabbed his mostly empty backpack and flipped it to Stuart. "I got you a present."

"What's that?" Stuart said opening the pack. There were a couple dozen pill bottles and paper bags in the back pack.

"Find some of the ibuprofen and amoxicillin in there, and take a few before we head out," Patrick said.

Stuart felt himself begin to tear up at the thought of Patrick keeping him in mind with all that they just went through. "Thanks…" Stuart said as he began rifling through the bag.

After everything was stowed and tied off, they all climbed into the boat. It was tighter than they had imagined with an extra person. Stuart and Sawyer sat next to each other precariously in the middle of boat, each near the edge. None of them seemed to care much about the tight quarters as they shoved off from the dock because they were too enthralled in their own stories. They mostly talked about Patrick and Mackenzie's experience with the cloud and their hike to South Dakota. They were just getting to the part where they met up with Stuart when they landed on a small beach a half of a mile or so down-stream from where they had been docked.

They continued to tell Sawyer all about them and their travels while they setup camp on the beach and gathered some fire wood as the sun slowly set. About the time that the water was boiling in a cook pot by the small fire that they were all sitting in the sand around, they reached the point in their story where they had entered the drug store early that morning.

"And that's where we met you," Mackenzie said looking across the fire to Sawyer. "And you decided to spray George's creature-brains all over me," she said with a coy smile and a slight laugh, but Sawyer didn't take the comment well.

"They're called Scaveys," he said flatly. "They don't have names anymore. And I don't enjoy shooting them."

The whole feeling around the fire felt tense and Mackenzie shifted her weight around in the sand. She had clearly become uncomfortable with Sawyer's response, but was not sure how to rectify what she had said.

"Sorry," Mackenzie started. "I didn't mean to…"

Patrick interjected to ease the tension "So why do you call them Scaveys?"

"It's not just me that calls them scaveys, everyone calls them scaveys," Sawyer said as he leaned back in the sand and rested on his elbows. "They're scavengers. The scientists and doctors on the television say that the first ones ate the meat from the dead animals that were killed by the cloud. Or even ate meat from their refrigerators or from the store that was tainted by the cloud. Once they ate it, they weren't the same." Sawyer paused and stared into the fire for a while. The others thought that he was trying to gather the courage to continue.

After what seemed like too long of a pause, Stuart asked "What does it do to them?"

"It changes them," Sawyer said. "They aren't human anymore; they're scaveys." Sawyer continued to stare into the flicker of the small fire on the beach. This time the others just waited for him to continue. "They got my folks," he said after a while. He reached up and wiped an undiscernible tear from one of his eyes. "We live outside of a little town called Hubbard that's just west of Sioux City. We have a small farm with a few head of cattle. My little brother and I had finished our chores and were waiting for the bus that morning when my mom had come flying down the driveway in the old red truck. We thought that she might be running the truck down to us that morning to take into town. I'm old enough to drive, but my folks like it when I ride the bus with my little brother because it saves gas money. Sometimes though, they have me drive him in when there's something special going on."

Sawyer took a swig of the coffee Patrick had made and shifted in the sand a little before continuing. "Not that morning though. Mom had heard about the cloud on the radio, and that they were evacuating everyone east as quickly as possible. She was so frantic that she just about didn't get the truck slowed down in time, and Aaron and I had to jump out of the way. We got into the truck and mom cranked the radio that was tuned to a local talk radio show as she tore across our freshly planted fields in that old truck to make it out to Dad in the north forty."

Sawyer continued to tell the others about his experience that morning, but his tone turned somber as he reflected, "That radio announcer had been on the radio in the mornings for as long as I could remember. He usually gave the ag-reports and told everyone what to expect for weather for the next few days. When you listen to someone like that for that long, even though you've never met them in person; you kind of feel like you know them. I could hear the fear in his voice. He was telling of the satellite images they were showing on the news stations of the orange cloud moving as fast as a single engine airplane across the mid-west, killing everything in its path. He was begging people to leave. To drop what they were doing and head east with just the clothes on their backs. His fear came through the radio. I understood why Mom was so whacked out."

"Did they say that it started at Yellowstone?" Stuart asked. The ibuprofen had cut his fever and while he still looked worn down, he felt better than he had in the last couple of days.

"No. They didn't know that at first," Sawyer answered. "The announcer that we were listening to said that they had all kinds of conflicting reports, but the most common was that China had hit us with a missile that released a toxic gas."

Sawyer stared into the fire as he continued his story "My dad jumped down off the tractor and ran out to meet us as he saw Mom bouncing across the fields driving like a banshee. Mom told him what was going on, but he had to stick his head in the window and listen to the radio for a moment before he comprehended what she was telling him. He opened the door and got behind the wheel as Mom slid over. Dad took off across the field and left the tractor idling there in the field. Part way back to the house, Dad started barking orders out to Aaron and me. I had to go get the camper trailer ready to hook up while Aaron went to get gas cans. Mom and Dad headed to the house to grab stuff, then came out and hooked up to the camper. We took off and headed east listening to different radio stations trying to figure out what was going on. Mom tried to call different relatives and friends all over, but the phone service was all jammed up and the phones didn't work at all."

Sawyer sat up and poured some more coffee in his cup before continuing. "The roads were terrible. My dad was smart enough to take the highways instead of the interstate, but it was still like rush-hour in down-town Sioux Falls. All the radio stations were saying to stay off of the interstates because they were pure grid-lock. People were driving in the barrow ditch, the medians, and cutting across people's fields. My dad said it was just like rats from a drowning ship. All they did was make the traffic worse."

Sawyer stared into the fire quietly as if he was lost in his own memories. Finally, Mackenzie broke the silence. She asked "How far did it go? The cloud I mean."

"The Stafford Line has all of Wyoming and Colorado in it. Most of Idaho and Utah. The better parts of South Dakota, Nebraska, and Kansas are in it too." Sawyer paused and sipped some more of his coffee, then added "They said that if they hadn't dropped the bomb, it could have been most of North America."

"Bomb?" Stuart exclaimed. "What bomb?"

Sawyer took a deep breath before he continued with his story. "We drove all day and most of the night with the other rats as we all headed east as fast as the clogged highways would let us. We made it to a town called Waterloo in Iowa where we ran out of all of the gas we had taken with us. The gas stations there for the most part had been looted and taken over by scum. They were charging people thirty dollars a gallon with cash only. We didn't have enough money to buy a full tank if we had wanted to. We had been hearing on the radio for the last several hours that the government was planning to drop a special bomb on the epicenter that they thought might stop the cloud. So my dad found an underground parking lot in the downtown area and we pulled the truck and camper down into it. We couldn't get radio signal down there, so my dad left and scouted the area out for what seemed like forever. He eventually came back and we all walked down the street to a casino where other people were gathering to watch the news coverage on flat screens that were mounted around the inside of the building."

Patrick could read the tenseness in Sawyer's face. He could only imagine how terrifying the experience must have been for Sawyer's family and all those people. He couldn't help but ask about the cloud that had mesmerized him for hours. "What did it look like from the satellite?" Patrick asked.

Sawyer thought for a moment before answering "It was amazing."

"What do you mean?" Stuart asked.

Sawyer thought for another moment. He finally turned to Stuart and said "It's hard to explain. It was a thick orange and dark yellow fog that just continued to boil out of the epicenter. You couldn't see anything through it. It didn't waft like a cloud, it kind of crawled along the ground. You could just feel death coming from even the pictures of it. The news stations kept looping some footage that a jet took as it flew above the cloud, and it reminded me of a big bowl of that nasty warm cereal that Mom would make for us in the winter before school."

Sawyer dug a flat can with a metal lid out from his back pants pocket. He thumped the lid twice, then opened it up and put some tobacco in his front lip. He put the lid back on and held the can up to Patrick, offering him a pinch but Patrick shook his head. Sawyer sat the can down on a rock next to him and turned his head to spit.

Mackenzie's stomach tightened and Sawyer somehow didn't look near as handsome to her as he did a moment before. She told him "That stuff isn't good for you, you know."

"Yeah; I know," he said.

"So, what about this bomb?" Stuart asked again.

Sawyer turned his head to spit again before continuing. "Well," he said. "The government supposedly figured out how this cloud was coming out of the ground and built a two-stage bomb to stop and dissipate the cloud." Sawyer held up one finger as he said "The first stage was like one of those bunker busting bombs that was supposed to go deep into the ground before exploding so it would plug whatever hole that stuff was coming out of." Sawyer took the time to turn his head and spit again before holding up two fingers and continuing. "The second stage let off some top-secret explosion in the low atmosphere that was supposed to cause the cloud to dissipate. They called it the EMD stage, but I never heard them explain what that was."

"Isn't that what you guessed happened Dad when all the electrical stuff got fried?" Mackenzie asked her dad.

"Kind of," Patrick replied. He was deep in thought and trying to absorb all what Sawyer was telling them. "I thought it was an 'EMP' caused by a bomb. That stands for an Electro-Magnetic Pulse that occurs when a big nuke detonates. It causes a voltage surge in anything inductive that burns out electronics and electrical things. I don't know what an 'EMD' is, but it sure sounds similar."

"It does sound almost the same," Sawyer said. "We didn't get to see any footage of the jet flying the bomb in, but they had a countdown clock in the corner of the screen that started with thirty-eight minutes on it that was supposed to be the time for when they dropped the bomb. The casino was full when we got there, so we had to make our way around to a television near the back wall to watch all of this. We'd stood there all day long and into the night before that count down timer was on the screen. People kept trickling into that casino all day long. The place wasn't exactly shoulder to shoulder by then, but it felt like we were packed in like there like sardines."

Sawyer turned his head and spit again before continuing. "They talked about the bomb pretty much the whole time the counter was on the screen. They had a press conference from some talking heads at the Whitehouse that talked about the two stages of the bomb, without really saying anything about it. The newscasters then just kept saying the same things that they had talked about at the press conference over and over again. Finally, they cut to a live satellite feed just before the counter reached zero." Sawyer spit again, and then shook his head for emphasis. "Nothing happened. It was almost three minutes later before the video cut back to the newscaster and he said that he wasn't sure what had happened, but they were awaiting word from the military. Then – the power went out. The whole place was dark. Just the exit signs were lit up. You could feel the tension that was already as thick as that cloud get thicker. People were starting to panic and think that it was the end; just when the lights came back on."

"So, there's still power back east?" Stuart asked.

"Well, the casino had a backup generator that came on," Sawyer replied. "I think that the power went out everywhere for a while, but it is back up on the east coast now I think." He turned his head and spit once more. "We stayed and watched the television for a couple of hours, but they really didn't say much more. They did say that the bomb was a success, but they wouldn't show anymore satellite images for some reason. My brother, mom, and me headed back to the camper and crashed while Dad stayed and watched the television. In the morning, Dad was back early and said that he had found someone to sell us some gas for a reasonable price. We got gas and headed back home."

"Back home?" Mackenzie asked.

"Yeah," Sawyer said understanding her concern. "We're farmers. The cloud was gone and we had fields to plant and critters to take care of."

"Hadn't the animals died?" Mackenzie asked.

"Yeah; they had," Sawyer responded. "But when we started back we were hopeful. The front edge of the cloud didn't look like it had made all the way to our place from the last satellite images we saw."

Patrick stood up and put some more water on to boil so they could make some more coffee. He could tell that there was a lot more conversation to be had. Sawyer continued to tell them about the trip back and how there wasn't hardly anyone moving west by the time they headed back. Also that all of the radio stations were off the air or replaced by the emergency broadcast system message that told people to stay away from the areas that the cloud had covered.

"I've only seen my dad cry a couple of times, and that was one of them" Sawyer started as he was telling them about how their farm looked when they pulled up the drive. "The house; tractor; barn; everything was just as we left it, except the animals. They had just fallen over where they lay. The pigs had all gathered in one corner of the pen like they had been trying to get away from the cloud. Most of the cows were just spread out in the pasture. The calves were laying right next to their moms."

Sawyer was getting choked up some, and took a second to collect himself before continuing, "We all went in the house and rested a while. The power was still out and there was no school, so my brother and I spent the next day helping Dad load all the carcasses up with the front-end loader on the tractor, and piled them out in the bean patch. We thought that the worst was behind us. If only we had known."

"It's okay son," Patrick told Sawyer. "We've all been through some pretty dark days and seen a lot of evil things in the last few weeks. Take your time and tell us at your own speed"

Sawyer collected himself for a little while longer. He spit to the side a couple of more times before starting his story again. "Well, with the power being out; several of our neighbors were trying to cook up all of the meat in their freezers before it spoiled. The Rancombs had almost a full deer left in their freezer that they were trying to consume before the warm days ruined it all together. They gave my folks several packages of meat when we were over there visiting one of the first evenings. They had made it as far as Minnesota before they turned around and came back."

Sawyer reached up and wiped his eyes again as he tried to relive what had been so dreadful for him. Mackenzie stood up from the opposite side of the fire where she had been sitting and walked around to where she could sit next to Sawyer. She put her hand on his forearm in an offering of comfort.

"Well," Sawyer said as he sucked some snot from his nose, turned and spit again. "I told you that whenever that cloud touched meat and people ate it, they turned into scaveys. Well, that's what happened. We had been eating on food that we'd gotten in the camper and all of Mom's canning stuffs. We were going to eat some of that deer that night when we got home, but the meat had gone rancid and Mom just threw it in the trash. Early the next morning though – the Rancombs came…" Sawyer hung his head and sobbed a couple of times. Mackenzie rubbed his forearm.

"Uhhhhhhh, well," Sawyer said again when he lifted his head. "I guess that I'll have to tell you the rest of that story some other time." He turned his head to spit again. "My brother and I made it though. We hopped back in the truck with nothing but a shotgun and this pistol," he said as he patted the holster on his waist. "We drove east until we ran out of gas, which wasn't very far. We weren't sure what we were doing, but we thought that we'd try to get to Minneapolis to find our Aunt Julie. Neither of us cared for Aunt Julie very much; she was kind of a city mouse and never liked coming out to visit us. But we didn't know what else to do."

Sawyer continued to tell the others about how he and his brother survived in those first few days. He said that he wasn't proud of some of the stuff that they did, but it was either that or starve to death. Nobody seemed to believe them at first about the scaveys, until more reports came waffling in from others that were headed east. The radio and television stations were useless and continued to broadcast repetitive messages from the emergency broadcast system, but never provided any news or real information. Cell phones were useless and didn't work even if you could find a generator to charge them. There were a few landlines that were operational, and people would pay large amounts of money and stand in line for hours for a chance to try to call a relative. Other people were the only way to get information about things that were going on elsewhere, and Sawyer and Aaron weren't sure who they could trust.

"My brother is fifteen, and quite a bit smaller than me," Sawyer told the others as the first light of the morning started to peak over the horizon. "He could get into places and hang around within earshot without looking conspicuous. There was a group of men that always huddled up and talked at night at the YMCA we were staying at. They got Aaron in on their conspiracy theory that the whole thing was a ploy by the government. They had all kinds of reasons and notions about what they thought and what so-and-so had heard, but it all sounded like gibberish to me. Idle hands and all. Against my brother's wishes, I had decided that we needed to go someplace else because

I was worried about the load of manure they were filling his head with. We were fixing to leave the next morning; just walk out. But that night, a huge convoy of Humvee's, tanks, and armored personnel carriers rolled through town heading West. You can imagine all the things those conspiracy kooks were spewing by the next morning. I was still bent on leaving and dragging my brother out of there by the scruff of his neck if I had to; but then the President came on the television, and I changed my mind."

Sawyer told them about the live presidential address. How the president told the nation that martial law had been declared. There was to be a curfew at dark and anyone not obeying military orders could be arrested and tried by the highest ranking local official. He said that it was all temporary until they resolved the issue of the cloud and scavengers, and then life would return to normal.

Sawyer spit again and the others could see the look of vile on his face as he continued telling them about the address and the days following it. "That's when he told everyone about the Stafford Line. He said congress gave the power to quarantine the portions of the country that the cloud had affected, and the television showed a map with a red line on it. He said no one was allowed to cross the Stafford Line under penalty of treason, and that there was no reason to cross it as there were no survivors. I never liked or trusted the president to begin with, but listening to him that morning about made me puke. You could tell that he was lying about everything other than the martial law; and that he was covering up something big."

"Like what?" Stuart asked.

"I don't know," Sawyer answered. "You could just tell. If you ask any of those conspiracy nuts, they'd give you a handful of different stories to pick from. I don't really know what he was lying about, I just know he was lying. That's why I'm headed to the Park."

Sawyer told them that he and his brother left to go see what the military was doing on this imaginary Stafford Line. Aaron brought a new friend along named Howard who was a scrawny college freshman who had lost everyone he had known as well. The three of them traveled south along the Stafford Line stopping in towns and encampments along the way talking with the locals and trying to find out whatever they could. Their little band grew in numbers as they went, and ended up being around sixteen people by the time they made it to New Yankton.

"New Yankton?" Stuart asked bewildered.

"Yeah – the town of Yankton, South Dakota is inside the Stafford Line. So a lot of the locals made an encampment just outside of town and call it New Yankton," Sawyer explained. "That's where they started calling us the 'Truthers'."

"Who did?" Patrick asked.

"The town's folk," Sawyer answered. "Some people in our group didn't have a problem telling others why we were there and that we didn't believe in the martial law. There was a ruckus one evening when a lady was walking across the 'street' to get her teenage son that was in one of the large tents where we were staying. He had been listening to some of the rhetoric when a squad of soldiers stopped the lady. Evidently, they tried to arrest her for being out past curfew when some of the towns people told the soldiers that they weren't going to arrest her. We all went out and took the lady back from the soldiers and brought her in the tent with us. The crowd cheered, and our numbers doubled that night."

"How did you get the lady away from a whole squad of soldiers?" Stuart asked.

"We just grabbed her and brought her back into the tent," Sawyer said as a matter of fact. "The squad could have mowed us down if they had wanted to, but I don't think that they really signed up for shooting their friends and family. We just grabbed the lady and brought her in with her son. Anyways – after that, they called us the Truthers."

Sawyer stood up and stretched with his arms above his head before he began talking again from a standing position. "Aaron kind of became the leader of our little group. Nobody voted on it or anything. Everybody just knew that he was sharp and they trusted him. He came up with the vision for us to get across the Stafford Line and go to the Park to see what really happened. It took a little while, but he sold me on the idea hook, line, and sinker. The day after the ruckus, a couple of guys found us and told us that they had just came up from Norfolk, Nebraska. He said for whatever reason, they had seen a spot just north of Norfolk where the standard troop spacing between each other left a small ravine open to where he thought some scaveys could sneak through. That was just what Aaron had been waiting for. He schemed up a plan for six of us to slink up the ravine while the rest of the group made diversions for the two squads north and south of the ravine. It was a good plan. It almost worked."

Sawyer was so tired he was having difficulty standing, and he began shifting his weight back and forth on each leg to keep himself awake. The others were compassionate with him, but they were too enthralled with the story to offer him to tell it later.

Sawyer continued. "Howard and I snuck out of the encampment that night and walked down to scope out the hole in the line that the others had told us about. Sure enough, it was just as they had said. There was a mostly dry creek bed that cut a small hill in two for almost a quarter mile. We took lots of pictures on cell phones and hoofed it back to show Aaron and the others. Our whole group left the next day and walked down to Norfolk. We made final preparations, and it was decided that Aaron, Howard, myself, and three other guys would be the ones to get across while the rest of the band split and would go cause trouble for the soldiers on either side of the hill. Once it was totally dark, we crawled on our bellies towards the ravine and stopped just short of it and waited until the diversions started. Once they were going full stream, we GI Joe'd fast down into the ravine and started hoofing it as stealthily as possible through the creek bed. The creek bed was only a few feet wide and a couple of feet deep, so we had to go single file. I had been the quickest, so I was out front when I heard a soldier yell 'Halt!" Sawyer mimicked the soldier yelling and all those around the campfire jumped a little.

Sawyer held an imaginary rifle out in front of him as he continued to impersonate the soldier. "'Halt I said!' the soldier screamed out to us. I just froze where I was at. I could just barely see him out of the corner of my eye standing at the bank to the creek bed. Howard was not too far behind me, and after a second he clamored up out of the ravine and took off sprinting away from the soldier. The soldier yelled again at him, and when Howard didn't stop; he fired. I could see in the muzzle flash that he had on night vision goggles. The soldier cursed a couple of times and then directed us to get up out of the creek with our hands up. We all stood up one by one, except Aaron and I. The others got out of the creek bed with their hands-on top of their head and walked back to where the soldier was standing. 'You too!' he yelled and Aaron finally stood up. I don't know why he couldn't see me with those goggles on. I must have just blended into the creek bank good enough to not be seen. The soldier took all the others back towards their Humvees at gunpoint, and I just laid there. I laid there until it hurt. I didn't know what I should do. Then I made my mind up that I was getting to the Park, and that a hundred soldiers with night vision weren't going to stop me. I crawled on my belly, just moving inches at a time away from the line. By the time it was morning, I was worried that I wasn't far enough away and that they would spot me so I picked up the pace a little. When I got far enough away that I couldn't see them, I figured they couldn't see me and I hightailed it away from there."

Sawyer stretched one more time with a big yawn before saying "I'm sorry guys, but I've had it. Can I crash in one of these tents and we'll finish the story tomorrow?"

None of them wanted the story time to end, but they all finally conceded and divided up who was going to take what watch.

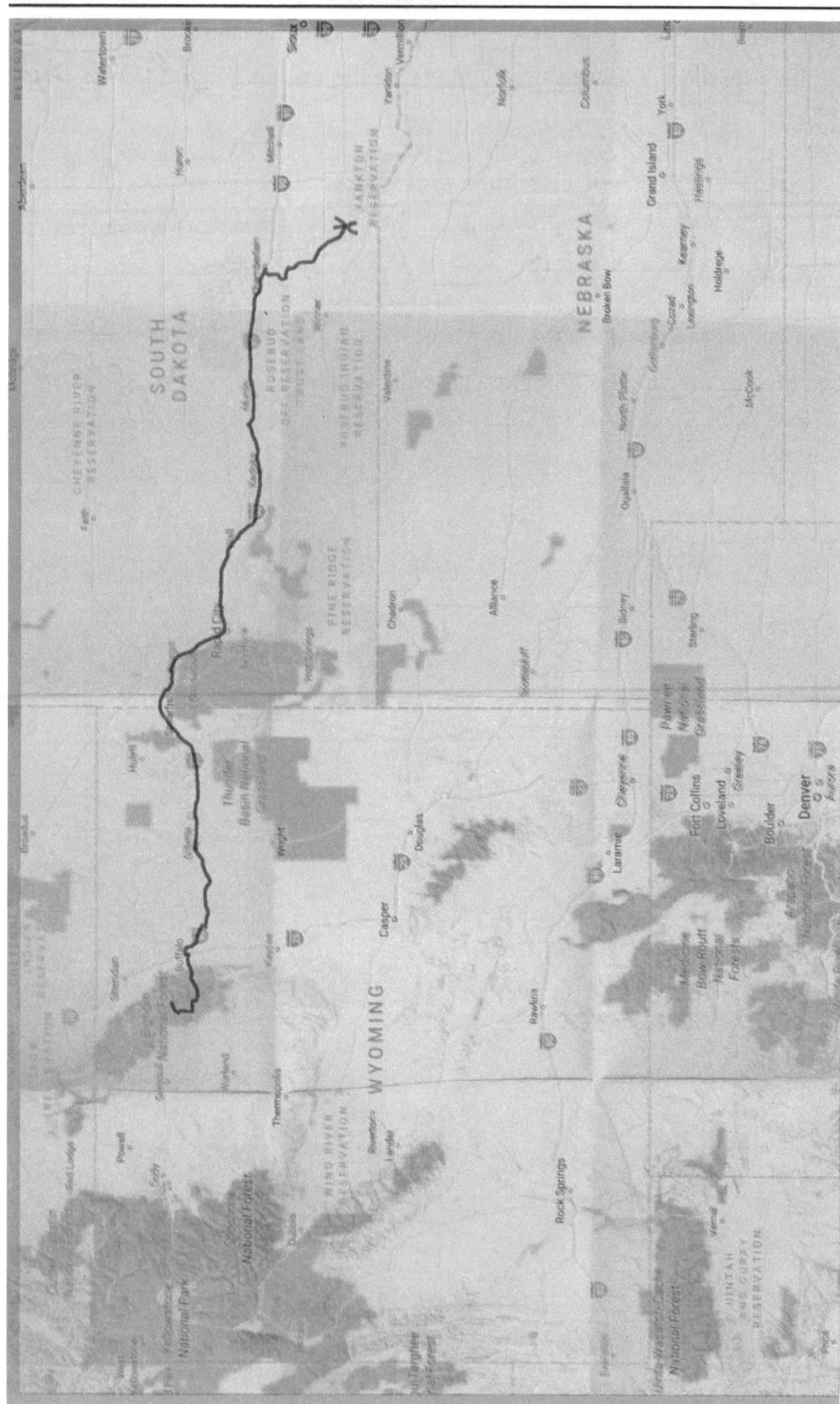

CHAPTER 20

STUART HAD COLLECTED more firewood and had water warming on a small campfire again when Sawyer climbed out from Stuart's tent. It was mid-morning and Sawyer stretched and yawned before exchanging quiet morning pleasantries with Stuart. Sawyer left camp for several minutes, then returned and joined Stuart by the fire.

"Do you have any of that coffee made? That sure hit the spot last night," Sawyer asked in a low tone as not to wake the others.

"No, not yet," Stuart answered. "It's working on it though." After a few minutes of silence, Stuart asked "Why don't animals turn into scaveys?"

"Not sure," Sawyer replied.

"I mean, it's kind of weird that people turn into these creatures after they had eaten the tainted meat, but the same meat doesn't affect animals," Stuart said half as a statement and half as a question.

"Well, it affects them all right," Sawyer offered. "It just kills 'em. It doesn't just have to be the meat that was tainted by the cloud. If you get some of the scaveys' blood or saliva in you, it'll get you just as well."

"Really?" Stuart asked.

"Yeah. I hadn't ever seen it first hand, but they have strict orders on those soldiers that man the Stafford Line," Sawyer answered. "Whenever they rotate back off the line, they are quarantined for four days to make sure they don't have any symptoms."

They both sat quietly for a while thinking about things that they had heard and learned talking with each other the day before. When the water started boiling, Stuart made both him and Sawyer a piping hot cup before sitting back down in the spot that he was in before.

"So how did you plan on getting gas for that four-wheeler without any electricity?" Stuart asked, respectfully keeping his voice low for the other two that were sleeping.

"Siphon hose," Sawyer replied before sipping on his coffee. "I had to do it a few times by the time I got here."

"You just go up to cars and suck out the gas?" Stuart asked confused.

"Yeah. I made a siphon hose from some clear tubing I got at a hardware store when I ran out of gas the first time. It took me a while, but I also figured out that I needed to carry a long screwdriver too. The newer cars have something down there that you have to knock out of the way before you can get the hose down in the tank."

Stuart sat quietly and thought about Sawyer siphoning the gas along the highway. Stuart started talking again, but this time he had forgotten to keep his voice low. "You know, there was one thing different that I heard between the story that you told and the Kincaid's version."

"What's that?" Sawyer asked intrigued.

"Mackenzie told me that the cloud had left them on the mountain, and then the bomb had exploded," Stuart said and then paused to make sure that he had what he was thinking right in his mind. "Remember? I think Patrick talked about it yesterday too. He said that a strong wind came up, and by the next morning the cloud was gone. But the bomb wasn't dropped until that night when they were driving down the mountain. Why would they have needed to drop the bomb if it had already stopped and was going away by then?"

Sawyer thought about what Stuart had said for a moment before responding. "See; that's why I have to get to the Park! I could tell that S.O.B. president was lying through his teeth when he came on the television. The other thing that is totally fishy is how they could figure out what happened and build a special multi-million-dollar bomb to fix it in less than two days. Most of the time, the government can't even figure out how to blow their own nose in two days."

"Yeah;" Stuart said as Mackenzie crawled out of her tent still looking like she was half-asleep. "You're right! How could they have figured out exactly what that mysterious cloud was, where it was coming from, and how to fix it in two days?"

"What are you guys all excited and talking loud about?" Mackenzie asked as she cut half-closed and sleepy eyes to Stuart and shuffled her way to the fire.

Stuart said "We're just talking about how the government came on the TV and said they needed that special bomb to stop the cloud, but you told us that the cloud was already leaving by the time that bomb was dropped."

Mackenzie pursed her lips and then nodded her head before pouring herself a cup of coffee and added some water back to the pot.

"I'm going with you!" Stuart blurted out.

"What? What do you mean?" Mackenzie turned and asked Stuart. She turned so quickly that some of the hot coffee sloshed from her cup and onto one of her fingers before hitting the ground. She immediately stuck the hurt finger into her mouth.

"You bet," Sawyer exclaimed. "That would be awesome!"

"Whaaat arrruuuu thhhtoing?" Mackenzie garbled around the finger in her mouth to Stuart. She was looking up at him with large forlorn eyes that reminded him of those anime comics.

Stuart took a step forward and put a hand on Mackenzie's shoulder. "Listen Mak," he started. "I've gotta do this. I helped get you guys across South Dakota, and I can help Sawyer get back across it too."

Mackenzie pulled her finger out of her mouth and looked quickly at the pink flesh on the side of her finger that would blister soon. She then looked up at Stuart with tears in her eyes and said "Don't go."

After a brief pause, Stuart said "I have to. I don't belong back there with everyone else. I'm good at stuff out here. Besides, I think that he's right. I need to go see what happened at the epicenter too."

Mackenzie looked up at Stuart for a moment longer, but when the first tears spilt down her cheeks she threw her cup and all its contents on the ground at their feet and stomped off away from camp. When she was just past the tents, she yelled back at Stuart in anger "Does he even know that your gay?"

She didn't stop and wait for a response, she just kept stomping.

Patrick came out of the tent shirtless and his pants unzipped looking around quickly trying to size up the commotion that had awakened him.

"You're gay?" Sawyer asked Stuart with his chin pointed down and looking up at him from under his brow.

"What's wrong with Mackenzie?" Patrick asked forcefully as he was wiggling his shoes on his feet without any socks.

"She's pitching a fit," Stuart answered Patrick. Then looking back to Sawyer, Stuart said "Does that change your mind about me going?"

"Which way did she go?" Patrick asked Stuart. Stuart pointed in the direction that Mackenzie had headed without looking away from Sawyer. Patrick took off trotting in the direction that Stuart had pointed.

Sawyer bent down and poured himself another cup of coffee. "Nah. I guess you can still go," he said. After he stood back up he added "We're sleeping in different tents from now on though."

Stuart laughed a little and stuck his open hand out to Sawyer. Sawyer took it and they shook hands.

Stuart and Sawyer talked excitedly more about scaveys, Sawyer's plan on how to get to Yellowstone Park, Stuart's Dungeon, and a few other things by the time Patrick had coaxed Mackenzie back into camp. Her eyes and nose were beat red and she sniffled as she stormed past the two boys at the campfire and climbed into her tent.

Patrick went into the tent as well and returned with a shirt that he put on. He also had the road map that he'd gotten from the sheriff office in Buffalo. He motioned for the other two to join him and they made their way over to a large rock some ways off from the fire and the tents. Mackenzie could still probably hear them if she was trying to, but it would be difficult if they kept their voices low.

Patrick opened with "Mackenzie doesn't want either of you two to go back. We've spent every waking second for the last few weeks trying to get out of this place and get back home, so she can't believe that you guys would rather go through that instead of go back to civilization with us. But I get it. If what you say is true Sawyer, then I would have had a strong pull to join your Truthers as well. With my kids though, I probably would have chickened out; but I would have wanted to. Do you have a route planned to Yellowstone yet?" Patrick unfolded the map and laid it out on the rock in front of them. They each peered over it and pointed as they discussed the best way for them to get to Yellowstone under the circumstances.

They planned and talked the better part of the morning. It was early afternoon when Patrick braved going back into the tent to pack things up and try to smooth Mackenzie over enough to join them again.

"You up?" he asked her as he entered the tent.

Mackenzie was laying in her sleeping bag reading a book. She didn't look up or even acknowledged that her dad had entered.

"You mad at me?" he asked incredulously.

Patrick kneeled at the foot of his sleeping bag and began to stuff it into its stuff sack. Mackenzie turned the page on her book while Patrick thought about what he could say to her.

"Listen," Patrick started as he continued to put his bag into its sack. "I know that you don't want them to go back, but they feel that they have to. It's like a higher calling, or a duty."

Mackenzie turned a page on her book without looking over to her dad. Patrick pulled the drawstring closed around the stuff sack and began picking up the odds and ends from around his side of the tent and put them in the different zippered pockets on his backpack.

"Those two don't have a mom and brother waiting for them in Columbus. They don't have that something to look forward to back in civilization," Patrick said as he continued to stow things in his pack.

"They have us," Mackenzie finally said as she looked at her dad with a quivering upper lip.

With that, Patrick sat his pack down on the tent floor and sprawled out next to his daughter and her bag. He put one arm around her, and she snuggled her nose down into his shoulder and began to cry some more.

"They do have us. And if it wasn't for this calling to find out what really happened, I think that would be enough," Patrick said trying to think of what he could say to comfort her. He couldn't come up with any gems, so he just continued to tell the truth. "If it wasn't for you, and James, and Mom; I'm pretty sure that I'd be right alongside of them."

Mackenzie craned her neck to lift her eyes out from Patrick's shoulder to look at his expression to see if he was serious. "Yeah," he said with a slight chuckle as he looked at her.

She rested her face back in his shoulder and asked "Why?"

He thought about how to respond and then said "The truth is a powerful thing."

Mackenzie pulled herself back, laid on her back and rubbed the tears from her face. "What do you mean?" she asked.

"I think that I believe what Sawyer told us about his story. If that's true, then there are quite a few things that don't add up. It also doesn't sound like it's going to be the same world that we left."

Mackenzie sniffled, and then pulled herself up on one elbow so that she could get a better look at her dad. "I still don't get it," she said.

"Maybe it's because we are Americans," Patrick started. "But I think that it's just because we're human, and we know human nature. We naturally suspect people in power have their own interests in mind instead of ours. The way our government is today, they take any chance they can get to grab more power; and martial law is a pretty extreme way to get power."

"You think that our own government would kill off all of those people to get more power?" Mackenzie asked.

"I hope not," Patrick answered. "But it wouldn't surprise me that they would take advantage of a situation to grab more power."

Mackenzie was quiet and thought about that for a moment, and then asked "I heard Stuart talking this morning about how the bomb was dropped after the cloud started disappearing."

"Yeah, that doesn't really add up either," Patrick said. "I could see if it was supposed to dissipate the cloud faster maybe. I don't know."

Patrick sat up and finished putting the things away in his pack as he continued talking, "You see how if you were back home milling around and talking to your friends how you would have those kinds of questions?"

"Yeah, I guess," Mackenzie answered.

"And how you'd be almost compelled to go and find out if you didn't have me or Mom, or anyone with you," Patrick finished.

Mackenzie was quiet for a minute, and then said "I still don't want them to go."

Patrick leaned over and gave her one last hug and said "I know that you don't Darlin'. They know it too."

Patrick grabbed his back pack and opened the tent flaps that served as the door. He called back into her as he was walking out "Get up and around now. We need to break camp and make tracks."

After putting her things away hastily, Mackenzie emerged from the tent. Stuart and Sawyer were standing next to each other down at the boat. Mackenzie walked down towards them and put an arm around each of them initiating a group hug. Neither of the boys were comfortable with the situation, but they each patted her back with one of their free arms.

"I wish that you guys would come with us," Mackenzie said to them as she released them and took a step back.

"We are," Sawyer said and started walking towards Mackenzie's tent that was only thing remaining in the camp.

"What do you mean?" Mackenzie asked as she turned to follow him.

"We're going to ride with you until Yankton," Stuart said. "Sawyer thinks that you guys will run into a bunch of scaveys between here and there, and you'll need our help."

"Really?" Mackenzie asked as they reached her tent and started breaking it down. "Isn't that a long way out of your guy's way?"

"Yeah," Sawyer answered. "But Stuart says that he knows where the motorcycle dealer shop is in Yankton, so if we can find some gas we could be back here in a day."

"Cool," Mackenzie said. "How long until we get to Yankton?"

Stuart answered as he was putting the tent poles into the bag. "Your dad thinks that we should be able to get there by tomorrow night if we hustle and paddle some."

"Depending on how many scaveys we run into I'd say," Sawyer added.

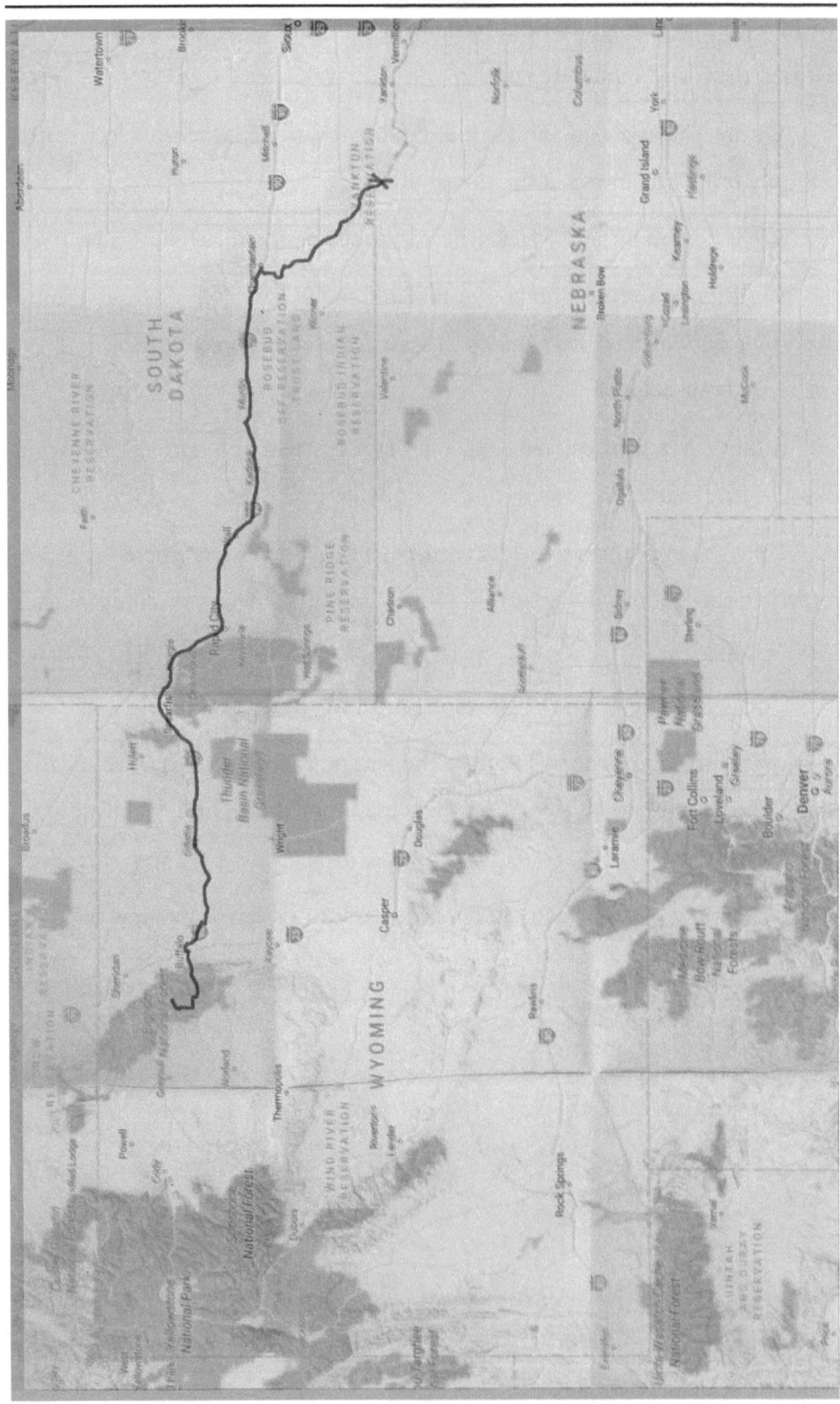

CHAPTER 21

THE BOAT WAS cramped with all four of them and their gear in it. Still, they made due as Sawyer and Stuart sat in the middle seat again and did most of the rowing. It seemed to Mackenzie that they were going a lot faster than they had at any other leg of their trip. They all continued to talk throughout the day and share notes about where they came from, the scaveys, and what they thought might have really happened to cause all of this. Mackenzie hadn't seen Stuart be as open and excited about anything since they had met.

The topography of the river had gradually changed in the last hour or so as the sun began to set. The normally wide river that they had been floating down was becoming choked down, with smaller channels crisscrossing and intersecting one another like a delta. The trees that had lined, and then dotted the river banks, now were sparse or non-existent. The normally slow current of the river was almost gone altogether.

It was almost fully dusk when the boat ran aground. Mackenzie wasn't expecting the sudden stop and came out of her seat a few inches. She felt herself involuntarily make circles with her hands to keep her balance and not fall forward out of the boat.

"Whooa," Patrick said loudly. "What the heck was that?"

Sawyer extended his oar out the side of the boat and slapped the water. "Feels like we've hit a sand bar," he said. He dug around in his pack that was stuffed under the bench he was sitting on and brought out a small flashlight. Mackenzie was so used to not having artificial light for the last few weeks, she was amazed when it came on when Sawyer clicked the button on the end of it.

Sawyer pointed the flashlight over the side and peered into the murky water. "Yeah," he said. "We bottomed out on something sandy." Sawyer handed the flashlight to Mackenzie, flipped the oar around so that he was holding the wrong end, and submerged the handle in the water. He gave several big pushes with the oar and they were floating once again.

"How well can you see the bottom up there with that thing?" Patrick asked Mackenzie.

Mackenzie got on her knees and peered over the front of the boat with the flashlight pointed down into the water. "Ummm, a little bit I guess," she answered.

"I guess we're going to have to try and find a place to camp for the night," Patrick said. Looking around at the banks and not seeing what he wanted he said "Let's see if we can make it a little further first though. Mak, you keep a look out for sand or rocks and yell out if you see anything."

"All right," Mackenzie answered as she tried to settle in and get more comfortable leaning over the edge of the boat.

They paddled slowly that way for another hour or so until it was fully dark. The moon was a little more than half-full, so there was some ambient light, but not enough to navigate the larger channel with. They made their way to the south side of the main river and Patrick directed them to dock at a concrete boat ramp when it came into view.

Mackenzie's back was aching and it screamed at her as she climbed out of the boat after they had gently beached it in the mud next to the boat ramp. They all were stiff and stretched some as they got out of the boat and pulled it further up the bank.

Sawyer took the flashlight from Mackenzie and snapped it off in a hurry.

"Hey," Mackenzie said. "What's that about?"

"Sorry," Sawyer answered. "It will attract scaveys."

"We haven't seen any on this side of the river," Mackenzie said.

"Yeah, but I bet there's a town nearby with this boat ramp here," Sawyer said. "If there's a town, there's bound to be scaveys."

"Should we pitch the tents over there?" Patrick asked the group as he pointed over to a picnic bench and fire ring on the other side of the boat ramp. They could just make it out in the moon light.

"I don't think that we should stay in tents tonight," Sawyer said.

"What do you mean?" Patrick asked.

"If there is a town close by, we'd be overrun in minutes in tents down here," Sawyer replied.

"So, what do you think that we should do?" Patrick asked.

"Let's scout it out a little bit. If there's a farm house or some place to hole up for the night, we'd be better off," Sawyer suggested.

Patrick didn't say anything, he just stood there and pondered Sawyer's suggestion.

"You asked if we'd come along and help you get past the scaveys," Sawyer started. "I'm telling you, you don't want to be down here in tents if they start to swarm us. Let's grab our rifles and scout out the area a little."

"Alright," Patrick said. "Grab your rifle Mak."

They spread out side by side and walked up the boat ramp. When they crested the small hill from the river, the boat ramp and empty parking area turned into a well-maintained dirt road that had a road sign that said "4th Street". The ground was flat, and the road went straight south as far as they could see with barren fields on either side of it.

"Not really a sprawling metropolis," Patrick whispered.

Sawyer gave him a sideways glance and started walking down the dirt road. Patrick shrugged as he looked at the other two, then started after Sawyer. Mackenzie was glad to be out of that boat and able to get a little exercise. She normally wasn't one for exercise, but it felt good to be out walking instead of bent over the bow of the boat searching for the bottom with the flashlight.

The small group walked in silence along the road. The air wasn't cold, but much cooler than it had been throughout the day and it felt refreshing. The smell of the river was giving way to the smell of earth as they walked further away from the boat. Sawyer suddenly came to a halt and held his right hand up in a fist like some of the platoon commanders do in the war movies. The whole group recognized what he meant and stopped immediately. Mackenzie peered into the darkness lit only by the moon and stars, but didn't see any-thing except for the same extending road up ahead. Sawyer motioned with his right hand for them to walk along the edge of the road, so they all joined in single-file as he began to move again.

After they had walked for several more minutes, Mackenzie recognized the dark shape of a building or house up ahead on the left. Just when she was going to whisper to Sawyer if that is what he had seen, Sawyer walked to the barb wire fence on the left-hand side of the road. He stepped on the bottom wire and pulled up the other strands so the others could pass through. Mackenzie was first and dipped down to go under, but her dad put his hand on her shoulder to stop her.

"Huh-uh," he whispered as she turned around to see what his concern was. He motioned for her rifle that she had slung across her back. She looked at him quizzically, and he motioned again to it. She took the rifle off her back and handed it to her dad. He then motioned for her to crawl through and handed it back to her once she was across. He then handed her his rifle and then climbed through himself. They helped the other two across, and then they made their way across the field at a diagonal line towards the farm house. When they were a few hundred feet from the house, Sawyer started walking hunched over and low to the ground, so the others followed suit.

They reached a row of elm trees and a mesh fence on the north side of the house, and Sawyer motioned for them to get down. They all readied their rifles and squatted down in the moonlight shadows of the trees and listened. Mackenzie's thighs started to burn from the squatting position she had taken when Sawyer reached down and grabbed a large clod of dirt from the field and lobbed it over to the side of the house. The clod hit with a large thud and partially broke up when it hit the siding near the second-floor window. They all looked and listened intently for any kind of sound or response, but heard nothing but their own group's breathing in the quiet new world.

Sawyer reached down to grab another clod of dirt, but Patrick grabbed his wrist and then shook his head. Patrick handed Sawyer his rifle, and then climbed over the mesh fence to the farmhouse's yard. He recovered his rifle, then scurried over to the corner of the house near where Sawyer's clod of dirt had hit the siding. Patrick peered around the corner for a moment, and then quietly dashed to the front porch and tried the front door. It was open, so he turned the handle and entered.

The others watched and waited for a noise or Patrick for what seemed like too long. Stuart stood up and tried to hand Sawyer his rifle, but Sawyer motioned for him to squat back down. Stuart complied, but from the look on his face he wasn't happy about it.

Finally, Patrick emerged from the front door and waved for the others. They each made their way over the fence and joined Patrick in the entry way of the large farm house.

As they filed in, Patrick reported to Sawyer in a low voice "The house is clear of scaveys. There is one empty bed upstairs, the other bedrooms have some scenes that I'd rather Mackenzie didn't see."

"Any food?" Stuart asked in a low voice as well.

"I didn't check very good yet, but the kitchen has been thoroughly tossed," Patrick answered.

Sawyer told Stuart "Why don't you see if you can scrounge up any food and then meet us upstairs. No meat. Got it?"

"Got it," Stuart said as he headed off to what looked like it was the kitchen from the entry way.

"Can you see anything from that bedroom without the bodies?" Sawyer asked Patrick.

"Not sure. Let's go look," Patrick responded.

The three of them walked single file up the stairs and then turned right down the hallway. It was dark in the hallway and Mackenzie reached out and grabbed a belt loop on the back of her dad's jeans to help guide her. Sawyer walked a little too fast and bumped into the back of Mackenzie. He kept his hand on the small of her back as they crept down the hall to tell where she was in the darkness. Mackenzie liked the way that his warm firm hand touched her and was glad that it was almost pitch dark in the hallway because she could feel her face blushing.

The empty bedroom was small, but was on the south-west corner of the house and had two large windows on each exterior wall that let some moonlight in. Patrick went around the bed to the south window, and Sawyer went to the other. They each opened the curtains as wide as they would go and peered out into the darkness.

"I think that I see a gas station sign," Patrick said still in a low voice but loud enough that the others could still hear. "And maybe a stop light. Just a little further up the road we were on."

Mackenzie joined her dad first and then Sawyer did as well when he couldn't make anything out from the window he was standing at.

After looking through it for a minute, Sawyer said to them "We'll see what Stuart finds down there. If it's empty, I'll head into town to see what I can get for groceries."

"I don't think that's a good idea," Patrick said almost immediately. "We have enough food to get us to Yankton."

"Yeah, but Stuart and I aren't going to want to spend time messing around in Yankton while you guys are crossing the Line. It'd be better if we could stock up now on a few things to get us through for a few days."

After a brief pause, Patrick argued some more, "At least wait until morning so we can cover you from here if we need to."

"Nah," Sawyer answered shaking his head. "It'd be better to go tonight. The scaveys swarm when they see or hear something, so the darkness would be to our advantage. I know what I'm doing. Trust me."

Mackenzie involuntarily giggled.

"What's so funny?" Sawyer snapped.

"Nothing," Mackenzie answered.

"Tell me," Sawyer said again.

Mackenzie looked into her dad's eyes and said "It's just... my dad always told me never to trust a man who says 'Trust me'."

Sawyer turned quickly and stepped back to the other window.

Patrick gave his daughter a wry smile and then looked back out his own window. "Listen Sawyer," Patrick started. "I know that it's fun to play army, but we have to go about this smart."

Sawyer turned and faced Patrick. His chest was going up and down and he was clearly upset. "You think that this is playing army?" he said. His voice came out much louder than he had meant it to, and he immediately quieted himself back to a hushed voice before continuing. "Playing army," he said disgustingly. "If you'd seen some of the stuff that I went through, you wouldn't call it playing army. Killing the neighbor boy with my bare hands; holding off a swarm of more than fifty by myself in a strip mall; sleeping with one eye open behind a barricaded door while those things paced back and forth outside a bedroom in a townhouse... It's only been a few weeks, but I feel like I've fought a whole war against those things. If you think precautions are playing army, then you know a lot less than what I gave you credit for."

"Hey!" Mackenzie said. Her pulse was racing and her blood was warm from this boy practically yelling at her father.

Patrick grabbed her shoulder. "It's okay," he said to her softly. Then to Sawyer he said "You're probably right son. I haven't seen or been through what you have. I just want us all to make it through this thing."

"Well, then I'm telling ya," Sawyer answered with some vindication in his tone. "Stuart and I need to get some food so that we're good past Yankton; and if there isn't any here then going into this town tonight will be better than going in the morning."

"Okay," Patrick responded. "Let's wait and see what he finds here first."

After only a few minutes, they heard Stuart coming up the stairs. Sawyer went into the hallway and helped guide him into the bedroom.

"Get anything good?" Mackenzie asked as she sat on the bed.

"Zilch," Stuart said as he sat on the opposite side of the bed. "It was pretty gross actually. Everything had been ransacked, but there was also blood, and mud, and hair, and just nasty stuff everywhere."

"Were there bodies and stuff?" Mackenzie asked.

"No. Not that I seen," Stuart answered. "Just nasty stuff everywhere."

"There's a gas station and some other buildings just up the road there," Sawyer told Stuart. "I'm going to head up there and see if I can find some food for us."

"I'll go with you," Stuart said.

"You sure?" Sawyer asked.

"Yeah, I don't want to just wait around here all night wondering if you found anything," Stuart said.

"Alright," Sawyer said as he turned towards the door. "Let's go then."

"Hey," Patrick said stopping Sawyer in the doorway. Sawyer turned with his jaw set. "If you get in trouble, fire three quick shots."

"Okay," Sawyer said visibly relieved that he didn't have to verbally spar again with Patrick.

"Three quick ones or we're not coming out of here," Patrick repeated.

"Gotcha," Sawyer said as he turned to leave and waved for Stuart to follow him. "Three quick ones."

After they left, Mackenzie walked over to the window to watch them leave and Patrick closed and locked the bedroom door. He knelt at the edge of the bed with his head down and said a silent prayer. Mackenzie watched the two boys sneak down the edge of the dirt road together until she could no longer see them.

Patrick joined her at the window and asked quietly "You still see them?"

"No. They played leap frog army all the way up the road," she said coyly.

Patrick smiled at her, patted her on the shoulder, and then lay down on the bed with his hands behind his neck.

"Why did you let him go if you didn't think that it was the best thing?" Mackenzie asked her dad as she continued to peer out the window to try and catch a glimpse of the other two.

"He was probably right," Patrick said.

Mackenzie turned and gave her dad an unbelieving look.

"What?" Patrick asked.

"I just don't think that I've ever heard you admit that you're wrong," Mackenzie said.

"Darlin', I'm wrong a whole lot more than I'd like to admit," Patrick answered.

"I know Dad," Mackenzie said with a chuckle. "You just don't ever say that you're wrong."

"That's just the engineer in me," Patrick chuckled back at her. "I still don't think that it's smart to go into that town that we don't know in the middle of the night when there are clearly scaveys around here, but he has had more experience with them than I have."

After a few more minutes of staring out the window, Mackenzie asked "What was the thing back there at the fence?"

"What do you mean?" Patrick asked her from behind closed eyelids.

"With the gun. Why did you have me hand my gun across when I was climbing through the fence?"

"A hunter safety thing," Patrick said opening his eyes. "Every year it seems like someone gets accidently shot by their son or their buddy when the fence catches the trigger while they're climbing through. Always hand your gun across when you can."

"You're such an engineer Dad" Mackenzie said as Patrick closed his eyes again.

After a while, Mackenzie sat down on the corner of the bed so that she could still see half-heartedly out the window. Patrick's even and deep breathing told her that he was full on into a hearty nap. Her mind turned to her friends and her mother. She was thinking about what it would be like to run and wrap her arms around her mom. The smell of her perfume, the loving and gentle hug, the feel of her mom's curly hair. Then she heard the first shot and her legs instinctively propelled her up off the bed, and the image of her mother vanished from her thoughts. Adrenaline was coursing through her veins as her dad joined her at the window a split second later.

"Do you see them?" Patrick asked her quickly.

"No," Mackenzie said.

Patrick reached down and tried to open the window, but it didn't budge. He found the clasp, opened it, then pushed the window up to the open position. He knelt by the open window and readied his rifle. He swept the scope back and forth looking for any movement.

After seeing what her dad was doing, Mackenzie knelt next to him and did the same. She couldn't see hardly anything through the scope on her small rifle and switched quickly between looking through the scope to looking with her naked eye, and back again. She couldn't make out anything in the darkness.

After a few seconds, she heard something coming from near the front of the house. She stood up and went to the other window and caught a glimpse of figure running down the road towards the town. She ran back over and knelt at her prior position and found the figure in her scope. She could see that it was a male scavey. He looked like he would have been in his late twenties and was dressed in a dirty white t-shirt and jeans. He was running as fast as he could up the dirt road towards the town. She trained her scope reticles on the back of the scaveys' neck and flicked her safety off with her index finger.

"Whooa," her dad whispered. "Don't shoot."

"Why? I got him," Mackenzie said.

"If you shoot they'll know we're here," Patrick said. "I don't think one more of those things is going to make a bit of difference to whatever they've gotten themselves into."

Mackenzie took a deep breath and put the safety back on. She continued to watch the scavey run for a few more seconds until he was totally out of view in the darkness.

"I hope that you weren't wrong twice tonight," Mackenzie said.

They both knelt at the window and sat on the corner of the bed quietly for several more hours waiting for something else to happen. The first signs of light began to show as a deep red glow came from the east. As the light grew in intensity, the more they could make out of the small town several blocks away. The gas station sign and the stop light silhouettes became more distinct.

Then they could begin to make out the shapes of a couple of houses and a few buildings around the street corner that was in their view. Then they could start to make out the colors of the buildings and the few cars that were parked along the road and streets.

"Where do you think that the shot came from last night?" Patrick asked Mackenzie as he stared through his scope trying to make out more details as the sun rose in the sky.

"I don't know; I was – " she stopped abruptly as another gun shot rang out.

This time with the window open, they both were sure that it was considerably West from where they could see. It must have been further along the main street past the stop light that they could just make out.

Then another report, but the last one sounded different. It was from the same general area as the first, but it sounded like it was from a different gun.

"That's his pistol I think," Patrick said blankly as he was still trying to see anything out of his scope. "Open that other window and man that post," Patrick told his daughter. She wasn't exactly sure what he meant, but she scrambled over to the other window and struggled to open it. After fighting with it for a few moments she finally got it to open and readied her rifle. She couldn't see as much down the street from that vantage point, but she could see the driveway to the front of the house and the empty fields to the trees that must have hidden the rest of the town from her view.

They heard two more quick reports from the gun that Patrick thought was Sawyer's pistol. They were from the same general area, but they sounded like they were getting closer.

"I think that they're headed back this way," Patrick shouted over to Mackenzie. Then he added "Make sure that you know what you're shooting at before you pull the trigger. Aim small, miss small."

One more shot from a different gun was heard. This time it was definitively much closer than before. It seemed like they were making their way down the main street back towards the street light and gas station.

"Was that three shots?" Mackenzie asked her dad. "Should we go get them?"

"No," Patrick answered. "I told him three quick shots or we were staying put."

Two more shots from the pistol. It sounded like they should be able to see them any minute.

Out of the corner of Mackenzie's eye, she saw a Scavey running down the road toward the town in almost the same path that the last one had taken. This one was much larger though. He looked like he had been in his fifties and was considerably overweight with a balding head. He loped more than he was running, but he was still making good time up the road.

Mackenzie flipped the safety off from her rifle and drew a bead on the neck of the loping scavey. She could see through her scope that one of the shoulder straps from his overalls was unattached and flapped against his back with each of his loping step. Mackenzie thought to herself *Aim small, miss small.* She let out her breath and slowly squeezed the trigger as she kept her target in sight.

The little rifle was loud in the small bedroom. So much so that she involuntarily closed her eyes and didn't see the impact of her shot. When she opened her eyes again, she saw the large man lying in the street face down and motionless with one hand clasping the back of his neck.

"Here they come!" her dad yelled across the room. She craned her neck to peer down the street and saw Stuart and Sawyer sprinting down the dirt road towards them. Stuart was in the lead, and Sawyer was running with his pistol pointed behind him. "Watch the front door!" her dad yelled again.

Mackenzie turned her attention to the front door and the driveway in front of the house looking for any movement. She felt her arms starting to shake, so she closed her eyes and took a deep breath. As she was letting the air from her lungs, her dad fired and operated the bolt on his rifle to load another round. She looked down the street and saw a scavey explode backwards off its feet just as it turned the corner chasing after the two boys.

Suddenly both boys stopped in the middle of the road about half-way to the house. Stuart dropped to his knees and aimed his gun down the road in the direction towards the river and passed the house. Sawyer turned and aimed his pistol behind them watching the corner that they had just came around. Stuart shot once, then twice. Mackenzie swung around to the other side of the window to try and see what Stuart was shooting at. She heard him fire again, and again, and again. The elm trees that they had come through blocked her view, and she couldn't see what Stuart was shooting at.

Her dad fired again and the sound made her flinch. When she opened her eyes, she saw a woman scavey running down the driveway towards the front door of the house. She brought her rifle up quickly and fired a shot just as the long hair of the woman vanished from her field of view, and she heard the screen door slam on the front door.

"I missed one Dad!" Mackenzie screamed. "I'm sorry – I'm sorry!"

"Did it make it inside?" Patrick yelled back over to her without looking up from his rifle.

"Yeah," she screamed again. "I'm sorry!"

Patrick took the revolver from his belt and slid it across the floor to his daughter. "Cover the bedroom door with this," he said.

Mackenzie grabbed the revolver with her right hand and looked back out the window. Stuart fired two more times then got back on his feet. The two of them were sprinting back to the house again. Her dad fired once, loaded another round and shot again.

Mackenzie watched Stuart and Sawyer running down the road. Just as they neared the drive way in front of the house, footsteps bounded down the hall to the bedroom. Mackenzie raised the revolver and cocked the hammer back as the creature hit the door and let out a scream that didn't sound like any human sound she had ever heard before. The door held.

Patrick put his rifle on safety, bounded over to where his daughter was kneeling by the window, and took the revolver from her. Just as he grabbed the revolver, the woman scavey hit the door again, but this time the jam gave way where the door handle was. The creature fell into the room with both arms above her head and her mouth wide open in the middle of a full non-human scream. Patrick squeezed the trigger of the revolver and the top half of the creature exploded into the hallway and the small bedroom.

Mackenzie cringed at the sight and sound and closed her eyes tight.

"It's us! It's us!" Stuart called out as they bounded up the stairs.

"Let's get out of here!" Sawyer yelled to them.

Patrick grabbed his rifle and went back to Mackenzie. He lifted her up and guided her to the door. She didn't want to, but she couldn't help but catch a look at the scavey body lying on the floor next to the bed. She looked away and closed her eyes tight again just as fast as she had looked. Mackenzie wished that he hadn't seen the sight. She was sure that the picture of the woman missing most of her parts above her neck would haunt her dreams for years to come. And the blood. The blood was everywhere.

"Let's go Mak!" Patrick yelled at his daughter as he was trying to guide her quickly down the hallway.

Mackenzie finally forced herself to open her eyes when she reached the top of the stairs. Stuart and Sawyer were standing on each side of the open front door looking out in both directions.

"You alright?" Stuart asked her as she and Patrick bounded down the stairs.

"I think so," she told him.

"We need to get out of here," Sawyer told them. "I'll watch the rear while we high tail it back to the boat."

Patrick said without hesitating "Let's go!"

Patrick shouldered his rifle sling and kept his revolver in his right hand while he grabbed Mackenzie's with his free hand. They headed out the front door at an all-out run while Stuart fell in right behind them with a duffle bag that they must have found in town the night before. Sawyer watched the road behind them for a minute, then took off after the rest of the crew.

Mackenzie's lungs were burning and her legs felt like jello by the time they crested the hill and first seen the boat beached in the same spot that it had been the night before. Stuart had overtaken them on the run back, and was half-way down the hill by the time her and her dad started down the boat ramp.

Sawyer fired twice for the first time since they left the farm house. He hadn't come over the top of the hill, so she couldn't tell what he was shooting at when she turned her head around to look.

Stuart reached the boat first and threw his rifle and duffle bag into it. He then struggled to push the boat from the dry ground out into the river.

Patrick dropped Mackenzie's hand and told her to hop in as he helped Stuart push from the front of the boat. As soon as Patrick added his weight to the effort, the boat moved suddenly and quickly out into the river. Patrick stepped into the bow with one foot and made his way to his seat in the back as Stuart knelt in the knee-deep water and turned to wait for Sawyer who had just reached the top of the boat ramp and was sprinting towards the boat.

When Sawyer was almost to the edge of the water, three scaveys came over the top of the hill as well. Patrick readied his rifle and aimed at the lead scavey.

"Go! Go! Go!" Sawyer yelled to those in the boat.

Stuart pushed off and hopped into the boat. Patrick fired his rifle and missed. He loaded another shell into the chamber as Sawyer reached the boat and lunged onto the side. Mackenzie thought that they were going to tip over at first because the boat listed under Sawyer's weight. The boat held though and he scrambled up onto the middle seat. Both Stuart and Sawyer began to paddle quickly away from the shore as Patrick shot again. This time, his aim was true and the teenage boy that was leading the pack dropped like a sack of potatoes on the boat ramp.

Stuart and Sawyer started paddling down river. Stuart was going frantically enough that they started to turn back towards the bank with the scaveys.

"Slow down," Sawyer yelled at him just as Patrick squeezed off another round and the second scavey fell just as he reached the water's edge. He fell face first into the river and part of him bobbed there while his feet remained anchored on the bank.

The third scavey looked like he had been a good looking young business man from his haircut and the way that he was dressed. He reached the water's edge and let out a loud hissing sound with his mouth wide open as he looked at it.

"Don't they like water?" Patrick asked Sawyer.

"I don't know," Sawyer responded and turned his attention to watch the creature. The scavey paced back and forth where the boat ramp met the river a couple of times, then it decided to run along the river bank following the boat. "At least that one don't," Sawyer said and Patrick fired again dropping the creature instantly. Patrick dug in his pack and loaded both of his weapons up again.

When they were down the river enough to where they couldn't make out the boat ramp any longer and their nerves had calmed down some, Mackenzie asked "So what happened last night?"

Sawyer and Stuart looked at each other. Stuart started to explain while they both continued to row. "We checked out a few places along the way that had been scavenged. But we found a mom and pop restaurant on the other end of town where none of them had made it into a walk-in pantry that they had in the kitchen. We filled up this bag with all kinds of good stuff – "

"No meat," Sawyer cut in.

"Yeah," Stuart confirmed with a grin. "No meat. We left the restaurant and headed back when we saw a big scavey crossing the street up ahead of us. I got excited and shot him when I probably shouldn't have."

"You can say that again," Sawyer chimed in.

"As soon as I shot, they all came out of nowhere," Stuart said. "We high-tailed it back to the restaurant and holed up in the pantry. I wanted to shoot to have you guys come get us, but Sawyer said that it would be better if we waited until dawn. We barricaded the door with some of the shelves in the pantry and waited until we saw light coming in under the doorway. Those things paced back and forth and scratched at the door all night. For whatever reason, they slowly left just before dawn and we decided to make a break for it. We ran back to the house shooting them as we saw them. You know the rest."

Mackenzie normally would have asked a dozen questions about their adventure, but now her mind was overloaded with all that she had seen and done in the last twenty-four hours. She turned and leaned over the front of the boat looking for rocks and sand bars that would hinder their progress back to her mother.

THE HIKE

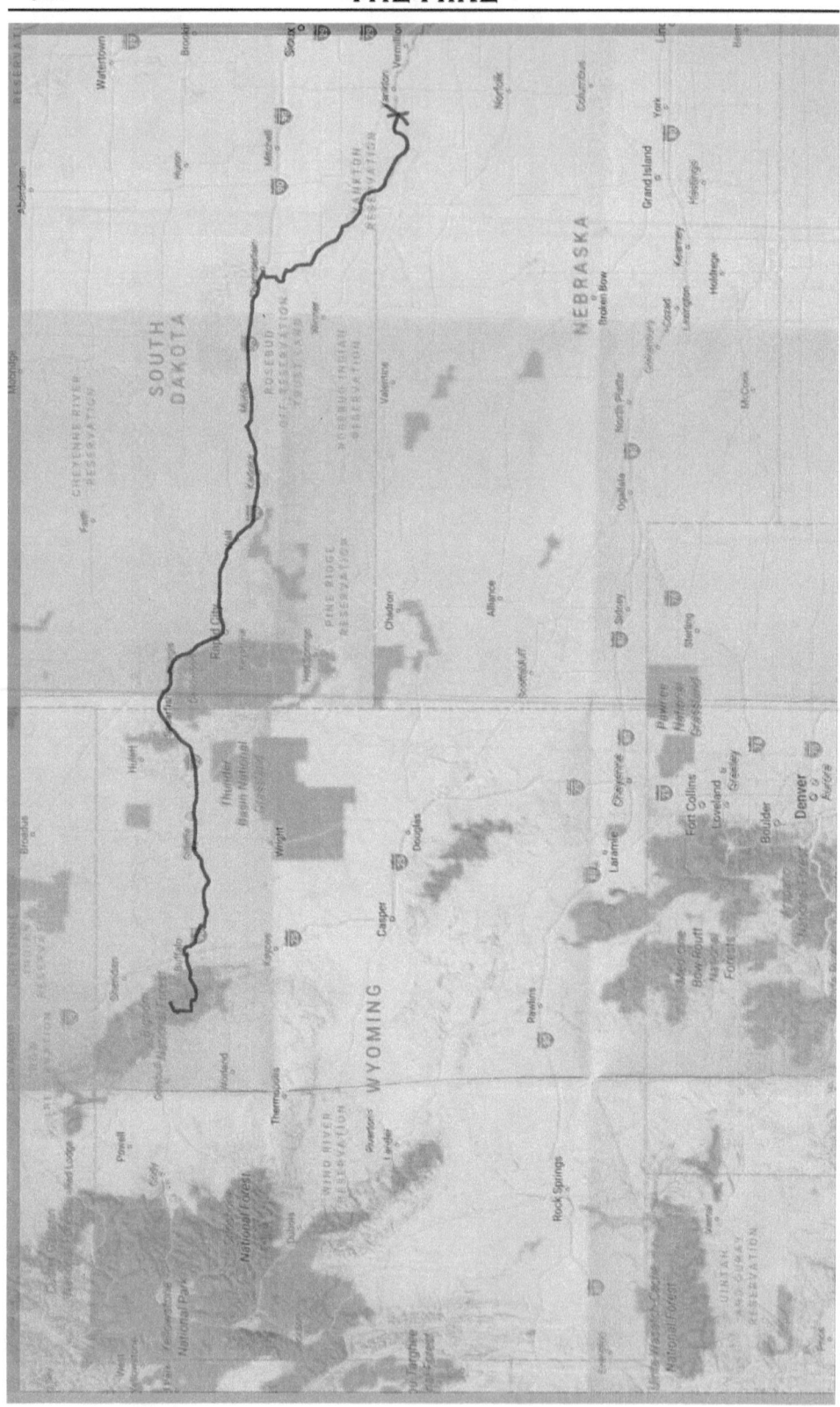

CHAPTER 22

THE WHOLE BOATING party took turns rowing, looking over the bow, and scanning the river banks for more scaveys throughout the day. While they took turns doing each task, they remained in their normal positions for most of the trip. By early afternoon, the narrow slow moving delta gave way to a large open lake.

"I think that we're getting close," Stuart said.

"Why's that?" Sawyer asked.

"Because I think that this is the lake right at Yankton. Lewis and Clark Lake I think. I fished here a couple of times when I was a kid," Stuart answered.

"How far do we have to go?" Patrick asked with excitement clearly in his voice.

"I don't know for sure," Stuart answered as he turned in the boat so that he could see Patrick. "It's been a long time since I've been here. A couple of miles I guess."

"And the town is right on the lake?" Sawyer asked and Stuart turned back around front.

"Pretty much. There's a dam at the end of the lake, and the highway to Yankton is right there." Stuart thought for a moment and then added "There's an old fort and campgrounds on the north side of the lake about half-way across I think. We could probably make out the dam from there with binoculars."

"Sounds like a plan," Patrick said.

The group paddled quietly for the next hour or so hugging the north edge of the lake looking for the campground and fort that Stuart had told them about. They reached a point on the lake where they could see the dam before they reached the campground that Stuart had told them about, so they decided to stop early. They beached the boat in a small bay that had an asphalt boat ramp and several parking lots around it.

They grabbed some of their gear and cautiously made it to a stand of trees near a brick building that served as restrooms. There were nice beaches all along the lake's edge that would have been a perfect place to frolic and relax under different circumstances. There weren't a lot of trees or other cover that broke their line of sight, so they could see in almost all directions with their binoculars and rifle scopes without obstruction. After they each took turns using the restrooms, they decided to cook an extremely large can of vegetable soup from the restaurant on the last of the available camping stove gas. While the soup was cooking, they finalized their plan of how to safely get Patrick and Mackenzie across the line, without getting Stuart and Sawyer caught. They relaxed, napped, and talked in low tones after lunch until dusk.

Sawyer was cleaning up the dishes and stowing the food back in the duffle bag they had found when Patrick sidled up to him. Patrick held something out to Sawyer for him to take.

"Thanks for all of your help," Patrick told him. Sawyer took the folded map from Patrick and looked at it for a moment before standing up and sticking his hand out to shake. Patrick took his hand and pumped it a couple of times before bending in and giving him a quick man hug with the other arm. Patrick let him go and said "I wish you the best. Take care of Stuart for us."

"I will," Sawyer told him and continued putting the food stuffs up.

Patrick walked over to Stuart where he was sitting in the grass visiting with Mackenzie. Mackenzie gave him a hug and was crying a little when Patrick approached.

"Uh, sorry," Patrick said.

"It's okay Dad," Mackenzie said.

"I didn't mean to interrupt," Patrick said.

"It's alright Mr. Kincaid," Stuart said as he stood up to face Patrick.

"I wanted to give you this," Patrick said as he held out his hand with his bible in it.

"Ahhh. I can't take that," Stuart told him.

"You can, and you will," Patrick told him. "You're going on an adventure with another young man that is smart and brave; but neither one of you are wise. Whatever questions you have are answered in that book." Stuart didn't move. "Take it," Patrick said and motioned the book towards him. Stuart apprehensively reached out and took the bible. "Those answers are sometimes hard to find, but if you read it daily and ask for His help; you'll get the wisdom that you need."

Stuart reached out quickly and gave Patrick a bear hug. Patrick wasn't expecting it and he about fell over backwards.

"Thank you, Mr. Kincaid," Stuart said with considerable emotion in his voice. "Thank you for everything."

"Okay Stuart," Patrick said after a moment. "You can turn me loose now."

Stuart let him go and used the back of his sleeve to wipe his nose.

"You sure that you want to go with him?" Patrick asked him.

"More than anything," Stuart answered.

"Good luck then. We'll be praying for you," Patrick said. Mackenzie stood up and the three of them had a big group hug with runny noses all around for each of them.

Sawyer brought the display of affection to a halt as he walked by on his way to the boat and said "We'd better get going."

Patrick told Stuart after they separated and started towards the boat "Oh – and when you find the Answer to your questions; tell Sawyer about Him."

They shoved off again and started paddling towards the dam. The sun had set by the time they all made it into the boat and the last light was disappearing as they got into a rhythm of rowing. They heard some commotion along the bank not far from where they had put in. The bank rose quickly into tall bluffs. They couldn't see anything and the noise didn't seem to be following them as they passed by, so they continued on their way trying not to make any noise of their own.

It didn't take them long and they had reached the dam. The dam at the end of the lake was huge, just as Stuart had told them. There was also a large marina next to it as he had explained over lunch. There were dozens of sailboats and larger motor boats docked on piers all next to the marina. The group pulled into an empty slot on one of the piers and tied their small drift boat off to it. They unloaded all the gear that they wanted to take and fastened it to Stuart's and Patrick's bikes.

They walked east along the highway together towards the town. Stuart and Sawyer walked next to the bikes while the other two walked abreast down the center of the highway. As they neared town, they could see artificial light coming from the other side of it that shown dimly on the horizon. The light cast an eerie glow that they weren't used to seeing in the new world.

When they reached the edge of town and the first main street that headed north, Stuart and Sawyer found a low spot next to a building to lay their bikes down. They joined the other two and said their goodbyes. Stuart said goodbye to Mackenzie first and they both were emotional after the quick hug and few words. Stuart thanked Patrick again and gave him a quick hug. Sawyer talked to Mackenzie for some time in hushed tones that Patrick couldn't make out from where he was standing. He was beginning to get upset with the secretiveness when Sawyer leaned forward and gave Mackenzie a hug. Mackenzie wiped her eyes dry and Sawyer stepped up to shake Patrick's hand one last time.

"Good luck young man," Patrick said.

"Good luck to you," Sawyer repeated. "You're gonna need it."

Patrick nodded to them both and they turned and headed east down the street that was lined with residential houses. Patrick unbuttoned the strap on his pistol holster and said to Mackenzie "Let's go find Mom and James."

Mackenzie nodded and started walking abreast with her dad. She had to try to keep the skip out of her step at the thought of seeing her mom. After they went several blocks, the side street that they were on turned into the main road. The artificial light on the other side of town was much brighter now, and they could almost make out where it was coming from. They both slung their rifles and tied the white towels they had brought along to the muzzles. They carried the rifles in front of them kind of like the color guard does at big assemblies.

The two of them walked several more blocks and passed some vacant commercial buildings and two gas stations. Patrick took out his revolver and fired two shots into the air. That was the signal to the other two that they were getting close and to let the soldiers know that something was coming.

Patrick leaned into his daughter and said "Don't forget about what we talked about."

"I know Dad," Mackenzie said with disdain in her voice. "I won't say a word about Stuart and Sawyer."

"Well I know you won't, but I just want to make sure that our stories are straight," Patrick said. "Whatever Stuart had done, tell them that was me; and whatever Sawyer had done, that was you."

"I know Dad," Mackenzie repeated still irritated. "Now let's find Mom."

They started walking again, but now they lifted their rifles with the towels tied to them well over their heads and waved them.

"It's just us! Don't shoot!" they both yelled and repeated together as they walked along towards the lights. "It's just us! Don't shoot!"

After less than a block, they heard a loud diesel engine headed their way. They stopped where they were, but continued to wave their towels and yell out "It's just us! Don't shoot!"

The engine sound got louder and louder. A Humvee came rolling down the street headed straight at them at a rate of speed that was much faster than the town's sheriff probably would have allowed under other circumstances. There were bright lights from all over the vehicle pointed at them. The driver of the truck slammed on the brakes several yards in front of them and the tires slid several inches with a screech on the pavement. A deep voice from one of the soldiers standing with the top half of his body extruding from the roof of the Humvee called down to them "Drop your weapons."

Patrick and Mackenzie both carefully laid their rifles down on the pavement in front of them and stood back up slowly.

"All of them," the deep voice said. "Drop all of your weapons."

Patrick suddenly remembered his revolver and reached back to his belt, unsheathed it, and laid it on the ground next to the rifle.

Four soldiers each jumped out of the Humvee's doors simultaneously. One from each side of the vehicle ran forward to Patrick and Mackenzie while the other two leaned against the front of the truck with their rifles trained on their targets. Both running soldiers simultaneously stopped about ten feet in front of the father and daughter. "Hands on your head," one of them said and both Patrick and Mackenzie complied.

"On your knees," the other one called out.

"It's okay" Patrick whispered to his daughter and they both knelt in front of the soldiers.

Both soldiers advanced and stood behind them as they knelt in on the pavement flooded in the bright lights of the Humvee. Patrick felt the soldier behind him grab both of this thumbs with his gloved hand and squeeze them tight. The soldier gave him a quick pat down, then pulled his hands down from his head and placed them in the middle of his back. The soldier then zip-tied his hands together and put another one on from his hands to his belt loop.

Patrick heard his daughter gasp as the other soldier must have been doing the same to her. "Hey – go easy on her. She's just a girl."

The soldier behind him hit him on the back of the head with the heel of his hand and said "Hush up!"

Patrick took a deep breath and tried to calm himself.

"Get up!" the soldier yelled to Mackenzie. The one behind Patrick grabbed his wrist and lifted to encourage him to move as well.

They walked them both back to the Humvee and slid them into the back seat through one of the side doors. The two soldiers who they'd taken their spots stood on the running boards outside of the vehicle as the driver put it into reverse and mashed the accelerator. He then stopped and mashed the accelerator again to go forward.

The soldier who was clearly in charge was the one who had been half standing in and out of the vehicle through the hatch in the roof. He bent down into the main cab so that he could look at his two new passengers. "How in the world did the two of you sneak passed the Line?" he asked them.

"What do you mean?" Patrick asked.

"You know what I mean. You could have just as easily gotten yourselves shot. Not only are you violating mandated curfew, but you are beyond the Stafford Line! My crew now has to spend four days in the pokey due to whatever your selfish motives were" the soldier said clearly upset at the predicament that his new passengers caused for him.

"We didn't sneak anywhere," Patrick informed him. "We're survivors."

"Yeah right," the soldier said incredulously.

"It's true," Mackenzie half yelled at the young man.

"Whatever. We'll get to the bottom of it when we get back to base," and with that he was standing again with his head out of the vehicle and clearly out of earshot.

When they reached the base, the crew of soldiers weren't any less rough with their captives. When they entered the building, one soldier took Mackenzie into one door while they marched Patrick down another hall.

"Dad!" Mackenzie yelled to her dad out of fear.

"It'll be okay Mak!" Patrick yelled out to her as she was pushed through the doorway.

The place they were in looked like a big truck stop instead of a military base. They led him to a row of showers, threw him a bar of soap, and told him to scrub up. Patrick thought that the shower felt great, and hoped that Mackenzie was getting the same treatment.

One of the soldiers yelled for him to hurry up. Patrick shut the water off and stepped out of the stall.

"Close your eyes!" one of the soldiers yelled right before he doused him with a bag full of white powder. "Turn around!" he yelled again at him. Patrick complied and was doused with the white powder on his back side.

One of the soldiers handed him a towel and a white jumpsuit, both folded neatly. Patrick unfolded the towel and started to dry off.

"Nuh-uh," the soldier said and motioned with the muzzle of his rifle for Patrick to leave the shower room.

Patrick felt cold and embarrassed walking nude out of the shower room. The soldier stuck the barrel of his rifle in Patrick's ribs and told him to move down the hall. They came to a room with a small window in the door, a drain in the floor, and a cot that took up most of the space. The soldier shoved Patrick into the room hard enough that he almost fell down across the cot.

"Four days," the soldier said, then left and locked the door from the outside.

Patrick dried off, then put the jumpsuit on. He decided that he hoped they treated Mackenzie a little different instead.

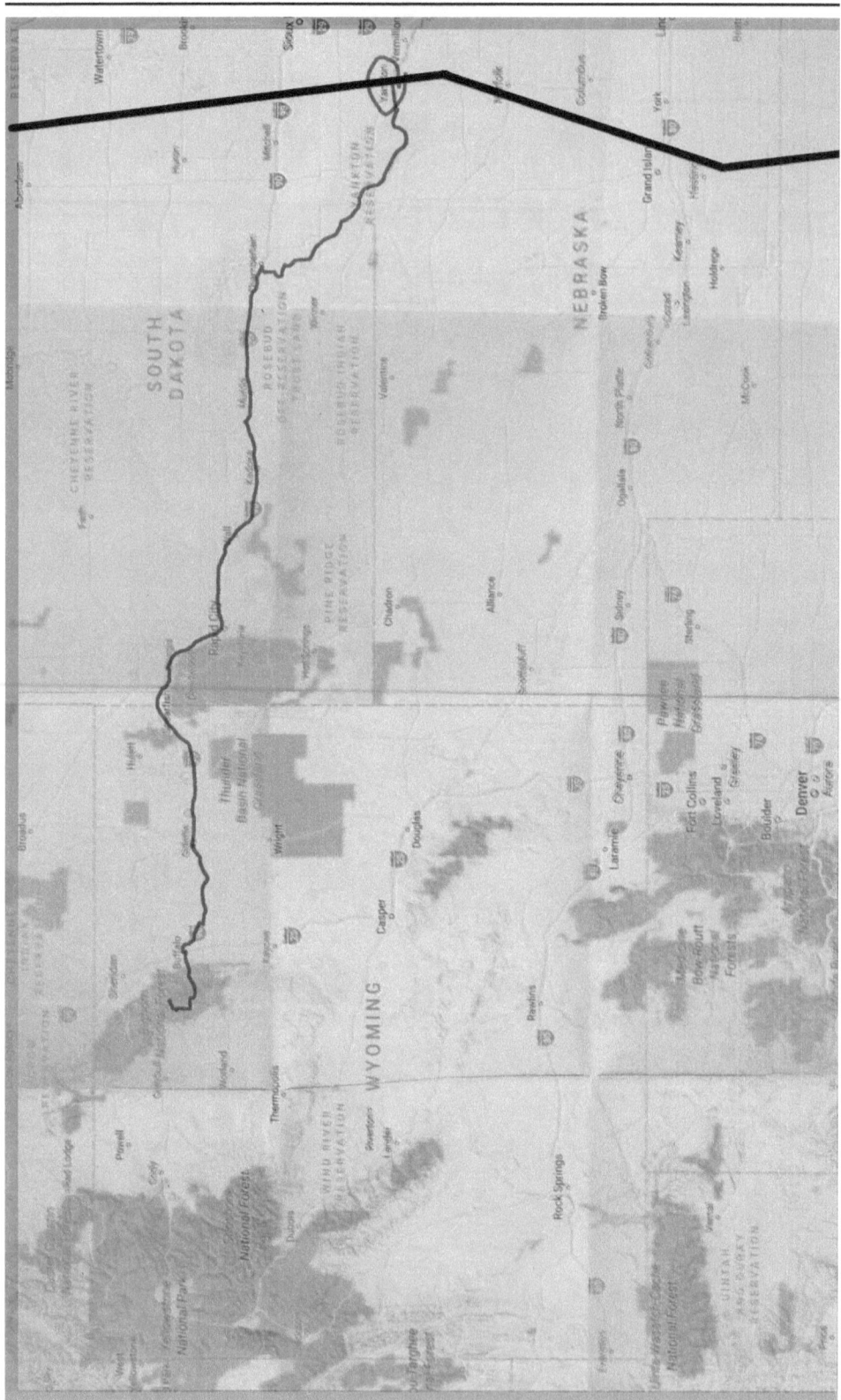

CHAPTER 23

THE FOUR DAYS felt like twenty. Patrick hadn't seen a
soul the whole time. It wasn't until the second day when he was looking for a way to escape that he found bottled water and MRE's left under the
cot near the foot of the bed.

He used the drain in the middle of the floor to relieve himself, and
counted himself lucky that he didn't have to go number two. The only light
came from the fluorescent fixtures outside the door that let light in the small
four-inch by eight-inch window high up in the center of the door. He once
thought that he had seen someone walk by, but by the time he jumped to the
window to look he couldn't see anything.

Four days of wondering. Four more days of longing to see his wife and
son again. Four days of hopefulness and faith that this had been the right
decision and that his government wouldn't harm his daughter. Four days of

playing the events of the last several weeks through his mind, and imagining how he was going to tell the story to others without mentioning Stuart or Sawyer.

Finally, on the fourth day that felt like the twentieth; a young man with a gas mask and face shield appeared at the door. Patrick jumped up and stood at the door waiting for him to unlatch it. Patrick's anxiety and the four days of solitude made him think of himself as a golden retriever standing in front of the door to be let out after being cooped up all weekend. Finally, the gas mask man opened the door and Patrick bounded out.

"Whoa there," the young man in the gas mask and smock said to him.

"Sorry," Patrick said to him. "It just feels like I've been in there forever. How's Mackenzie?"

"Who?" the man garbled through the gas mask.

"Mackenzie! My daughter!" Patrick yelled at the young man.

"Oh! Settle down sir. She's fine. We're releasing her now as well. Now please; let's exit the quarantine area," the man in the mask said and pointed to a door at the end of the long hall.

Patrick turned and complied with the man in the gas mask. He walked down the long hall to the door at the end and his bare feet were frigid by the time they reached the end. The man in the mask stepped passed Patrick and opened the door. Patrick stepped through into what looked like a bustling office building. There were all kinds of what looked like soldiers and marines talking, staring at laptop computers, and talking on radios. Mixed among them were a spattering of people wearing white lab coats like the man in the gas mask.

Once they had stepped through the door and the man in the mask had secured the door behind them. He removed his mask and took a deep breath.

The man had a dark trimmed goatee and looked to be in his mid-thirties. Patrick thought that his wife probably would think that he was a handsome fellow.

The whole room came immediately to a standstill when they heard the door close. They all were staring at Patrick. Then the whispers started. People from all over the room leaned to each other and started whispering and talking in hushed tones without taking their eyes off him. The gas-mask man lifted a hand and gestured down another hallway and said "If you please."

Patrick turned and walked down the hallway that was lined with more doors like the ones where he had been quarantined.

"We're in here," the man with the goatee said as they reached a door a few from the end of the hall and opened it. They both stepped into the room that was dimly lit. There was a metal folding table in the center of the room with four chairs set up around it. At one spot on the far side of the table was a laptop computer and a few manila folders set next to it.

The man with the goatee extended his hand and said "Abram Meyer."

Patrick shook the man's hand and replied with his name.

"Nice to meet you Patrick. Please sit down," he said and gestured to one of the chairs opposite of the laptop. Patrick sat down and folded his hands on the table as Abram sat down across from him. As Patrick sat down he saw that there was a large mirror on the wall behind Abram that no doubt was a one-way mirror for monitoring these types of interrogations.

"I apologize for the stares and jeers out there Mr. Kincaid," Abram said. He picked up an electronic cigarette that was sitting next to the laptop and took a drag from it. "But rumor has it that you and your daughter are survivors from the cloud and not just two scoundrels that escaped across the Stafford Line."

"We are survivors," Patrick replied.

"Yes, we know," Abram said before taking another pull on his cigarette. "We found your wife Mr. Kincaid. She explained to us the expedition that you and your daughter were on."

"My wife?" Patrick exclaimed unable to resist his joy at the knowledge that she was alive. "Mary's okay?" he asked as he felt himself rise out of his seat a couple of inches.

"Yes, Yes," Abram said calmly and opened the top manila folder and peered at some printout of information. "And your son James as well. They both are alive and well."

Patrick leaped from his seat and walked around in a small circle. He was exhilarated from top to bottom.

"Mr. Kincaid…" Abram said calmly.

Patrick forced himself to stop. He stood behind the chair that he had been sitting on and put his hands on the back of it. He ignored Abram's calling and bowed his head and closed his eyes to give thanks.

"Mr. Kincaid…" Abram repeated but with clearly more irritation this time.

Patrick ignored Abram again while he was giving praise and thanks. Abram typed something on the lap top and moved the mouse around some while he waited for Patrick to respond.

Patrick finished his prayer and then forced himself to sit down again. Patrick cleared his throat and said "I'm sorry Mr. Meyer. It's just that you gave me the best news I think that I've ever gotten." He felt a tear forming at the corner of his eye and reached up to wipe it.

Abram finished typing something on the keyboard and paused for a minute before looking at or responding to Patrick. "No, I understand Mr. Kincaid. Please forgive my abruptness," Abram said flatly. He took another drag from the e-cigarette before continuing. "It's just that your wife and son are here at the facility, and the sooner that we complete this debriefing, the sooner you will be able to leave with them."

"Well, let's get it over with then," Patrick said.

"Okay," Abram said as he placed a microphone that was connected to the laptop in the center of the table. He pushed a button on the keyboard, then leaned back in his chair with his arm's folded and the electronic cigarette in one hand that was close to his chin. "Let's start from the beginning Mr. Kincaid," Abram said and then tilted his head to take another draw from the e-cigarette.

"Okay. The beginning…" Patrick started.

Patrick spent the next several hours telling the entire story of their adventure and interaction with the cloud. He omitted telling Abram anything that he thought would lead to suspicions of Stuart or Sawyer. Patrick had gone over the story in his mind so many times in the last four days that he could tell that it is was coming off a little rehearsed, but Abram didn't let on about any suspicions. Abram asked very few questions throughout Patrick's monologue, and the ones that he did ask only seemed to Patrick to be clarifying questions and not probing ones. Patrick finished the tale with being taken into custody by the soldiers and he added several snide comments about how he and his daughter were treated roughly.

After Patrick had finished, Abram sat for several seconds with a thoughtful look on his face staring at Patrick without moving or saying anything. Finally, he reached forward and pushed a button on the keyboard and then asked "Thank you for your story Mr. Kincaid. I only have one more question for you before we dismiss you."

Abram let silence and anticipation hang in the air. Patrick felt his stomach muscles tighten as he anticipated questions about Stuart, Sawyer, or maybe something different that Mackenzie had told him.

"You and your daughter both referred to the infected people that you saw as 'Scaveys'. Where did you hear that term?" Abram asked without any emotion.

Patrick could feel his pulse begin to race, and he felt sweat start to form at his temples although it was quite cool in the room. He could tell that he was taking too long to answer the question, but finally said "I think that we must have heard it from the soldiers when they were bringing us in. We kept calling them 'creatures', and one of them said 'You mean scaveys?'"

Abram pursed his lips and then nodded slightly. "I see," he said. Abram leaned forward and tipped the computer screen on the laptop down. "We do appreciate your willingness to share your story with us Mr. Kincaid. The more that we learn about this event, the faster we can heal those infected people and get our country back to what it was before the catastrophe."

Patrick felt himself relax and his pulse slow.

"There are two things that I need to inform you of before you are dismissed," Abram said.

Patrick nodded his head instead of verbally responding. He didn't want to say anything more that might screw up his chances of seeing his family again.

"The first thing is that you and your family will be allowed to return to your place of residence since it is outside of the Stafford Line, but you will be under house arrest until otherwise notified."

"House arrest?" Patrick blurted out without restraint. "What did I do?"

"I think that you understand your government's concern with potentially wanting to know more about your adventure in the future as more facts become available," Abram said wryly. "You may have a clue that unlocks the nature of the events that you haven't recognized or that we don't know how to ask today. The alternative to the house arrest is an extended stay at one of our military bases such as this one, until we are sure that we no longer have any need for information that you might have. Will you be able to comply with the house arrest directive?"

Patrick's blood was boiling. All that Sawyer had told him was true about the martial law and the absence of freedom. Instead of releasing a diatribe about freedom and the glory of the United States that he felt welling up within him, he replied through semi-grit teeth "I will comply."

"Excellent," Abram said flatly. He took another drag as he seemed to ponder how to relay the second piece of information. "Now, more importantly; there is an issue with your story that we need to correct."

Patrick replied only with a furrowed brow that communicated his lack of understanding.

"For whatever reason, you are mistaken about how some of the events took place regarding the cloud. We're not sure why your memories are jumbled, it could be due to your close interaction with the cloud itself. In any event, the bomb that was dropped caused the cloud to dissipate. It did not dissipate on its own prior to the bomb explosion."

Patrick understood what Abram was trying to do, but couldn't restrain himself from prying. "So, you mean that my daughter and I didn't drive part way down the mountain before the explosion that caused the EMP?"

"No. No. We believe that your memories of that event are correct," Abram said quickly. "There were two bombs that were dropped. One must have occurred the first night you were on top of the mountain that caused the cloud to begin to dissipate. The second bomb detonated the following night that caused the EMP."

Patrick thought about it for a few moments before honestly responding "Yeah; I guess that could have happened that way."

"Good," Abram said as a small smile approached his face. "It is imperative that you know that and that is included in your story to any others. Is that clear?"

Patrick looked Abram square in the eyes and said "Crystal."

"Good. Good. Now let me go get your daughter so that we can begin your dismissal," Abram said as he stood up and left the room.

Patrick sat in the chair and waited for what seemed like a long duration before the door opened again. Mackenzie stepped through and a soldier behind her closed the door from the hallway.

"Dad!" Mackenzie exclaimed.

Patrick jumped up and they embraced each other. Patrick then held her at arm's length and looked her over up and down. She looked clean and unharmed.

"You okay?" Patrick said as he felt tears start to well up again.

"Yes! You?" Mackenzie answered as her tears were already beginning to fall. Patrick nodded and embraced her again.

"Did they tell you about Mom and James?" Mackenzie asked.

"Yeah. They said they're fine and that we get to see them in a little while," Patrick said.

"I can't believe that it's over," Mackenzie said and snuggled her nose in her dad's shoulder.

"I know. Me neither Darlin'," Patrick answered and held her tight.

"Did they make you say that'd you lie about bombs?" Mackenzie asked in a hushed tone.

Patrick couldn't believe that she was asking a question like that in here. He hesitated before responding, but then said quietly "Glurp," and darted his eyes to the mirror across from the table. He hoped that she caught it. He then said to her a little louder "I don't know if it is a lie. I suppose that there could have been two different explosions and we only heard the second one."

Patrick motioned for them to sit down in the chairs at the table opposite of the laptop. They both sat in silence and waited for whatever was going to happen next.

Abram finally opened the door and was accompanied by two soldiers with helmets that had M.P. insignias engraved on them. He stood in the open doorway and said "Mr. Kincaid, you are hereby dismissed under the conditions that we had previously spoken of. You are free to join your family. These gentlemen will escort you outside and see to it that you make it home safely."

Patrick and Mackenzie practically jumped up out of the metal chairs that they were seated in and bounded to the doorway. Abram stiffly stuck out his hand for Patrick to shake as they met in the doorway. It made Patrick's skin crawl, but he grasped the man's hand and gave it a pump before shouldering past him to the hallway.

The soldiers gestured for them to walk down the hallway, then had to take large steps to keep up with the brisk pace of the father and daughter. Patrick reached the door first, but realized that it was locked. He had to wait for the soldiers to catch up and wave a badge in front of a panel on the side of the door. The panel beeped, a green light lit, and this time the crash bar opened the door when Patrick pushed on it.

The door opened into a yard with a very tall fence that was lit from above. There were several soldiers and a few civilians milling around, most of them puffing away on cigarettes in the night air. Patrick eye's locked onto Mary and James sitting at a metal bench in the middle of the yard. He sprinted towards them as soon as he recognized who they were. Mary barely had time to stand up by the time that he reached her, and his momentum was enough that they almost spilled over with her going backwards when they collided. Patrick squeezed her so tight that he was scared he was going to break her, but he couldn't make himself let up. Mackenzie slammed into them both seconds later.

James yelled "Dad!" from somewhere by Patrick's knee and he scooped him up into the mass of family. Patrick's whole mind and body was in relief.

THE LONG HIKE WAS FINALLY OVER.

Follow the interactive blog with your favorite
characters at

www.THE HIKE NOVEL.COM

QT FOTOGRAPHY

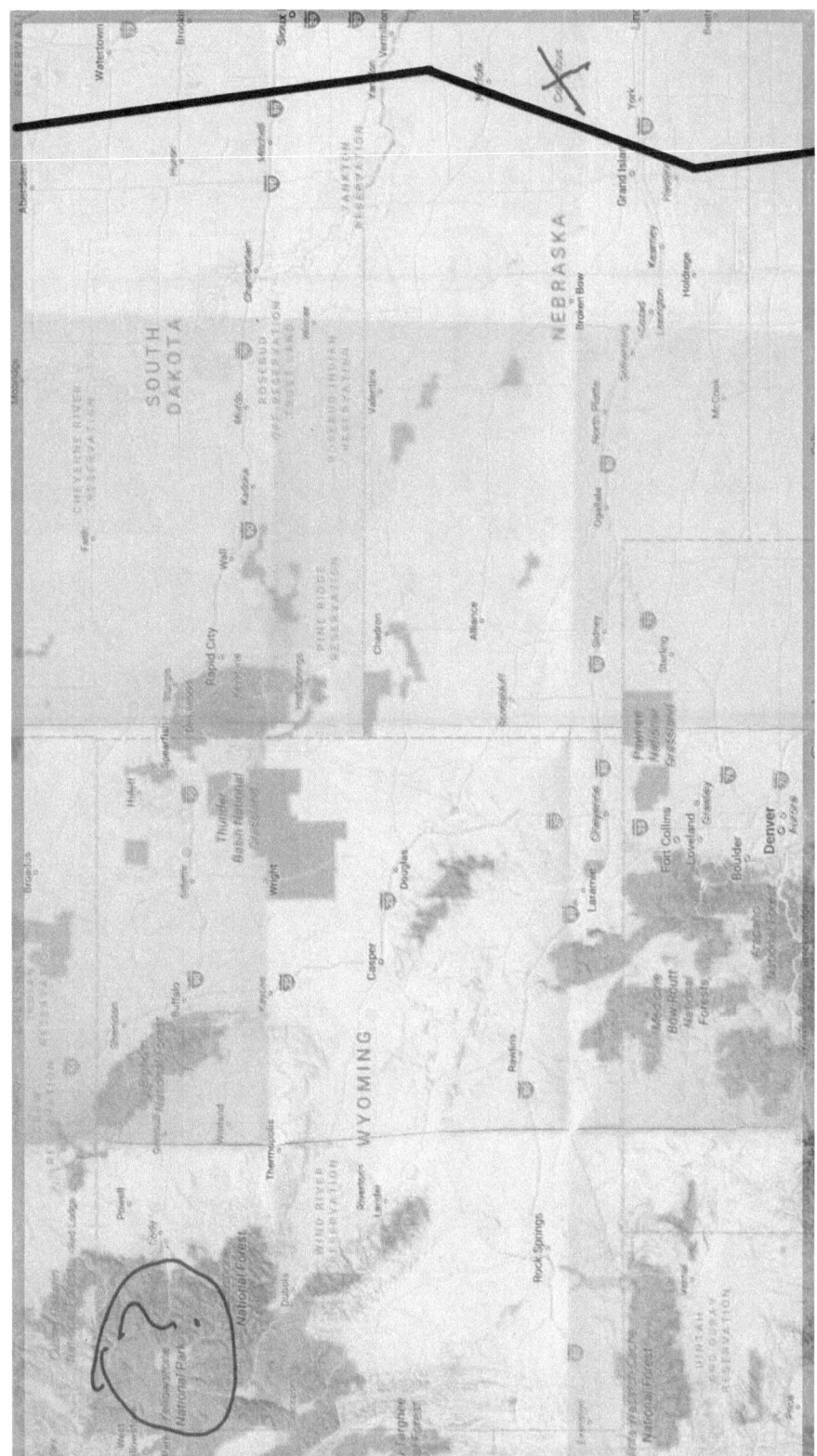

Jelly-Smooth

Dream Big